THE CONDUCTOR— THE BEST DELIVERER OF DEATH ALIVE

His name is Rene Santos, but security services the world over know this supreme terrorist as The Conductor. He does not use his own hands to wield instruments of destruction. Rather he uses an army of others as he orchestrates flawless symphonies of slaughter.

For over thirty years he has mocked the law. Now he has a new face and a new life, and a new job to do if he wants to save himself from exposure by his old employers. One more time he has to do their bidding, and he will go to any lengths to achieve this, his greatest, deadliest, most savage triumph.

A human earthquake of cunning and carnage is about to rip apart San Francisco. . . .

THE CONDUCTOR

THE
CONDUCTOR

Jerry Kennealy

A SIGNET BOOK

SIGNET
Published by the Penguin Group
Penguin Books USA Inc., 375 Hudson Street,
New York, New York 10014, U.S.A
Penguin Books Ltd, 27 Wrights Lane,
London W8 5TZ, England
Penguin Books Australia Ltd, Ringwood,
Victoria, Australia
Penguin Books Canada Ltd, 10 Alcorn Avenue,
Toronto, Ontario, Canada M4V 3B2
Penguin Books (N.Z.) Ltd, 182-190 Wairau Road,
Auckland 10, New Zealand

Penguin Books Ltd, Registered Offices:
Harmondsworth, Middlesex, England

First published by Signet, an imprint of Dutton Signet,
a division of Penguin Books USA Inc.

First Printing, August, 1996
10 9 8 7 6 5 4 3 2 1

 REGISTERED TRADEMARK—MARCA REGISTRADA

Printed in the United States of America

PUBLISHER'S NOTE
This is a work of fiction. Names, characters, places, and incidents either are the
product of the author's imagination or are used fictitiously, and any resemblance
to actual persons, living or dead, events, or locales is entirely coincidental.

BOOKS ARE AVAILABLE AT QUANTITY DISCOUNTS WHEN USED TO PROMOTE PROD-
UCTS OR SERVICES. FOR INFORMATION PLEASE WRITE TO PREMIUM MARKETING DI-
VISION, PENGUIN BOOKS USA INC., 375 HUDSON STREET, NEW YORK, NY 10014.

For Shirley
Siempre

ACKNOWLEDGMENTS

Sincere thanks to my literary agent, Dominick Abel, for sticking with this project.

Many thanks to my editor, Ed Stackler, for his many valuable suggestions and encouragements.

I greatly appreciate the help so gladly given by members of the San Francisco Police Department, including Inspector Don Kennealy, Inspector Chris Sullivan, and Captain Mike Dower, and I am indebted to attorneys Jim Biernat and Mike Bracco for all that free legal advice on the courtroom scenes.

Special thanks to Marci Bastiani for guiding me through the catacombs of the Opera House.

Most of all, thanks to my wife, Shirley, for always being there and for putting up with me all these years.

Prologue

Lima, Peru

Victor Petrov stood with his hands on his hips, surveying the pewter gray sky. He was a tall, slender man, his thick silver-blond hair combed straight back from his forehead. His eyes dropped and slowly scanned the deck. The wood was a moldy dark green color, patched with envelope-sized pieces of sheet metal. The pale pink, Spanish-style house had seen better days: small holes in the stucco, tiles missing from the roof, the walls dripping with unpruned bougainvillea, the garden area overrun with unkempt fruit trees. The smell of rotting vegetation assaulted his nostrils. "How can you stand to live here, Rene? How long has it been?"

"Awhile," Rene Santos responded cryptically. Petrov no doubt knew exactly how long he'd been in Lima. How had he found him? An informer? A mistake on his part? Or was it just luck? Bad luck.

It had been eight, no, nine years since he last had met with Petrov. That meeting had taken place in a much warmer climate. A two-story tent in Libya, where priceless Kerman rugs were placed directly on the sand as if they were no more than cheap coco mats. Petrov was wearing a suit for that meeting with Qadaffi, a typical cheap, box-like Russian's suit. Years earlier, in Cuba, he'd worn a uniform. A crisply ironed uniform, the chest littered with ribbons, in direct contrast to Fidel's faded battle fatigues. The three of them had stood on a beautiful Havana beach, tossing a baseball casually back and forth as they discussed the possibility of bombing the United States Embassy in Mexico City.

Now Petrov was back in civilian clothes. But the materials were not made in Russia, and it wasn't a vodka-drenched Russian seamstress who had been responsible for their final appearance. The dark blue Italian-cut slacks and cream-colored silk shirt were both obviously tailored expressly for his trim figure. Alligator skin loafers replaced the thick-soled, laced-above-the-ankle shoes that had been a prerequisite of the entire Russian military and diplomatic establishment.

Petrov shrugged his shoulders. "Damn, it's chilly. Is it always like this? I expected some heat."

"They call it *garúa*. Feels like a London mist, doesn't it?" His tone turned hard. "What do you want, Victor?"

"Why, you, of course, Rene. I have a job for you, the great El Cabecilla, the world-famous terrorist," Petrov said in a mocking tone. Santos's face remained completely expressionless. If the man sweats, he sweats ice water, Petrov thought. He could not read anything in Santos's coffee brown eyes. The eyes were about the only thing that resembled the old Santos. The ugly duckling had turned into a handsome swan. The face belonged to a different person. He took a few steps forward and examined Rene closely, his eyes going from the tip of Santos's scalp down to his leather sandals, the immaculate white slacks and shirt, the shirt unbuttoned to the waist, exposing his hairless, muscular chest and stomach. He still had an athlete's body. "Amazing. I would have never recognized you, Rene. You look like you could go back to the circus and climb up on the trapeze. I don't think anyone would recognize you. Are you ready to go to work?"

"For who, Viktor?" Santos asked, leaning back against the rusty iron railing. "Surely the GRU has no use for me now."

"The GRU is a thing of the past, Rene. I'm an entrepreneur now. Can you imagine that?"

"Entrepreneur," Santos said. "Isn't that just another word for criminal?"

"You wouldn't believe Russia now. It's amazing. Like one of those American movies." He did a parody of a cowboy drawing guns from two holsters. "Everyone is walking around armed. Shootings, killings; the civilians, the ex-army people. There's no control." He holstered his imaginary guns. "Everything is up for grabs. Everything."

Santos fingered the silver cross dangling from a chain around his neck. "What is it you want me to do, Victor? Join your little Russian mafia?"

"In a way. I want you to do what you do best. Kidnap some people. Perhaps kill them. Come on. Let's go inside where it's warm."

The fluorescent lights stammered to life, drenching the room in a sticky pallor. The walls looked as if they had been originally painted white. Now they had a saffron yellow tint. Dusty mahogany shelves covered one wall, the shelves half filled with books that looked as if they hadn't been touched in years. Ancient black furniture stood in museum-like arrangements around the perimeter, under old, dark paintings of overdressed men on horseback.

A big, bearish man with a dark beard and thinning black hair plastered to his scalp came onto the deck carrying a tray with black bread and slices of creamy white cheese and a bottle of wine in a clay ice bucket. He placed the tray on a table that was covered with a leather cloth fringed with tasseled rope. He spoke to Santos in Spanish: "Anything else?"

"No. That will be all."

Petrov watched the man leave. As big as he was, he walked with easy, economical movement and balance. He wore baggy white canvas pants and a blue denim shirt that stretched down to his knees. A sensible outfit if one's plan was to cover a variety of weapons, Petrov thought. "Is that the man who was at the window with a rifle when I arrived?"

Rene answered with a noncommittal nod and poured a glass of wine, handed it to Petrov, then poured a smaller measure into the glass he had chosen for himself. "Get to the point, Victor."

Petrov grunted, then placed a briefcase on the table. He opened the case, shoved it to one side, and spread a series of maps on the table.

"I know you have been to Russia many times, Rene, but never here." His blunt-tipped finger trailed over the map, moving from Moscow in an easterly direction, stopping at a town called Tyumen. "The Houston of Siberia, my friend. Samatlor is the biggest-producing oil field in the world right now." The finger moved again. "And here is Kazakhstan. The Tengiz oil fields. Hell on earth. In the summer it's one hundred thirty degrees, the rest of the year it's thirty below zero. They estimate there are nine billion barrels of oil under the ground. Deep under the ground, unfortunately. But it's there. When you fly over, you can see the black ice. Some idiots hack into the pipes with axes, fill up all the cans they can find, then drive away, leaving lakes of oil to sink into the ice. Black lakes. Worth billions, Rene."

Petrov dug another map from the briefcase and unfolded it slowly. Santos could see stacks of American currency in the bottom of the case. Petrov unfolded the maps, revealing the outline of the United States.

"You have been to America, Rene?"

"New York City. Years ago."

"What did you think of it?"

Santos took a small sip from his glass. "Too big. Too noisy. Too American."

Petrov's finger stabbed at the map. "California. The land of sunshine and movie stars. I want you to go there. Kidnap a couple of Jews. You will make more money than you ever dreamed of." He caught Santos's eyes. "I know your present position. All your money is tied up in Swiss banks. And they'll never release it to you. You know that. What I'm offering you is a chance to double the money those bastards in Switzerland are keeping from you. Berlin, that's where you want to keep your money. The Germans. They're the ones to work with now, not the Swiss." Petrov snorted, one hand going to the small of his back. "Rene Santos. El Cabecilla himself. Living like a shopkeeper in this shithole of a country, scratching out a living in the drug trade." He shrugged his shoulders. "And the Jews. They still want you, don't they? And if they come, find you, see what you look like, then what, my friend? More surgery? You must be getting tired of that."

Santos ran a hand gently across his chin. More surgery. Yes, he was tired of surgery. More important, the doctors had told him that he had reached the limit as to what could be done. His fingers moved to the silver cross. Petrov was clever with his threats. *Either I go to work for him, or he will tip the Mossad.*

He reached out to the leather briefcase. Vuitton? Bally? Certainly not Russian. He shifted the neatly stacked packs of bills and found a small plain brown envelope containing six computer diskettes.

Petrov's voice became more assertive. "That's everything, Rene. Everything in the GRU and KGB files on you. I purged them after making those copies. Your time at school in Moscow. Your operations in Spain, Morocco, Greece, England, France, Italy, all of it."

It was the files relating to Rene's early life that had most interested Petrov: his having entered a Catholic monastery at age thirteen, then his departure six years later. The killing of four priests. The GRU psychiatrist theorized that Santos had been raped, possible gang-raped, repeatedly for years and had suddenly snapped. He got away, joining a circus, and became an accomplished acrobat and juggler. He'd put his athletic skills to use as a burglar, but was captured in Turkey and sent to prison. He escaped, and after that became more of a planner than a participant. El Cabecilla. The conductor.

"Thank you for these," Santos said, placing the diskettes gently on the table.

"What are friends for?" Petrov reached for the wine bottle. "Now, let's get down to business."

* * *

It was dark when Petrov left. The woman's bare feet made no noise on the warped wooden floor.

Santos pointed at the maps. "We're going to the United States, Naimat. California."

"Why? Because of the Russian? I could follow him. Kill him."

"Victor Petrov is a hard man to kill." He saw her shoulders stiffen.

"How did he find us?"

Us, Santos thought, his fingers massaging the cross. An informer? Maybe Petrov had found him through Cesar. Or had it been Alejandro Liberto? Or Naimat? They had been together almost ten years now. She had become his right hand. She had changed. The soft baby face that had been such an asset in convincing young Israeli soldiers that she was just a poor, defenseless woman had hardened. Lines were showing in her forehead, around her mouth. Her hair was cropped short, in part to make it easier for her to don a wig. In part because she liked it that way. Her mannerisms were becoming stronger, more masculine. She'd spent most of her life in the company of men. Hard, totally ruthless men.

"Get Cesar. And Liberto. I want to be out of here by the morning." His fingers went to the cross again. Perhaps Petrov's visit will turn out to be a good omen, he mused. I've been in Lima too long. Perhaps the change of scenery will restore my luck.

Chapter 1

San Francisco

Inspector Jack Kordic sat at his desk in the Homicide detail, staring out the window at the freeway traffic, jammed in its usual bumper-to-bumper pattern, approaching the Bay Bridge. He was contemplating his birthday, less than a month away. Forty-three. Not old. But he felt old. What would he do on his birthday? Where would he go? Where was there to go?

He glanced at his watch. Almost five-thirty.

Kordic had once been one of those commuters, waiting until the moment when he could get out of the office, into the car and follow that necklace of taillights to the East Bay maze, through the Caldecott Tunnel, and finally, if traffic wasn't too bad, an hour later he was home in Walnut Creek. Home with Linda, with Danny, with—

He wanted a drink, but not badly enough to go across the street to the Lineup and maybe run into some cop who hadn't seen him in a while, who didn't know what had happened, who would, with all good intentions, ask the wrong question. Or worse, someone who knew what had happened and was embarrassed by it, embarrassed for Kordic. He plopped his feet back on the floor. The Homicide detail was a large, L-shaped room, separated from the hallway by a partition sealing off the receptionist's desk. The lieutenant's office was tucked away against the east wall. There were sixteen desks scattered around the room, all dull gray metal, made in, of all places, San Quentin Prison. His was the only one with no personal memento—no family photograph of wife, girlfriends, kids, or pets. The desks butted up against one another so that the partners were seated directly across from each other. Partners. At one time the thought of a member of the Homicide detail working without a partner would have been unthinkable. But the detective divisions were going the way of the old two-man radio car, slowly sinking into extinction.

He pushed himself to his feet and began digging through the desks, finally finding an almost full pint of Jack Daniel's in Lieutenant Chris Sullivan's desk. He took the whiskey over to the water cooler, filled one of the paper cups halfway with Daniel's, added some water, and then wandered slowly back to his desk. He pulled the venetian blinds up and looked out onto the snarled traffic on the James Lick Skyway. He raised the paper cup, drained half of it, and silently toasted the unending line of headlights.

He swallowed the rest of the whiskey, then crumpled the cup in his hand and tossed it in a wastebasket, his eyes drifting back to the freeway. Don't think about *it*.

Don't think about *them,* the doctors had advised. Not when you're drinking. Just don't think about it.

Kordic held the pint bottle up in his hand and took a swig. Easy for them to say. He grabbed a pencil from his desk and drew a small line on the label, directly across the notation showing the liquor had won a gold medal in Liege, Belgium, in 1905. God, who cared what had happened in 1905? Still, the pencil mark was an identifier. A mark. More than a mark, a commitment. The psychiatrists had advised him to quit. He'd tried AA, but just didn't fit in. He didn't consider himself an alcoholic. He hadn't been a heavy drinker before Linda and Danny were killed. An old-time sergeant had slapped some sense into him. Literally slapped it into him. "If you're going to drink, Jack, me lad, then do it. But don't become a fuckin' drunk. Limit yourself." The sergeant had grabbed a bottle of whiskey, waved it under Kordic's glassy eyes. "Find an amount you can handle." He took a key out and scratched a line across the glass. "Find your line and go that far and no farther."

That far and no farther. It worked. For now. He stowed the whiskey in his desk drawer, and went back to staring out at the freeway over the tips of his unshined shoes.

"Hey, Jack, don't hang around forever, huh?"

Kordic swiveled around and saw Lieutenant Chris Sullivan striding toward his office.

Sullivan was a tall, heavy-shouldered man. Since his divorce a couple of years ago, he'd turned into an exercise fanatic: weights, aerobics, and daily jogs from his Chestnut Street flat over and back across the Golden Gate Bridge. He wore tailored suits and shirts just so no one would miss the results of his exercise regimen. The shirts were monogrammed, both over his chest and on the French cuffs, with CBS, for Christopher Bernard Sullivan. "Just do your ABC's for CBS and everything will be fine" was the department's summary of Sullivan.

"No, just finishing up a few things, Chris. Where you going?"

Sullivan buttoned his shirt collar and adjusted his tie. "I've got to meet somebody at the New Pisa. Why don't you come along?"

Kordic was shaking his head, trying to come up with an excuse he hadn't used before, when Lieutenant Wesley Tilson entered the room.

Tilson was in his early thirties, and his hair was muddy brown color, thinning rapidly from a high forehead. He had a sharp, pointed nose and quick brown eyes that, put together, made him look a bit like a fox. Always alert and watchful. He was barely five foot six in stocking feet. Not too many years back, the height standard for a police recruit had been five foot ten inches. Kordic remembered seeing applicants being carried into the testing room on stretchers, so a precious fraction of an inch would not be lost when they stood in front of the height chart. Others had glued pads to the bottom of their feet. One overzealous individual had supposedly had his girlfriend bop him over

the head with a wooden mallet out in the hallway before he went into the exam room, hoping that the lump
on his head would get him to the minimum height figure. But the height and weight standards had been
dropped. "Now a three hundred pound midget can get
in" was the way one disgusted sergeant had summed
up the situation.

Actually, Kordic had argued, a three hundred pound
midget could be a great advantage in certain circumstances.

Tilson looked even smaller standing next to the six-
foot-two Sullivan. He gave Kordic a sour look, then
said, "Chris, the chief wants to see you first thing in
the morning on the assignment shuffles."

"Yeah, okay," Sullivan replied wearily. "I'll be
there."

Tilson turned his gaze back to Kordic. "Fine. I'm
going home now. The wife and kids are waiting."

Kordic's eyes narrowed, watching Tilson's retreating
back.

"The little jerk's got it in for you, Jack," Sullivan
said. "You ever going to tell me what it's all about?"

"It's not worth mentioning, Chris. See you in the
morning."

Sullivan hesitated a moment, then said in a deep,
bottom-of-the-barrel voice, "Okay, but don't work too
hard, pal. It'll all be there in the morning."

Kordic plopped back into his swivel chair, the chair
groaning in protest as he titled it back as far as it
would go and propped his feet on his desk.

Sullivan was right. Tilson did have it in for him.
Tilson was a paper-pushing protégé of Chief Fletcher.
Though no one could deny his intelligence, he had few
friends in the department, having spent his past few
years in Internal Affairs.

Before Tilson made lieutenant, he'd been an assistant inspector, and for three weeks was Kordic's partner
in the Sexual Assault detail. They'd never gotten
along. Tilson was a stickler for the book even then. He
had no interest in a long lunch, a drink, just work.

Kordic had to give him his due, he could work—behind a typewriter or on the phone.

But not in the street. He still remembered the night. Dark, cold, windy, a thick fog slickening the streets. A hot prowl in the Richmond District. A serial rapist had picked the wrong victim this time. A tough young Swedish secretary, who told Kordic later that she woke up to find a strange man standing over her. "He didn't look anything like Robert Redford, so I kicked him in the balls."

The man had carried his aching balls out the window to the fire escape and up to the roof. Kordic and Tilson were less than a block away when the call came in. They went up after the suspect, who made his way down the street, moving from roof to roof.

Shots were fired. Kordic and Tilson split up. Uniformed officers arrived. More shots were fired. Kordic thought he saw the suspect hiding behind a chimney. He crept up slowly, gun in hand. Suddenly there were three more shots, whizzing past his head, gouging chips from the chimney bricks.

Kordic had wheeled around, arms extended, his Magnum thumb-cocked, his finger already pressuring the trigger. He barely recognized the man not ten feet from him. Assistant Inspector Wesley Tilson—crouched over, shoulders shaking, his gun clasped between both hands, his deer-in-the-headlight eyes bulging almost out of their sockets.

Kordic grabbed Tilson, but Tilson's hands were locked onto the gun. In the struggle another shot went off, the bullet passing through Kordic's jacket sleeve. He had to hit Tilson, hard, knocking him to the gravel rooftop, finally kicking the gun from his hand.

"I didn't know it was you," Tilson repeated time after time in a frightened monotone. "I didn't know it was you."

The uniformed officers cornered the suspect minutes later. Kordic had to help Tilson down to the street.

Tilson pleaded with him not to report what had happened, and Kordic agreed, on the condition that Tilson request a transfer to another detail. Tilson agreed, but only after writing up a report that made it look as if he'd been responsible for the rapist's capture and arrest.

At that point Kordic had held Tilson's career in the palm of his hand. Had he made a formal complaint, Tilson would never have been promoted, never made full inspector, never have had the chance to take the lieutenants' test.

He had let Tilson off the hook, and somehow Tilson had never forgiven him for it. Maybe he was afraid that Kordic had spread the story around. Whatever, Kordic now knew that it had been a mistake, because Tilson now had his career in the palm of his hand. And he wasn't going to let Kordic off the hook. Ever.

The seven uniformed patrol officers stood in an uneven line. There were five men, two women: four Caucasians, two blacks, one Asian. Though the command given was "Attention," their positions varied from arms folded across their chests to hands clasped behind their backs to leaning against the booking desk.

Lieutenant Frank Harris read out the watch order, which consisted of felonies reported during the two previous shifts.

"Sometime between twenty hundred hours yesterday and oh-eight hundred this morning, the safe at Cordes' Creamery was jackhammered from the floor and removed." Harris raised his eyes from the clipboard. "Repeat, jackhammered from the concrete floor. They opened the place this morning and the whole damn thing was gone." His gaze settled on Charlie Whitman, a tall, slope-shouldered man with a jaunty white mustache and pot belly, who looked as if he'd be more at home on a Mississippi River gambling boat at the turn of the century than in his unpressed police uniform. "That's your beat, Charlie."

Whitman replied in a lazy drawl, "Must have gone down on the midnight shift, Lieut. I checked that place out a couple of times. Drove by it just before I went off duty."

"Sure you did," Harris responded with a lack of enthusiasm. "All right, people. Go out there and do your duty." He crooked a finger at Officer Larry Falore. "See me in my office before you hit the streets."

Falore questioned his partner, Donna Frazier, with his eyes.

She shook her head. "Beats me. See you in the car."

Ingleside Station was one of the oldest in the city, built back in the days when horses were a mainstay of the force. The horse stable had been converted into a garage fifty years ago. The building itself was a high-ceilinged Victorian, the interior painted that pea green color that civil servant administrators seem to favor for police and fire stations, but not for their own offices.

Falore followed Harris back to his office, a cramped cubbyhole alongside the stairs leading to the second-floor changing room. Falore had been at Ingleside less than two weeks. He knew little of Lieutenant Harris, except that he was known as a hustler, a former jazz musician with lots of irons in the fire.

Harris slid into the swivel chair behind his desk, leaned back, and locked his hands behind his head. "You want a little side work, Larry?"

"What kind, Lieut?"

"Security. Working for me. Fifteen bucks an hour." He paused. "Cash."

Falore remembered someone telling him that Harris had a small security firm and used off-duty station officers. The latest department budget crisis had curtailed all overtime work for the uniformed forces, so Falore, saving every cent he could for a down payment on his first home, jumped at the chance. "Yes. Sounds good to me."

Harris pulled a red vinyl-covered binder from his desk drawer. "Jim Dykstra broke his leg. He'll be off on disability for six months at least. I need someone to pull his shifts, starting tonight. From midnight to eight."

Falore cleared his throat carefully. "Ah, there's a problem. I don't get off until midnight, Lieut."

"No problem," Harris said with a tight grin. "Take off at eleven. I'll cover you."

Falore had one more problem. He'd have to call his wife, Jennie, and give her the news. She left for work at eight in the morning, so he'd miss seeing her. Then he'd go back to work at four in the afternoon, before she came home. He took a deep breath. "Where do I go?"

Harris plucked a gold Parker pen from its holder and began scribbling on a small pink scratch pad. "You know who Paul Abrams is?"

Falore hesitated a moment. "You mean the rich guy? The real rich guy?"

"That's the guy," Harris agreed. "Abrams Oil. Abrams Manufacturing." He tore off a piece of the note paper and slid it toward Falore. "That's his address. Your job tonight is just to sit in the house. It's wired, state-of-the-art. It would take a tank to get in there, but Abrams insists on one guard in the house at night. Armed guard." He pointed the tip of the pen at Falore's holster. "So bring your weapon."

"You want me in uniform?"

"Definitely not. Plain clothes. I've got people working on this around the clock, Larry. Two with Mr. Abrams during the day, plus a full-time driver. One or more with his wife. We all wear the same outfits. Gray slacks, blue blazer, white shirt, red tie. He likes to be able to spot us right away. Abrams supplies the clothes, and they're top-of-the-line stuff, no JC Penny's catalog crap. Tuxedos, with red bow ties, for big social events."

Falore glanced at the address on the note pad. "What is this guy, paranoid or something?"

Harris shifted his weight on the chair, the movement producing a soft, creaky noise. "How old are you, Larry?"

"Twenty-six."

Harris closed his eyes a moment, trying to remember when he was twenty-six. What he knew. What he didn't know. He didn't know a lot, he remembered that. "Paul Abrams's brother, Donald, was kidnapped in New York City over ten years ago. Held for ransom. The perps were dumb. Dumber than most. Donald

Abrams tried to escape. They beat him up. Beat him to death.

"Paul Abrams bounces around in *Forbes* magazine's most wealthy individuals list every year. Sometimes he's number two or three, sometimes he drops down a few notches. But he's always there. In the top ten. So he's a target, Larry. A real target. Man's got the right to be a little paranoid." Harris splayed out his hands. "And he can afford all the security he needs. And I provide it. Here in the Bay Area, most of California. When he travels out of state, either we go or I have someone, usually local cops, sometimes private firms, waiting to meet him at the airport. Mr. Abrams has his own network of bodyguards overseas, but when he goes, one of us flies with him, in his personal jet, and stays with him until he's handed over to the local talent. Abrams may not look tough, but he's a ruthless bastard. I've seen him crack the whip and scare the shit out of state senators and bank presidents. He uses his money like a club, and if you're in his way, he beats you over the head with it. If he likes you, you're fine, but cross him and he cuts you off right at the knees. I don't want to lose Abrams. I've had him for six years now. He's happy. I want to keep him that way, okay?"

"No sweat, Lieut. You tell me how you want to handle it, and I'll do it."

Harris tapped the pen rhythmically against his knee and smiled benignly. "Piece of cake tonight, Larry. Guy you're relieving will show you how the alarm system works. So you can just sit around. Help yourself to anything you want in the kitchen. Roger, the butler, is the majordomo around the place. He starts kicking ass around six in the morning."

Harris paused, studying Falore, liking what he saw: over six feet tall, athletic build, wavy dark hair. Good-looking. Maybe too good-looking. "Mr. Abrams lives by his own clock. Sometimes he'll get up in the middle of the night, come downstairs, and start plinking away at his piano. He may go into his studio and do a little painting. He may just wander around his art gallery. Or he may study his coin or stamp collection. Sometimes he talks to the guys on duty. Maybe he'll even ask you to play chess. You play chess?"

Falore shook his head.

"Anyway," Harris continued, "Abrams may talk to you, or he may look right through you like you're not there. Depends on the mood he's in." He paused again, giving Falore what he called one of his X-ray stares. "Mrs. Abrams's name is Adele. She's twenty-four. He's in his mid-fifties. She's gorgeous. She's also a prick teaser, Larry. Likes to strut around and show the boys what they're missing." Harris slammed his fist down on the desk hard enough to knock the pen holder to the floor. "And they are missing it, Larry. Anyone who fucks with Mrs. Abrams and screws me out of this gig is going to be in deep shit. Get it?"

"Got it, Lieut," Falore responded calmly.

"Good. Now, take off when you want to. Just make sure you get out there before midnight."

Chapter 2

"It is a beautiful view, isn't it?" asked Ellen Edmondson. "You can see from the Golden Gate Bridge all the way past the Bay Bridge." She pointed a long, brightly enameled finger toward the bay water. "That's Alcatraz, of course."

Rene Santos nodded his head in agreement. "Beautiful, indeed." He leaned over the balcony. A chill wind was blowing, but the rain had stopped. His eyes roved over the buildings below. Some were huge mansions, others multi-unit apartments. They were all well maintained, the gardens neatly groomed, many of the roofs turned into small little green spots, with potted plants, gazebos, deck chairs, and small splashes of blue water that he later learned were spas and hot tubs.

His eyes drifted down to Paul Abrams's impressive four-story redbrick mansion on Vallejo Street, which was the only view he had any real interest in. "How soon can I take possession?" Santos asked the attractive realtor.

"Well, you did want a year's lease, didn't you, Mr. Citron?"

"Definitely. As I explained on the phone, I'm interested in taking possession immediately. I wish that I had more time, but"—he waved a hand vaguely—"you know how the business world is."

Ellen Edmondson certainly did. And the real estate market in San Francisco had never really recovered from the earthquake of 1989. Still, she had been conned into leasing property to some well-spoken scoundrels before. And Citron was definitely well-spoken. What was it about a rolling, throaty French accent that made a person seem more sexy than he was? Not that Citron wasn't sexy-looking: thick dark hair, trim mustache, lean body encased in a charcoal suit whose tailoring made it obvious it was not bought off a rack. The Polo-style overcoat draped over his broad shoulders was definitely cashmere. She knew that without touching it. His shoes were polished brightly enough to be used as a mirror. Shoes had always been a tipoff to Ellen. People investing in a wardrobe just for show would put all their money into the suit, or sports coat, or a fancy coat. But they would draw in the purse strings at the shoes. Not this Frenchman, though. He looked solid gold from top to bottom. "I see no problem, as long as we can work out the financial details."

Santos gave her the full wattage of his smile. "Would a money order speed things up, *mademoiselle*?"

"Yes, indeed," Ellen responded, thinking that now was the time to toss out a light pass. "Are you sure you're wife will be happy here, Mr. Citron?"

She was disappointed with his response.

"Of course." The big smile again. "She is easily pleased. She married me."

"Do you like it?"

Larry Falore swiveled around so fast that he almost dropped the bottle of Coors to the floor. The sight of the woman in the black silk pajamas froze him for a moment. "Yes. A Matisse," he said, glancing back at the still-life painting, which depicted five apples and a water jug on a rumpled blue tablecloth. "Beautiful, isn't it?"

"Ah, you actually know something about art. How interesting."

She padded barefoot toward Falore. The first two buttons on her pajama top were undone, showing an expanse of lightly tanned cleavage. Her tawny blond hair was slightly damp and looked finger-combed, as if she'd just gotten out of the shower. Falore cleared his throat, then said, "How are you tonight, Mrs. Abrams?"

"Bored. Do you enjoy paintings?"

Falore let his gaze wander slowly around the room, which stretched out a full fifty feet. "Your husband has some wonderful things here."

Adele Abrams arched her back, her hands going to her buttocks as she stretched and yawned. "My husband, yes. Actually, Officer—"

"Falore. Larry Falore, ma'am."

Mrs. Abrams made a sour face. "Ma'am. God, that makes me sound positively ancient, Larry. Shame on you," she chided him. "They're not just my husband's paintings, Larry. They're half mine now. Were you just lucky with the Matisse?" She pointed at a canvas alongside the Matisse. "Try that one."

Falore grinned confidently. "That's easy, ma'am—ah, Mrs. Abrams. A van Gogh." His eyes moved down the room. The walls were ten feet high and covered with pale ivory, embossed wallpaper. Track lighting hung from the ceiling, perfectly spotlighting each ornately framed painting. He ticked off the names of the artists: "The clowns are by Georges Roualt, the London Bridge by Andre Derain, the Picassos from his Cubism stage, and the crucifixion scene is a Chagall." He looked back at Adele Abrams. "I'm not sure about the ones down on the end there," he said, indicating two large canvasses that looked like nothing more than square blobs of yellow and black paint to Falore. "I'm not much on the modernists."

"Very impressive, Larry Falore. Very impressive. How long have you been working for us?"

"Almost three weeks."

She went into the arching-her-back pose again, causing her breasts to push out. Falore could make out her hardened nipples pressing through the silk. Lieutenant Harris was right. She was a grade-A prick teaser.

"Where did you learn so much about art, Larry?"

"College, ma'am. I was an art major."

"From an art major to the police department. That's rather a dramatic change of careers. Why the police?"

Falore smiled wearily. "Got married. Needed a job.

I wasn't much good in school anyway. I can't even tell if these are originals or copies."

"Oh, they're originals, Larry. Believe that. My husband does not tolerate anything but the best." Her hands began toying with the buttons on her pajamas.

"I hope he doesn't mind my being in here. I was told it was okay to look around."

"Paul's in Russia. He won't be back for a couple of days. So by all means look around." She tilted her head to one side and bulged out her lower lip with her tongue. "There's so much to see, isn't there?"

Falore took a deep breath, like a skin diver getting ready to go to the bottom, watching as Adele Abrams turned slowly and exited the room. He waited until she was out of sight before exhaling.

Chapter 3

Mary Ariza exited the elevator and hurried out of the building, joining the lunchtime crowd on Montgomery Street. Tall, trim, dark-haired, with a heart-shaped face and dark, almond-shaped eyes, she got more than her share of stares, looks, and glances, but today more so. Her smile. She just couldn't take the smile off her face. She had them. The insurance company settlement conference she'd just come from had gone her way. The opposing attorneys were nervous. They didn't want to go to trial. Mary did.

Her client was a twenty-seven-year-old department store clerk. Admittedly gay. No arrest record. No prior civil cases. Well thought of by his coworkers. He had wandered into the Tenderloin District during his lunch hour, on his way to a favorite restaurant, when he was assaulted on the street, in broad daylight, a knife stuck in his back, forced into an adult bookstore by two men dressed in motorcycle leathers, taken into one of the store's cubicles where patrons watched X-rated videos. He was then sodomized and forced to perform oral copulation on both of his assailants.

The police department's investigation of the incident showed that her client had been taken to Central Emergency Hospital, where it had been confirmed that there was semen in his rectum. Laboratory tests showed that there were actually two separate strains of semen, thus confirming his statement regarding two assailants. The suspects were never apprehended, so if her client was not going to see justice done in the criminal courts, he was damn well going to go after the bookstore in a civil trial.

The insurance company attorneys representing the bookstore had tried to laugh off the case at first. The victim was an admitted homosexual. Living with another man. There were no witnesses.

But the law offices of Pontar & Kerr had taken the case. And dropped it in Mary's lap. Her first big case since coming to San Francisco.

Mary had visited the bookstore several times herself over the past couple of months. Grotesque inflatable plastic "love dolls" of both sexes and various races hung from the ceiling. Vibrators of plastic and rubber, varying from the size of a pencil to that of a little leaguer's baseball bat, were for sale. A fishbowl filled with condoms was set alongside the clerk's register. Customers could select videotapes featuring scenes the store described as "Straight, Gay, Bi, Group, Dominate, or Religious." Mary had been curious about the "Religious" designation, but not enough to ask the store's owner, a sleazy-looking man whose eyes bounced from Mary's eyes to her breasts every few seconds.

She couldn't wait to get him on the stand. She was going to crucify him. Where was your security? How do you protect your customers?

The defense attorneys insisted that a security guard had been on duty, but Mary's investigator had interviewed the man, who admitted his main duties were to sweep the cubicles of Kleenex and handkerchiefs left behind by the customers.

Her client's latest medical report showed him HIV-negative, but the doctor, her expert witness, would testify to the fact that the AIDS virus could be there in a dormant state, ready to become active at any time, in the near future or up to five years from now.

That's what terrified the defense attorneys. The jurors thinking about AIDS. Attacking her client would only make them appear homophobic.

The traffic light changed, and she darted into the street, her heels almost catching on the cable car tracks, her mind already going through the stack of files on her desk that demanded her attention.

When she reached the sidewalk, a middle-aged man with lank brown hair bumped into her shoulder. Mary's hands instinctively went to her purse, clutching it to her chest. "Why don't you watch where—" Her protest was cut short when she saw the man crumple to the ground, his face rapidly changing from red to gray.

Mary dropped down alongside him. "Are you all right?" she asked, sensing that the man was seriously ill. She reached for his carotid artery, but there was no pulse. "A doctor, please," she yelled at the people hovering over them. "Find a doctor. Call an ambulance!"

It had been years since she had taken a course in CPR. The fallen man's glasses had slipped down in front of his mouth. Mary brushed the glasses away, then ran a finger inside his mouth to see if the teeth were false. They weren't. She tilted his head back to open his airway, pinched his nostrils shut, then used her other hand to lift his jaw forward. She took a deep breath and blew air into his mouth, her eyes fixed on his chest, watching it rise. She gave him three quick breaths, then pulled away. Mary ran her hand across his chest, found the sternum, moved her hand one palm upward, placed the heel of her hand in the center of his chest, wrapped her left hand over her right wrist for leverage, then pushed down forcibly, compressing his chest fifteen times. She repeated the sequence, three breaths and fifteen compressions, hoping all the while that a doctor would suddenly kneel beside her and take charge.

The man's eyes suddenly opened, and he started to speak in Spanish.

Mary looked up at the crowd. "Did you call an ambulance?" she asked no one in particular.

"One's on its way," someone responded.

The man grabbed Mary's hand, struggling to sit up. She pushed him back to a prone position, placing her purse under his head. "A doctor will be here in a minute."

The man's hand grabbed hers again, pulling her close. Mary could smell tobacco and alcohol on his breath. He was speaking rapidly in Spanish now. At first Mary could not understand what he was saying, then it came to her.

"Perdone, Padre, porque e pecado." Forgive me, Father, for I have sinned.

"Relax, a doctor will be here soon," Mary replied in Spanish, mildly surprised at how quickly the language came back to her. "Just stay still. You're going to be all right."

The man again pulled her close, whispering hoarsely into her ear. *"Perdone, Padre,"* he repeated, *"porque e pecado."*

He rambled on for a couple of minutes. Mary paid little attention, her eyes darting up frequently, looking for help. For anyone with more expertise than she possessed.

Finally a policeman arrived on the scene. He bent over at the waist, hands on knees, peering down at the stricken man. "How's he doing, lady?"

"I think he's had a heart attack. He needs medical treatment. I think he—"

She heard a siren wailing in the distance.

"Ambulance is on its way," the policeman said. He motioned the crowd. "Okay, everyone, back away, back away. Give us some room."

The ambulance stewards arrived, one cracking open an oxygen bottle as he knelt down. Mary told them briefly what had happened, what she had done. An oxygen mask was placed on the man's face, and he was loaded onto a portable gurney.

Mary watched as the ambulance drove away. She reached down and brushed her pants at the knees, noticing that the material was scuffed and soiled from the dirty sidewalk.

The policeman came over to her. "You did a hell of a job, lady." He looked around, finding that the sightseers had dispersed. "No one gave you any help, huh?"

Mary found that she was shaking all of a sudden. "No. No one else helped."

"Did you know the guy?" the policeman asked.

"No. I never saw him before. He must have been in shock. He thought I was a priest."

The policeman pulled out a notebook. "Can I have your name, please?"

She glanced at her watch, hesitated, then dug in her purse for a business card. "I'm late for an appointment," she said, handing the policeman her card, then spinning on her heel and walking rapidly up Montgomery Street.

The cop sighed, then slipped her card into his notebook. "Nice hoop on that lady, huh, pal?" he said to the man standing beside him. "That guy must have been in real bad shape. He thought she was a priest."

"*Sí. Muy bueno,*" Cesar Davila mumbled. He used his bulk to push his way through the crowd, then took off after Mary Ariza. He cursed under his breath. What the hell had happened to Liberto? Where would the ambulance take him? They'd finally had the chance to follow Paul Abrams from his house to his office, but Abram's Mercedes had disappeared into the building's garage. Cesar had run down the concrete parking ramp, only to be turned back by a uniformed security guard. Liberto was to wait out front and see if the bodyguards came onto the street. Cesar had wandered around the building's vast lobby, hoping to find the elevator Abrams would use to get to his office on the forty-first floor, but it was useless. The building was a maze. Too many people. Too many elevators. By the time he got back to California Street, the ambulance was pulling up. He saw the woman, on her knees, beside Liberto, Liberto clutching her, pulling her to him, talking into her ear. Liberto looked bad. Like he was dying. Maybe he was already dead. What did you tell her, my stupid friend? Rene would want to know.

Cesar Davila hurried after the tall, dark-haired woman. She had a long stride and weaved her way through the crowd, her arms swinging purposefully. He edged closer and could hear the heels of her shoes making sharp, decisive explosions, like the bark of guns, as she increased her pace.

He kept an eye on the street signs, reciting each to himself to help his memory: Leidesdorrfs, left on Sansome, then past Halleck, a right on Clay. Where the hell was she going? Why couldn't she walk in a straight line? He felt hemmed in by the crowds, the tall buildings, the traffic: diesel-spouting buses, double-parked trucks of all sizes, and line and lines of cars barely moving in the congested streets, horns honking at the double-parked trucks.

The woman came to a halt at the corner of Clay and Battery, just as rain started to come down. Davila edged up close behind her, close enough to smell her perfume. It smelled good. What was it the police officer had said? "Nice hoop on that lady." If by hoop he had meant her ass, he was right, Davila thought. Even the man's-style black suit could not completely disguise the figure beneath it. Her hair was dark brown, cut in a short style that did not appeal to Davila. He preferred his women with long hair. He wondered briefly if she was a *lesbia*. The suit. The haircut. It was certainly possible. But this was America. All the women acted like they had balls. Like Naimat.

It started to rain harder and the woman looked up at the sky, showing her profile to Davila. If she is a lesbian, it is a terrible waste, he thought. The traffic light changed and she started across the street, Davila at her heels again.

The rain had driven much of the crowd from the streets. The woman turned into one of the tall buildings. The streets were no longer paved in concrete but in swirling white tiles that somehow reminded Davila of Rio de Janeiro. Up an escalator, then along a shopping plaza on the building's mezzanine, past restaurants, clothing stores, jewelers. The mezzanine opened to the sky again, and they crossed a bridge some twenty feet above street level, over to yet another building. Davila swiveled his head skyward. The building looked exactly like the three surrounding it: tall, flat, a narrow box of windows. The woman held her purse over her head to protect herself from the rain. She started to trot, to run, and Davila's heavy frame caused him almost to lose his balance on the slippery tile as he raced to keep pace. She turned left, into a lobby with six elevators. Davila's stomach started to grumble. If he lost her here, it would be impossible to find her. The lobby was jammed with people, men in raincoats and business suits, women in dresses and pants outfits like his quarry. Davila almost bumped into her as they got into the elevator. He felt uncomfortable in his leather jacket, but none of the fifteen or so other passengers seemed to pay any attention to him. There was no conversation as the elevator streaked upward some twenty-five stories before coming to its first stop. Then it stopped at almost every floor. There were only three people remaining in the elevator when the woman exited on the thirty-fourth floor.

She walked down a carpeted hallway in that hurried stride of hers, never looking back, toward two Plexiglas doors, black-stenciled with the inscription LAW OFFICES OF PONTAR & KERR.

Davila paused, watching the woman push her way through the doors. She stopped briefly at a half-circle desk and spoke to a young woman with frizzed red hair. The redhead handed her several small pieces of paper. The woman glanced at them as she made her way down a corridor, disappearing from sight.

Davila took a deep breath and shoved open the doors. The redhead looked up at him with a polite smile on her face. "Can I help you, sir?"

"Yes, please. That young secretary that just came in. She looks so much like an old friend of mine. Her name wouldn't be Shirley Lopez, would it?"

"No, that's Mary Ariza. And she's an attorney, not a secretary."

"Attorney," Cesar Davila said, his face twisting in a sneer. Rene wasn't going to like that. He wasn't going to like it at all.

Inspector Jack Kordic's feet made crunching sounds in the sand as he crossed over to the fire engine. Four lengths of one-inch nylon rope were attached to brackets on the engine's chrome bumper. He followed the taut lines over to a group of three men standing near the edge of the cliff. Two were outfitted in heavy black canvas jackets and scuffed fire helmets; the third was wearing a navy cardigan and white military-style cap.

Kordic pulled out his badge and identified himself. "How's it look, Chief?" he asked the man in the white hat.

Battalion Chief Voelker walked him over to the edge of the cliff and pointed at the rocks below. "I've got two men trying to pull a body out of the water." He handed Kordic a pair of binoculars. "Tough work. They've got to wade in to get it, but the waves keep coming in and knocking them back."

Kordic peered through the binoculars, feeling a quick surge of vertigo as he looked straight down at the two firemen fighting the surf to get at the body. It was wedged between twin cone-shaped rocks some fifteen feet from a small, desolate beach. The top portion of the rocks was black-gray and looked slick and sculpted from centuries of surging tides. The rocks were exposed for less than a moment; then the next wave would crash in and cover them completely in an explosion of greenish-gray water and foam. Kordic looked at the body caught between the rocks until a wave came in and submerged it from sight. "Jesus," he said, more to himself that the fire chief. "What a mess."

"Ain't it, though?" Voelker agreed.

Kordic handed him the binoculars and retreated a few steps. They all watched for several minutes as the two firemen waded cautiously into the water, only to be driven back by the pounding surf. Kordic looked west, toward the Farallone Islands. The sky was a tie-dyed mixture of dark grays, heavy with cauliflower-topped cumulus clouds. The breeze was freshening. It looked like rain was on its way. A squadron of seagulls circled lazily overhead. "What do you think the chances are of getting the body off the rocks, Chief?"

Voelker grimaced, as if he was in pain. "Best bet is to let the waves knock it free." He held his portable radio to his mouth and relayed that very message to the men below. "Adams. You and Gallegos take it easy. Let the water free him, then make a grab. If you miss, he goes out to sea." He looked at Kordic with an unblinking stare. "There's not much more we can do."

Kordic nodded in agreement, peering down over the cliff again, then backed away slowly. His hands went to his pockets, patting them out of habit. You gave up smoking six months ago, stupid, he told himself. He felt the rain in his hair before he saw the drops plop onto the sand. "Good luck, Chief," he said, then turned and headed back to his car.

Kordic sat in the unmarked police car for almost an hour, his fingers drumming on the steering wheel, watching the activity of the firemen. The windshield wipers were beating a steady rhythm, clearing the sporadic bursts of rain. He wished he had a cigarette. Wished he had a drink. Wished he had his old partner, Benny Munes, with him, so he wouldn't be there alone, in a rundown city vehicle waiting to see the remains of the poor bastard who somehow ended up at the bottom of the cliffs off Lands End. A merchant seaman? A yachtsman? Or maybe one of those tough Italian fishermen who kept their little one-cylinder boats moored beneath the restaurants at Fisherman's Wharf so they could look up at all the curious tourists while they mended their nets and washed out their crab pots. Now he had something else to wish for. A nice crab Louie. Or some sand dabs. He glanced down at his wristwatch. Past lunchtime. Way past. He thought of driving over to Clement Street to pick up a sandwich or some dim sum, then noticed that the firemen had started moving. The chief waved to the driver of the engine, circling one hand over his head like a cowboy about to rope a steer.

Kordic turned off the ignition and climbed out of the car, pulling his raincoat collar up. The clumps of ground cover, thick, finger-sized leaves of ice plant, had turned slick with rain. He took the long way around, through a stretch of wind-shaped cypress trees. By the time he got to the edge of the cliff, the fireman had the ketchup-colored fiberglass basket stretcher on level ground. A wet gray blanket covered the body on the stretcher.

The two fireman who'd been down in the water retrieving the body stood alongside the chief, their turnout coats soaked through, their pants plastered to their legs.

"Nice job, guys," Chief Voelker told them. "Take my buggy, get back to the house, and dry off. I'll come back with the engine." He looked over at Kordic. "Hope whoever's in there was worth the risk to my men." He bent down and undid the Velcro straps securing the blanket. The straps came apart with that sticky envelope sound, then Voelker pulled back the blanket. "Jesus Christ," he said, his hand snapping back as if a snake had bitten it.

Kordic stared down at the body. Or what was left of it—the head had been severed. He knelt and dragged the blanket all the way down. It was the body of a man. He was sure of that. They had at least left his penis in its proper place. The hands were cut off at the wrists and there were puckered black marks across the stomach, chest, and thighs.

"He's all yours, Inspector," the fire chief said, drywashing his hands in a Pontius Pilate gesture. "All yours now."

Kordic covered the body with the blanket. "Thanks. I'll make sure the coroner gets the stretcher and blanket back to you."

Voelker shook his head slowly from side to side. "Tell them to keep the blanket. Either that or burn it."

The parking was a problem. A major problem. As bad as in any city Rene Santos had lived or worked in, including Paris, Rome, London, and Beirut. Well, maybe not as bad as Beirut, he conceded. There was a slightly better chance that the motorcycle would still be waiting for him when left on the streets of San Francisco than in the battle-scarred alleyways of the Middle East. He humped the Kawasaki ZX7 up the curb and edged the machine in between two BMW sedans in an area marked PHYSICIAN PARKING ONLY. He took off his helmet and looped the bike's safety chain through the helmet's ear holes, and then around the rear wheel with indifference. If the machine was stolen or towed away, he'd simply steal another one.

Santos glanced in the motorcycle's sideview mirror, tilting his chin up as he studied his reflection, going over his face from hairline to chin. The trim nose, the lowered hairline, the high cheekbones, the firm jaw, smooth skin. A little tightness around the eyes. It was a face that in no way resembled its original: no more pockmarks, no hooked nose, no sags, no sunken chin. A face that pleased him. A face that had taken years of work—nine different surgeries. A face he did not want to give up. A face that would allow him to travel without fear of being recognized where he wanted and when he wanted. The last surgery had been just that—the last surgery. "It's not like the cinema," the doctor had told him. "I can't just go in and change everything over and over, as if your face is a jigsaw puzzle." There was nothing more he could do—there was just so much cartilage, so much bone to work with—to go further could lead to negative results. "I could disfigure you perhaps," the doctor advised, "but I don't think you'd be happy with a face like that."

No, Rene had the face he wanted. The face he had always wanted. But Viktor Petrov now knew the face.

Santos fingered the small silver cross hanging beneath the Roman collar. It was the same cross he'd been given by his mother when he entered the monastery. It was all he had left from those days. Except for the bad memories.

The rain had let up and a few blue patches were emerging between the clouds. Santos hurried up the wide brick steps toward the hospital's main entrance. Alejandro Liberto having an attack on the street was bad luck. And Santos had found that luck ran in streaks—bad and good. Liberto was not quite fifty. But a hard fifty. His face ravaged by chemical abuse, his nostrils eaten away by cocaine, almost blind without his bottle-thick glasses. Not an ideal soldier for an operation like this. But Santos no longer had the pick of Qaddafi's military elite, or the top graduates from the PLO terrorist schools. Now he had to take what he could get. Especially when operating in virgin territory. He had been in San Francisco for several weeks, much

of that time spent in locating an apartment, then a safe
house to keep his prisoner, studying maps, driving
around town, scouting personnel. The city itself had
surprised him. He had expected it to be much larger. It
was only forty-nine square miles, much of them verti-
cal. The cultures stayed in their segregated sections:
blacks, Hispanics, whites, Chinese, Japanese, even the
gays had their own territory staked out. There was
much mingling at the borders of the separate domains,
but nonetheless, an interloper soon looked out of place
if he didn't take precautions. And taking precautions
was what had kept Santos free and alive while his
more celebrated confederates were underground—
some of them literally, others stuck in hellholes in the
Mideast, afraid to leave their apartments, much less in
the country.

He had mixed feelings about working in America.
The openness of the system was certainly a plus; he
could travel anywhere without having to show a passport. The negatives were dealing with the customs, the
languages, and the bureaucracy. Always there was the
bureaucracy. The local laws, including an idiotic rule
about having to wear a helmet when driving a motorcycle. The motorcycle was not Santo's first choice for
transportation, but he had learned long ago that a bike
was the best way to conduct an initial surveillance in a
metropolitan area. It was easy to hide in traffic, easy to
park, easy to dispose of. But a simple thing like being
pulled over for not wearing a helmet might ruin the
whole operation. The driver's licenses and Social Security cards needed for identification were amazingly
unsophisticated and easily acquired. Viktor Petrov had
provided him with a variety of the necessary papers.
The easy access to credit cards was an advantage. No
wonder all those banks and savings institutions had
gone bankrupt.

Learning to cope with the intricacies of the system
was a continuing challenge. All Cesar Davila could tell
him was that Liberto had been taken away by an ambulance. Where to? Which hospital? He had to call three
hospitals, then go through the city's Health Department

before learning that anyone picked up by a city ambulance was taken to San Francisco General Hospital on Potrero Street.

A gray-haired woman in a red-and-white-striped apron sat behind the information counter. She smiled widely when she saw the Roman collar.

"Yes, Father, how can I help you?" she asked.

She listened with her chin in her hand as Santos explained his problem. "A man was brought here in an ambulance earlier this afternoon. I believe he had a heart attack at California and Montgomery streets."

"His name, Father?"

"That I don't know," Santos said, holding his palms up in a gesture of helplessness. "A woman called me, told me that her friend had collapsed. She was very upset. Said he was a Catholic and needed the last rites. She hung up before I could get any more information."

The woman smiled warmly. "Well, we'll just have to do a little digging." She picked up her phone and went through four separate conversations before getting the information. "They have him listed as John Doe, Father. He had no identification on him. But the man in Room 414C was brought in from California and Montgomery streets. I hope he's the right person." She wrote the room number on a piece of scratch paper and directed him to the bank of elevators past the gift shop.

"I'm sure he is," Santos replied. He shared the elevator with several nurses and a doctor who was too busy studying a chart on a clipboard to notice him. One of the nurses, a thin black woman, glanced at his collar and gave him a friendly nod. Santos nodded back solemnly. He located Room 414. There were four beds, two were empty. One was occupied by a man who appeared to be in his eighties, wearing a pale green smock. His emaciated milk white arms dangled from the sleeves. He was propped up by several pillows, his bald head shaking back and forth, his rheumy eyes fixed on the television set hanging from the acoustical tile ceiling. He gave Santos a quick glance, his lips peeling back to reveal freckled pink gums. Then he turned his attention back to the television set.

Liberto was in the third bed, against the far wall. He was asleep. Santos grabbed the edge of the pale green curtain, the rings atop the material making a rasping sound against the metal rod as he pulled the curtain closed. He stared down at Liberto. An intravenous tube was hooked up to one arm, a demand-valve oxygen mask taped to his face. Santos pulled a handkerchief from his pants pocket and gently removed the mask. He pinched Liberto's nostrils shut, then covered his mouth with the handkerchief. Liberto's eyes opened briefly, and he made a futile effort to push Santo's arms away. Santos kept the pressure steady, his eyes riveted on Liberto's. He held his position for several minutes, even after he was sure Liberto was dead. The rasping sound of the curtain being opened startled him. His right hand pushed away his raincoat and grasped the knife handle.

"Issh he gonna die?"

It was the old man from the next bed. He stood there wobbling on skinny legs, his wattled neck quivering as he tried enunciating without the benefit of his teeth.

He repeated his question. This time Santos understood. "We are all going to die, my friend. Some of us sooner than others."

He placed his hand on Liberto's head and began administering the last rites, the sacrament of the sick. *"Commendatio Ánimae . . ."*

Chapter 4

"Moose's Restaurant in North Beach," Adele Abrams called from the Mercedes's backseat.

"I was told you were going to a luncheon at the Hilton, ma'am," Larry Falore said, applying slight pressure to the accelerator as the stretch sedan glided effortlessly up the steep slope of Broderick Street.

"Pull over to the curb, Larry. We have to talk."

Falore glided the Merc to a stop, set the parking break, then swiveled around to look at Mrs. Abrams.

"Do you believe everything you're told, Larry?"

"No, ma'am." She was wearing a muted indigo blue plaid jacket over a matching skirt. According to what Falore read in the papers, short shirts were out, long ones were in. Adele Abrams apparently didn't read the papers. She leaned back, took off her dark glasses, and smiled at him, stretching her legs apart. Falore couldn't help wondering if there were panties above those thighs.

"You're still on the 'ma'am' kick, Larry. I asked you not to call me that. It makes me feel positively ancient."

"What would you like me to call you?"

She put her dark glasses on and pursed her lips as if about to blow him a kiss. "You'll think of something. I'm sure you will. Now, who told you I was going to the Hilton?"

"Don Hansen, the man on the night shift. He had your schedule for the day." Falore pulled a three-by-five index card from his jacket pocket. "Says right here. Mrs. A. Charity luncheon, Hilton Hotel, twelve noon."

"Well, there's been a change in plans, Larry. I often change my plans. But there's no need advertising it, do you know what I mean?"

"Yes, I think I do."

She crossed her legs slowly, running a hand across her thigh. "Good, Larry. I appreciate that. You can take off now." They drove several blocks in silence, then she said, "Do you like picnics, Larry?"

"Sure. Everyone likes picnics."

Adele Abrams dug a gold cigarette case from her purse. "Think of a spot, Larry. A nice quiet spot for a picnic." The car phone rang and Adele picked it up, then pushed a button on the armrest. The window that separated the rear of the vehicle from the front seat hissed upward. The window, like all the glass on the Mercedes, was coated with Limotint, Smoke 5, the darkest tint allowable on the road. Visibility was near normal from inside, but if you stood outside and peered in, all you saw was your reflection. Falore took a glance at the rearview mirror, then patted the soft leather seat. "Not a bad spot for a picnic," he said softly.

Falore dropped Adele Abrams off at the restaurant on Stockton Street. She told him to come back for her in three hours. Long lunch, Falore thought as he pulled around the corner onto Filbert and spotted a parking spot in a white zone in front of St. Peter and Paul Church. He crossed Washington Square, noticing that the little park's lawn areas were empty, but due to a break in the weather, the green wooden benches were filling up with the usual mixture of old-time North Beach residents and the street people that were slowly taking over the park. He bought a meatball sandwich at the Bohemian Cigar Store, then wandered slowly back toward Moose's Restaurant. A half-dozen parking attendants, clad in purple windbreakers the color of the neon moose hanging over the restaurant's front door, were busy handling the lunchtime crowd. He found an empty bench with a view of the restaurant, wedging his way in between two old women. One read a foreign-language newspaper. The other, who had a small, sad-eyed black poodle in her lap, threw pieces of bread to a gathering of pigeons.

Falore was munching away at his sandwich when he saw Adele Abrams come out of the restaurant. She was not alone. A man with sun-bleached hair, no more than thirty, wearing a bronze leather jacket and chinos, had her by the arm. He gave the parking attendant a ticket. The couple chatted, laughing at each other's jokes until the attendant came back with a silver Porsche 911. Adele Abrams showed a lot of leg climbing into the small car. As Falore watched the Porsche accelerate down Stockton Street, he speculated on just where they were headed. The man's apartment? A motel? Some picnic spot he knew of?

The woman on his right nudged him with her elbow. "Are you going to finish that?" she asked, pointing an arthritic finger at the remains of Falore's sandwich.

He handed it to her, expecting to see her toss some to the pigeons or feed it to her dog. She set the dog on the pavement and took a bite of the sandwich, nodding her head in thanks as she chewed on a meatball.

Mary Ariza massaged her eyes with the palms of her hands. She had been reading the deposition transcripts relating to her client's rape case for almost two hours straight. First her client's, then the plaintiff's, then the bookstore owner's, and finally the police detective's.

She was reaching for another of the blue-bound deposition folders when her intercom buzzed.

The office receptionist's voice came over the line. "There's someone to see you, Miss Ariza. A priest. Father Torres."

"A priest? What's it about?"

Mary could hear Wanda asking the priest that very same question. "He says it's about the man who had the heart attack yesterday."

"Oh, all right. Send him in," Mary said, standing up, stretching to relieve the tension in her back and running a hand through her hair. She opened the door to her office, poked her head into the hallway, and saw the priest heading in her direction. She waved a hand. "This way, Father. It's easy to get lost around here."

"Yes," the priest answered. "A regular rabbit hutch. How many attorneys are there in your firm?"

"Twenty-two at the moment," Mary said, gesturing with her arm for him to enter the office. "Have a seat please, Father."

Mary studied him as he walked over to her "client's chair," a red leather high-back, the leather old and starting to crack. It was supposed to impress the client. "High quality, expensive, but old. Well used. Shows them that we're here for the long run," a senior partner in the firm had told her when he wheeled the chair into her office the first day she came to work for Pontar & Kerr. The priest didn't have the inflated stomach that she associated with most middle-aged men of the clergy. He was lean, athletic, with well-brushed hair and tinted aviator-style glasses. A handsome priest. She suddenly remembered a crush she'd had on a priest when she was in grammar school. Everyone said he was too good-looking a man to be a priest, as if only the homely should get a calling from God. She extended a hand. The priest seemed reluctant to take it and when he did, Mary noticed his hand was rough, heavily callused. It looked somehow out of place, not part of the package. Not the type of hand to offer a host at the altar. Maybe he was the type of priest who worked in a monastery where they tilled the soil, grew their own food.

"Please sit down, Father," she repeated, making her way back behind her desk. "How is the gentleman? Did he make it?"

Rene Santos gave her a mournful smile, feeling strangely off balance. The woman reminded him of someone. Who? "Sorry to say, no, he did not. But his family is very grateful to you for what you did. It was very courageous. Nowadays people don't want to get involved. It's nice to see a young woman like yourself is an exception to the rule."

Mary wondered what the priest wanted with her. "What brings you here, Father?"

Santos crossed one leg over the other, smoothing the crease to avoid wrinkles. "His family was wondering if he had any last words that they could take comfort from."

Mary brushed a lock of hair back from her forehead. "Well, to tell you the truth," she confided, "he thought I was a priest. He started to tell me his confession."

"Are you a Catholic?" Santos asked, finally placing who she reminded him of. The same face—the haughty Castillian features. The same eyes. The same nose, but it was the brushing of the hair gesture did it. Sister Angela. The angel. The nun who had visited the monastery twice a month. She seemed so pure, so chaste, her robe and white habit so immaculate. Untouchable. He had wondered what she looked like under that robe, under that habit. Was her head shaved? Was her body round? Flat? And one night he'd found out. Had watched through a crack in the door, saw her with the priests, a-straddle one while two others suckled at her breasts. Her skin was smooth alabaster, like the statues in the chapel. Her hair was short, like this one's. She'd brushed it back from her forehead when she bent over to engulf one of the priest's cocks. He still remembered the look on her face when he approached her on her next visit. He'd taken a bottle of wine from the kitchen—drinking to build up his courage. Finally the time had come. He found her alone in a deserted alcove. He stammered something about seeing her with the priests, then reached out to touch her, pulling his robe up, exposing himself. She'd laughed at him. Called him *carantamaula,* ugly face. Then she reported him to the priests. And watched while they punished him. Urged them on. It was a memory that had haunted him for years—but one that he had purged from his mind. Until now. Now it was back.

"Yes, I'm a Catholic, Father. But I have to admit, it's been a while since I've been to Mass."

"Just what did he tell you, if I may ask?"

"Well, it was rather strange. He spoke in Spanish."

"*Hable español?*"

"*Sí, poquito,*" Mary said, slipping directly into

Spanish, then grinning. "Though not as well as I used to. But I still understand it quite well."

"Where did you learn?"

"My parents are Spanish. My grandfather still lives in Spain. I visited there often during the summers when I was a girl."

Santos leaned forward, his elbows dropping to his knees. "What part of Spain?"

"Fuengirola."

"Ah, just near Málaga."

"You know Spain, Father?"

"A little."

"It's a small town, on the Mediterranean coast, the Costa del Sol."

Santos didn't need the geography lesson. His village of Pozoblanco was no more than a hundred miles away from the famed Costa del Sol, the Spanish Riviera. He had spent almost a full summer commuting between Málaga and Gilbraltar, often stopping at the rich little town of Fuengirola for something to eat. Gibraltar, where he'd killed three British bankers. "So, what did he tell you in Spanish?"

"Well, it was rather strange. He kept rambling, but there was something about killing. Someone called Rose."

Santos pressed his palms together in a prayer-like gesture. "He said he killed Rose?"

"Yes, I think so. It was confusing. Did he actually kill someone?"

"Perhaps, in his eyes. Rose was his daughter. She became pregnant. There was a family dispute. He forced her to leave the house. She died in childbirth."

"Oh, that's unfortunate," Mary said sincerely.

Santos fingers went to his cross. "Obviously, he never forgave himself. What else did he tell you?"

"Well, he was rambling quite a bit. Most of it was about Rose. And Peru, I think. Lima, Peru. Does that make sense?"

"He lived there for a short time," Santos confirmed in a soft voice. "Anything else?"

"Yes, there was something else. A man with a strange name. The conductor."

Santos's fingers tightened on the cross. "The conductor?"

"Yes. *El Cabecilla. Como se llama esto?* That's what it means, doesn't it? Conductor. Orchestra leader."

"Yes, exactly that. His father had a small band, played at weddings and things like that."

Mary looked at the priest with a questioning expression on her face. "He spoke strangely of his father. He was afraid of him. He kept repeating something about being afraid of the conductor."

Santos heaved himself out of the chair, brushed the seat of his pants, and said, "Was there anything else, Miss Ariza?"

"Not really. Not that I remember. He just rambled on and on. I wish I could be of more help, Father."

"Well, I've bothered you long enough." He stared at her for a moment, his mind once again racing back to Sister Angela and that night at the monastery. "Well, you were very kind. An act of mercy. I'm sure his family will take comfort in the fact that he thought of them in his last moments. Good day to you."

It wasn't until several minutes after the priest left that Mary realized he hadn't mentioned the name of the dead man.

Chapter 5

"Inspector Kordic. Line six."

Kordic stopped his two-finger assault on the typewriter and picked up the phone.

"Hey, Jack. Doc Phillips down at your friendly neighborhood coroner's office. That body you hauled in from the ocean yesterday. I've got something interesting. Come on down."

"Two minutes," Kordic said, settling the receiver back on its cradle.

Kordic took the elevator, keeping his expression blank as a group of scruffy, finger-snapping men, all in their late teens to early twenties, got on at the second floor. They laughed and patted one of their buddies, a tall, pasty-faced lad with carrot-colored hair pomaded into spikes. "I told you that judge didn't know from shit, didn't I, man?" The redhead turned and looked at Kordic, a smirk on his face. "Fuckin' cops suck too."

The others started laughing.

The elevator came to a stop at the first floor. Kordic elbowed his way to the front, making sure to step on the redhead's foot as he passed by.

"Hey, you mother—"

Kordic unbuttoned his sports coat, exposing the grip of his revolver. "Watch your language, Red. You may be celebrating too soon."

One of the teens pushed the button to send the elevator to the basement. Just before the doors closed, all of them gave Kordic the finger and began laughing again.

"And justice for all," Kordic muttered. He wondered just what charges the charming group had beaten in the courtroom: a stolen car, drugs, robbery, rape, attempted murder. All of the above? He exited the Hall of Justice's rear doors and walked less than a hundred yards to the medical examiner's office.

Assistant coroner Alvin Phillips greeted him warmly. He was forty-two, a bachelor, with a lean, ascetic face. Despite his occupation, he always seemed as if he was about to break into a smile. "Hey, Jack. This is some little mystery you dropped in my lap."

"I know you get tired of the routine stuff, Al. Just trying to help out."

"Come on. I'll show you what I've got so far."

Though he'd been in Homicide for five years, Kordic's stomach always did little flip-flops when he entered the autopsy room. The stench of strong chemicals and human waste assaulted his nostrils. There were six stainless steel tables spread across the tile floor. Red rubber tubes, looking too much like giant veins to suit Kordic, were attached to each table, along with a sump sink. Alongside was a rubber-wheeled cart, made of the same stainless steel as the autopsy tables. It held a variety of knives, saws, and a scale to weigh the victim's organs.

Dr. Alvin Phillips was a tall, thin man. He moved like a bird, head on skinny neck bobbing with each step. He walked over to one of the tables and pulled back a bloodstained sheet. The body rescued from the ocean was stretched out on the table. A large cut, from sternum to naval, had been sewn up with big cross-stitches.

"Good thing you didn't decide to go in for plastic surgery, Doc," Kordic said.

Phillips chuckled. "I don't need much of a bedside manner in this job either, my friend. Your victim is no kid. I'd say somewhere in his mid to late seventies. In excellent shape. A jogger maybe. With his head attached, he'd be about five-five or five-six. Probably weighed a hundred forty pounds. Burn marks on his stomach, thighs, testicles, and penis. Probably made by a cigarette, from the size and depth of the burns."

"Anal penetration?" asked Kordic.

"No. No sexual assault. This wasn't a romance. Hands and head were severed postmortem. Not a very neat job. Here's something interesting." Phillips pointed a ballpoint pen at the man's left forearm. "Take a look at the tattoo."

Kordic took a deep breath, then stooped over to examine the tattoo. It looked like it had been there for some time, a row of pinkish flowers that might have been red when the tattoo was new. "Looks likes roses. Nothing special."

"Take another look," Phillips said, handing Kordic a round-lensed magnifying glass.

Kordic took his time. When he finally pulled his head up, he asked, "Is there another tattoo under the flowers?"

Phillips flashed a big grin. "Give the detective a star. Yes. Numbers. I can't make them all out. I'm having the crime lab come down and see what they can make of it. Come on into my office, Jack."

Phillips's office consisted of a gray metal desk, a matching file cabinet, two wooden chairs, and an old stand-up refrigerator, bare metal showing through around the handle. A St. Pauli Girl poster and a round office clock were the only decorations on the walls.

Phillips opened the refrigerator and took out two glasses and a flat plastic bottle filled to the top with a dark amber liquid. He poured them both a drink. Kordic picked up his glass and examined it. Then he looked at the bottle: IMPERIUM SUPER-CONCENTRATED EMBALMING FLUID, the brown and gold label read. Kordic ran the glass under his nose.

"Manhattan," Phillips said, flopping into his chair and leaning back with the air of a man who was through for the day. "Make them myself. At least I never have to worry about the night cleaning crew going through my refrigerator and stealing my stash." He held up his glass. "Cheers."

Kordic balanced the glass in his hand as if it were filled with gold and he was assaying its worth. He had made a promise to himself. Nothing hard before five o'clock. He glanced up at the clock. Not even close.

Still, he didn't want to offend the good doctor. He took a precautionary sip.

"Time of death is going to be a bitch, Jack. He was probably in the water a day or two. Not much more than that."

"Actual cause of death?"

Phillips patted his chest. "Ticker gave out. He must have been a tough old buzzard to last as long as he did."

"Any way to tell how he entered the water? Was it right there by the cliffs? Dropped off the bridge? Any ideas at all?"

"No. You'll have to talk to the Coast Guard or someone who knows about the tides and currents. A great many of his bones were broken. All postmortem, from that battering he took in the water. Still, it's interesting, isn't it? An old man is tortured, murdered, and then his head and hands are chopped off and he's dumped into the Pacific Ocean. I don't see much of a chance of identifying the body, unless a friend or relative reports a man that age with roses tattooed on his arm as missing." Phillips drained his glass and set it carefully down on the desk's blotter. "It's a mystery, Jack. But that's what they pay us for, isn't it?"

"Sometimes I wonder," Kordic said. He tilted his head and took a deep swallow. The whiskey hit the back of his throat, and he could almost feel it coating his teeth. "Sometimes I wonder," he repeated when he got his breath back.

Kordic tried it the easy way first, checking the missing persons lists. There were no reports for anyone matching the description of the headless victim. Clint Olsen from the crime lab dropped by his desk and gave him the photographs of the tattoo.

"Best we could do, Jack," Olsen said, handing Kordic a manila envelope.

Kordic studied the pictures. There were eight in all, four actual size, the rest magnified. He concentrated on the vines of the roses entangled with the numbers underneath. Kordic stuffed the photographs back into the envelope, chalked "out in field" in the space alongside his name on the Homicide roster list, and took the elevator down to the Hall of Justice garage. No hopped-up druggies on this trip, just the sad faces of victims, either of the criminals on the streets or the court system itself. Interspersed among the downtrodden were a few well-dressed, smiling attorneys.

Kordic drove four blocks to the 1100 block of Folsom, finding a parking spot next to a fire hydrant less than fifty yards from his destination: Bona's Tattoo Parlor.

Bill Bona looked like a yuppie businessman when he was dressed up in a conservative business suit, his chestnut brown hair cut military-style, his soft, oval face framed by tortoiseshell-framed glasses. You could just make out the start of a little coloring when he pulled up his cuff to look at his watch. That bit of color turned into a rainbow of interwoven tattoos picturing everything from daggers to tigers to tulips to smiling, voluptuous women, all covering some ninety percent of his body. Like many tattoo artists, Bona had the simple proclamation *Your Name* printed on the inside of one wrist.

Bona had been helpful to the police department numerous times in identifying tattoos, both the legitimate parlor types and the heated ballpoint pen experiments done in the privacy of a prison cell.

Somebody really had to want a tattoo to get to Bona's office, located on the second floor of a warehouse that catered to commercial photographers and artists. A rickety flight of stairs led to a small room, the walls blanketed with photographs of clients showing off the results of Bona's handiwork on various parts of their anatomy.

A young man with a ponytail and silver earring of interconnected pyramids dangling down to his shoulders greeted Kordic with the enthusiasm a kitten shows for a pit bull.

"Whatjawant?" he asked, an unlighted cigarette dangling from his lips.

Kordic showed his badge. "Where's Bill?"

"Inback. Youwannaseehim?"

It took Kordic a few seconds to decipher the boy's reply. "I'm a friend. I know the way."

He walked down a narrow hallway, the walls decorated with more pictures of tattooed flesh, past a cubicle with a padded leather dental chair and an array of drills. He was glad Bona wasn't plying his trade. On his last visit to the parlor he'd had to question Bona while he was putting a small valentine heart of the beefy buttock of a woman wearing motorcycle leathers. He found Bona in his office, dressed in faded jeans and a white tank top that showed off his handiwork.

Kordic fanned the photographs the crime lab had taken across the desk. "I've got a problem with this one, Bill," he said, then gave Bona a brief rundown on the condition of the corpse taken from the ocean.

Bona studied the photographs by holding them up to the halogen drafting lamp clamped to the corner of the desk, then taking a magnifying glass from his desk drawer, moving it slowly across the pictures, his nose only inches from the glass. "Yeah, I see what you mean. The roses are a cover-up. I can only make out three of the numbers." He reached into his desk drawer again, took out a Lucite ruler, and maneuvered it around one of the pictures. "This one is life-size, I take it."

"You take it correctly," Kordic said, ignoring the irony of life-sized photographs of a portion of a corpse.

"Room for eight, maybe nine numbers, I make it," Bona said, pursing his lips and holding the picture up to the halogen lamp again. "The numbers you can see look faded, old as hell." He turned an eye to Kordic. "Might be some of Hilter's concentration-camp work. The stiff old enough for that?"

"Yes. He's the right age. Can you tell me anything about the roses?"

"I can tell you who did it," Bona said, letting the photograph fall softly to the desk. "Looks like Al Vasso's work."

"How can you tell?" Kordic asked, picking up the photograph Bona had been studying.

"If you look closely, you'll see the stems at the bottom of the roses form a V. Vasso's autograph."

Kordic looked at the picture again. "Wouldn't the stems normally end like that?"

"Sure. But they're exaggerated. I couldn't testify to it in court, but I'd lay down some of my own money that Vasso did it."

"How can I get in touch with Vasso?"

"You'd need long-distance, Jack. Real long-distance. He worked out of Los Angeles. Died about five, maybe six years ago. Sold his business before he cashed in. I don't know who's running it now, but if they kept Al's old records, you still might be in luck."

Bona reached out and began spinning his Rolodex. He pulled a card loose. "Here. Last address and phone number I had for Vasso. Hope it helps."

Chapter 6

The hook-shaped pier at Aquatic Park was almost deserted. A few Vietnamese youths, the oldest no more than twelve, leaned against the chipped and weather-stained concrete bulkhead, watching the tips of their rods intently, occasionally pulling on the rope attached to their crab pots. A couple in their twenties, the man ill-dressed for the weather in a suit and tie, the woman in jeans and a cable-knit sweater, stood nearby. They were having an argument, the woman with her hands jammed into her jeans pockets, unmindful of the wind whipping her hair across her face, the man solemn-faced, a look of resentment stitched into his features.

A man in a putty-colored trench coat and black nylon rain hat hunched his shoulders against the wind. He passed the children and wandered slowly, giving the quarreling young lovers a wide berth. His eyes were fixed on the figure at the end of the pier, decked out in a navy knit watch cap, khaki hooded canvas parka and, despite the gloomy weather, wraparound sunglasses.

"Any luck?" asked the tall man in the trench coat.

"It takes more than luck," Rene Santos answered, looking out into the choppy bay waters. "It takes great skill."

"I've never had much skill."

"You must be Russian," Santos replied, glad that the silly code game was over. He had recognized Boris Zorkin immediately, having watched from the other room while Zorkin, an unknown Russian technician, and Naimat had interrogated Joseph Rose, the petroleum engineer. Rene leaned his fishing pole against the pier wall and studied the Russian, seeing a solid,

weather-worn man in the prime of his early forties. He
had small, button-like black eyes. Shifty eyes. The
eyes of an assassin.

"The information we obtained from Rose was excellent," Zorkin said. "Viktor was quite happy."

"Your engineer got all the information he needed before Rose died?"

A gust of wind caused Zorkin to clamp a hand on
his hat to keep it from flying away. "Yes. All we
needed. Now the old Jew is dead and buried. But only
we know that for sure, right? His staff thinks he's still
alive, and in Russia."

"Right," Santos said, then added, "I lost a man."

"What? How did that happen?" Boris Zorkin demanded, the wind dropping his voice down to a whisper.

"That most confusing of circumstances. Natural
causes. Brought on by a lifetime of neglect. A heart attack."

That seemed to appease Zorkin. "What of Paul
Abrams? How long until you get him?"

Santos moved his jaw as if chewing gum. "He con-
tinues to be a problem. No set pattern. He goes to the
office some days, some days he does not. When he
does go, it can be anywhere from nine in the morning
to four in the afternoon. He works a great deal of the
time at home. When he does go out, there are always
the bodyguards."

Boris grunted, a trace of contempt in his voice. "We
told you that. It's because of his brother's kidnapping
years ago. He is paranoid about security. We told you
that also."

Santos tapped a finger against the Russian's chest.
"You didn't tell me that the bodyguards were San
Francisco police officers."

Zorkin brushed a hand across his chest as if to wipe
away Santos's touch. "What difference does it make?
Are you saying you can't handle the job?"

Santos's voice turned ice-cold. He began raising his
right arm slowly, stopping when it reached shoulder
level. He spoke in Russian. "Listen, you piss ant of a

man. You worthless piece of dog shit. Don't ever question me like that again. If I raise this arm another few inches, your head will be blown off your body and I'll heave what is left of you into the bay. Do you understand what I'm telling you?"

"I meant no disrespect," the Russian assured Santos testily. "It was merely a question. Do you need help? Men? Equipment? What? I am here to help you."

Santos let his arm drop to his side. "I'll be in touch. You may go," he said dismissively. He watched the Russian stalk off, his pace increasing with each stride.

He lingered a full five minutes, then left the pier. The Vietnamese boys waited until Santos was well past them before running down to the end of the pier and retrieving the unattended fishing rod. One of the boys reeled in the line. "Look," he yelled to his companions when the weights at the end of the line banged against the rod's tip. "No hooks. The man had no hooks."

Cesar Davila shuffled up alongside Santos, his large feet barely raising themselves above the pavement. "Zorkin was alone. A Ford Taurus, gray, four-door, California plates number 2UKZ3321."

"He came straight from the embassy?"

"Yes," Davila answered. "No one followed him."

"Good work. Let's get a drink somewhere. I'm freezing. I've got a job for you. One you should enjoy."

They hiked along the shoreline, past the Maritime Museum, a white two-story building that looked like the upper deck of an ocean liner. The bay waters lapping up to the cobblestone path had a murky, brownish tinge. Two park rangers on horseback, in dark green uniforms and cowboy-style hats, rode by, the horses breaking up a stream of high school students in berry-colored sweatshirts jogging down toward the pier. They cut through a small park ringed by old-fashioned streetlights, then up Hyde Street to a neon sign advertising the Buena Vista Café. The saloon was filled with tourists. Santos picked up excited conversations in German, French, and Dutch. A sign over the bar claimed that the drink Irish coffee had been invented on the premises.

Davila ordered a brandy; Santos decided to try the house specialty. The mixture of coffee, whiskey, sugar, and heavy whipped cream was one more American disappointment to Santos. He wiped the mustache of cream from his lip and signaled to the bartender for a brandy.

They took their drinks to the only open area available, by the front door.

"How was Zorkin?" Davila asked.

"Arrogant. A typical Russian. I don't know what Petrov is up to, Cesar. It doesn't feel right."

"We can always go home."

Santos swirled his brandy, watching it bathe the glass. Home. Where the hell was that?

Davila said, "The old Jew, Rose. You got his checks, didn't you? His credit cards? We could squeeze a lot out of those."

"Forget him. We still have to get Paul Abrams. But first there's the woman Liberto spoke to. This Mary Ariza. I want you to kill her. Liberto told her too much. He mentioned Peru, and Rose, but she didn't know what it meant."

Davila pulled his size-eighteen neck in like a turtle. "Where shall I do it?"

Santos dug a piece of scratch paper from his jacket pocket and passed it to Davila. "Her home address." Finding Avila's address had been easy. He had spent days digging through public records on Paul Abrams. He knew his political affiliation, the amount of property he owned and its estimated worth, the permits for the work he had done on his home, including the security alarm system. All the information was public record, there for the asking. Locating Mary Ariza had taken just one trip to the San Francisco City Hall. She was an upstanding American citizen. A registered voting Democrat, her name, address, even her birth date duly recorded in the data base, available to anyone who came to the voter registration desk and entered her name into the computer. She had registered less than a month ago, so the address was bound to be valid. "Get her when she comes home from work tomorrow."

Davila shrugged. "Consider it done."

Santos sipped the brandy, imagining the look of terror on the Ariza woman's face when she saw Davila. The look that would have been on Sister Angela's beautiful Castillian face if she had been at the monastery when he killed the priests. It was his only regret about that night—that the nun hadn't been there. Ariza had said that her grandparents were from Spain. Fuengirola. So close to where I was born. So close to the monastery. Could she be related to the nun? A cousin? A relative of some type? "Use a knife, Cesar. Make it look like a sexual attack."

Jack Kordic stood and rubbed the small of his back. It had been a long and, so far, uneventful day. The telephone number that Bill Bona had given him for the Los Angeles tattoo artist Vasso had been reassigned to a carpet shop four years ago. Vasso was well-known, but the consensus was that when he died, his shop had been disbanded. No one had taken over the business. No one knew what had become of his old records.

Lieutenant Chris Sullivan's raspy voice broke into Kordic's thoughts:

"Hey, Jack. You're starting to make a habit of working late. I can't justify writing in any more overtime. How you making out?"

Kordic rubbed his forehead with a hand, as if soothing away the pain. "Okay, Chris. Not having much luck in identifying that stiff from the ocean."

"Forget the case, Jack. I'm talking about you. How's it going?"

Kordic perched on the edge of his desk. The detail room was empty, all the inspectors having left at, or just before, the stroke of five o'clock. Kordic could remember times when the room would be a beehive of activity far into the night, the detectives working on cases whether they could pull in overtime or not. Or they'd be waiting for their partner to finish his report before hustling over to Cookie's or the Lineup for a drink. The department's budget had eliminated overtime, but the real reason the room was empty at quitting time was that somehow, over the last several years, the whole department's spirit had been broken. Not just in Homicide and the other detective divisions, but in the station houses, the traffic division, everywhere a "do nothing, then you won't get in shit" attitude had developed. The only people who seemed to buck the trend were the members of the Stress unit. They had more work than they could handle, but handle it they did. Kordic was living proof of that.

The malaise had started years ago and survived through numerous administrations and a series of chiefs. One had come up from southern California, another had been a former cop and city supervisor who lasted less than a month after he ordered his men to remove underground newspapers from their racks because they contained an unflattering story about him. And on and on. They came, they stayed, mostly for a year to get the added benefits to their pensions, then left. And it seemed to make no difference. The enthusiasm, the camaraderie, the "us against them," the "good guys against the bad guys" feeling was gone. The kind of cop who used to stay well beyond the time needed for their pensions now retired at the earliest opportunity. They couldn't wait to get out. Kordic was just the opposite. He was afraid to get out.

"I'm doing fine, Chris, just fine," Kordic said, wondering how long his mind had been wandering.

Sullivan slipped on his suit coat. "I'm sorry about not being able to hook you up with a partner yet, Jack. You know the problem. Soon as I get the okay, we'll get another inspector in here. What do you hear from Benny?"

Benny Munes, Kordic's partner before Kordic had been put off duty for almost a year on stress disability, had retired. "He's doing good. Got a letter from him yesterday."

"Good. And don't worry about Tilson. I can handle him."

"He won't be satisfied until I'm out of here."

"Yeah. It came up in the meeting today. But I'm on your side. Anything you need, you just ask, okay?'"

"I know. Thanks, Chris."

Sullivan seemed as if her were about to say something, then he just patted Kordic on the back. "Hang in there, Jack. You sure you're okay working alone? I can bounce you into Public Affairs or the Permit Bureau until the purse strings loosen up."

Kordic shook his head. He had spent two months in the Permit Bureau when he first came back on duty. Only the report from Dr. Flaherty authorizing Kordic to return to his old assignment had gotten him back into the Homicide detail. The doctor wanted monthly feedback from Kordic's supervisor on how he was doing. And Chris Sullivan was doing just that. They had worked together at a couple of district stations, when Kordic was a patrolman and Sullivan a sergeant. Sullivan was a throwback, a sharp, solid, caring man who took a personal interest in every person who worked for him. Too many of the new breed seemed to be interested in nothing but taking courses in "Mid-Management Training," "Public Awareness," or "Crime Prevention Through Environmental Design." Architectural police courses. Everyone wanted to be an architect, no one wanted to be a plumber. Sullivan was a plumber who didn't mind getting his hands dirty.

"No, I'm fine," Kordic said. "Just fine."

"Okay. Something will pop up on your stiff. Either that or there'll be another one to take his place," Sullivan said ruefully. He couldn't remember a time when there had been so many homicides—the victims shot, beaten, tortured, knifed, burned, hung, drowned, buried alive—the killers ranging from pimple-faced adolescents to crusty senior citizens. The slightest thing could set them off. A careless remark, a traffic violation, a radio too loud. Throw in the gangs, the hard-core robbery and assault victims, and it came close to epidemic proportions. "One thing we don't have to worry about is a lack of work. See you in the morning."

Kordic watched as Sullivan left the room, his thoughts turning to Wesley Tilson. That not too subtle crack he'd made the other night. Tilson leaving, "going home now. To the wife and kids."

He looked at the calendar. It was close to an anniversary. Almost a year ago. A year ago that his wife and young son had been killed. It was a scenario he'd gone over in his head a million times. Linda and Danny coming in to the city to do some shopping, then they were all going out to dinner. Linda had driven across the Bay Bridge, taken the Fifth Street off-ramp, and was heading toward a parking garage when someone stuck a gun in the car's window. Got her to open the door. Then shot them both. Danny had died right on the spot, but Linda made it to the hospital. She was able to tell Kordic what happened before she died. She was getting out of the car, offering no resistance. Neither was the boy. Kordic had drilled them on what to do in a crisis situation. Something spooked the bastard. Kordic never found out just what. Perhaps it was the police department credit-union sticker on the car's window. Something spooked him, or maybe he was just wasted on drugs. He shot them both and drove off. Never was caught. The car was found abandoned near Candlestick Park.

Almost a year. It didn't seem that long ago. But then, Kordic admitted to himself, he'd been dead drunk much of that time.

Chapter 7

Cesar Davila started his day with a visit to the auto-salvage yard. The map of San Francisco that Rene Santos had given him identified the area as the Potrero District. The streets were either numbered or had names of states, such as Mississippi, Indiana, Tennessee, Michigan, and Illinois. He had checked several wrecking yards and found the one on Michigan the most to his liking. The neighborhood consisted mostly of rundown, metal-front shop buildings. Now and then there was a row of dilapidated houses looking as if they would all fall down if they weren't leaning against each other. The streets were wide, full of potholes and cracks that sprouted foot-high weeds. The people walking the streets were almost all black. There was a smell of incinerated garbage in the air. He coasted his motorcycle to a stop alongside a flatbed truck stacked with what once had been automobiles. Now there were smashed metal carcasses no more than two or three feet high, piled one on top of the other. Davila counted three stacks of six to a stack. He examined the hulks carefully, but in their present condition he could not tell just what make or model they once had been.

A sleek black Doberman came charging toward the chain-link fence, snarling, his teeth bared. Davila called out to him in Spanish, "*Quieto, hombre, quieto.*" He reached into his pocket and shoved a ball of ground meat through the fence. The dog skidded to a stop, his dark eyes bouncing from the towering man to the meat at his feet. Davila continued to soothe him with his voice: "*Ah, hombre, lechero, lechero, comer.*" The dog ducked his head to the meat and took a tentative lick, then gobbled the whole ball in one bite.

Davila shoved two more balls of the meat laced with Valium through the fence. The Doberman soon dropped to the ground, not asleep but groggy. Davila heaved his bulk over the fence, dropping down along-side the animal. He bent down and lightly patted its haunches, then surveyed the yard. There had to be a hundred vehicles of all types: big trucks, small trucks, sedans, sports cars, vans. All were in various states of disrepair: doors, bumpers, engine parts cannibalized before being sent to the crusher. He decided on a red late-model Chevrolet. He pulled a screwdriver from his jacket pocket and began removing the license plates.

Davila climbed back over the fence and drove to an-other parking lot in the downtown area, one whose billboard advertised IN & OUT PRIVILEGES. He spotted a Chevrolet that would suit his purposes perfectly, a beige four-door sedan. The parking attendant, a tall, l nky young man with a freckled face and flax-colored hair, was too busy wedging a BMW convertible into a spot at the back of the lot to notice Davila slipping into the Chevrolet. The key was in the ignition. He turned the engine over and hit the accelerator, and the car moved off quickly and quietly. He drove aimlessly for a few blocks, then pulled over and examined his new acquisition. Nothing fancy. The glove compartment held a pair of inexpensive, plastic-framed sunglasses, a small box of Kleenex, and some crumpled food wrap-pers. He checked under the seats, then took the keys out of the ignition and walked around to the back of the car to check the trunk. A blanket, a set of golf clubs, golf shoes, a scuffed red plastic tool box that held an array of hand tools. Certainly nothing worth stealing. Davila bounced the car keys in his hands. The man who owned these keys would undoubtedly report his car stolen. Perhaps try to sue the idiots who ran the parking lot. He tossed the keys in his hands again, then slid back behind the wheel. It would have been a sim-ple matter just to hot-wire a car, or steal one with the keys in it. But Santos had been specific in his instruc-

tions. And Davila had to agree with him. Once he replaced the plates with the ones taken from the car at
the junkyard, the Chevy was as good as invisible. And
he had the keys. Amateurs made the mistake of stealing a car by starting it up from exposed ignition wires.
The wires were easily spotted by soldiers, police, nosy
neighbors. And without the car keys the vehicle had to
be left unlocked. The keys made all the difference.

He dug a map from his jacket pocket and found the
place Santos had marked, a clothing store on Market
Street, just a few blocks away. Since parking tickets
were of no concern, he left the car in a bus stop directly in front of the store. Davila picked out a dark
blue vinyl jacket and a baseball cap of the same color
and handed them to the man behind the counter.

"What do you want on them?" the man asked, impatiently tapping his fingers on the counter.

Davila passed him the paper with the instructions
from Rene Santos. The man nodded his head. "What
size print?"

Santos's instructions hadn't taken the print size into
consideration. Davila's face registered confusion.

"Usually we do two inches on the jacket, one inch
on the caps. That okay?" The man was middle-aged,
with a Buddha-like stomach, his sparse gray hair carefully arranged to cover an expanse of waxy scalp. The
look on his face and the tone of his voice made Davila
want to reach across the counter and slap some respect
into the bastard, but he simply said, "*Sí. Perfecto*. It's
okay."

The man took the garments and shuffled toward his
press. Davila thought he heard him mumble something
about "fucking beaners," but he paid little attention.
He was excited now. He could feel himself starting to
get an erection. All the tedious preparation was done.
Now he could get the woman. He rubbed his hands together like a man anticipating a gourmet meal and
started to whistle.

The man glanced up from his machine and gave him
a crooked smile.

* * *

The librarian looked up at Rene Santos, her mouth drawn in a tight, disapproving line. She examined the request form. "I can't give you more than three rolls at a time," she said.

"I understand," Santos said, his voice soft and eminently reasonable. He had been coming to the reference section of the main library for several days, dealing with the same pinch-faced young woman who released the microfilm copies of the newspapers as if she were passing over secret documents from CIA vaults.

"Do you want the *Chronicle* or the *Examiner*?"

"Both, please."

"You can only have one at a time, you know."

"Yes, I know."

"And you have to leave your library card or driver's license with me."

Santos sighed, staring at the young woman's long, crane-like neck. The urge to wrap a hand around that neck was getting stronger and stronger with each visit. He fished his wallet from his pants pocket and handed her one of the three California driver's licenses neatly tucked among the half-dozen credit cards.

The woman took the license, squinting as her eyes bounced from the license photograph to Santos. Satisfied at last, she rose from her chair, walked over to the grimy gray metal filing cabinet, returning with three cigarette-pack-sized cardboard cartons. "These are the *Chronicle*. You'll have to return them before I can give you the *Examiner*."

Santos nodded his thanks, then took the materials over to one of the reviewing machines. The library was crowded again, all but one of the machines taken. Santos snapped in the cartridge, threaded the end of the microfilm through the lens, then pressed the forward button, slowly monitoring the pages of the last year's newspaper as the grainy images flashed on the screen. He went through each edition studiously, starting at page one and going through every section of the paper except the classified. It was a long, arduous task, but one that he could not trust to anyone else, partly because he was not sure what he was looking for. Over the past several days he had seen numerous stories on Paul Abrams: some on the front page, others in the business section, the gossip columns, and the society pages. He made copies of the photographs showing Abrams at his wedding, with his young wife at social functions. Abrams usually wore a stiff, formal tuxedo, his wife a low-cut, clinging gown. Most of the photos had been taken at the opening of a visiting Broadway production or a charity ball for one of those causes the rich seemed to prefer: AIDS, the homeless, gay rights. The fact that these causes also were the ones given the most attention by the press was not lost on Santos. In several of the photographs he could see Abrams's ever present bodyguards hovering in the background. He found nothing of interest on the microfilm covering August or September.

Paul Abrams was a difficult subject. Santos had seen presidents and generals with less protection than Abrams had. The newspaper articles had described him as an eccentric. His hobbies were those of a collector: paintings, stamps, coins, rare books. No golf or tennis matches for Mr. Abrams. Santos wondered about the man's passions. The young wife, that was one obvious passion, but what of others? What drove him? His collecting? Money? Born to money, what else was there to do but make more money? The old cliché of the one who dies with the most toys had all too much truth to it. The ultra-rich studied the publications that rated their wealth with all the intensity that a jeweler gives a raw diamond about to be cut and polished.

Santos stood to stretch his muscles, glancing around the gloomy room at his fellow time travelers, wondering what brought them to use the antiquated screening machines. What was it in those back issues that would be of interest to the old man in the dirty tweed sports coat with a heavy smoker's hack? Or the young woman with an infant strapped to her back in a papoose-type harness? The two men in expensive business suits: lawyers? Perhaps some type of policemen? No, they wouldn't be police. The police would have other, quicker means to dig up the desired information. Santos sank back into the hard wooden chair and started on the tape for last October. He was almost at the end when the décolletage of Adele Abrams caught his eye. She was walking up a staircase, her husband trailing dutifully behind. Other middle-aged couples filled the photo, the men all tuxedoed, the woman dressed in flowing gowns, their necks encircled with elaborate jewelry.

The caption over the photograph proclaimed: Paul and Adele Abrams were among those hurrying to their seats at the Special Grand Opera Charity Performance.

A companion story featured more pictures of the rich guests, "all done up in their best for the party of the year. Each event seems to get better and better," the writer gushed. "A tremendous alfresco pre-opera feast featured caviar, champagne, oysters, all served by gorgeous hunks dressed up as palace servants out of one of those old Ali Baba and the Forty Thieves movies, and oh, so many beautiful people having a beautiful time. If you could only make one party a year, this was definitely the one. I can hardly wait till next year, darlings."

Santos glanced at his watch, focusing on the day-date calendar. "Next year is almost here, darling," he murmured softly.

Kordic received some good news the following morning. The messenger was Dr. Phillips of the coroner's office.

"Jack, I've got a definite on those numbers under the rose tattoo."

Kordic reached for a pencil. "Shoot."

"Shouldn't you think of a better phrase for the remittance of important information?" Phillips replied dryly. "Anyway, here they are: 2036082."

"Nice work, Doc. How'd you decipher them?"

"Simple. I just peeled off the tattoo and looked from the inner side of the skin."

Kordic winced at the thought of the procedure Phillips had performed, thanked the good doctor, dropped the phone on its cradle, and stared at the numbers. Seven digits. The same as in a standard telephone number. Who would put a telephone number on his forearm? His stomach tightened as he recalled a summer vacation with his late wife and son at a resort in nearby Lake County. Kordic thought of the people in the cabin next to them, Marty and Judith Newberger. Marty was a building contractor from Napa. Danny had noticed that there were numbers tattooed on his forearm, and in childlike innocence asked about them. Newberger had made a small joke about the numbers being his phone number. Then one night over cocktails he loosened up and told Kordic and Linda about his life in Germany. Where was it? Not Berlin. Hamburg, that was it. The Nazis took the family. Marty was only sixteen, but already a skilled journeyman painter and carpenter in his father's business. That was how he survived. Having usable skills. Painting and carpentry.

Kordic had seen all the movies, the television shows, read dozens of books about Nazi atrocities, but it wasn't until that warm August evening on the cabin's deck, sipping martinis, listening to Newberger's story, that the true horror of it all hit him. Newberger had been forced to help build labor camps. At one camp the Nazis would interrogate Polish officer, having them stand in front of a gray-painted wooden wall. If the questions were not answered to the interrogator's satisfaction, he'd simply shoot the man. Marty and his crew's job was to drag the body away, clean up the mess, mop up the blood, and putty and paint the wall if the bullet had passed through the victim's body. There were other stories, so graphic that Kordic had sent his son on an errand to the store, afraid the boy would have nightmares if he listened to any more of the horror. To the truth.

Maybe just for once it would be simple. He punched the numbers into the phone. There were two rings, then a phone company-recorded message came on informing him that the call could not go through. He tried the operator. There were no 203 prefixes in the Bay Area.

He dialed the FBI number from memory, but after

being transferred to six different extensions and telling his story, all he learned was that the FBI did not have a list of German prisoner-of-war numbers.

Kordic dug through the phone book for the local number for the Central Intelligence Agency. There was no address listed, just the number, though Kordic knew from past experience that the CIA's offices were located just a floor away from the FBI's at the Federal Building on Golden Gate Avenue. The receptionist took Kordic's name and number, and advised him that she'd have someone get in touch with him "as soon as possible."

Dale Jarvis, the CIA agent that called some forty minutes later, did not seem all that interested in Kordic's problem. "That's old stuff, Inspector. We've got nothing on file. All the big-time Nazis are either long dead or already in some Israeli jail. Are you sure those numbers are from a German camp?"

"No," Kordic admitted, "not sure at all."

"Could be anything," Jarvis suggested. "Some of the European countries tattooed their army and navy ID numbers on their arms. The Russians too, I think."

Kordic thanked Jarvis for his input. He stared down at the numbers on the pad again, then began doodling, covering them with a crudely drawn rose. The man had wanted the numbers hidden, camouflaged by the flowers. Why? He picked up the phone book and looked up the number for the Israeli Consulate.

The Israeli Consulate and the Israeli Government Tour Office shared the same address, 220 Bush Street. Kordic rode the elevator to the twelfth floor. A small buzzer and intercom were set at eye level alongside the entrance door. Kordic pushed the buzzer, then looked up at the mini-TV camera mounted on the ceiling.

Static crackled over the intercom, then a female voice asked, "Can I help you?"

Kordic identified himself and the door clicked open. He entered a waiting room with a long mahogany table in the center. Against the far wall a young woman sat behind a glass window. It reminded Kordic of the type of windows in prisons: thick, tinted glass with a slot at the bottom for passing papers. The glass had that light green, slightly wavy look that bullet-proofing does to a surface.

Kordic showed his badge to the gamin-faced girl on the other side of the glass. She appeared to be no older than twenty-five. He gave her a brief explanation of the purpose of his visit.

"I'll have Mr. Freeman help you, sir. He'll be with you in a minute."

Kordic wandered around the room, looking at the travel posters that covered most of the wall space. One of them should have received whatever type of award they give to the best travel posters, he thought. The picture was of a lush green valley dotted with orchards. The print stated:

ON THE SEVENTH DAY HE RESTED
GUESS WHERE?

A short string-bean of a man in his fifties, dressed in a conservative dark blue suit, entered the room. What was left of his hair was gray and cut very close to his scalp. A curved briar pipe was clenched between his teeth.

"Max Freeman, sir. How can I help you?"

Kordic took out his badge again and showed it to Freeman, who, unlike most people when shown identification, took the time to study it carefully.

"Here's my problem," Kordic said. "I've got a body of a man somewhere in his seventies. The head and hands were amputated. The only identification I've been able to come up with is a tattoo on his arm. Seven numbers." He took a note pad from his jacket and read off the numbers: 2036082.

"And you believe that these numbers may be German concentration camp numbers?" Freeman asked.

"It's just a possibility. There was another tattoo. Roses that covered the numbers. The roses were put on after the numbers. We don't know how long after."

"As if to conceal the numbers?"

"It kind of looks that way. It took quite a bit of work for our medical examiner to come up with the numbers." Kordic gave Freeman a description of the medical technique Dr. Phillips had used.

"Very interesting," Freeman said. He sat still for a moment, tapping his pipe stem lightly against his teeth.

"Unfortunately, Inspector, as thorough and as methodical as the Nazis were, they did not keep very accurate records on their concentration camp prisoners. Seized property, valuable art or jewelry, that they recorded with a passion. But human life was too cheap. Especially Jewish human life. Not worth the effort. There are some records we have come across, but I have no idea what the odds are that your particular numbers are on file. I will send a cable and see what turns up. That's all that I can promise."

Chapter 8

The double shifts were getting to Larry Falore. He leaned back in the Mercedes seat, folded his arms across his chest, slid down as far as he could, and closed his eyes. He could hear the soft patter of rain falling on the car's roof. He'd gotten off work at Ingleside Station just before eight in the morning, drove directly home, showered, shaved, and changed into the required blue blazer, gray slacks, white shirt, and red tie while his wife got ready for work.

The double shifts were getting to Jennie, too. Now almost seven months pregnant, going to work at the insurance company was becoming a chore. But she wanted to work as long as she could. They had talked often about the sacrifices they were making, but both had decided it was worth it. Once they got enough for the down payment, they could buy a house. The house was the goal they were working for. Making all the sacrifices for. But once the goal was achieved, the money saved, another decision would have to be made. Where to buy? For the same price they would pay for a forty-year-old two-bedroom home in San Francisco, they could get a new three- or four-bedroom home in the suburbs. The downside was the commute from the town of Fremont in the East Bay to San Francisco. Forty-five minutes when traffic was clear, which it never was during commute hours. It wouldn't affect Larry that much. His shift either started at four in the afternoon or at midnight. But Jennie would have a hell of a time getting to the insurance company on Montgomery Street. If she had to give up her job, they would barely be able to afford the house payments.

There would be no dinners out, no Giants or 49er games. No weekends at Lake Tahoe.

Falore groaned out loud at the thought of what the baby would cost. The department health plan would cover the hospital bills, but what was he going to do after that? He might have to hang on to this security job for years. Jennie was already complaining that she barely saw him.

No, he'd have to keep the gig as long as possible. And that might not be easy. Not with the way Adele Abrams was acting. She'd come down to the security room in the house two nights ago. He'd been sitting at the desk, half dozing, watching TV. She hadn't said a word, just put a finger to her lips to hush him to silence, then unbuttoned the pajama top and shoved her breasts into his face, while unzipping his pants and moving onto the desk. They made love right on the desk. There was a comfortable couch nearby and the carpet was thick and plush. But she insisted on doing it on the desk. She grunted, moaned and groaned, but didn't say a word. When it was over, she just patted him lightly on the cheek, then picked up her pajamas and walked out of the room.

Falore thought about the conversation he'd had at the squad room with Lieutenant Harris. Harris had called him into his office, asking how he liked working for Abrams.

"How's it going, Larry? You and Mrs. Abrams getting along okay?"

"Yeah, sure, Lieut. No problems. Why? Is she complaining?"

"No, no complaints, Larry." Harris leaned forward, took an envelope from a desk drawer. Larry caught it, squeezing it in one hand, liking the feel of the cash.

Then Harris asked him a question that made Falore sweat. "What do you think of Adele, Larry? She coming on to you?"

Did Harris know? How could he know? Falore answered as best he could. "A little. She comes on to everyone. I think she's screwing some bartender."

"That's her business, Larry. As long as you're not

screwing her. 'Cause if you screw her, you screw me. Don't forget that."

The back door opened, snapping Falore out of his musings.

"Sleeping on the job?" Adele Abrams asked, climbing into the back of the sedan.

"Thought you were going to be in there another couple of hours, Mrs. A."

"You thought wrong, Larry. Boring. A bunch of boring old ladies watching skin-and-bone, chalk-faced models pitching some fag designer's idea of what I should be wearing. Let's get out of here."

Falore hit the ignition and ease into congested Sutter Street traffic. "Back home, Mrs. A?"

"Mrs. A. Is that the best you can do, Larry? It's better than ma'am, but still not good enough." She reached into her purse, took out a pack of cigarettes, then crawled on her knees until she was close enough to offer Falore a cigarette through the dividing window.

"No, thanks," Falore said.

"Just light it for me, Larry."

Falore dutifully took the cigarette, punched in the dashboard lighter, and when it popped out, got the cigarette going and handed it back to her. She drew in a lungful of smoke and blew it out, aiming at the back of Falore's head.

"That was nice, the other night, Larry. I enjoyed it. My husband is off on another one of his trips. A short one, this time. Have you thought of any good spots for that picnic yet, Larry?"

"Oh, yeah, lots," Falore said, trying to keep his tone light—not quite sure how to handle the situation, yet not able or willing to resist the rewards. "Lots."

"Like where?"

"In this boat, just about anywhere, Mrs. A. Your car's bigger than my first apartment. But there's Golden Gate Park, by one of the little lakes, out by the beach with the wave watchers."

Adele rolled her chin against the leather partition directly behind Falore. "Wave watchers. Who are they?"

"People who park out by the beach. Just sit there and watch the waves. We find a lot of suicides out there. They just watch those waves, get hypnotized or something, I guess. Then they blow their brains out."

Adele took another deep drag on the cigarette. "Is that right? Have you got your gun, Larry?"

Falore patted his chest. "Never leave home without it."

"And your handcuffs?"

"Yeah, those too. Why? You planning on having me arrest someone?"

"No, Larry. I'm planning our picnic. Are you working for us tomorrow?"

"Yes. Day shift."

"Be sure and bring your handcuffs."

The mailbox name plate was brass, nicely polished. M. ARIZA was neatly printed above the label for Apartment 4D. The apartment entrance door was a joke, and Davila easily slipped the bolt with a piece of celluloid. He crossed the lobby, heading for the stairs. The elevator door opened and an elderly woman in a heavy red woollen coat walked out. She backed up a few steps, at first intimidated by his size, then gave him a hesitant smile after glancing at his coat and hat, the words BOB'S LOCKSMITH relieving any fears she might have of the husky, swarthy-faced man.

Davila decided he might as well use the elevator. The hallway on the fourth floor was empty. He knocked on the door of 4D. You never know. She could be sick and have taken the day off work. She could have a roommate. A visiting relative. He knocked again, waited a full minute, then dropped to his knees and examined the lock and frame. The door was solid wood. He shook the handle. It didn't budge. He tried the celluloid strip he'd used on the entrance door, but it would not slip into the crack between the door and the frame. He opened the tool box he'd found in the back of the Chevrolet, took out a wallet-sized plastic holder containing his pick tools, and selected an L-shaped torque wrench and a double-ball pick. Although the actors on the television shows are able to pick locks in the blink of an eye, it normally takes an experienced locksmith up to five minutes to get the job done. Davila had more experience than most locksmiths. He got the job done in under two minutes. He snatched up the tool box and entered the apartment cautiously, closing the door quietly behind him. He leaned against it and let out a long breath as he studied the room. There was a couch covered in indigo blue fabric with red and yellow flowers. A matching chair. A dark wood table in front of the couch. Magazines fanned out neatly on the table. Davila leafed through the magazines: *The Atlantic, Smithsonian, California Lawyer, Newsweek*. Nothing there for him.

A swivel-based TV console was set against the far wall, next to a stereo unit in a glass-door cabinet. There was a photograph in a silver frame atop the TV. A man and a woman. A palm tree in the background. The man in a business suit. A confident smile stitched across his Anglo features, his arm around her. The woman he had followed. Ariza. In a white dress that showed her figure off much better than that stupid man's suit had. Who was the man in the photograph? A boyfriend? Husband? Ex-husband? Just the two of them. No children. Just as well, for if there were children, they would soon be motherless.

He checked the CDs stacked in the bin alongside the stereo and muttered, "*Mulda,*" under his breath. Musicals. Symphonies.

The small kitchen held the necessities: stove, refrigerator, cupboards filled with dishes, glasses, pots and pans.

The bedroom was more to his liking. A big American-style bed with a brass headboard and footboard dominated the room. The silk-like bedspread was shiny white. The furniture was white with gold-leaf trim. A full-length mirror was positioned alongside a shoulder-high armoire. Davila sat on the bed and smiled at himself in the mirror, then abruptly hauled himself to his feet and dug through her closet, finding rows of suits, dresses, and jackets, hung neatly on wooden hangers, dangling over fifteen or more pairs of shoes.

All women's clothes, all the same general size. She lived alone. His heartbeat sounded in his ears. No man to worry about. There was one shoe box. He opened it, finding a pile of photographs. He thumbed through them. The woman appeared in all of them, sometimes alone, sometimes with young men, young women, or older people. Several included the man from the silver-framed photograph. There were two he particularly liked: one with her in a yellow two-piece bathing suit, the other a head shot, her hair longer then, staring right at the camera. He slipped them into his pocket, a souvenir, then turned his attention to the dresser drawers: sweaters, jeans. He slowed his pace when he found the drawer filled with lingerie. He discarded the plain white bras, deliberated over a red one that fastened in the front and a low-cut black model, settling for the red one when he found a pair of matching bikini panties. He tossed the bra and panties on the bed, then continued digging through the drawers until he finally found the bed sheets. He used his knife to cut four long strips from the sheets. He attached one strip to each corner of the brass headboard and footboard, arranging the four ends so they formed an X in the middle of the bed. He placed the bra and panties in the approximate spot he anticipated Mary Ariza's body would end up. Santos wanted it to look like a sexual attack. And so do I, Davila admitted to himself. He threw his cap so it landed on the bed's pillows, then went to the kitchen in search of a drink.

Walter Slager slide the hand-printed note across the table to Mary Ariza. She gave it a quick look.

I think number seven is in love with you.

Mary looked toward the jury. Juror number seven was gazing at her, a half smile on his face. She tapped Slager on the knee and whispered, "One down, eleven to go."

Walter was her co-counsel, a bright young man who was excellent at research and trial preparation, but lacked the "fire in the belly" to be a top-notch trial lawyer.

Mary steepled her fingers and waited as the insurance company attorney queried his client, Oscar Lofton, the bookstore owner. Lofton was a short, cadaverously thin man with a prominent Adam's apple. His hair was short and neatly cut. When Mary had met him at the bookstore, it had been long, greasy, and held back from his face by a leather headband.

Lofton had been well coached. He responded to each question with a short, concise answer, leaving no room for Mary to enter the questioning. She'd just have to wait her turn. When the judge said, "Your witness, Miss Ariza," she was ready.

"Mr. Lofton. Can you tell me how long you have been in business at your present location?"

Oscar Lofton folded his arms across his chest and tilted his head to the ceiling. "Three years now."

"And where were you before that?"

"You mean my business?"

"Yes."

"Los Angeles."

"And what type of business were you in, in Los Angeles, sir?"

"Same thing. Books, movies, entertainment."

"Adult entertainment?"

"Yes," Lofton answered quickly. "It was all legal."

"Was it, now?" Mary asked, walking back to the table and accepting the folder that Walter Slager handed her. "You were on Sunset Boulevard, correct?"

Wayne Miller, a Brooks Brothers-suited defense attorney with a well-tuned voice, objected. "I see no relevance in where my client conducted his business prior to the incident in question, Your Honor."

"Sustained," the judge said in a tired voice.

Mary went back on the attack. "Mr. Lofton, in your deposition you stated that you had three employees at the time that my client was attacked in your store—"

"Objection," roared the defense attorney.

"Sustained." The judge, a droll-faced man of sixty said, "You know better than that, Ms. Ariza. At least you better, if you plan to continue practicing law in my court."

"My apologies, Your Honor. Mr. Lofton, at the time of the alleged incident, you swore in your deposition that you had three employees. Correct?"

Lofton's head gave a quick forward jerk, like a hiccup. "Yes."

"And only three?"

"That's all I had. All I could afford. I work there myself six days a week. You got my payroll records."

Mary riffled the documents in her hand. "Indeed I do. Right here. Yourself. Your brother, Tony. A Mr. Albert Seedman, whom we have not been able to find, and the security man, Jasper Riley. Correct?"

"Yep. That's the lot."

"And your establishment is located at 185 Eddy Street, correct?"

"That's correct."

Mary addressed the judge. "Your Honor, I subpoenaed the records of the San Francisco Police Department for records relating to Mr. Lofton's place of business. I believe the department clerk is here in court with the records."

"Is the clerk present?" the judge asked woodenly.

A heavy-set woman with black-ringed eyes stood up and approached the banister separating the spectators from the attorneys. "Yes, Your Honor. I have the subpoenaed documents."

She handed them to Mary, then hurried from the courtroom.

There were two famous tenets of law that had been drummed into Mary early in her career: Never ask a question in court if you don't already know the answer, and never open a document in court unless you already know the contents.

The Pontar & Kerr investigator had accessed the police files, so Mary was aware of exactly what was in the police reports. She took her time, spreading the papers on the table in front of Walter Slager, found the reports she wanted, gave Slager a quick wink, then turned her attention back to Oscar Lofton.

"Now, Mr. Lofton. Do you know a Miss Mary Phillips?"

"Can't say I do."

"How about a Terry Linard?"

Lofton hunched forward. "Nope. I don't know none of them."

"You're sure about Ms. Linard. How about Elisabeth Feller?"

The defense attorney let out a long sigh. "Your Honor, my client is being harassed. He says he does not know these people. What's the point of all this?"

"Good question, Mr. Miller," the judge confirmed. "Is there a point, Ms. Ariza? If so, I'd like to hear it. Now."

Mary slowly ran her finger down the pages, then waved them at the jury. "Your Honor, I have a list of thirty-three names, twenty-nine women and four men, all of whom have been arrested on prostitution charges and all of whom have listed their business address as 185 Eddy Street, the location of Mr. Lofton's adult bookstore. Do you want to hear the rest of the names, Mr. Lofton? Would that refresh your memory?"

Lofton started to say something, but it was as if his tongue were stuck to the roof of his mouth.

Wayne Miller stood up, throwing an arm in the air. "Your Honor, my client's store is located in a rough area. We do not contest that. It is an area known for drug deals and prostitution, but he is not in the business of providing prostitutes to his customers. He runs a legitimate business, licensed by the city. He has no control over who walks the street in front of his establishment, or of anyone who may have claimed his address as their own on an arrest sheet."

Mary smiled at the jury. It was the smile of someone holding four aces. She waved the documents in her hand. "I will be happy to subpoena each and every one of these people to court and ask them if they split their fees with Mr. Lofton, who was, I believe, their pimp."

The defense attorney protested again, then asked if they could approach the bench.

"This is a stretch, Ariza," he said between clenched

teeth. "Even if any of this crap is true, pimping is not a felony. You can't—"

"I can show that sexual acts took place on the premises," Mary declared confidently. "I can show that Lofton knew of it. That his dirty little cubicles were used for more than just masturbation and watching pornographic videos. That his so-called security man wouldn't have paid any attention to the protests of my client, because he was used to acts of sex going on in the store all the time. That Mr. Lofton was indeed acting as their pimp. I can."

Miller held up a hand in mock surrender, then turned and looked at the judge. "Somehow, Your Honor, I get the feeling that Ms. Ariza had access to those police records earlier. And that she already has these potential witnesses lined up."

The judge nodded his head knowingly. "That's the way I would have done it when I was practicing law, son."

Miller fumed inwardly. "Can we have a recess, Your Honor? I'd like to talk to Ms. Ariza."

"Yes, I'm sure you do. You can use my chambers." He slammed his gavel and announced, "Court is recessed for twenty minutes."

Chapter 9

The conference in the judge's chambers lasted over an hour, then moved to the courthouse hallway, where both Mary and Wayne Miller made frequent use of the public telephones. The insurance company was reluctant to give in to Mary's demands—one million dollars. But they were finally convinced, and Mary had her first "trophy settlement."

Attorney Wayne Miller snapped his briefcase shut and held out a hand to Mary. "Congratulations. I never did want to take this one to trial. You really had me by the balls on this one."

Mary gave his hand a firm shake. "It was a nice feeling, Wayne."

Mary's client and Walter Slager had been pacing the corridors nervously throughout the negotiations. She gave them a thumbs-up sign after shaking Miller's hands. Walter Slager let out a loud whoop, then rushed to Mary.

"I knew we could do it," he shouted. "I knew we could do it."

Her client, in tears, almost numb, appeared as if he'd lost a close family member rather than won a large settlement.

Oscar Lofton loped by, caught Mary's eye, smirked, and said, "Hell. It ain't my money anyway, lady."

"No, but my client will spend it like it was."

"What timing," Walter Slager said excitedly. "The office party's tonight. We can really celebrate."

Pontar & Kerr's office party? Mary had forgotten all about it. Walter was right. It was perfect timing.

Walter Slager's car was in the underground garage

across from City Hall. He insisted on driving Mary to
the party, after calling the office and advising them of
the settlement.

It was raining as they hurried across Polk Street. A
car skidded on the wet pavement, causing Mary and
Walter to jump out of its way. Mary's right foot landed
in a puddle.

"Shit," she exclaimed, shaking her damp foot.

"Relax," Slager advised her. "We just won a big one."

Mary nodded in agreement. "I'll have to go home
and change now, Walter. I'll get a cab and meet you at
the party."

"No way. I'll drive you." He smiled mischievously.
"I've always wanted to see your apartment."

Mary liked Walter. He was young, good-looking,
and bright. But the last thing she was interested in was
an office romance. In fact, since moving to San
Francisco there had been no romance of any kind. The
breakup with her ex-husband still haunted her. How
had she misjudged him so? How could a man change
so completely in a year? Ric had been charming, sexy,
and sweet before they married, and he remained that
way for several months after the wedding. Then he became jealous and possessive, arguing over trivial
things. Then he accused her of having an affair with
one of the lawyers in her office.

Maybe it was because his check from the real estate
business was suddenly less than hers. Maybe it was his
pride that caused the change. Then he'd done the un-
forgivable. He slapped her. A hard slap across the face.
He had apologized profusely—but an apology wasn't
going to settle their problems. She moved out that
night and filed for divorce. Had she acted hastily?
Should she have given Ric another chance? No. The
first slap was always the first of many.

Slager found a parking spot almost directly in front
of Mary's apartment.

"I'll only be a minute, Walter. You can come up if
you want."

"I'll call the restaurant and tell them we'll be a few
minutes late. I'm sure it won't be a problem."

Mary wriggled her foot in her shoe, frowning at the squishy feeling. The elevator made its usual bouncy stop. "It would have been quicker if we had walked. It's the slowest elevator I've ever been in," she said, searching in her purse for her key.

"Here, allow me," Slager said, taking the key, then putting an arm around Mary's shoulder as they walked down the hall. He slid he key in the lock, turned the handle, and said, "After you."

Mary crossed the threshold, saw a strange man, and screamed.

Slager pushed her aside and rushed into the room. "Who the hell are—"

A knife blade suddenly slashed across Walter Slager's throat. Mary watched in horror as blood cascaded down his chest. She ran back out into the hall screaming as loud as she could: "Help! Help!"

A hand grabbed her from behind. She swung her briefcase backward as hard as she could, feeling it make contact. She pulled away and began running, screaming.

"Hey, you!" someone yelled.

Cesar Davila turned and saw an old, fat man come out of the apartment near the stairs. Davila chased after Ariza, grabbing for her with one hand, the knife in the other, ready to strike. He caught her briefly, surprised at the strength she showed in pulling loose. He lunged, slashing with the knife, hitting her arm.

A loud, braying voice was yelling, "Police, police. I called the police."

Davila thought he heard sirens. Ariza was on the floor, holding her briefcase in front of her. He reached out, his eyes marking her neck as the knife's target, then another voice, a woman's yelled, "Get your gun, John! Get your gun!"

Davila kicked at Ariza as he ran by, then pounded down the stairs, two at a time.

Jack Kordic was once again the last man to leave the Homicide detail. He was almost at the door when the phone rang.

"This is Communications. Granados and Pittman around?"

"No. This is Inspector Kordic. What've you got?"

"Central Station called in a 187 on Hyde Street. Granados and Pittman are on call. I tried catching them on the radio and beeper, but no luck."

"Give me the address," Kordic said. "I'll handle it."

The black-and-white patrol car was nosed into the curb in front of 1147 Hyde Street, the dome lights spinning blurred streaks of red into the gusting rain. Kordic parked fifty feet away just in case there was a need for the black-and-white to get away in a hurry. He recognized the uniformed officer guarding the apartment house's front door as Greg Monroe, a bright young cop out of Central Station.

"How's it going, Greg?"

Monroe tipped his cap back. "Hey. Jack. Long time no see. I just got a quick look at the victim. He's room temperature. Not a nice way to go. Neck slashed. Blood all over the place. Fourth floor. The second victim is a young woman, Mary Ariza." He spelled the last name out. "She got cut too, but from what I saw, she'll be okay. Just nicked on the arm. Ambulance took her over to San Francisco General."

"Good. Do me a favor, will you? Radio the hospital. Tell them to keep this Ariza woman there until I can talk to her."

"Will do," Monroe said, pushing his cap back down and running out to the radio car.

Kordic entered the building, saw that the indicator arrow on the elevator was stopped on number four, and decided to use the stairs.

There were knots of people standing around the landings on the second and third floors. Kordic brushed off their questions by saying, "I just got here. Someone will be down to talk to you in a minute."

Officer Pat McCarthy, Monroe's partner, greeted Kordic as he got to the fourth floor. "Crime lab's on the way, Inspector. Witnesses are in Apartment 4C. I've taken brief statements." McCarthy had straight blond hair, and at six three was a full half foot taller than his partner, earning them the nickname of the "Mutt and Jeff team." He pulled a spiral notebook from his uniform pocket. "Mr. and Mrs. Landon. Both of them got a good look at the perpetrator. The other tenants on this floor stayed in their apartments until it was all over. Didn't see a thing."

"Good job," Kordic said, slipping on a pair of disposable sterile gloves. He was pleased to see that McCarthy already had his gloves on. "Let's take a look at what we've got."

McCarthy had sealed off the entrance to the Ariza apartment with a strip of yellow crime-scene tape at waist level. Kordic ducked under the tape and entered Apartment 4D. The body of Walter Slager lay on its right side just inside the door, his left hand near the gaping wound in his neck. Kordic bent over the body carefully. A thick pool of blood had formed an amoeba-shaped pattern on the carpet.

"Found him just like that, Inspector," McCarthy said. "I checked for a pulse. Obvious he was gone."

Kordic nodded, straightened up, and looked around the room. "You check out the place?"

"Just to make sure nobody was hiding in the bathroom or under the bed. Witnesses said the perp took off down the stairs."

"Okay. I'll be with the witnesses in a minute."

Kordic did quick inventory of the apartment, finding little of interest in the front room, kitchen, or bathroom. The bedroom was a different story.

"You see this?" he called out to McCarthy.

"Yep. Sure did. Looks like the perp was waiting for the lady to come home."

"Sure does," Kordic said, fingering one of the torn piece of bedding material tied to the bed frame and shaking his head at the positioning of the lacy red bra and panties. He picked up the blue baseball cap, examining the label. "Made in Taiwan. Looks brandnew. See if you can find a local listing for Bob's Locksmith." On a chair near the window was a grimy red plastic tool box. He unsnapped the box. Pliers, hammer, cable jumpers, and a black vinyl envelope. He flipped open the envelope. "Hmmm. Our boy was a pro. That's a first-class set of lock picks."

He waited for the crime lab and medical examiner to arrive, pointing out the tool box to the lab attendant. "Take care with that baby. It might be all we get."

While the lab was busy taking photographs, Kordic drew a rough diagram of the apartment, including a stick figure of the position of the body.

"You see his ID?" the medical examiner inquired. The M.E. was new to Kordic, Chinese with long, dark hair and a face that tapered to a narrow chin. He handed over the dead man's wallet.

Kordic perched on the edge of the sofa and flipped open the wallet. The driver's license showed the name Walter Slager, with an address on Union Street. Mastercard, Visa, American Express, all to the same name. Three hundred and twenty dollars in cash. A tarnished St. Christopher's medal. And business cards showing Slager was an attorney at the firm of Pontar & Kerr in the Embarcadero Center.

The M.E. was removing the victim's pants, preparing to take his temperature. Kordic handed him the wallet. "Thanks, Doc." He took one more stroll around the apartment, then went to see the witnesses.

John and Paula Landon were both in their early sixties. He had gray hair and a potbelly, and wore brown slacks and a green turtleneck sweater that rode up on his stomach. She was thin, with black hair that bore an unmistakable orange tint. Her shiny lavender designer jogging suit looked brand-new.

"Oh, it was just terrible, Officer," Mrs. Landon said. "I heard her scream and opened the door and the poor thing was running toward us. The man was chasing her. With a knife. It was—"

"It looked like a good-sized blade," John Landon said, pushing his wife gently aside and holding out his hands some six inches apart. "Damn good-sized. He was a tough-looking bastard. Big. Over six feet. Big shoulders. Mexican-looking. He was wearing a blue jacket. Bob's something, I think, but I can't be sure."

"That's quite a description, Mr. Landon."

John Landon pushed his chest out until it almost reached the dimensions of his stomach. "I was an M.P. in the army," he said, his voice full of pride. "Japan. Lot of shit going on over there then, I can tell you."

Kordic turned his attention to Paula Landon. "Did you see what he was wearing?"

Mrs. Landon touched her hair, rearranging a curl. "I saw the jacket, but I couldn't tell you what the writing on it said. I don't even remember seeing any writing."

"White," Mr. Landon said. "White print on blue. I saw that knife and headed for the bedroom. Got a forty-five Colt semi-automatic. Would have liked to have blown that guy's head off. He was gone by the time I got the gun. You could hear him going down the stairs. Sounded like a cattle stampede."

"We brought the poor girl into our place," Mrs. Landon said. "Mary Ariza. She's only been here a few months. I've only spoken to her a few times." She pointed at a dining table, the top littered with yellow towels streaked with bloodstains. "We stopped her bleeding. John called the police."

"Nine-one-one," John Landon said. "Got connected right away. Then I went over to this Ariza girl's place. Saw the body." He held his right hand out flat, then jammed the thumb downward, like a decadent Roman emperor decreeing death. "Dead as a doornail."

"You touch anything?" Kordic asked.

Landon looked insulted. "I told you, I was an M.P. Looked around, made sure no one was there, but I didn't touch nothin'."

"You've both been very helpful," Kordic said sincerely. "I'd like you to work with our police artist. See if you can help us to come up with an accurate sketch of this man."

"Be a pleasure, Inspector," Mr. Landon said. "I just wish I had been closer to my gun. Could have saved you boys a lot of trouble."

* * *

The emergency ward at San Francisco General Hospital was in its normal state of pandemonium. An ambulance was backed into the double doors leading to the four crisis operating rooms as a petite, lean-cheeked nurse with a perpetually mournful look about her features helped two stewards lift a gurney from the back of the ambulance.

Jack Kordic stopped long enough to give them a hand. The victim, a stocky man with turban-like bandages covering his head, was moaning. "She didn't have to hit me. Damn, she didn't have to hit me."

Kordic threw a questioning look to one of the stewards as soon as the gurney was on the ground.

"Wife," said the young steward. "Baseball bat. Said he was messing with their nine-year-old daughter."

Kordic wiped his hands on his raincoat as the gurney was wheeled indoors. He was glad the case wasn't his. Homicide seemed like a nice, clean job compared to juvenile sexual assaults. At least most of the time.

The same nurse he'd seen outside was standing behind a chest-high counter, logging an entry onto a clipboard.

"I'm looking for a young woman, came in an hour or so ago," Kordic said, taking his badge from his pants pocket and waving it at the nurse. "Name of Ariza. Mary Ariza."

The nurse's eyes flicked briefly to the badge. "Uh-huh. Dr. Harper's patient." She went back to scribbling on the clipboard. "One of your people is with her, I think." She waved the hand holding the pen over her shoulder. "Try Room 5A."

Kordic walked by a group of lonely, frightened-looking people sitting on hard-back benches. A man in bib overalls sat holding his left wrist, rocking back and forth in pain. A chubby platinum blonde holding a towheaded baby a few months old cooed softly into the baby's ear and looked hopefully up at Kordic. Her eyes dropped back to the baby when she saw he wasn't a doctor. Two teenagers, their shaved heads revealing scrapes and welts, dressed in silver-studded motorcycle leathers, cigarettes dangling from their sullen mouths, stopped their conversation until Kordic passed by.

Kordic knocked lightly on the door to Room 5A, then twisted the handle. A paunchy uniformed cop Kordic recognized but whose name he could not recall was leaning against the wall. He straightened up, taking his cap from under his arm and jamming it on his head. "You the inspector handling this thing?"

"Yes. Where is Miss Ariza?"

"Behind that curtain," the policeman said, tugging his belt, which was weighted down with a long-barreled revolver, handcuffs, a black nylon pouch holding a spray can of Mace, and a portable radio. No billy club, which meant he had a flat, leather-covered sap in his back pants pocket.

"You don't need me anymore, do you?" the officer said, his tone nonchalant, as if Kordic's response made no difference to him.

"No. Thanks for hanging around." Kordic approached the green plastic curtain. "Miss Ariza. I'm Inspector Kordic. Can I speak to you for a minute?"

"Yes. Certainly" came the soft, almost whispered, reply.

Kordic pulled back the curtain. An attractive dark-haired woman, her eyes wide, filled with anxiety, was sitting on the hospital bed, legs dangling toward the floor. She wore a black skirt and white blouse. The blouse's left sleeve had been cut off at the shoulder. A bandage the width of a playing card was wrapped around her biceps. Pin-sized dots of blood colored the front of her blouse.

"Tell me," she said anxiously. "How is Walter?"

"You mean Mr. Slager?"

"Yes. The man at my apartment. Is he going to be all right? No one would tell me anything."

"No, I'm afraid he won't be all right, Miss Ariza. He's dead."

Mary Ariza flinched, as if she'd been slapped. "Oh, no!"

Kordic wished he could have broken the news to her easier. Wished he could break it to them all a lot easier. How many times had he had to deliver the bad news? How many ways are there to tell someone that their friends or loved ones have been murdered? He remembered his own reaction when Chris Sullivan had told him about Linda and Danny. Even though they were lifelong friends, and Sullivan had known his wife and son, Sullivan had been professionally blunt. There's really no other way to do it. He reached out and touched Mary lightly on the shoulder. "Yes. I'm very sorry about Mr. Slager. Do you feel up to talking about it?"

Mary tilted her head back and pinched her nose between thumb and forefinger. "Yes, give me a moment to pull myself together, Mr. . . ."

"Kordic. Inspector Kordic. Jack. Tell me what you can about the man with the knife."

Mary Ariza grimaced and closed her eyes. "He was big and had dark hair, and a beard, that's all I remember. I never saw the man before. I opened the door to my apartment. Actually, Walter opened it, I had just handed him the key. Walter went in and this—this lunatic started swinging a knife." She opened her eyes and stared into Kordic's. "Do you know who he was?"

"We don't know yet. He was inside, waiting for you, Miss Ariza."

"No one has a key to my place." She paused a moment, then repeated, "No one," in a strong, definite tone.

"Did you call a locksmith? Or ask your landlord to call one?"

Mary's eyebrows knitted together. "A locksmith? No. Why do you ask?"

"Did anyone know that you and Mr. Slager were going to your apartment together?"

"No. They couldn't have. Walter—Mr. Slager and I work at the same law office. Pontar and Kerr. We had just settled a case. We won a judgment of a million dollars. We were both happy as hell. We were going to an office party at Ernie's Restaurant." She winced as she pulled her left wrist up slowly and looked at her watch. "Damn. The party's still going on, and none of them know anything about this."

"I'll contact the restaurant for you," Kordic said. "So you and Mr. Slager decided to stop at your place before going to the party?"

"Yes. I stepped in a puddle as we were leaving City Hall. It made a mess of my shoes and stockings. We were just going to stop at my apartment long enough so I could change, then go right to the party. Do you suppose that he was a burglar and we caught him in the act?"

"No. He was waiting for you, Ms. Ariza. He had some of your garments, a bra, panties, laid out on your bed, along with bindings cut from your sheets. He had carefully planned a sexual assault. At the very least."

The realization of Walter's death, his murder, and the fact that the killer had been waiting for her, waiting to rape her, were just sinking in. She shook her head, hoping it would clear her thoughts, then looked at Kordic closely for the first time, figuring him to be in his early forties, with shaggy salt-and-pepper hair matted down from the rain. There was a sadness in his green eyes. Two deep clefts formed between his eyebrows, another split his chin. He seemed to be genuinely concerned about her. She had deposed policeman, cross-examined a few in court, but never really got to know any of them. They'd always answered her questions in crisp, jargon-bloated responses: "The victim encountered the suspect at approximately . . ." Kordic somehow looked different.

She slid off the bed, straightened her skirt, slipped her feet into her shoes, and noticed they were still damp. "Can I get out of here now, Inspector?"

"Sure. Have you got someone you can spend the night with?"

Mary considered the question. "No, I don't."

"I'll call Ernie's and let your fellow workers know

what happened. Maybe one of them can put you up for the night."

"Thanks, Inspector, but I'll make the call." Her hand went to her bandaged shoulder. "You find the maniac who killed Walter."

Chapter 10

"Cesar was sure you were going to kill him," Naimat said, watching as Santos did a set of fingertip push-ups. "Or he thought I would do it."

"Yes, I know," Rene Santos replied, his voice normal, showing no strain from the exercises. Cesar had every right to think that he would be killed. Had they been back in Peru, or anywhere in the Middle East, even Europe, Santos damn well would have killed the fool. One foul-up was intolerable, and the old man's body popping out of the ocean had been just that. But now he had botched the simple task of killing that damned attorney.

"We are going to have to get rid of Cesar," Naimat said, her eyes on Santos's rippling muscles. His body was lean, strong, marred only by the belt-wide faded scars crisscrossing his back—mementos from his days in the monastery. It was an athlete's body, built up during the time he had been an acrobat in the circus, and rigorously attended to. Even in the training camps, in the scalding heat of the desert, while the others were getting drunk, trying unsuccessfully to get her in bed with them, Rene would concentrate on his exercises, pushing his body to the limit. It was a shame he seemed to get so little pleasure from it. Not from a woman, or a man, as far as she knew. How did he relieve his sexual tension? Somehow she just couldn't picture him masturbating.

Santos rolled gracefully over onto his back, positioned his arms behind his head, and began doing sit-ups. "I thought you liked Cesar."

"I do." She did like Cesar because he was afraid of

her. That was the only way she could tolerate men. When they feared her. She hated the pigs she'd been forced to seduce, to take to bed, to lure into traps. And the ones who pawed at her, treated her like a trinket, a toy to be played with. But Rene wasn't like that. He had treated her like an equal from the beginning. But he was changing. And not just his looks. Or was it because of the change in his appearance? She had liked him better before the surgery. He seemed preoccupied lately. Not himself. "But Cesar is turning into a bungler."

Santos concentrated on his exercises, counting silently to a full hundred before jumping to his feet. "A bungler, true. But who do I have to replace him with?"

Personnel. It had never been a problem before. In Beirut, Tehran, Tripoli, even Tel Aviv, he'd be able to pick and choose his accomplices. In the whole of Europe, he knew exactly where to go, who to see to do his recruiting. He was always able to count on professionals, or reliable, dedicated amateurs whose passion for a cause had turned them into something better than professionals. These amateurs were willing to take their own lives without hesitation. In other words, they were fools—fools he could well use. But now he was stuck. His hard-core cell consisted of Cesar Davila, Naimat, and Alejandro Liberto. Poor, stupid Liberto had picked the worst of times to have a heart attack. Viktor Petrov's man Zorkin was willing to provide help, but Santos did not want the Russians involved in the operation. The less they knew of his plans, the better.

But here everything was different. He'd read the books, seen the movies about the Italian Cosa Nostra, so feared, so powerful. A joke. At least in San Francisco. Amazingly enough, there was no one in charge. No one person. No one who could be called the "The Man." There was no single dominant crime organization. And the town was wide open, especially to narcotics. Idiots, complete idiots were making fortunes peddling drugs. Every nationality had its own section, its own territory: the Chinese, blacks, Filipinos, Latins, and Irish. And each group had splinter groups whose only purpose was to destroy the others. And the Latins were the worst. The local Mexican connection he was being forced into using was a prime example: gangs, not cells. Chaos, not organization. Machismo was all that seemed to count with them. But he desperately needed help. Someone to create a diversion. A big diversion.

He grabbed a towel and dried himself off. "What have you learned of Adele Abrams?" Santos asked.

"The bitch is fucking her policeman, Rene."

"The bitch? You mean our dear Mrs. Abrams? You are sure?"

"Yes, I'm sure. They stopped out at the beach. He got out of the front seat. Joined her in the back," she said, waving her head slowly back and forth. "He was fucking her, all right."

Santos leaned against the balcony railing, his thumb and forefinger kneading the cross dangling from the chain around his neck, digesting the information. How could the fact that his wife was having sex with one of her bodyguards help him get to Abrams?

"I think I should kill her, Rene."

"Kill who?" Santos snapped. "Adele Abrams?"

"No. The attorney. Ariza. Let me kill her."

Santos considered the request. No, not Naimat. A man would do the job. It should be a man. "I think not. I've got more important things for you to do. I need you to keep an eye on Cesar. He's meeting with the local gang lord tonight. Get dressed. We have work to do."

The red graffiti on El Condado's faded orange outer wall identified the turf as surely as the neatly lettered gold leaf on a bank president's office door or the stenciling on the bow of a battleship. The number 22 set inside a diamond figure indicated that a faction of the 22nd Street gang was in charge. The designation C/S stood for *Con Safo,* a hex mark: "Anything you write over or below what we wrote goes back to you twice as bad."

Cesar Davila walked straight to the bar. The smell of fried food and spilled beer permeated the room. The bar itself stretched out forty feet, ending at the entrance to a small dining area. The walls were paneled with bamboo mats, of the type used at the beach. Crude oil paintings of ocean scenes and volcano-spouting mountains dotted the mats. Davila rested his elbows on the zinc bar and called out to the bartender for a double Mount Gay rum on the rocks.

Gus Melendez, the bartender, a stocky, slope-shouldered man with a lantern jaw, wiped his hands across his stained apron and bent down for the liquor bottle. He didn't recognize Davila at first. He looked quite different. The beard. The beard had been shaved off. But it was the same man—the big, ugly hombre was a *ventrano,* one who has been around. A direct connection to the *talco,* the cocaine that makes the world go 'round. They said he could also supply all the *mota,* hashish, and *carga,* heroin, you wanted. He had been hanging around for two weeks now, and always ordered the same drink. Not the cheap rum in the bar's well, always the expensive Mount Gay, which upset the bartender because he never charged Davila. The *ventrano* always put money on the bar, but Melendez never touched it. He had seen the way local *jefitos* treated him. With much respect.

He poured a hefty measure of rum into a glass and placed it in front of Davila. "You changed, huh? The beard. I didn't know it was you."

Davila accepted the drink, said, "*Gracias,*" then, when the bartender walked away to service another customer, muttered, "*Lambion.*" Kiss ass. Which was all right with Davila. Right now he needed someone to kiss his ass. Rene had taken the news of the botched attempt on the woman attorney stoically, his face betraying no sense of outrage. He could not read anything in Santos's coffee brown eyes. No hatred, no contempt, no anger, nothing. All he did was tell him to shave off his beard, stay away from the Ariza woman, and have the shopkeeper who sold him the hat killed. No harsh words. No threats. His instructions were to get Moreno, or one of his gang members, to kill Ariza and the shopkeeper, then stay on Moreno. Make sure he had a plan, an appropriate site picked out to create a diversion, and help him in any way necessary. Santos made it sound as if Davila's future actions were all-important. The job could not be done without his input. But Davila knew just how lucky he had been. He scratched his bare chin. If it had been up to Naimat, he would be dead. He knew that. He could read her eyes.

The thought of having Naimat as an executioner was not a pleasant one. The Russians had used drugs and needles on the old Jew, but when they finished, Naimat went at him with a knife, pliers, and cigarette butts. And he was sure she had enjoyed every single moment of the torment. But Santos was a man who never forgot. Davila knew that once he was of no use to Rene, he was a dead man. Which meant that he would have to strike first. And he would need help. Perhaps from the Russian—Zorkin. He gulped down his drink and placed the glass on the damp bar napkin. Within moments it was filled to the rim.

"Have you seen Tony Moreno?" Davila asked.

"He's in the back eating. You want him?"

"Why else would I ask?"

The bartender backpedaled toward the beaded curtain that separated the eating area from the bar.

Davila glanced around at his fellow drinkers. All were younger than him, some still in their teens. They dressed in black: black pants, black sweaters, black leather jackets. Some of the jackets were black and silver with the insignia of a pirate's face and two crossed swords. The Raiders, the patches said. He was surprised to learn the emblem was that of an American football teams. He doubted if any of the *cholos* wearing the garment knew anything about football.

The women wore black too. Or jeans with holes in the knees, the ass, everywhere. Davila thought again how strange these people became when they lived in this crazy country. The ripped, tattered jeans actually cost more than brand-new ones. It was like all their clothes, their tattoos, their cars, their jewelry. The purpose was to make a statement. To identify yourself. *Pendejo*. Stupid, Davila thought. He had been trained to blend in, to look invisible. If you made a statement, the police would be among the first to decipher it.

He saw Tony Moreno swagger through the curtains. Rene had gotten Moreno's name from a dealer in Lima, Peru. Moreno was dressed in the usual manner, all black, the leather jacket studded with chrome, the crease in his pants sharp enough to slit a throat. A thick gold chain, weighed down by a gold cross the size of a child's hand, hung from his neck. The sleeves of the jacket were pushed up to the elbows to show gold bracelets, the rings on his fingers. His hair was wet-combed straight back from his forehead, a short, tapered ponytail trailing over the back of his coat collar. He was twenty-three years old and had heavy facial features, thick lips, broad cheekbones, and protruding eyes shadowed by thin, arched brows.

Moreno greeted Davila with a pat on the shoulder. *"Ese vato, hombre?* What's happening? You shaved, man. It looks good." He lowered his voice. "Any business going down?"

Davila was mildly amused by Moreno's casual attitude, his mixture of Spanish and English. Since most of the clientele at El Condado spoke nothing but Spanish, English was the far safer language in Davila's opinion. Moreno's version of English was that of a *tinto*. Black man.

"I have some work for you, Tony. The instructions come from *el jefe*."

El jefe. The boss. The man. Moreno had never met the boss. But he sounded like a major player, all right. That tough, cool, "don't fuck with me" voice on the phone. Never dropping his own name, but he had given Moreno the right names. The man was super-connected. The boss. Moreno liked to think that he himself was *el jefe*. And in his own small world he was. He liked dealing with the big man from Peru. He was *lacayo*, a flunky to his boss, but he was quick to deliver with money, or whatever Tony wanted. Colombians were *pinchies*. Chicken-shit dudes, and they wanted too much for their precious *talco*. He'd string Davila along for a bit longer. Then cut off the old man's balls and find the cool dude. "That's what I do, man. Work. Good work."

Davila picked up his glass and carried it over to an empty table near the front window. Moreno followed, waving a hand at the man and woman at the nearby table. They got up without protest and moved to the bar.

"This is wet work," Davila said.

"Work is work," Moreno said as he hooked a chair free from under the table with a snakeskin cowboy boot and sat down opposite Davila. "How you gonna pay?"

"Whichever you prefer. Cash or powder. The work must be done quickly. Two targets. Separate targets. A shopkeeper and a woman."

Moreno leaned back and looked at the toes of his cowboy boots reflectively. "Your woman?"

"No."

Moreno nodded. He had not seen the man with a woman. He wondered if he was a *joto*. A queer. "How do you want them done?"

"The man, I don't care. Make it look like a robbery." He gave Moreno a description of the shopkeeper where he'd purchased the baseball cap and jacket and the store's address.

"Anything in this place worth pissin' on?" He saw the confusion in Davila's eyes. "Worth stealin', man?"

Davila fanned away a fly with his hand. "The cash box, that's about all."

"And the woman?"

"I want you to hit her when she leaves her apartment in the morning, when she goes to work."

"Where's this *ruca* live?"

Davila gave him the address. "Put your hand under the table, Tony."

"Huh?"

"Under the table, *amigo*."

Moreno scooted his chair forward and reached below the table, his hands taking a paper bag from Davila. His fingers felt the outline of the *guette*. A pistol. A smile came to his face when he felt the bulb at the end of the barrel.

"The woman's picture is in the bag," Davila said. "Now, what of your plans? Have you picked your spot?"

"Yeah. I sure have. My old high school It's a few blocks from here. They kicked me out. I guess this will get me even with them, huh?"

"Good. As long as it ties up the city. I'll help you with the explosives."

"*Orale,* man. I like it. We should celebrate. I've got some prime powder." He tossed his head toward the bar. "You see anyone you like? Pick one, we'll party on my boat."

"You have a boat?"

"Shit, yes, man. Just got it. Took it over from some *tinto* who was running *carga* up from Mexico. Big, beautiful boat. Sleeps six." He paused and smiled. "Fucks twelve. You want to play?"

Davila eyed a young woman at the bar. Long, straight hair, smooth skin, her pants so tight on her ass he imagined he might have to pry them off. He pointed a finger at the girl. "That one." He had missed his party with the attorney. This would make up for it.

Moreno swiveled around, heaving a sigh of relief when he saw Davila's choice. He wasn't a *joto* after all.

Chapter 11

Naimat slid low behind the motorcycle's handlebars when she saw Cesar Davila and a group of five, two men and three women, exit the El Condado. She glanced at her watch: almost two o'clock in the morning, closing time for bars in California. She was pleased to see that Davila looked drunk. His arm was draped around the shoulders of a sulky-faced girl wearing jeans and a leather jacket. He was swaying and looked as if he needed the girl's support to keep from falling to the pavement. The girl appeared to be in her teens, slim, well built. The other two girls were similar in age and appearance. Even dressed alike. She recognized one of the other men, a boy really, as Tony Moreno. Rene had taken several clandestine pictures of Moreno. The second man was a little older, maybe in his late twenties, reed thin, barely taller than the girls. Moreno was gesturing wildly, swaggering as he signaled the others to follow him to his car. The pale blue Cadillac was parked near the restaurant, in a red zone. Moreno stopped to take a parking ticket from the dash. The girls all laughed as he tore up the tag and tossed it into the air as if it were New Year's Eve confetti. They all piled into the Caddy, Davila nuzzling the girl's neck and patting her ass before climbing into the backseat.

The Cadillac pulled from the curb with squealing tires, made an illegal U-turn, and headed south. There was not much traffic. Naimat kick-started the motorcycle. She had no trouble keeping the light blue car in sight. They drove down a street called Valencia. After less than a half mile the Cadillac turned left on Army

Street. Naimat tried to get her bearings. East. They were traveling east, she was sure of it now. The Cadillac picked up speed as it turned onto a freeway approach. Naimat narrowed the gap between them as the Caddy surged ahead. She checked her speedometer. Seventy-five. She felt strangely uncomfortable on the massive five-lane freeway. She much preferred chasing a quarry down dark streets. Alleys were even better. They were going south now. A green highway sign showed the next exit was Candlestick Park. In a few seconds she saw the huge shell of the stadium off to her left.

Moreno had the Caddy pushing eighty in the outside lane. She saw his taillights flash as he slowed down and swerved to the right, suddenly darting into the curb lane and zipping off the freeway at the Sierra Point turnoff.

Now there was no traffic of any kind. Naimat dropped back several hundred yards. She had no idea where they were. The road curved left, dipping under the freeway, winding past the empty parking lots of deserted office buildings. The Cadillac's brake lights came on, and she doused her headlight. A forest of masts, looking like trees shorn of their limbs, some decorated with strings of Christmas bulbs, bobbed up and down in the dark bay waters. BRISBANE MARINA, declared a floodlighted sign.

The Cadillac pulled to a stop. Naimat did the same, turning off the ignition and pulling up behind a row of eucalyptus trees. She watched as they exited the Cadillac. Moreno waved a bottle over his head. She could hear singing. Or attempting to. She couldn't make out the words. She watched their progress as they walked over a small concrete bridge that connected the parking lot to the boat piers. Cesar Davila was still using the girl's shoulder as a crutch. She had never seen him that drunk. Or was he drunk? Was he merely playing a game for Moreno? She waited until they were across the bridge and on the pier, then followed. Her shoes made faint kissing sounds as she ran over to and across the bridge. Moreno was in the lead,

waving his bottle and singing. She could hear the
words now. They were singing in Spanish, something
about dancing: "Baila, baila baila me." They stopped
in front of a white cruiser, docked stern first, with blue
canvas awnings covering the aft deck. Tony Moreno
unsnapped the canvas that covered the door to the
boat's cabin. The three girls were shivering, holding
their arms across their chests, their legs doing little
dance steps, their shoes rattling on the wet decking.
The canvas was finally opened enough to permit
boarding, and they trooped onto the boat, Davila swaying badly, almost falling down. They disappeared inside. A few minutes later, a light came on inside the
cabin.

Naimat moved cautiously, like a tightrope walker,
maneuvering between mooring posts and neatly coiled
lengths of rope and water hoses. As she got closer, she
could hear the sound of rock music coming from the
white cruiser. It looked quite big up close. She had little knowledge of pleasure boats. Her time on the water
as a child had been spent in smelly wooden fishing
boats. She estimated the gleaming beauty to be some
fifty feet in length, all fiberglass with teak trim and an
overhanging deck so it could be steered from above.
Bright red, cigar-shaped rigging fenders kept the hull
from banging into the dock. Very fancy, she thought,
wondering if Moreno had purchased the boat with the
proceeds from his drug operation or if he had stolen it.
Some of the boats moored alongside were much less
grand. They were small, of patchy, weathered wood
with old car tires as bumpers.

She could make out a portion of the deck-level
wheel house. A cluster of polished chrome levers
shone through a crack in the boat's curtains. She tip-
toed to the rear of the boat, noticing the name *Olé*
neatly painted on the stern.

She stood for a moment, head cocked to one side.
She could hear human voices over the drone of the music, but the words were indistinguishable. Then there
was a shout from one of the girls. Then a scream. Then
laughter. Naimat retreated, stopping at the bridge for a

final glimpse. A thin smile came to her lips. The *Olé* was rocking in the water much more than its neighbors were.

"Party now, Cesar," she whispered softly to herself. "For soon the party will be over for you."

The dainty china coffee cup with hand-painted tulips looked out of place in the beefy policeman's hand. He was sprawled out on the floor, legs hanging down the stairway. He dropped the newspaper he was reading when he saw Jack Kordic and stood up, brushing crumbs from his uniform pants.

"How's it going?" Kordic asked.

"Quiet as hell, Inspector. Can I get out of here now?"

Kordic pointed a thumb toward Mary Ariza's door. "She inside?"

"Yeah. Only came out to bring me coffee and a roll. The guy next door, Landon, he wanted to bullshit all night." He held the coffee cup by the handle, between his thumb and forefinger, pinky extended. "You want to give her this?"

Kordic took the cup and knocked lightly on Ariza's apartment door. He glanced down at the carpet and saw the uneven trail of bloodstains. Were they from Slager's wound? Did they drop off the knife? Or were they from the nick on Ariza's arm? He'd have to wait for the lab report to find out.

The uniformed cop yawned as he waited for the elevator. "Light was on under her door all night. Bet she didn't get much shut-eye."

Mary Ariza's voice sounded tired when she asked, "Who is it?"

"Inspector Kordic."

The door opened slowly, an inch at a time. Kordic could make out one dark, doe-like eye. Then the door was shut and there was the rasping sound of the safety chain being slid back.

Her hair was ruffled, her face swollen on one side, with deep, wavy crease marks across her right cheek.

She wore a robe of white toweling that stretched down to her ankles, and was tightly belted around her waist.

"Here's your coffee cup," Kordic said. "It was nice of you to think of the officer."

Mary Ariza put a hand in front of her face and tried to stifle a yawn. "Oh, it was nothing." She stood aside. "Come in, Inspector, please."

A jumble of blankets covered the living room couch. Ariza immediately went over and started folding them. Kordic ran a hand across the rough texture of the couch, which had undoubtedly been responsible for the marks on Ariza's face. "Were you able to get some sleep?"

"Not really. Just dozed off and on. You know how it is."

Yes, Kordic thought. I certainly do.

"Is there any news, Inspector?"

"No. Nothing yet. Whoever he was, he left a baseball cap with a logo for a locksmith company. So far we haven't found such a company. Clever idea. People see a man with a cap and jacket that shows he's a locksmith, they don't pay any attention if he's bent over a door, working with tools. A tenant on the second floor saw him enter the building at approximately three p.m. He was here for a couple of hours waiting for you. I was hoping you could come down to the Hall of Justice with me. Look at a few pictures. As you know, he was armed with a knife. Were you able to check? Are you missing any knives? Or anything else?"

"No." She waved a hand in frustration. "I mean, yes. I checked. I haven't gone over everything, but nothing valuable, worth stealing, is missing."

"How's your arm?" Kordic asked to change the subject.

"Sore," Mary said, unconsciously flexing her shoulder. "I spoke to my boss, Matt Pontar. They're arranging a memorial service for Walter Slager. His family is from New York. He'll most likely be buried back there, but Matt wants to have some kind of service for him here. They will have to—"

Her knees buckled and she looked as if she was going to sink to the floor. Kordic reached out and grabbed her elbow. She yanked her arm away, yelling, "No!"

Kordic backed off a few feet, holding his hands out in front of him. "Sorry. You looked a little unsteady there."

"I know, I know," Mary apologized. "Please. Help yourself to some coffee. I'll change and be right with you."

Mary felt embarrassed once she was alone in her bedroom. The police inspector had been right. She felt as if she was about to faint. She was having a difficult time dealing with the fact that she was a victim. She sank onto the edge of the bed and rubbed her face roughly with her hands. She took a deep breath, counted to ten, let it out, then repeated the exercise. She had to get control of herself. Identify this man and put him behind bars.

She went to the closet, wondering what was appropriate for a visit to the Hall of Justice. Her sense of humor returned. Something in stripes?

Mary Ariza was sickened by the number of men pictured in the eight binders Inspector Jack Kordic had stacked on the interrogation room table. The spine of each binder had an identifying tab: *White Offenders, Black Offenders,* and *Latin Offenders.* Kordic had dumped the *Black Offenders* binders on the floor and instructed her to go through the Latin first, and if unsuccessful to go through the white. The brief view Mary had had of her attacker's face was frozen in her mind. Each page of a binder had four sets of entries, full-face and side-view photographs of each taken after his arrest. At first she had studied each picture carefully, noting the suspect's name and scanning the type of crimes he had been arrested for. The modus operandi also was listed: "Always uses a gun." "Always a knife." "Claims to be a police officer." "Victims all blond." She stopped reading after seeing the notation "Uses hammer and bolt cutters."

She kept turning pages, checking the photographs.

She was starting to feel a little claustrophobic in the small room. Inspector Kordic stopped by with a cup of coffee in a paper cup when she was about halfway through.

"How are you doing?" Kordic asked.

"I haven't spotted him yet. What I can't get over is that about half of them are smiling, as if they were being photographed for a family album."

Kordic chuckled dryly. "You're right. It's a natural reaction, I guess. Someone points a camera at you and you smile. For some of these guys, about the only family they have are cops or prison cons. Keep at it, Miss Ariza. I'll be back in about fifteen minutes."

Lieutenant Wesley Tilson passed Kordic in the hallway, studiously ignoring him. There was a rumor going around that Tilson was being considered for a chief's position in a Los Angeles suburb. Kordic didn't put much faith in the rumor. It would simply be too good to be true.

A message from the crime lab was waiting for him when he got back to his desk. The lab was just around the corner from the Homicide detail, so Kordic decided to walk over. Tom Sato, the head of the lab, was sitting at his desk, the desktop piled high with bulging manila folders. He rose to greet Kordic. Sato was small-boned, his coal black hair styled in the same crewcut he'd worn in his college days twenty-five years ago. His shirt pocket drooped under the weight of a half-dozen pens and pencils.

"Jack, good to see you again. Glad you're back. I may have something on that Walter Slager case for you." He began digging through the folders. "Yes, here it is. We were able to pull a good set of prints from the tools in that case. The chisel blade especially. We used Androx stain and it popped right out at us." Kordic nodded as if he knew what Sato was talking about and accepted the black-and-white photograph and computer printout Sato handed him. "We got a bingo. Ran the prints. They belong to a guy by the name of Douglas Reese. I ran a rap on him. As you can see, not much there."

Kordic looked first at the ultraviolet photograph, which clearly showed the arch, loop, and whorl of a fingerprint. He quickly checked the rap sheet. Douglas Reese had been arrested twice. For drunk driving. The last time over a year ago. Nothing else.

Sato showed Kordic the baseball-style cap with Bob's Locksmith printed across the front. "Looks brand-new. Made in Taiwan. He left a few strands of hair. He's got type A blood. That's about all we've got so far."

Kordic thanked Sato for his efforts and hurried down to the record room. Each police detail and station had a computer hooked up to the record room and could tap into local, state, and national criminal records systems. But to get an actual mug shot he had to go to the record room.

There was a long, serpentine line of civilians standing in front of the one and only counter that sold copies of accident reports to the general public. Kordic waved his badge at the clerk and leaned his elbows on the counter marked POLICE PERSONNEL ONLY. The clerk gave him a tired look, finished ringing up the cash receipt for a world-weary-looking man in a rain-drenched parka, then sauntered down to Kordic.

"Whatcha need?" she asked between snaps of bubble gum.

Kordic slid Sato's report across the smudged formica countertop. "Original reports and a mug."

He waited almost five minutes, feeling the hatred from the eyes of the civilians. He could hear a few muttered comments, "Fucking cops" and "What about the taxpayers?" among them.

The rap sheet showed Douglas Reese to be a white male adult, five foot six, one hundred thirty pounds, fifty-eight years of age, brown hair, blue eyes. This was nothing like the descriptions given by Ariza or John Landon. Occupation: insurance adjuster. The mug shot showed a bald, wrinkle-faced man with a weak chin and protruding nose. Kordic stopped to show the photo to Mary Ariza.

She shook her head positively. "No way. It all happened so quickly, but that definitely is not the man."

Kordic trooped back to his desk and called the insurance company Reese worked for. The switchboard operator connected him with Reese. Kordic identified himself and was immediately asked, "Have you found my car?"

"Your car was stolen?"

"Sure was. I made a report. You mean you still haven't found it?"

Kordic blew air through his lips and closed his eyes. "Did you have a tool kit in the car, Mr. Reese?"

"Yeah. Sure. Tool kit. Blanket, flares, golf clubs. Some junk. Why?"

Kordic questioned Reese as to his whereabouts at the time Walter Slager had been killed.

"I got off work at five. Went to find my car at the lot and it was gone. Took goddam near an hour for you guys to come and take the report. I know you're busy, but Christ, man—"

Kordic broke in to thank him for his time, then hung up. He went over to the computer and punched Reese's name in, requesting any recent reports. Sure enough, the stolen auto report was there. He copied down the license plate number. It was already on the station hot sheets, but he would update it, connecting it to Slager's murder. Deep down he knew it was futile. The slasher would have dumped the car by now. Or changed plates. Still, it was worth doing. It hadn't taken him long in his police career to figure out that there were very few master criminals walking the streets, which is why he pulled the yes lever on any new bond issues on the ballot for more prisons. The need for more prison space was becoming acute. Hard timers were being kicked out of county jail after serving just a few months of a sentence that fifteen years ago would have put them in San Quentin for four years. Most of them were high on drugs or high on the need to steal something to get them more drugs. Or just plain stupid.

Somehow he didn't think the Slager slasher was stupid. He had shown a good deal of expertise in getting into Ariza's apartment. He had been waiting for her, all set to dress her up in a sexy outfit, to tie her to the bed. But why pick Ariza? She was attractive, all right, but the city was filled with attractive women, a lot of them living alone. Why Ariza? What was the connection? The slasher had made two mistakes. The tool kit and the cap. But so far neither had turned up much of anything. There was no Bob's Locksmith in San Francisco or the neighboring communities, according to telephone information.

Kordic reached for the phone book, letting his fingers run through the yellow pages. He groaned inwardly at the number of listings under Sporting Goods Dealers. Forty, he estimated. He riffled the pages as if they were a deck of cards, stopping at Garments, Printing and Lettering.

His mind was so focused, he didn't hear the detail secretary calling out for inspectors Granados and Pittman. "Just came in. Confirmed 187. Clothing store on Market Street. Clerk shot to death. Crime lab and M.E. are rolling."

Chapter 12

Mary Ariza heard the tap on the door. She looked up and saw her boss, Matt Pontar. "We didn't expect you to come into the office today, Mary."

She stood up, dusting the arms of her jacket. "I've got a lot of work lined up, Matt."

"Don't get me wrong," Pontar said. "We're happy to have you back. But if you feel you need a few days off, by all means take them."

She shook her head determinedly. "No. I'm fine."

"I went over the settlement on the adult bookstore. Nice job. Damn nice job. A million bucks. I didn't think the insurance company would go that high."

"In a way I wish they hadn't," Mary confessed. "I think we would have gotten more from the jury."

"You never know with a jury. You done good, kid. Listen, I know things are a little unsettled for you right now. My wife and I would be happy to have you come and stay with us for a while."

"No. That's nice of you, Matt. But it's not necessary. They had a policeman at the door last night. And I'm sure that man would never come back again."

Pontar looked back into the hallway, then came into Mary's office, closing the door behind him. "Are you satisfied with the way the policeman is handling the case?"

"Inspector Kordic? Yes." She had to admit that she'd been pleased with the actions of the police so far. "Why do you ask?"

Pontar cleared his voice, like a man coming down with a cold. "I know some people in the department. If you don't think Kordic is doing all the right things, I could probably get the case assigned to someone else."

Mary's forehead corduroyed in confusion. "Is there something I should know about Kordic?"

Pontar perched on the arm of the leather chair. "He's gone through some tough times. About a year ago his wife and young son were killed. A car jacking. Whoever did it was never caught. Jack Kordic went off the deep end. Problems with booze. A suicide attempt. He had a nervous breakdown. Frankly, I'm surprised they let him back on duty. To top it off, his partner retired from the department while Kordic was going through all this. They haven't replaced his partner, so he's working on this alone. I'm not sure he's up to handling it."

"My God. The poor man," Mary said quietly. "I thought there was a look of sadness in his eyes."

"He's got reasons to be sad," Pontar conceded. "But that doesn't alter the fact that someone tried to kill you, Mary. And we want the best people available handling the investigation."

Mary's temper flared. "I can handle this myself, Matt. Don't worry about me."

Pontar pulled a face as if he had suddenly bitten into a particularly sour lemon. "Me and my big mouth. I don't want to interfere, Mary. But I am worried about you. And that offer of staying at our houses was sincere. Think about it. Please." He strode toward the door, turning on his heel as he reached for the knob. "Does Kordic have any leads?"

"I was down at the Hall of Justice looking at mug shots. Didn't do much good. Kordic told me that they were able to get some prints off the tools he left behind, but it turns out they came from the trunk of a stolen car. I think he's trying to trace the baseball cap that was left behind. He suggested I go through all my files. All the cases I've been involved in since I came to work here. I've just started, but I can't make a connection. I think it was just some weirdo who happened to pick my apartment."

Pontar opened the door, took a deep breath, and let

his shoulders drop. "Poor Walter Slager. He just happened to be in the wrong place at the wrong time."

Mary Ariza's right hand went to her neck. Walter had no doubt saved her life by pushing her aside and confronting the man with the knife. What would have happened if they hadn't stopped at the apartment for the change of stockings and shoes? Would the man have left? Given up? Gone in search of someone else? The thought of her lingerie and the torn bed sheets popped into her mind. He definitely had been waiting for me. Why me?

"Don't bullshit me, now. How's it going, Jack? Any problems?" Lieutenant Chris Sullivan asked.

Kordic took a sip of the dark brown beer. He licked the foam from his lips, his eyes flicking around at the crowd. "No, no problems, Chris. I'm still waiting to hear from the Israeli Consulate on the tattoo numbers on the body from the ocean. And there's nothing new to report on the attorney that was killed. Walter Slager."

Sullivan took a long swallow from his stein, a light, filtered German-style ale. Like Kordic's dark beer, brewed right on the restaurant's premises. The building had once been the home of the Hills Brothers Coffee Company. Both Kordic and Sullivan could recall inhaling the delicious smell of the roasting coffee drifting out onto the Embarcadero. An enterprising young man had converted the main floor into an upscale beer hall, and now Gordon Biersch's was a big hit. The lunchtime crowd was mostly workers from nearby office buildings. After dark the music was cranked up. The chablis and camembert crowd came in, some no doubt thinking they were slumming. Sullivan had brought a date along one night. He felt as if he had dropped in at high school party celebrating a football victory. He clinked his glass against Kordic's. "How's that stuff treating you?"

"No problem," Kordic assured him. "A beer at lunch, a drink before dinner. Maybe a glass of wine. No problem."

The waitress delivered two huge platters containing hamburgers and French fries. Kordic picked up the ketchup, idly wondering how restaurant ketchup bottles were always filled to the top. The night crew topped them off everyday, but what about the ketchup at the bottom of the bottle? Did it ever rise above halfway? There must be restaurants with ten-year-old globs of ketchup stuck to the bottom of the bottles.

"What do you hear from Benny?" Sullivan said.

Benny Munes, Kordic's partner, had pulled the plug on his fiftieth birthday, the earliest available date for retirement from the department. He had moved to Idaho, of all places, vowing to take up hunting and fishing with a passion. Munes, who had been born in Mexico and who had complained of the cold on mild spring days in San Francisco. "Probably up to his ass in snow," Kordic said. "I get letters. He seems to be enjoying it. Sent me a picture. He's holding a trout that must go ten pounds."

"Knowing Benny, he probably bought the damn fish in a supermarket." Sullivan took a bite out of his burger, his attention drifting to the bar, where two women in their early thirties were busy warding off the smirks of four kids who looked like they should have been carded before being served a beer. He wondered how Kordic was doing in the woman department. Wondered but didn't ask.

"Anything I can help with on the stiff from the ocean, or the Slager killing?" Sullivan asked.

"Well, I could use someone to help with the legwork on running down that baseball cap the perp left in Mary Ariza's place."

"Baseball cap? Tell me about it, I haven't seen your report yet."

"The perp left two things in Ariza's apartment. A tool box that checked out to a stolen car and one of those gimme caps. The words Bob's Locksmith printed on it. No such company in the area. Not a bad pretext, though. Ariza has a good Schlage lock on her door, so the man who picked it knew what he was doing."

Sullivan drained the rest of his beer, emitted a light

burp. "So maybe he is a locksmith. From out of town somewhere."

"Yeah. Could be. I'm working on it."

"I got a brief look at this Ariza when you had her going over the mugs. Nice-looking lady. She's an attorney, right?"

"Right. Been in San Francisco for about eighth months. Lived back in Florida before that. Handles mostly civil cases. No connection there so far."

Sullivan picked up the remains of his hamburger. "You might check with Granados and Pittman. They caught a run this morning. Shop owner on Market Street. You know the kind of joint, sells sports stuff, silk-screened shirts. Also makes up sweatshirts, caps, with whatever you want printed on them. The owner was killed. Maybe there's a connection, Jack."

A hand-painted sign was tacked to the middle of a weathered sawhorse: CLOSED UNTIL FURTHER NOTICE.

Kordic edged around the sawhorse. An elderly man was pushing a vacuum cleaner around the carpeted floor. Kordic tapped him on the shoulder and the man jumped, dropping his hold on the vacuum's handle, his hands going up to his protect his face as if he were about to be hit.

"Easy, mister," Kordic said over the noise of the up-turned vacuum. He took his badge from his coat pocket.

"Shit, man, you scared the hell out of me." He stooped down gingerly, righted the vacuum cleaner, and hit the off button.

Kordic estimated him to be in his early seventies. He had nicotine-brown skin spiderwebbed with wrinkles.

"Other officers said I could clean up. It's okay, isn't it?"

"Absolutely," Kordic assured him. "I just wanted to check out a few things. Have you been working here long?"

"Yeah. Couple of years. But usually in the evenings. I clean the place up. Help out on Saturdays, or whenever it's busy and he needs me. My name and number was on the cash register. I guess that's why you people called me."

Kordic took in the room. Two walls were covered with racks of jackets and sweaters, most with the emblems of major league baseball and football teams. A center aisle displayed neat rows of sweatshirts. The wall behind the counter was covered with white T-shirts, all embossed with team emblems, outlines of the Golden Gate Bridge, the city's skyline, or pictures of sports superstars: Joe Montana, Jerry Rice, Barry Bonds. Alongside the counter was another row of clothing, nylon windbreakers in black, green, yellow, blue, and red. Baseball-style caps of matching colors were arranged directly above the jackets. Kordic picked up a cap. It was identical to the one left at Mary Ariza's apartment.

The old man was looking at Kordic with an air of resignation. "You think his family will keep the store open?"

Kordic shrugged his shoulders. "No idea. You need the job, Mister—?"

"Singleton. Elmer Singleton. I've got a small pension, Social Security, but you know how it is." He made a tight circle with his right arm, finishing up with his palm upturned behind his back.

Kordic nodded. The old timer was getting his money under the table. Probably below minimum wage. "What was the owner's name?"

"Burris. Harry Burris."

"And he was the man who was killed?"

"Yes, sir. He was all alone. Used to have a kid working for him, but the kid stole a dollar for every two he rung up."

"When Mr. Burris sold something, like one of these jackets or caps, he would put your name on them if you wanted, right?"

"Yep. Sure. Your name. Team name. Anything you wanted. Some of the people came in here wanted some strange things on their clothes, I can tell you. I used to press them on."

"Shoe me where, please, Elmer," Kordic said.

The press was in the back, a small cubicle six feet

square. "You want it right away, we just pick out the letters and press them on." Singleton pointed at a counter tray filled with numbers and letters of the alphabet. "You want it fancy, embroidered, we have to send it out."

"Did Burris keep an inventory? When he sold an item, what kind of receipt did he give the customer?"

"We just write down the date and the price, the number of letters."

"Show me the receipt book."

The counter area still had some yellow crime-scene tape blocking the area near the cash register, and a chalked body outline of the late Harry Burris was visible on the carpet

Elmer Singleton nodded toward the register. "That open space under the register. Usually kept the book there."

Kordic leaned over the counter, groping until his hand struck a tablet. It was a standard eleven-by-eight-inch, carbonless-paper receipt book. "How much for one of the caps and jackets there?"

"Cap is $7.99. Jacket $19.99."

"How much for the lettering?"

"Depends on the size, Officer."

Kordic frowned. He should have brought the cap with him. He went back to the press room, dug through the cloth letters. They were neatly packaged in sizes ranging from a half-inch to two inches. He was sure the cap from Ariza's apartment had one-inch letters. He dug out the letters, carried them out to the counter, arranging them until they spelled out Bob's Locksmith. "How much for a cap, lettered just like this?"

Elmer Singleton rubbed his jaw with his hand. "We charge for the apostrophe just like it was a letter."

"How much?"

"Fifty cents a letter. So what you got there is seven dollars, plus the cap."

Kordic scribbled numbers on a blank receipt page. "So we're talking $14.99 for the cap and $26.99 for the jacket."

"That's $41.98," Singleton said with a grin. "I was

always good at numbers. But then you got the sales tax. Eight and a half percent." He gave a dry chuckle. "The governor's got to get his share."

Kordic went back to his scribbling.

Singleton interrupted him. "Three dollars and fifty cents tax, Officer."

Kordic looked up at Singleton, who smiled back, showing a full set of piano-ivory teeth. "I ain't that good with numbers." He tapped a tax code chart taped to the side of the register. "Got it from there."

Kordic added the two figures. "Forty-five dollars and fifty-five cents." He thumbed through the receipt book. There it was. A receipt made out on the fourteenth, the day of Walter Slager's murder, in the amount of $45.55. The only notation other than the date and the amount was a two-initial notation: *BL*. As in Bob's Locksmith. He slid the receipt book over to Singleton. "What else does this show other than the date and the amount?"

Singleton studied the tag for a moment. "Nothing. 'Cept this circled X at the bottom. Means the customer paid cash."

Kordic wasn't all that disappointed. He had the feeling that if this particular customer had used a credit card, the card almost certainly would have been stolen. He held out a hand. "Elmer, you've been a great help."

What was the connection? Had whoever killed Walter Slager killed the store owner, Harry Burris? Why? Why had it been necessary to kill Burris? Because he had seen the killer? Leaving the cap behind in Ariza's apartment had been a mistake. But a big enough mistake to kill Burris? Or was it just a coincidence? Another senseless robbery-killing?

If the attack on Mary Ariza and the killing of Burris were connected, then what was the common denominator? If Ariza was his target, why not just kill her on the street? Kordic had checked with the Burglary detail. There was nothing recent in a three-block area of Ariza's apartment—and no M.O. of anyone using a locksmith's cap. The same was true of the Sexual Assault detail—no serial rapist using the locksmith pretext.

There was nothing in Ariza's place worth stealing—just a normal TV, clothes, costume jewelry. Thieves who go in for those kinds of burglaries didn't bother picking locks. They just kick the door in. Only a real pro could pick that lock. And a real pro would know what was behind the door before he picked it.

There had been nothing behind Ariza's door. He had been waiting for her. Why Ariza?

Chapter 13

Pepe Fuentes was still on a high, partially from the killing of the shopkeeper, partly from the power of the cocaine Tony Moreno had supplied him with. Man, it was powerful shit. And the gun. The double deuce with the silencer. He couldn't get over just how silent the gun was. He remembered every moment of it, walking into the store, the old Anglo giving him a long, hard look and going to the cash register, like he knew what was coming. Then pulling the trigger. The .22 pistol spitting out the slugs, sounding like someone coughing. It was like those cool fucking spy dudes on the tube. Poof, poof, and the old man sagging down. Then strolling out of the store. Nobody on the street heard nothing. Beautiful. But this other one, the attorney chick, was turning out to be bullshit. Moreno had made Pepe study her pictures. He knew what she looked like, all right, but where the hell was she?

The rain made it impossible to watch her apartment house from across the street. Twice a woman had come out of the place and he had run across the street, only to find it wasn't her. Enough was enough. He'd go inside where it was dry. Watch her walk out her door, then pop her. What the hell was the difference if she died in the street or inside the damn building?

Pepe saw her name and apartment number on the mailbox. The door was locked. He was reaching for the slim jimmy bar in his back pocket when an elderly man came barreling to the door, opened it, and stepped outside. He was unfurling his umbrella when Pepe caught the door and slithered past him. He gave Pepe a suspicious look, but so what? We all look the same to the old white ones.

The elevator door was open and waiting. He punched the button for the fourth floor, hand gripping the gun. It would be something if the doors opened and she was there. But the fourth-floor hallway was empty. He edged down toward her door. He could hear something. People talking. About the weather. Radio or TV. He looked around for a good spot. The stairwell. He walked halfway down to the third floor. He could just make out Ariza's door. Perfect. Open the door, *chavala*. Then *adios*.

"I know, I know, I'm taking it out now," John Landon said grumpily as he reached under the kitchen sink and picked up the paper bag overflowing with garbage. He rested the side of the bag against his stomach and used his right hand to unlock the door. He was whistling "As Time Goes By," having seen *Casablanca* for the umpteenth time on TV the night before, when he noticed a young man backing down the stairs.

Landon walked to the stairwell, leaning over the rail just as the man retreated all the way to the third floor.

"Can I help you, son?" Landon asked, wishing he had put his glasses on before leaving the apartment.

"No, just waiting for a friend" came the reply.

"Waiting for Johnny Baker, I bet, huh? Don't ever get into a poker game with that kid, he'll take you to the cleaners."

"Yeah, don't I know," said the young man, turning his back to Landon.

Landon whistled more of "As Time Goes By" as he made his way to the hallway garbage chute. He quickly dropped the paper bag into the chute, then hurried back toward the stairway, noticing that the young man was now standing on the third-floor landing, impatiently slapping his right hand against his thigh.

Once back in his apartment, Landon ran to the bedroom. His wife was lying comfortably in bed, with both pillows behind her back, reading a paperback novel.

"What's the matter, John?" she asked, dropping the book and watching in disbelief as her husband went to the closet and took a .45 semi-automatic pistol from under a stack of neatly folded sweaters.

"Some kid is outside. I don't like the looks of him," Landon said, jamming the gun's clip in, then jacking a round into the chamber. "Better call the cops, Paula. I'm going to check him out."

Paula Landon pulled back the bedcovers. "For God's sake, don't do anything foolish, John."

Landon raced into the living room, where he found his glasses on top of the TV set. He went to the kitchen, took a large paper bag from under the sink, shook it open, and headed back to the hallway.

Pepe tapped his foot nervously on the carpeted stairway. He glanced at his wristwatch. Ten minutes to eight. Where the hell was she? Any minute more tenants would be popping out of their doors, like that nosy old fat bastard dumping his garbage. Hurry up, woman, hurry up.

His head jumped when he heard the sound of a door opening from the floor above. He took the steps two at a time, his right hand reaching into his coat pocket for the gun. Damn, it was just the fat man again.

"Hey, buddy," John Landon shouted. "What the hell are you doing around here?"

"I told you," Pepe said, trying to keep his voice friendly. "I'm waiting for someone. Giving him a ride to work."

"Yeah. So you told me. Said you were waiting for Johnny Baker. There ain't no Johnny Baker in this building, buddy. Never has been. What's your game?"

"Beat it, old man. I told you I'm waiting for someone. Go dump your garbage."

"I called the cops. Let's see what kind of a story you give them."

Pepe was ready to turn and run when he saw the woman come out of her apartment. She closed the door behind her with a loud bang.

Mary Ariza spotted John Landon. "Hi, Mr. Landon, how are—?"

She saw a young man in a black jacket race up the steps toward her. He held something in his hand. Mary started to scream. Suddenly there were a series of loud explosions and the front of the boy's jacket turned red.

Jack Kordic took a quick look at the body on the stairs, then walked down the hallway to Mary Ariza's apartment. A man of medium height, dressed in a well-tailored blue pinstripe suit, was leaning against her door, arms folded across his chest. "Are you Inspector Kordic?"

"Yes. Who are you?" Kordic demanded, studying the man. He had a voice of authority. A no-nonsense look to him. Though the suit was obviously very expensive, and he wore an immaculate white shirt with a spread collar over a heavy gray silk tie, the face had a tough, weathered look that made him appear as if he would have been more at home on a ship's deck or in a saddle.

"Matt Pontar. I'm Mary's employer." He held up a hand, as a traffic cop would to stop a car edging into an intersection. "Look, Inspector, I don't want to get in your way, but I'm really worried about Mary. We all are. I don't think she's safe here. I'd like to put her up at my house." His eyes flicked around the hallway. "And I'd like to do it right away."

"Sounds like a good idea to me, but it's up to the lady. She inside?"

Pontar moved away from the door. "Yes. Anything I can do to help, Inspector. Just let me know." He took a business card from his wallet and handed it to Kordic. "I'll wait outside in my car."

Mary Ariza was sitting on her couch, knees together, a cup of coffee clasped between her hands. She saw Kordic and stood up, brushing her skirt. "Inspector, I'd like to get out of here as soon as possible."

"I don't blame you. I just spoke to your boss. I think he's got the right idea. Just tell me what happened."

"Everything happened so fast," she said, carrying her cup to the sink. "I was leaving for work. I saw Mr. Landon standing there. I said hello or something like

that. Then this man—boy, really—ran up the stairs. He
didn't say anything. Just ran up. He had a gun." The
cup made clattering sounds as she put it in the sink.
"Suddenly there were shots. At first I thought they
were from his gun. The young man's. But no, it was
Mr. Landon. He shot the man." She turned to face
Kordic. "What is going on, damn it? Why are people
trying to kill me? What are you doing about it?"

"I'm doing the best I can, Miss Ariza. There's got to
be a reason for two attempts on your life. You're the
only one who knows what's been happening in your
life. You've got enemies out there. Who are they? You
tell me." Kordic's voice had gotten a little louder than
he intended.

They both stared at each other for several seconds.

Mary pulled her eyes away first. "I'm sorry, Inspector. I'm just—I don't know why anyone would want to
harm me." She looked directly at him. "I really don't.
Really."

Kordic remembered sitting through a four-hour
training class on kinesic interrogation techniques. The
long-winded professor had gone into excruciating details on the values of the kinesic approach, which he
described as a systematic study of the relationship between body movements, such as blushes, shrugs, or
eye movements, and communication. An entire hour
had been devoted to "flag expressions of the head,
eyes, eyebrows, nose, and mouth." Kordic felt the
course had been a waste of time—his, not the professor's, who was picking up a couple of hundred dollars
from the city coffers for each of the twenty-seven policemen attending the lecture.

Everything about Mary Ariza showed she was telling the truth. All her barriers were down. It was the
exact moment an investigator waited for with a witness. "Mary, let's work together on this. Help me. This
is not the same man who attacked you with the knife."

"No," she said positively. "He was much younger.
The man with the knife was older, bigger, and he had
a beard."

"Are there any cases you've been working on where

you could have made an enemy?" He tried the smile again. "Attorneys must make enemies."

"Yes, I know we're not very popular. But I've only been in San Francisco a few months. I think I told you, Walter Slager and I just had a big victory in court. For a million dollars. But the settlement was with an insurance company. There's no reason for anyone connected with that case to be after me."

"What about back home?"

Home? Florida. Her ex-husband? Ric. No. Not possible. The divorce settlement had been amicable. Much more so than their marriage. All she had wanted was out. No alimony, no support, and what little property they had was split down the middle. He had been jealous, but by the time the divorce was final, he'd already found someone else. The last she heard, they were engaged. "No, Inspector. No one back home would have any reason to do this."

"No clients who thought you done them wrong?"

"No."

"No boyfriends carrying a grudge?"

"No, I'm divorced. My ex would have nothing to do with this, believe me."

"Okay, how about something unusual happening to you? Something that you might not think important. But something unusual."

Mary leaned against the kitchen counter. "Well, just the man in the street, but there couldn't be a connection between that and these attacks."

Kordic's interest was immediate. "What man in the street?"

"I was coming back to the office after a settlement conference. A man bumped into me. He fell to the sidewalk. I could see he was ill. It looked like a heart attack. I gave him mouth-to-mouth resuscitation until the ambulance arrived."

"Who was the man?"

She combed her hair with her fingers. "I don't know. He was middle-aged, not very well dressed."

"Did he say anything to you?"

Mary pinched the bridge of her nose as if she had a

headache. "Did he ever. He thought I was a priest. He began telling me his confession. In Spanish."

"You speak Spanish?"

"Yes."

Kordic's eyes narrowed. "How did he mistake you for a priest?"

"Well, he had glasses. Thick glasses. They had fallen off when he dropped to the sidewalk, and I was wearing a black pant suit. I guess he was in shock."

"What did he tell you?"

"Oh, strange things. He rambled quite a bit. I didn't hear all of it. He thought he killed his daughter, Rose. Blamed himself for her death, anyway—at least that's what the priest said."

"Priest? There was a priest there?"

"No." Mary smiled apologetically. "I know it sounds confusing. The priest came to my office the next day. He told me the man had died. Told me about the man's daughter. What really happened."

"Which was?"

"His daughter had gotten pregnant, moved out, and died at childbirth, is what Father Torres said."

Kordic reached for his notebook. "Which church is Father Torres from?"

"I never asked, damn it. I guess the policeman gave him my address."

"Which policeman?"

"I didn't get his name. He was just there. After the ambulance took the man away, I gave the policeman one of my business cards."

Kordic tried to figure what significance all this could have with the attacks on Ariza. "You're sure the man had a heart attack? He wasn't shot? Assaulted?"

"Oh, no. Nothing like that. He just had the attack, and I gave him CPR. As simple as that."

Kordic asked her specific questions as to the time and place of the incident. He snapped his notebook shut, then asked, "Was there anything else he told you? While he thought he was confessing?"

"Oh, something about his father, being afraid of his father."

"Was the man local? From San Francisco?"

Mary shook her head. "I wasn't paying much attention, Inspector. My mind was on the case I was working on before this happened, and I was just trying to keep him alive. I think he mentioned something about Lima, Peru. But whether he lived there, I have no idea. Can I leave now? I'd really like to get out of here."

"Mr. Pontar is waiting for you. Would you mind if I used your apartment for an hour or so?"

"No, not at all." She picked up her purse, glancing around the room, as if she were looking at it for the last time.

"I'll lock up when I leave," Kordic assured her.

He watched her walk to the elevator: eyes straight ahead she advanced slowly, as if wading through water. What the hell was it with Ariza? he wondered. Smart. Good-looking. Seems to be telling the truth. The first attack could have been a sex nut. But two tries? This one by a different guy with a gun. What the hell was going on?

"No ID on him, Inspector," said the assistant medical examiner, as if reading Kordic's mind.

Kordic recognized him: Jerry. Jerry something, but he couldn't recall his last name. Tall, thin, receding red hair. "Nothing at all, huh?"

"Nope. Okay if we move him now?"

"Crime lab had their shot?"

"Yeah, all done with this guy," Jerry said, bending down and pulling the blanket from the body. Kordic dropped to his knees to take a close look. One bullet had hit him in the shoulder, the other had blown away most of the left side of his face. Alongside the body was a pistol in a clear plastic bag. Kordic picked up the weapon, weighing it in his hand.

The young medical examiner stared at the pistol as if it were a rare antique. "Never saw one of those things before, except in the movies."

Kordic stared at the silencer on the end of the gun. He had seen homemade silencers before—usually nothing more than baby-bottle nipples slipped over the edge of the barrel. Or a hollowed-out potato. Even plastic liter-sized Coke bottles. But this looked like the real thing. He stood up, feeling tension in his back. "Take him away. He's all yours, Jer."

John Landon was waiting in his apartment. For someone who had just killed a man, Landon looked amazingly composed. His first words were "You're not going to take my gun away, are you, Inspector?"

Mrs. Landon was standing alongside her husband, a defiant look on her face. "You should be giving John a medal, that's what you should be doing. Not treating him like a criminal."

"Who's treating your husband like a criminal, Mrs. Landon?"

"Those other policemen. The ones that were here first. They acted like they were going to arrest him."

"Hey, calm down, honey," John Landon said, patting his wife's shoulder with a ham-like hand. "They're just doing their duty." He looked at Kordic. "She doesn't understand. You don't unless you've been in the business, I guess."

"The man you shot. Any chance he's the same man that killed Walter Slager with a knife?"

"Nah, no resemblance at all. The guy with the knife was twice as big as this punk."

"You told me you were in the military police, didn't you?" Kordic asked.

"Damn right. Something about this guy just didn't look right to me."

"That why you shot him?"

"Hey," Landon said hotly. "I went out to dump the garbage. This punk was loitering around. I asked him what he was up to, he said he was waiting for a friend. I made up some b.s. about a guy who doesn't live in the building, and he fell for it. I knew something was wrong." Landon ran his hand across his stomach, as if he were hungry. "So I came back into my place, told the missus to call the cops. Got out my forty-five, hid it behind a brown bag, pretending I was dumping the garbage again, and went and checked him out. As soon as he saw Mary Ariza, he went after her with that silenced gun of his."

"You could tell the gun had a silencer?"

"Naw. Not till after I shot him." Landon waved his hands in front of him, an umpire calling someone safe sliding into home plate. "Don't worry. I didn't touch the damn thing. Just went over and looked at it."

"You're a pretty good shot, Mr. Landon."

Landon smiled, showing a broad range of tobacco-stained teeth. "Not bad, huh? Right through the grocery bag. I emptied the clip on him." His smile folded into a scowl. "You going to have to take my gun away?"

Chapter 14

"Paul, you should have woken me," Adele Abrams complained, her lips formed in a pout.

Abrams pushed his chair back from the desk. "I stopped by your room. You were sound asleep, darling. A smile on your face. You must have been dreaming. I didn't have the heart to wake you."

Adele draped her arms over her husband's shoulders, her lips nuzzling his neck. "It was you I was dreaming about, Paul. How was your trip?"

Abrams clasped her hands in his. "Successful." He stood and hugged her to him for a moment, then gently pushed her away, admiring her beauty. She was wearing oversize slacks and a man's-style one-button blazer, looking like a schoolgirl after raiding her daddy's closet. "You're all dressed up. I was hoping we'd have lunch together."

"I wasn't expecting you until tonight, Paul. I have a luncheon. Boring damn thing. It's a benefit at the de Young Museum." Her cheeks dimpled. "I can skip it. I'm sure they won't miss me."

"No, no. I have some calls to make. You go to lunch." His hand undid her blazer button and glided up across the silk blouse to her breast, his finger stroking the nipple erect. No bra. She was still young enough to get away with that. "We'll have dinner tonight, just the two of us."

"Sounds wonderful. I've bought some new outfits. You're going to love them. But I'd better get going now, darling."

"Have fun."

Abrams bent down and scooped up the cat, scratching it behind the ears. "Tell me, Shylock, have you been a good boy?" He carried the cat to the window, drawing back the velvet curtain and looking down at the street.

The driver, the new one, the young, good-looking one, had the car door open for Adele. She gave him a wide smile. Too wide a smile? "Is our girl being naughty, Shylock?" he whispered into the cat's ear. "Is she?"

He dismissed his wife from his mind, cradled the cat in his lap, and settled into his chair, spreading the documents from his most recent trip to Russia across his desk. It had been a grueling trip, but the results were well worth it. The meetings with his expert. A half-dozen stops at old well sites, then the visit to Tenghiz and the new oil fields. He had spread around plenty of *mah'sla,* literal translation—butter—but a bribe in any language, to the right people, and now he had a firm grasp on just what properties he wanted to bid on.

He'd dealt with the bankers in Moscow and St. Petersburg. The Russian bureaucrats made the people Abrams regularly dealt with in Washington, D.C., look like amateurs. The *Gazprom,* the super-monopoly that controlled the gas industry, had its nose everywhere. Then there were the thirty-two separate oil associations, each run by its own little general, whose main objective in life was to spread confusion while keeping his palm open for more *mah'sla.*

Finally, the *vory v zakone,* the Russian mafia, without whose cooperation nothing got done. His contacts there were solid. With all the circling sharks, the former Russian *prishlies,* the privileged class, and the ex-military men who wanted a piece of bloated oil pie, they'd have to be.

He heard light tapping on the door and looked up to see his attorney, David Blair, an oversize briefcase in hand.

Abrams dropped the cat to the carpet. "David, come on in. Good to see you."

Blair unloaded the briefcase on Abrams's desk.

"Good to have you back, Paul. The trip was a success?"

"Very much so. And how are things on the home front?"

Blair made a throwaway gesture with one hand. "Fine, just fine."

Abrams noticed a lack of confidence in his voice. "Any problems?"

"Nothing major. Did you see Joseph Rose in Russia?"

"Not on this last trip. But I did see him in Moscow a couple of weeks ago. Why? I thought his work was done there."

Blair unsnapped the case and extracted a manila folder. "We have all his reports, but I wanted to go over some specifics with him. His secretary says he's in Moscow. An unscheduled trip."

"Rose told me he was coming home for a while, to warm up his bones, then he was heading back to check out the oil fields near the Artic Ocean. Make contact with him. I don't like surprises, David. Not when we're this close."

"Neither do I," Blair admitted. "He's a reliable man. I'm sure we'll be hearing from him soon."

Abrams wasn't satisfied. Rose was a key to his operation. The old man had developed a way to heat oil in the ground, a flash-heat thermal-lance system. The beauty of Rose's system was that it greatly enhanced the recovery of oil from old wellheads and speeded up operations at new drilling sites, making it especially valuable in the Russian frozen wastelands. Rose estimated that the wellheads abandoned by the Russians still had thirty percent of their oil in the ground. "I wanted to buy out Rose, but he wouldn't go for it. He had to keep control of his little company. Do we have all his reports? His surveys? All we need?"

Blair smiled a harried smile. "Don't worry, we have it all, Paul."

Abrams slapped his hand on the desk, leaving a moist imprint on the wood. "I do worry, David. All the time. Find Rose. I don't want a single loose end in this deal. Understood?"

"Yes, sir," Blair answered firmly.

"Good. Now sit down. I'll tell you about those crazy Russian bankers."

"Thank you very much, Mrs. Pontar," Mary Ariza said, looking around at what had been described to her as "one of the spare bedrooms." It's almost the size of my entire apartment, Mary estimated, with windows opening right out to the Pacific Ocean. The room was filled with a half-dozen off-white whipcord-covered chairs and a loveseat. Pillows covered in blue and white stripes—the blue almost the exact shade of the ocean, the white a match for the foamy breakers—were scattered around the room. Mary vaguely wondered if they changed the pillows when the ocean turned gray.

A queen-sized bed with a trefoil-shaped wicker headboard butted up against one wall, the bedspread a match of the pillow material.

"Call me Mary, please," Mrs. Pontar said. "Two Marys. We'll probably confuse Matt, but he'll work it out. Make yourself comfortable. This door leads to the bathroom." Mary Ariza peeked in and saw the bathroom sink, a piece of pink marble delicately crafted into the shape of a seashell.

"You have such a beautiful home, Mrs.—Mary. I hate to put you to so much trouble."

"No trouble at all." Mrs. Pontar walked to the windows, folded her arms, and smiled. She was of medium height, and Mary thought she must be on the sunny side of forty. Her hair was a silky black and swayed when she moved. Her malachite green silk jumpsuit emphasized a voluptuous figure. "I'm glad the rain stopped. I never get tired of this view."

Mary Ariza edged up alongside Mrs. Pontar and looked at the sweeping horizon, which took in Point Bonita and the north tower of the Golden Gate Bridge.

Mrs. Pontar pointed at the phone on the bed stand. "Just punch one if you want to contact the kitchen staff." She took one of Mary's hands into her own. "I know you've been through a difficult time. Don't worry. You're safe here. Completely safe. You're welcome to stay as long as you wish." She released Mary's hand and smiled. "But don't feel as if you're a damned prisoner. If you want to go anywhere, use the convertible." She turned to the windows. "It's so nice to see the sun again, isn't it? I'll leave you now. Come downstairs whenever you feel like it. I'll be in my studio. My husband tells me you paint too."

"Not since college."

"Well, come down and join me. I need all the help I can get."

Mary Ariza watched her leave the room. God, what nice people. She wondered if she would be as gracious to someone who was being stalked by a killer. Or killers. She sat down on the couch, took a notepad and pen from her purse, and started writing. One word: Why?

Why, indeed. Why would anyone want to kill me? She wrote down the word *Enemies* and stared at it for several minutes, trying to think of anyone who might have something against her. She could not come up with one name.

She briefly thought of writing Oscar Lofton's name, the adult bookstore owner. But he was a weasel. Besides, he was right. The lawsuit hadn't cost him any money. Just his insurance company.

Who else? There was no one, damn it. No one. She couldn't believe her ex-husband, Ric, was involved, but just to get rid of any nagging doubts, she had called Miami and spoken to a friend of hers—of both of theirs really—that worked for the same realtor Ric did. She assured Mary that Ric had been in the office every day for the last week. She also told her that Ric and his fiancée had moved the date of their wedding up to the sixth of next month.

She dropped the notepad in frustration, stood up, and walked to the windows. What else could there be? Mistaken identity? A sudden surge of energy hit her. Yes, that could be it. It had to be. She went to the side of the bed and found a phone book in the cabinet drawer beneath the telephone. She thumbed quickly through the directory, found the A's. Her own number was not published. There were four listings under Ariza: Andrew, Donald, Michael, Robert. No Mary. No just plain M. Could one of the listed names have a wife named Mary? A daughter? She was about to call the numbers alongside the names when there was a knock on the door.

Mary Pontar entered the room. "There's a policeman to see you. Inspector Kordic." She cupped Mary's elbows in her hands. "He's not bad-looking."

Rene Santos surveyed the Hall of Justice from the back parking lot, tucked under a freeway. The sound of cars thundering overhead followed him as he paced off the length of the building, which took up a full block. The building itself was L-shaped, seven stories of concrete blocks sitting squatly between Harrison on the north and Bryant on the south, stretching to Seventh Street on the east and Harriet on the west. He speculated as to who Harriet was and what it was she had done to justify someone naming a street, even a squalid one like this, in her memory. A maze of communication antennas sat on the roof. There were two pedestrian entrances: one on Bryant, the other off the parking lot facing Harrison Street. There were dozens of marked and unmarked police cars in the lot alongside the north side of the building. A ramp led to the basement, a sign proclaiming: POLICE VEHICLES ONLY. He judged it a truly ugly building, but then he had never seen a police station that he liked.

Santos walked along a covered promenade, past the doors leading to the medical examiner's office, through two grimy safety-glass doors, and into the entrance to the Hall itself. His eyes darted around as he stood in line waiting to go through a metal detector. The group of people in front of him was an odd mixture. A third of them looked like vagrants who had spent the night sleeping in the streets, an almost one-to-one ratio of male to female, ranging in age from late teens to over sixty. Then there was the well-dressed, dark-suited crowd, with their shiny leather briefcases, the badge of attorneys worldwide. The rest appeared to be respectable, average-looking citizens, perhaps coming down to protest a traffic violation or file a burglary complaint. All dressed in clean but casual clothing, as Santos was. The collar stood up on his windbreaker, and a wool watch cap was pulled down on his forehead. A pair of cheap sunglasses completed the outfit. Nothing exotic, he thought, but more than adequate for the purpose he had in mind.

He shuffled his feet slowly along the marble floor, moving closer to the metal detector, which looked like nothing more than the skeleton of a door frame. He recognized the detector's brand name: RENS. Santos knew the model well. It had a sensitivity selector that could be adjusted so it would pick up the fillings in a person's teeth. Common practice was to set the machine so that pocket items such as keys, coins, or cigarette lighters would set off the beeping alarm. A policeman sat in a chair behind a battered wooden desk next to the detector. He was heavy-set, jowls in need of a shave, his stomach spilling over his belt buckle, an opened paperback book in his lap. He barely raised his head as he repeated his sermon: "Put your keys, any heavy metal objects, and tobacco on the desk."

Members of the suitcase crowd must have been regulars because even though they set off the alarm while passing through the RENS detector, the officer would take a quick glance at the proper-looking gentlemen and wave them through with a nod of his head.

Tempting, Santos thought, very tempting. But he had to be careful. He dutifully dropped his keys, watch, and small change into a yellow plastic bowl set on the desk, walked through the detector, and reached back for them. He noticed that as sleepy and unprofessional as the police officer looked, he had a heavy revolver holstered on his belt.

Santos wandered around the main lobby, checking for exits, surveying the crowd. The attorneys on their way to court. Defendants with worried looks on their faces. Groups of brash young men, talking in strange street language, smiles on their faces as if they thought the whole criminal procedure was a joke. It could be, Santos admitted to himself. But he knew from professional experience just how serious it could get.

There was a building directory near a newsstand. The county jail was located on the sixth and seventh floors. Courtrooms were spread among the first, second, and third floors. The various investigation squads, including Homicide, were located on the fourth floor. The office of the chief of police was on the fifth, the cafeteria listed as being in the basement.

Santos continued his stroll, getting the feel of the place. Enemy territory. It was a risk. But he had to find out just what the police knew. The second botched attempt to kill the Ariza woman had been a disaster.

First Davila, then Tony Moreno's incompetent hired hand. Could the police trace Moreno's man to Moreno, then to Davila? He had to know what they had. How close they were.

The walls were of pink marble, the flooring two-foot squares of green marble bordered in brass. The marble contractor must have made a fortune, he thought. He stood in front of a beige marble tablet, some three feet high and eight feet long, that listed the names of policemen killed in the line of duty. The first one was a John Croates in 1878. Santos counted off ninety-two names. The bloodiest year of all seemed to be 1957, with four victims claimed. Santos wondered just what had made that year so special.

He continued his inspection, finding that there were three staircases and a bank of six passenger elevators and one lone freight elevator leading from the basement to the upper floors. He dutifully marched up the full length of each stairway. One went from the basement to the third floor, the other two started in the lobby and climbed to the county jail floors.

He took the stairs to the cafeteria, finding it of modest size. Chairs of faded and torn imitation leather were tucked under streaked formica tables, most large enough to handle six to eight customers. A chalkboard over the serving trays listed the day's specials: sweet and sour pork, chow mein, and fried rice for $4.75.

Santos settled for a cup of coffee. The Asian who made his change barely spoke English. He carried his coffee to an empty table and watched the procession for fifteen minutes.

More of the briefcase brigade. Several uniformed policeman and what must be detectives: men in shirtsleeves with empty holsters on their belts. Empty holsters. Perfect, he thought. They must lock their guns away in their desks when they're wandering around the building. He studied the dress habits of detectives. Shirts in colors, stripes, patterns, nothing regimental there. Ties that matched or sometimes clashed with the shirts. The collar usually undone. They were joined by men in sports coats that Santos took to be more detectives by their talk and easy manner with the coatless bunch. He could see the butts of revolvers and pistols on their belts as they reached for their wallets. Probably just coming to work or getting ready to leave the building.

The small item in the newspaper detailing the finding of a headless, handless corpse in the ocean had listed an Inspector Jack Kordic's name and a telephone number. Kordic had requested anyone with knowledge of the victim's identity to contact him. Santos had called the number. A woman had answered, "Homicide, can I help you?" It made him chuckle, the voice apparently having no idea of the suggestion she was offering. "Homicide, can I help you?" Yes, Santos had been tempted to say, I'm working with a bunch of incompetents. I need some well-qualified killers. Instead he had asked to speak to Inspector Kordic. The detective's voice sounded irritated, tired. Santos had strung Kordic along, telling him of a missing uncle, trying to put a picture to the voice. Could one of the men at the table be Kordic? None of the voices seemed to match that of the man on the phone.

He left his coffee and took the stairway up to the fourth floor. The Homicide detail was located in Room 415. The door was open and he could see a ruddy-faced woman sitting behind a chipped green metal desk. She had a phone against one ear, her hands fiddling with a computer. A paneled wall behind her was littered with calendars, cartoons cut out from newspapers and magazines, and a sign proclaiming: NO VISITORS BEYOND THIS POINT. He walked past the door, then came back, stooping down to tie his shoes, his eyes flicking to the door's lock. It would not be a problem. There was a pay telephone just twenty-five feet away. He dug through the phone book for the police department's listing, dialed the number, and asked to be put through to Homicide. The woman sitting just a few feet away answered with her silly "Homicide, may I help you?"

"Yes. The killing this morning of the young Latin man on Hyde Street. I may have some information that will help. Can you tell me who is handling the case, please?"

"That's Inspector Jack Kordic's case, sir. He's away from the office now. Can I have him call you?"

The telephone suddenly felt slippery in Santos's hands. Kordic again. *De mala suerte.* Bad luck. He could feel it. He dropped the receiver on its cradle, his fingers unconsciously going to the cross around his neck. Kordic. He had to know what Kordic knew before he made his next move.

Chapter 15

Kordic parked himself in front of the computer and punched in the date, time, and location of Mary Ariza's encounter with the man who'd had the heart attack. Officially, it was listed as a 914: man down on the street. Since Kordic had no name for the victim, he entered Ariza's as the reportee and got a hit. He pushed some buttons, and the printer gurgled into action. He looked at the report as he carried it back to his desk. John Doe, age approximately fifty. Died at San Francisco General Hospital. Cause of death: massive coronary. The boxes showing next of kin, address, and date of birth were all blank.

Kordic decided to try the medical examiner's office. That file was as lean as the computer report. No additional ID. No personal items in the victim's possession other than a comb, a cheap ballpoint pen, and a pack of Camel cigarettes. He felt a strange tingling sensation at the back of his neck. No ID. That was wrong. All wrong. The street people, the legitimately homeless and the petty thieves, drug dealers, and borderline loonies that roamed the streets almost always carried some kind of identification: a Social Security card for picking up welfare checks, a soup-kitchen pass, a blood-bank card enabling them to sell the only item of value some of them possessed, some type of paper that would connect them to a source of income. But this man had nothing. The clerk took Kordic back to the morgue and pulled the heavy box from its refrigerated wall. Kordic studied the man's features. Nothing unusual. The blank face of death. He went back to the medical office and examined the dead man's clothes.

Nothing fancy: corduroy pants, a woollen shirt, a loden coat with wooden barrel-shaped buttons dangling from the loops. He ran his fingers along the coat's seams, then the shirt and pants. Nothing. The shoes were scuffed, worn down at the heels, a brand he'd never heard of.

He then checked the M.E.'s log, which recorded the names of visitors. Not a single entry. Where was the priest Father Torres? Why hadn't the good father arranged for the dearly departed's burial? Or at least made the identification? But maybe that's the way the family wanted it, Kordic surmised. It wasn't at all that uncommon, when a victim's family was too poor to pay for a funeral, to let him be buried as a John Doe, let the city pay the expenses.

Kordic closed his eyes and thought of the four refrigerated bodies not more than fifty feet from where he stood. The old gentleman with the tattoo. The heart attack victim. The punk that Mary Ariza's neighbor, John Landon, had blown away. Walter Slager, Ariza's boyfriend. Or had he been just a business acquaintance? Was there a connection among the four bodies? One had been decapitated and his hands chopped off to impede identification. The other two found with no ID on them. The punk, that was understandable. He was doing a job. But the other, the man who died at the hospital of natural causes—he should have had some type of identification on his person. Walter Slager was the only one who'd had a wallet on him at the time of his death, and he was just one of the unfortunates: wrong place at the wrong time. Or was he? Could he have been the target? No, Ariza said that was the first time Slager had ever been to her apartment. Kordic puzzled about it all the way back to his desk, then began making calls to the Catholic archdiocese. He drew blanks all over: San Francisco, Oakland, Marin County, San Mateo, and Santa Clara. No Father Torres. He could have been a visiting priest who had not bothered to check in, Kordic was told, "on vacation, on his way to a retreat." When Kordic mentioned Mary Ariza's description of the man's callused hands, several people suggested that perhaps the visiting priest was an ardent golfer.

The phone rang almost the instant that Kordic had hung up with the Marin County archdiocese. He picked it up. Good news for a change.

"Kordic," said Tom Sato of the crime lab. "We pulled prints off the stiff, your friend with the fancy gun. His name is Pepe Fuentes. S.F. number is 7640921. He's been a bad boy."

Kordic went immediately to the computer and entered the San Francisco Police Department criminal index number Sato had given him. The screen filled up with the subject's local criminal history. Pepe Fuentes, aka Pepe Ice. Twenty-two years of age. Seven arrests since his eighteenth birthday—burglary, armed robbery, rape, drug possessions. Almost all of the cases had been dismissed "In the Interest of Justice," an apologetic term for lack of evidence or, more likely, fear instilled in witnesses. He had pulled six months in the county jail on the rape charge.

Kordic printed the rap sheet, then ordered a state CI&I check and an Interstate Identification Index, commonly known as a Triple I, which would check Fuentes's records through most of the states in the union. Or at least the states that bothered to enter arrest records in their computers. The various police data bases were becoming less and less reliable. It was a by-product of the old computer adage: Garbage In, Garbage Out. Clerks or cops would forget, or get busy with something else, and not log an arrest on line. Recently the State Narcotics Division had uncovered a ring of clerks who were members of the Hell's Angels, and would routinely purge the system of their fellow gang members and anyone who would pay the Angels to get the records expunged. Kordic had once picked up a man whom he'd arrested just a year earlier for rape and aggravated assault. The man served nine months in prison, got out, then raped and severely beat the same unfortunate woman. When Kordic arrested him the second time, he ran a rap sheet on the man that came back negative. No record.

The local rap sheet on Pepe Fuentes showed a Folsom Street address. While at the computer Kordic had run a DMV driver's license and vehicle check. No cars were registered in his name, but the address on the driver's license was identical to that of the rap sheet.

He carried the printouts back to his desk, laying them out on the blotter, alongside the reports on Walter Slager and the John Doe who had died on the street. A tap on his shoulder brought him out of his reverie.

"Hey, pal," Inspector Dave Granados said, "come back to earth. You look like you're drifting off to never-never land."

Kordic leaned back in his chair until it creaked, like arthritic joints. "Dave, that shopkeeper up on Market Street. You got anything going on him?"

Granados was a tall, lean man who looked every bit the aging Don Juan that he was. Always impeccably groomed, with thick, dark hair, so dark as to be suspect, since Granados was a couple of years past fifty. His hairline was so straight it looked as if it were marked by a chalk line. He was the neatest man Kordic had ever met. Suits always pressed. Button-down shirt collars rolled just so, shoes always shined.

"Nope. Looks like a shoot and rake job. Don't know how much cash was in the register. Poor bugger probably lost his life over a hundred bucks or less."

"What type weapon?"

"Twenty-two caliber. Little stuff. Lately they've been using Uzis or ten-millimeter semi-automatics." He patted the holster on his hip. "Lot better iron than we carry."

Granados's partner, Barry Pittman, was new to the detail, having come in while Kordic was on his medical leave. Kordic hadn't formed a strong opinion of Pittman. He was young, looked eager, always seemed to have a smile on his face. He drifted over to Kordic's desk. "You ready to take off, Dave?"

Granados stretched and yawned without bothering to cover his mouth. "More than ready. It's been a long day. Let's go get a pop at the Lineup." He turned back to Kordic. "You want to come along, Jack?"

"Thanks, but I'll meet you over there. I've got a couple of things I want to clear up," Kordic said, standing up and handing Pepe Fuentes's rap sheet to Granados. "Ever run into this beauty?"

Pittman peered over Granados's shoulder at the report. "What's with this guy?"

"He was shot and killed in a homicide attempt. He was carrying a twenty-two semi-automatic with a silencer."

Granados's eyes bounced up from the rap sheet. "Silencer?"

"Yep. Intended victim was a Mary Ariza. Attractive young attorney. Apartment house on Hyde Street. She was lucky. Her next-door neighbor is a frustrated cop. Blew Mr. Fuentes away with his old army gun. Prior attempt was made on Ariza. She came home with a friend. He ended up getting his neck sliced open. Perp on that one was a Latin male, middle-aged, big, full beard. He left something behind. A blue baseball cap with Bob's Locksmith imprinted on it. No such firm. The cap and printing are identical to the stuff your man was selling on Market Street. I've asked the crime lab to check out the silencer job on the twenty-two slugs from your victim."

"Christ," Granados said, flinging the rap sheet back onto Kordic's desk. "Silencers. Uzis. They'll be cruising down Market Street in tanks and armored cars. They'll have cruise missiles pretty soon. Come on, Barry. Let's get a drink."

Kordic fiddled with the files for twenty minutes, coming up with nothing other than a headache for his efforts.

He reached into his desk drawer and pulled out the pint bottle of Jack Daniels, slipped it into his back pocket, picked up two cups from the water cooler, and made his way to Chris Sullivan's office.

Sullivan was sprawled out in his chair, feet up on his desk, a telephone jammed between his chin and shoulder.

"Yeah, yeah. I know, I know," Sullivan said, motioning Kordic to a chair. "But I can't do a hell of a lot about it."

Kordic pulled the whiskey bottle from his pocket and waved it at Sullivan, who bobbed his head up and down and silently mouthed the word, "Please."

Kordic filled both glasses and handed one to Sullivan.

"Right, right. Soon as I can," Sullivan said, terminating the call. "Thanks for the drink, Jack."

"It's your booze, Chris," passing the bottle across the desk. "I borrowed it the other night."

Sullivan shook the bottle. "You didn't do much damage." He forced a smile. "Let me give you some advice. Never take the lieutenant's test. All I am is a damn bookkeeper now. I'll be working on this reorganization crap all night."

"I'm having a hard time holding onto the job I've got now," Kordic said.

Sullivan pulled his feet from the desk, leaned over, dug through a pile of papers until he found the one he was looking for. "Your monthly evaluation sheet. I'll fill it out later." He winked at Kordic. "You're getting excellent marks. Anything you want to talk about?"

Kordic went over the files relating to the two attacks on Mary Ariza and the killing of the shopkeeper on Market Street. "I'm having a tough time running down this priest that came to her office."

Sullivan stood, stretched, and reached for his suit jacket. "You've got too much on your plate, Jack. I'm going to organize a task force. Put you in charge. Get some people in from one of the other details to do the legwork for you. I'm going out for a quick bite. See me first thing in the morning and we'll work it out."

Rene Santos waited until four-thirty to return to the Hall of Justice. He had changed his appearance: slacks, white shirt, striped tie, a herringbone sports coat straight off the rack of a downtown department store. He added plain-lensed, horn-rimmed glasses and a false mustache that filled up the area from his upper lip to his nose. He had noticed that San Francisco policemen seemed to favor that particular style of mustache for some reason. A cheap beige raincoat and matching hat completed the outfit. Under the hat his hair was sprayed to an almost helmet-like hardness. The holster he'd purchased at a sporting goods store was strapped onto his hip. The holster was all leather, except for the metal button and clasp which held a gun in place. He'd taken the precaution of removing the button and clasp, so as he went through the metal detector, the only metal objects on his person were his watch, his keys, and a few small American coins, which he dutifully placed in the yellow plastic bowl on the policeman's desk, along with an imitation leather clipboard. He passed through the metal detector and collected his possessions.

He used the stairs to the basement, purchasing a sandwich of stale white bread wrapped in cellophane and a cup of coffee. He sat at a table, chewing the tasteless sandwich, watching as the kitchen crew began cleaning the counters, storing the leftover salads, sandwiches, and bakery goods in an industrial refrigerator.

Santos pulled back the top slice of bread on his sandwich and examined the meat lying under a thin spread of yellowing mayonnaise. He had not been able to identify the meat by its taste, and looking at it gave him no additional clues. Whatever it was, he had eaten much worse in his time.

A Chinese boy, no more than eleven, was swinging a mop across the floor. He'd stop and dip the mop in a bucket occasionally. The smell of disinfectant was familiar to Santos. Bad food and disinfectants were staples of prisons and police stations all over the world.

Santos scraped his chair back as the boy with the mop approached his table.

"Closing now," the boy said.

Santos dug in his pocket, dropped a quarter alongside his empty coffee cup, then made his way to one of the stairways and walked up to the fourth floor. The walls and stairs were raw, damp concrete. He perched on a handrail, the clipboard in one hand, a ballpoint pen in the other, in case someone came by. But no one did. He checked his watch every so often, and when it reached six o'clock, he went through the double doors and out into the hallway. The rubber soles of his shoes made no noise on the marble floors.

He was glad to see that the doors to the various detective bureaus—robbery, burglary, fraud, general works, and the sexual assault detail—were all closed. He paused momentarily in front of each door, hearing nothing. No voices, no typewriters, computers, phones ringing—nothing. He slowed as he reached the door with the word HOMICIDE stenciled on its frosty glass partition, dropping to one knee as if about to tie his shoe. Again there were no sounds from the other side of the door. He straightened up and backtracked until he came to the men's room. He went into one of the stalls, locking the door behind him, then laid the clipboard on the toilet tank and hung his raincoat, sports coat, and hat on the door hook. Santos took a travel-sized plastic bottle of hair spray from his raincoat pocket, pumped a liberal amount onto the hair on the backs of his fingers and hands, then sprayed a glob of the liquid in his left palm. Using his right index finger as a brush, he layered the spray on his eyebrows. Satisfied, he returned the hair spray to the raincoat, digging in the pocket for a small bottle marked NEW SKIN. The container looked much like a bottle of fingernail polish, and the product's intended purpose was to form a temporary skin covering or bandage. It had never caught on with the general public, but people like Rene Santos found it very effective in blocking out fingerprints. He used the small brush attached to the bottle top and began brushing the clear liquid over his fingertips, one at a time, being careful to cover the entire area, from knuckle joint to nail ending. When all ten fingers were covered to his satisfaction, he went to work on his palms. His hands felt slightly stiff, and he blew on them to speed up the drying process. It would have been much simpler to slip on a pair of surgeon's gloves, but the chance of being spotted with gloves on was too high a risk for Santos. He had stayed alive by eliminating as many risks as possible.

He picked up his clipboard and went back out to the hallway. A short, thin black man in gray coveralls, with the headset from a Walkman-type radio covering his ears, was pushing a mop bucket down the far end of the hallway. He gave Santos a wave with one hand and mumbled some kind of greeting that Santos could not understand.

Santos waved back, ducking his head to his chest and bringing the clipboard up to cover his face. The janitor stopped, pushed a door open, and maneuvered his mop bucket inside.

Santos waited until the man was out of sight. The janitor had been a good thirty-five yards away. No recognition factor. A confident smile came to Rene's face. Dress the part and you're accepted. No matter where. It was a commandment preached to him at the terrorist camp, but one he had learned on his own long before he ever set foot in that blazing desert.

He tested the handle on the door leading to the Homicide detail. It turned effortlessly. He checked the hallway again, then slipped inside, letting the door come to a close behind him. The lights were on in the small outer office where he'd seen the secretary earlier that morning. The large, adjoining room was in darkness. He found the light switch, snapped it on, standing still while the fluorescent lights fluttered on. He stared at the abundance of desks and file cabinets confronting him. More than he thought there would be.

There were no name plates on the desks, so he had to go through each one, checking out the report folders, then the inside desk drawers, where he found boxes of business cards which had the police inspector's name printed on them.

He found Kordic's desk over by the window. Unlike his fellow officers, Kordic had no personal photographs on his desk. But in the desk's center drawer, under a box of business cards, there was one color photo showing a man, woman, and young boy, standing under a comically turreted castle. The woman was attractive. The man tough, competent-looking, the child smiling broadly. Why hide the picture? Santos wondered. Divorce? He studied the man's features, committing them to memory. It must be Kordic. He closed the drawer and began going through the manila files on the desk. They were there. All of them!

Walter Slager, the man Cesar Davila had killed instead of Ariza. Santos read through the file thoroughly, especially Kordic's interview with Mary Ariza. She had no idea why anyone would attack her. The description of Davila was vague. The only physical evidence was the cap and tool box that he had left behind. But there was a sketch of Davila. The resemblance wasn't very good; still, he was glad he'd ordered Cesar to shave off his beard. Clean-shaven, he looked nothing like the man in the drawing. Who had helped the artist? Mary Ariza? The fat man? The neighbor? "Damn Cesar," Santos mumbled to himself.

The next file was thicker than the first, and simply labeled OCEAN VICTIM. He heaved a sigh of relief when the victim was listed as "still unidentified." His stomach quickly did a flip-flop when he saw the follow-up reports, the photographs of the tattoo. He remembered the tattoo. Roses. Nothing more. His heartbeat ticked up as he read the medical examiner's report. Numbers under the tattoo. More photographs. A series of numbers—blurry in the first picture, gradually becoming clearer: 2036082. Serial numbers. What the hell were they? Why hadn't he noticed them? A handwritten note, pencil on plain paper, the words underlined: Israeli Consul, Max Freeman. The Israelis! Was Rose connected to the Israelis somehow? To Mossad? No, he would have told Naimat if he was. He had been telling her everything toward the end.

He quickly turned to the next file, which was listed under the name Pepe Fuentes. Santos took his time going through the typed report. Fuentes, Tony Moreno's incompetent hit man, had been identified through his fingerprints. Santos ran a fingernail down the page listing Fuentes's arrest record. God, he thought, couldn't that idiot Moreno find someone better than this? Moreno had to go. They would all have to go. Naimat included. But she was the best of the bunch, so she'd go last. He needed them all for now. Until he had Abrams, he needed them all.

How long would it take this Kordic to check out Fuentes? Find out who his friends were? Who had hired him to kill Ariza? Again there was a page with handwritten notes, some of which he could not decipher. The words that were clear burned into his eyes: "Silencer. Market Street hit?" His stomach muscles constricted. Market Street hit. The store where Davila had bought the cap and jacket. They'd match the cartridge from the dead sales clerk to the pistol Davila had turned over to Moreno. He turned to the last folder on the desk, listed simply as a John Doe. It was slim. Three pages, a typed report headlined JOHN DOE— AIDED CASE. An unknown LMA, taken from Montgomery and California to Mission Emergency—died following day.

Santos groaned out loud. LMA. Latin male adult. It was Alejandro Liberto! That fat pig Liberto! How had the policeman connected him to the other deaths so quickly? It was the woman—Ariza. She must have told the police about stopping to help Liberto. About his talking to her. Hearing his confession! The next page was nothing but a report from the coroner. The final page had more handwritten notes. Telephone numbers—then the name Father Torres, circled in pencil—followed by a series of question marks.

The file folder made a loud snapping noise as Santos slammed it back to the desk. He jumped when he heard someone demand, "What the hell's the problem?"

Santos turned on the balls of his feet. He saw a hard-looking gray-haired man, his suit coat thrown casually over one shoulder, a finger hooked through the loop inside the coat's collar. He had a leather holster on his left hip, similar to the one Santos was wearing, the difference being that this one was filled with a snub-nosed revolver.

"Just dropping off a file," Santos said in his best American accent.

"Who are you, pal?" Chris Sullivan asked.

"Davis, from Burglary," Santos answered confidently. Davis. It was a good American name. Not as common as Smith or Jones, but common enough. There must be more than one Davis on the force. "Kordic wanted some information on that Slager murder. Thinks it might have been a burglar caught in the act."

Santos could see that the big man wasn't buying his story.

"I don't recognize you. You new in Burglary?"

"Just got dispatched there this week," Santos answered, putting his clipboard in his left hand, his right going into his pants pocket. He edged backward, his legs bumping into Kordic's desk.

Santos didn't know that the local police jargon for a transfer from one assignment to another was "detailed." You got detailed, you didn't get dispatched. He didn't know the nature of his mistake, but he knew he had made one. The big man dropped his coat to the floor, his right hand moving toward his holster.

Santos took a step toward the policeman.

"Hold it a sec—" was all that Lieutenant Christopher Sullivan had time to say before Santos pulled a small black piece of hardened fiberglass-filled nylon from his pants pocket. He forced his heels into the ground, thrusting his right arm out while swiveling his left hip backward, driving the tip of the lethal knife, known in the trade as a CIA letter opener, into Sullivan's chest, his target the initials CBS embroidered on the blue shirt. The blade tip penetrated between the C and the B, and once the blade was in, Santos twisted it sharply left and right while bringing his knee up between Sullivan's legs.

Blood was gurgling from Sullivan's chest wound and lips as Santos pushed him to the floor. He pulled the knife free and quickly took Sullivan's revolver from its holster, then ran to the door, where he paused, took several deep breaths, then snapped the lights out.

Santos opened the door slowly, one hand setting the door's locking mechanism, and peeked out into the hallway, his breathing already back to a normal rhythm. He stepped outside, closing the door behind him, twisting the knob, making sure the lock had set. He had no doubt that the janitor had a pass key. He reached into his pants pocket, his eyes darting up and down the hall while his fingers searched, finally finding what they were looking for. He shoved several toothpicks into the door's lock, broke them off, then, after wiping the tip of the fiberglass knife under his armpit, ground the blade into the lock.

He hurried back to the bathroom. Still no sign of the janitor. He put on his sports coat and hat, draped the raincoat over his right arm, making sure it covered the policeman's gun in his hand, then headed back for the stairway, taking the steps two at a time.

Once back on the ground floor, he mingled with a crowd of scruffy men who appeared to have just been released from jail. The men were in a joking mood, and the main topic of conversation was "those fucking cops." A couple of them glared at Santos. There were several uniformed policeman mulling around by the Bryant Street exit, but none of them even glanced his way.

He spotted a break in the traffic and sprinted across Bryant Street, his lungs gratefully sucking in the exhaust-filled air. He hurried down the alley to where he'd parked the car, then drove around for several blocks before finding a gas station with a pay phone. He thumbed through the phone book's yellow pages for listings under newspapers and found the number for the *Chronicle,* which he recognized as being the city's major morning newspaper. He dialed the number and told the receptionist that he wanted to be connected to the news desk.

"News. Glazer."

Santos put a handkerchief over the receiver, deepened his voice, and, using a heavy Latin accent, said, "We killed the motherfucking cop in his own fucking office. We gonna keep killing the fuckers 'til they stop killing us."

He heard the screeching of brakes and a horn blaring. He looked behind him, seeing that a car had rear-ended a pickup truck in the middle of the intersection.

He slammed the phone down, went back to the telephone directory, cursing as he had to struggle through the maze of listings under City and County of San Francisco, finally locating the row of numbers for the police department. He knew if he simply dialed 911, the police emergency number, or the main number, the call would automatically be recorded and the location of the phone would pop up on the operator's computer. That wouldn't do. He picked through the confusing list of agencies, finally settling for Central Station. He had no idea where that was, but it sounded like a reasonable choice. He looked over his shoulder at the accident site. A man in a yellow slicker had got out of the truck, and was shaking a fist at a frightened-looking woman who was holding up her hands in a gesture of helplessness. Santos dialed the police number, keeping his eyes glued on the two people involved in the accident, knowing they'd probably be coming over to use the phone in a matter of minutes.

A young male voice answered the phone: "Central Station, Martel."

Santos repeated his message, then hung up and exited the booth. It was raining again. He pulled up his coat collar, undid the empty holster on his belt, and sprinted back to his car, pausing to jam the policeman's gun and the fiberglass knife into the holster and drop it into a sewer grate.

Chapter 16

Mary Ariza felt like bolting from the funeral parlor. She wished that she was somewhere in the back, where she could slip away without being noticed, but here she was in the front row, opposite Walter Slager's parents. Mr. and Mrs. Slager were two solid-looking natives of New England, both in their sixties. He with a shock of white hair over a ruddy face. She short, bundled up in a heavy black woollen coat and a small hat with a veil. The veil wasn't thick enough to disguise the hatred in her eyes when she looked at Mary.

"Oh, you're the one," Mrs. Slager had said in a frosty voice when Mary was introduced to her by Matt Pontar.

She knelt down in chorus with the small, assembled group for the liturgy. Most were attorneys and staff members of Pontar & Kerr. The unknowns were two young women who'd come in from Boston with Walter's parents. Mary didn't know who they were, but their glances were certainly no more friendly than those of Mrs. Slager. Sisters? Cousins? Girlfriends? Mary realized just how little she had known of Walter Slager's life.

The priest gave a blessedly brief eulogy, then started in on the rosary, Mr. and Mrs. Slager booming out the words to each prayer. Finally, the service ended. Mary took a final look at Walter in his casket, her mind numb at the actual sight of the body, knowing that there was a gaping wound hidden by the shirt collar and tie. She edged her way outside, huddling in the backseat of the Pontar limousine.

"God, that was grim, wasn't it?" Mary Pontar volunteered as she climbed into the car. "I'm so glad it's over. Thank God we don't have to go to the cemetery. They're flying the body back home."

Both women watched as the casket was carried to the hearse. Mary could see Mrs. Slager looking around at the sparse crowd, her eyes finally settling on the Pontar limousine. She took her hat off and glared into the car windows, standing statue-still until her husband grabbed her by the elbow and led her to a waiting car.

"Poor woman," Mrs. Pontar said, coughing into her hand. "It must be terrible for her."

Mary nodded silently, agreeing with the assessment. In a way, she couldn't blame Mrs. Slager for hating her. For blaming her for Walter's death. A chill ran down her spine as the vision of her own funeral came to mind: her body in the coffin, the jagged knife scar visible on her neck. Her parents grieving. She shuddered involuntarily.

The apartment was right over a Mexican restaurant. The aroma of spiced meats filled the air and triggered a memory—bringing Kordic back to the first apartment he and his wife had shared after they were married. It had been above a Thai restaurant, and they used to joke about how good everything smelled and how they wished they could afford to eat there.

The woman who came to the door was barely five feet tall. She opened the door a crack, smiled and nodded, then opened the door all the way.

"Mrs. Fuentes?" Kordic asked.

The woman, who appeared to be in her fifties, nodded her head again and smiled, showing a missing front tooth. Her skin was saddle-leather brown, her dark eyes had a sad, mournful look. She was wearing a heavily embroidered red and silver smock over black pants. "Sí, sí," she said in a soft voice.

Kordic showed her his badge and the smile faded. "Do you speak English, ma'am?"

"Ingles? No, no." She turned her head and fired off some rapid Spanish. A few moments later a boy in his early teens joined her. At the sight of Kordic he rolled both hands into fists and shoved them into the pockets of his baggy pants.

"I'm a policeman," Kordic said, flashing his badge again.

"You didn't have to show me the badge. You look like a cop," the boy said. "Why are you bothering my mother?"

"I've got bad news, son. About Pepe. Are you Pepe's brother?"

"Yes. I'm Manny." He squared his shoulders, rocking on the balls of his feet. "Pepe's not here. You got a warrant or something? If you don't got a warrant, then quit pestering us."

Kordic's eyebrows knitted together. "How old are you, Manny?"

"Thirteen. What's that got to do with it? I'm telling you, Pepe ain't here." He grabbed the door and started to close it.

Kordic put his palm against the door. "This is serious, son. Maybe I should come inside."

Mrs. Fuentes might not have understood very much of the English language, but she seemed to be getting the message. She pulled her young son to her, a hand going to his head. *"Pepe. Donde esta Pepe?"*

"My mother wants to know where Pepe is. Is he in jail? Is that it? Or are you trying to put him there again? What's the hassle this time?"

"Has your brother been living here?" Kordic asked, his eyes taking in the room, which was crowded with mahogany furniture. A silk-screened painting of the Madonna holding the Christ child in her arms hung over a white-tiled fireplace.

"I told you, man, you want to come in here, you should get a warrant. I ain't tellin' you nothin'. I don't know where Pepe is."

Kordic studied the youngster. He was a couple of inches taller than his mother. His hair was cut short in front and on the sides, the telltale small ponytail at the back. An earring in the shape of a cross dangled from his left ear. Thirteen going on thirty.

"I know where your brother is, son. He's at the morgue."

The boy stared at Kordic, his dark, defiant eyes widening, slowly filling with tears. "For real? Pepe's dead?"

"I'm very sorry to have to inform you and your mother of this, but Pepe was shot to death. Early yesterday morning."

Manny Fuentes rested his arms around his mother's shoulders and whispered into her ear. The woman's eyes on Kordic's as she heard the news of her son's death.

"You. You the man that killed my brother?" Manny Fuentes cried out, leading his mother to the couch.

"No, I—"

"But it was a cop, wasn't it? One of you *chotas*."

"Calm down, son. Your brother was not shot by a police officer. He was shot by a private citizen. In an apartment house on Hyde Street. Your brother had a gun on him. He was attempting to shoot a woman."

Manny waved the accusation away with a chopping motion. "No way! No way! How come he was killed yesterday and you didn't notify us till now?"

"Your brother had no identification on him. We found out who he was through his fingerprints."

The woman started sobbing. Her son helped her to her feet. She gave Kordic a scalding look as she passed. Kordic watched them disappear down a hallway. He tapped his foot on the vari-colored carpet while waiting for Manny Fuentes to return.

"My mother wants to see his body," Manny declared when he came back to face Kordic several minutes later.

"I wouldn't advise it. He's not a pretty sight."

Young Fuentes clenched his teeth, the jaw muscles working so hard his cheeks were moving like fish gills.

"Where's your father, son?"

Another violent chopping motion of his arms. "Dead. Six years ago." His eyes met Kordic's. "You say my brother was trying to kill a woman?"

"Yes. Mary Ariza. An attorney. Does the name mean anything to you?"

"No."

"Do you have any other brothers? Sisters? An uncle?"

Manny's face softened and he looked more his true age. "No. No one else."

Kordic backed up and sat on the arm of a floral-covered couch. The arm was covered with clear plastic and squeaked slightly as he settled on it. "Tell me about your brother."

Some defiance returned to the boy's eyes. "How do I know you're telling me the truth? How do I know it wasn't you that killed Pepe?"

"I've no reason to lie, son. Your brother's body is down at the morgue. They'll release him to you in a couple of days."

"Release him?" Fuentes's voice showed his confusion.

"For burial. Looks like you're going to have to be the man in the family now. Help your mother."

"I have been the man," he said hotly.

"Tell me about your brother," Kordic said again, this time in a whisper.

Manny Fuentes stared at the floor for a long time, then his head snapped up, the decision made. "Pepe hasn't been around much lately. He'd stop in, raid the refrigerator, bring Mom some flowers or a present. Give her some money. He always had money. Told Mom he sold television sets. I haven't seen him in about a week. Maybe longer."

"Does he have his own room here?"

"Yeah, sure."

"Where does he stay when he's not here?"

Manny Fuentes ran the fingers of his left hand down the side of his cheek hard enough to leave four distinct red marks on his cheeks. "Who knows? He wouldn't tell me. Treats me like a kid because I go to school, because I help—"

He choked back a sob. "You want to see his room?"

"I'd appreciate it," Kordic said.

The room was small, eight by ten feet. The walls were covered with posters of movie stars: James Dean walking down a rain-slick street, a cigarette in hand. Madonna, head tilted back, spike bra pointing straight ahead. An advertisement for a Mexican beer, with a busty girl in a bright red bikini, leaning forward, her elbows pushing her breasts out against the minimal restraints of the swimsuit. On the nightstand by the bed, a stack of magazines: *Hustler, Penthouse, Playboy*. Kordic opened the nightstand drawer, finding more reading material: untitled magazines with pictures of men and women bound to chairs, chained to garage ceilings, tied awkwardly over footstools. A large, uncapped jar of Vaseline was set alongside the magazines.

"Your brother was quite a reader," Kordic said, turning to see Manny Fuentes's blushing face, giving Kordic the feeling that the boy had made full use of the room's contents in his brother's absence.

Kordic went to the closet. The door had been removed, the opening covered by a moldy yellow curtain. Several pairs of pants, all black, a leather black bombadier-style jacket, a black woollen sports coat. Nine shirts, four of them solid black, the others stripes and patterns, but all with some black in them.

"Pepe wasn't much on colors, was he?" Kordic said, running his fingers through the clothing and stooping to check out a pair of black leather cowboy boots on the floor. He gave the rest of the room a quick toss, finding nothing of interest, just underwear, socks, and two skinny black silk ties. He patted the bed's pillow and checked the mattress, again finding nothing of interest. He dropped to the floor, peering under the bed, seeing nothing but a few dust balls. He got to his knees and leaned back on the heels of his shoes, looked up at Manny Fuentes and said, "You ever see your brother with a gun?"

"Never. My brother was tough. He didn't need a gun."

"Well, a gun was the last thing he ever held in his hand," Kordic said, grabbing onto the bed to help himself to his feet. "The very last thing. Who gave him the gun, son? It was a special gun. A hit man's gun. With a silencer. Was your brother a hit man? A killer of women?"

Manny Fuentes fell onto the bed like a runner whose legs had given out.

"Who would give him the gun? Who does he hang out with? Who tells him to go out and kill people, Manny? Who?"

The boy pulled his knees up to his chest and buried his head in his arms. Kordic listened to him cry for a minute, then walked silently from the room.

Kordic's plan upon leaving the Fuentes's apartment was to contact Mary Ariza again. He looked at his watch. Maybe there was time for a late dinner, a drink, or just a cup of coffee. He felt comfortable with her, the first time he'd felt comfortable with a woman since his wife and son had been killed.

He decided to wait until the morning to dig into Pepe Fuentes's background thoroughly: check his arrest reports, see who he had been involved with in prior busts. From the look of the corpse, his dress, his residence address, gang activity seemed a certainty. Kordic was friendly with Rocky Taylor of the Gang Task Force. The task force kept its own files on the proliferating number of gangs staking out their territories in the city.

The silencer. He'd have to check that out too. That was puzzling. Most of the gang punks enjoyed hearing their weapons go off. The louder the better. The bigger and louder the gun, the bigger the man pulling the trigger, in their minds. Dave Granados had been right about the armament the bad guys were packing around. They had the police outnumbered and outarmed with their machine guns and fully automatic assault rifles. A Criminal Intelligence Forecast from the Department of Justice had come across Kordic's desk the other day advising that one of the Asian gangs had made a purchase of three hundred bulletproof vests. Three hundred! Kordic could remember a time when bulletproof vests were a fantasy from the movies as far as the San Francisco Police Department was concerned. Now half the uniformed force wore them, even if they had to purchase the vests with their own money. Requests for upgraded hand weapons had come up against the same old budget stone wall, so here again individual officers were buying their own 9mm and 10mm automatics, handguns. A silencer, though. That added a new dimension. A terrifying one.

Kordic kicked over the car's engine and pulled out onto 20th Street, his eyes scanning the streets for a pay phone to call Mary Ariza, his mind trying to remember the name of the guy he knew at the Federal Bureau of Alcohol, Tobacco, and Firearms, a real weapons expert. The crackling of the radio caught his attention: "All units, all units, a 187 at the Hall of Justice. Victim Lieutenant Christopher Sullivan. All inspectors to respond to the Hall immediately."

Kordic flicked on the siren, stabbed the accelerator, and the car's motor growled and he made a skidding right turn onto Folsom Street. Chris Sullivan! A 187! A homicide! At the Hall of Justice! "Jesus Christ," he shouted hoarsely, his hands pounding on the steering wheel in frustration.

The broadcast was repeated again and again, but Kordic's mind was spinning, trying to imagine what could have happened in the short time since he'd left the office. "Jesus Christ," he shouted again. "What happened, Chris?"

Chapter 17

Usually Kordic got a friendly wave or nod from the uniformed officer guarding the entrance to the police garage, but not this time. Two motorcycle cops stood side by side, their leathers glossy black from the rain. Each held a three-cell flashlight in one hand, the other resting on the butt of their Magnums as they stopped each car pulling into the garage.

Kordic pulled his face away as the flashlight beam was waved in his eyes. "Inspector Kordic, Homicide. Put that light where it will do some good, will you?"

The motorcycle officer dropped the beam, spraying it around the inside of the car, including the backseat.

"Let's see some ID, buddy."

Kordic reached into his pocket for his badge holder.

"Slowly," the officer warned.

Kordic took out the badge and tried to get a look at the face behind the helmeted visor. He thought he knew most of the bike cops, but all he could see in the visor was his own reflection.

"Okay, go on in," the officer grumbled nastily.

Another bike cop, this one cradling a shotgun, was standing guard by the door leading to the elevators. Kordic recognized him. "Everybody's a little uptight, huh, Don?"

"You bet, Jack. The chief's got this place surrounded like a prisoner-of-war camp." He patted the shotgun's stock. "Too bad about Sullivan."

"Yes," Kordic said, his eyes tearing as he bumped the door open with his shoulder. "It sure is."

When he got off the elevator on the fourth floor, he was confronted by a horde of TV, radio, and newspaper reporters, who greeted each new arrival as if he were a movie star about to attend the Academy Awards.

Kordic held up a hand to shield his eyes from the lights. Someone yelled, "He's from Homicide," and suddenly microphones were thrust inches from Kordic's face and questions were shouted at him from all angles.

"Can you tell us what happened, Inspector?"

"Are there any suspects?"

"Who was the last person to see Lieutenant Sullivan alive?"

Kordic pushed the microphones away with both hands and started saying "fuck" over and over again, louder with each repetition. The lights were pulled away, the microphones dropped.

"Hey, Inspector. Give us a break, will you?" one reported yelled.

Kordic responded with another "fuck." It was a technique Benny Munes had taught him when they first teamed up. "You can't intimidate these media people," his old partner had said. "But if you ever get a camera jammed in your face and you want it out of there, just start swearing. And then hope you ain't on live TV."

Kordic didn't much care whether his little performance was live or not. He kept his head down and bulled his way through the crowd. A strip of two-inch yellow tape with the stenciled message CRIME SCENE DO NOT ENTER was stretched across the hallway.

Two more motorcycle cops stood glaring at the news people from the other side of the tape. No speeding tickets issued in town tonight, Kordic thought as he ducked under the tape, then merged with more uniforms and nervous-looking plainclothes detectives. The uniforms on this side of the tape had brass attached to the shoulders.

"Hell of a mess, huh, Jack?"

Kordic turned to see Jim Tomassi, a silver-haired inspector from the Fraud detail. "Yeah. They call you in on this too, Jim?"

Tomassi dug in his pocket for a cigarette. "Called in everybody. From all the details." He lit up and tilted his head to keep the smoke out of his eyes. "Everybody. How do you figure it? Chris getting it right here. Hell, we're not safe anywhere."

Kordic nodded in agreement and edged closer to the door leading to the Homicide detail. Strips of the crime-scene tape were stretched across the door at eye and belt level. Kordic poked his head into the room. Inspector Ray Tracey noticed him and gave him a welcoming wave. Kordic limboed under the tape.

Tracey, a big man with a linebacker's build, put a finger to his lips and whispered, "We can look, but we can't touch."

It appeared as if the entire staff of the crime lab was at work. Three men were taking photographs of the room, inch by inch, their strobe lights flashing every few seconds. Two men were on their knees running small hand-held vacuum cleaners near Kordic's desk.

"Is Chris's body downstairs already?" Kordic asked.

Tracey nodded. "From what I heard, Chris got it with a knife. Right in the heart. And right by your desk, Jack." Tracey pushed his jacket sleeve back and looked at his Mickey Mouse watch. "According to the deputy, we'll be getting the 'big picture' in the auditorium in about twenty minutes."

The Hall of Justice auditorium looked like an old neighborhood theater, with comfortable padded chairs set up in rows. Two aisles led to a stage, usually featuring prisoners being paraded in lineups. At a lineup there were usually no more than a dozen or so spectators, but now the small auditorium was filled, standing room only.

Instead of murder, rape, or assault suspects on stage, there was the autocratic presence of Chief Arnold Fletcher.

The majority of the assembled police officers would have been happier to see the suspects. Fletcher was not popular with the rank and file. He had spent much of his time in assignments most officers avoided: Planning and Research, Crime Prevention, Court Liaison, Administration, Noise Abatement, and Personnel. Just

about every cop Kordic knew could recite Clint
Eastwood's immortal words from the *Dirty Harry*
movies: "Personnel is for assssssholes."

Fletcher took off his heavily braided uniform hat,
placing it carefully on the podium in front of him. He
patted his hair in place, then leaned forward and in a
thick, modulated voice said, "Silence, men."

The noise level sank slowly, and Fletcher's eyes
darted about, seeming to memorize those who continued talking.

"Gentlemen," he commanded, then as if an after-
thought upon seeing the dozen women in the audience,
"ladies, I said silence. Now, let's get started. As I'm
sure you've heard, we've suffered a tragedy. Lieutenant Christopher Sullivan has died from a knife wound
inflicted to his heart. I'll wait until we obtain the coroner's report as to the approximate time of death, but
our best estimates are between eighteen- and nineteen-
hundred hours.

"An unidentified person called both a media representative and a member of this department and stated
that he was responsible. You'll be given a flyer with
his exact words." Fletcher's voice went up a notch.
"Unfortunately, neither the media representative nor
the policeman thought to make a tape of the conversation." Fletcher paused dramatically.

"The important thing for us to concentrate on now is
keeping this investigation where it belongs. Here, with
us. Naturally, the media has a legitimate right to the
story, but I'm warning you, men, there will be no leaks
on this." He pounded his fist on the podium to empha-
size his point, causing his uniform hat to fall to the
floor.

All eyes in the auditorium focused on the hat, wondering just how Fletcher was going to keep his compo-
sure while bending over to pick up the damn thing.
Fletcher's face, normally a light pink hue, darkened by
several shades.

Laura Jackson, a tall brunette working out of Burglary, nudged Kordic's elbow. "I guess we women

don't have to worry about leaking the story, Jack. Cheif's just warning you men."

"Now listen closely," Fletcher said in a nasally voice, "I'm forming a task force, men." Laura Jackson gave Kordic another elbow. "You will report directly to my office. Any information passed on to the press will go through me."

Tim Riordan, an inspector in Missing Persons, who was planning to retire in a month, was sitting in the front row. He stood up and raised his hand.

Fletcher gave him a withering look, but Riordan just waved his hand faster.

"We'll hold all questions until later," Fletcher said bluntly.

"Just wanted to tell you your hat's on the floor, Chief," Riordan said with a serious look on his face.

Fletcher's clenched-teeth reply was drowned out by laughter. "I'm glad you're finding time to be amused, men, because you won't have time for anything but work from now on." He placed both hands on the podium, dropped his chin to his neck so that he was almost looking down through his eyebrows. "Lieutenant Wesley Tilson will be in charge for the present. He will address you now."

Kordic groaned inwardly as Tilson stooped to the ground, picked up Fletcher's uniform hat, and presented it to him with the flourish of a West Point cadet whipping out his sword. There was a scattering of clapping and light boos.

Tilson's frozen expression didn't change a fraction. "Ladies and gentlemen, I've learned that a man, white, dressed in shirtsleeves, was seen approaching the door to the Homicide detail at approximately six o'clock this evening. If that gentleman is present, I would like him to meet me in Room 517 at the close of this meeting. If that gentleman is not forthcoming, I will be requesting that each and every one of you submit a report as to your exact whereabouts at that time."

There was a chorus of shouted complaints. Tilson's only reaction was to glance at his wristwatch.

A plainclothesman stood up and boomed out a question: "What about this guy that made the phone call? Why don't we concentrate on him rather than what the hell we were doing? Nobody here knocked off Sullivan, for God's sake!"

"Your rank and detail?" Tilson demanded.

"Inspector Ray Tracey. Homicide. And a damn good friend of Chris Sullivan's," he replied hotly.

"I'm sure we're all glad to hear of your friendship, Inspector. I want you and the rest of the people who worked under Lieutenant Sullivan to meet me in Room 517 in thirty minutes. Everyone else can return to your details. Your lieutenants will have specific instructions for you."

Tilson raised his eyes in a question to Chief Fletcher.

Fletcher gave him a curt nod, and Tilson turned his attention back to the auditorium. "This meeting is now over."

There were four television screens on one wall, each constantly monitoring a portion of the premises: the front door, the garage entrance, a wide-angle view of the street, and another of the rear garden. The main burglar-alarm hardware was housed in a cabinet built into one of the walnut-paneled walls. The desk had a red phone connected directly to the alarm company, a white phone that when picked up auto-dialed 911, and an elaborate black phone console with buttons for connecting anywhere throughout the twenty-six-room house.

"My wife tells me you have an interest in art, Officer," Paul Abrams said, startling Larry Falore so much that the newspaper he was reading dropped from his hands onto the floor.

Falore stood up, then bent down for the paper. "Yes, sir. I majored in art in college."

Abrams was wearing red velvet pants, a red and gray smoking jacket, and cradling the piebald cat in his hands. "Any favorites?"

Falore stood awkwardly, moving from foot to foot.

"Rembrandt, Vlamick, Andre Derain. So many, it's hard to choose."

Abrams curled his tongue against his teeth and whistled softly. "Yes, you have very good taste, young man. Are you married?"

"Yes, sir. First child on the way."

"Good, very good," Abrams said, weaving a hand through the cat's thick fur. "It must be difficult for your wife. Your working two jobs. Not seeing much of each other."

Falore laid the newspaper on the desk. "Well, sir, if we ever want to buy a house like this, I'll just have to keep at it."

Abrams chuckled, then the chuckle became a hearty laugh. "Yes, but I'm afraid you're going about it the wrong way. Pick rich parents. Believe me, that is the only way." He leaned down and kissed the cat on its neck. "Come, Shylock, let's go look at our stamps."

Falore waited until Paul Abrams strolled out of sight before flopping back behind the desk. The man sure moves quietly, he thought. Something to think about, since Adele had become so demanding. The sex was great, but it was the risks she seemed to like that worried him. Rolling the window down halfway in the car while having a screaming orgasm. Stopping near the polo fields in Golden Gate Park, pulling him into the bushes for a quick blowjob. She had a fixation with oral sex. The one thing he didn't have to worry about with Adele Abrams was getting her pregnant.

The cook had left him a corned beef sandwich, along with a baseball-sized scoop of creamy potato salad. He picked up half the sandwich and had taken his first bite when Adele Abrams knocked lightly on the door and slipped inside, closing the door behind her. She was wearing a white, multi-zippered cotton flight suit decorated with embroidered patches of the American flag and sports car logos. Her hair was parted in the middle, and hung down so straight it looked as if it were ironed. She leaned against the door, crossed her legs at the ankle, looped a finger through the ring on the zipper under her chin, and pulled it down slowly until it was past her waist.

"Guess what, Larry?"

Falore's throat muscles tightened. "Your husband just left," he said hoarsely. "Jesus Christ, Adele. Are you crazy?"

She swiveled her shoulders as she walked toward him, the flight jacket gaping open. "No bra, Larry. Isn't that the way you like them?" she said tauntingly.

"Get out of here. You'll get me fired, damn it." Paul Abrams had never before stopped at the small security office while Falore was on duty. Adele had. In fact, she was making a habit of it. But only when her husband was out of town.

"Adele, come on," Falore pleaded. "Get out of here. Your husband just left. He could come back any minute."

She put her hands on his chest and pushed him backward, until his legs bumped into the chair he'd just vacated. "I've got some news for you, Larry. Bad news, I'm afraid."

Falore's eyes bounced from her breasts to the door. "Adele, cut it out, please. I don't want to lose this job."

"Sit, sit," she coaxed in what he had come to call her little-girl voice, her statutory-rape voice. "Paul won't bother us. He's too busy with his stamps and his cat." She pushed Larry down into the chair. "That's his problem. He loves cats and hates pussy." She dropped to her knees and wriggled her arms free of the flight suit. "I was reading a book, Larry. About that ancient movie actress Marlene Dietrich. Do you remember her?"

"Adele, stop it," Falore said, his voice dropping almost out of hearing.

Her hands worked at his belt buckle. "She was a real swinger, Larry, but she said she didn't really like sex. 'Put it in, pull it out.' " She leaned back and looked up at Falore with gleaming eyes dilated, her tongue licking her lower lip. "Dietrich's daughter wrote the book, Larry, and she said her mother preferred fellatio, because it gave her power over her male partners. Isn't that kinky? Her own daughter saying that? Is it true, Larry? Does this give me power over you?"

"Shit," Falore groaned, tilting his head back and staring at the pale yellow ceiling. "Please, Adele. Give me a break. I need this job."

She leaned over him and sucked him into her mouth, her teeth nibbling at him, coaxing him to climax. Falore stared down at her, wondering how he was going to end it. Get her off his back. She was becoming insatiable. She stood up slowly, a triumphant smile on her face, the back of her wrist sliding slowly across her lips.

Falore jumped up straight when something brushed past his leg. It was the cat. The damn piebald cat. He looked toward the door. It was open a crack. He was sure that Adele had closed it after her. Sure he had heard the lock click home.

"Oh, I forgot, Larry. That bad news I was telling you about. The radio said that a policeman was killed. In his office at the Hall of Justice."

Falore stood and pulled up his zipper. "A cop. What was his name?"

"Sullivan. Lieutenant Christopher Sullivan."

Falore's eyes squeezed half shut in concentration. "Sullivan. He's in Homicide, I think. You mean to tell me he got killed in the Homicide office?"

Chapter 18

Jack Kordic wandered the hallway outside Room 517 for almost an hour. Members of the Homicide detail were being shuttled in and out at twenty-minute intervals.

Ray Tracey and his partner, Bill Swensen, a usually happy-go-lucky Swede who always had a few Mars candy bars squirreled away in his baggy coat pocket, were pacing up and down like horses waiting to be saddled and pointed toward the starting gate.

"Shit, I just don't believe it. Chris getting it and the chief assigning Tilson to the case," Tracey moaned. "What the hell are we waiting for? That son of a bitch Tilson is going to botch the whole goddamn thing up. What are we waiting for?"

Swensen offered Kordic a mangled candy bar. Kordic declined, instead accepting a cigarette from Tracey. His first smoke in a long, long time.

Dave Granados and Barry Pittman had been the first team to be interviewed. When they came out to the hallway their only message to their comrades in waiting was a rolling of eyes and a shrugging of shoulders.

Kordic and the others talked about Sullivan as they waited their turn. Tracey and Swensen were the final team of partners to be summoned into the room.

Kordic bummed another cigarette from Tracey, vowing it would be his last. Ten minutes later, he wished he had asked for a few more smokes. Ten minutes after that, he was debating with himself as to whether he'd have time to make it down to the cigarette machine outside the cafeteria door to buy a pack.

He idly wondered what cigarettes cost now. Two bucks? Three?

Tracey and Swensen finally came out. Tracey tried to slam the door behind him, but the pneumatic hinges prevented that and the door glided slowly to a close.

"Tilson says to wait a minute, Jack," Bill Swensen said. "He'll come out for you."

"What's up?" Kordic asked irritably.

Ray Tracey held up a hand in a gesture of contempt. "Tilson's orders. We're not to discuss the case with you. I don't know what kind of a bean he's got up his ass, but I'm afraid it's got your name on it." He dug into his pocket and threw a half-empty pack of unfiltered Lucky Strikes to Kordic. "Hang in there, Jack."

Kordic watched the two inspectors head toward the elevators. He shook a cigarette loose from the pack, stuck it in his mouth, then remembered he didn't have any matches.

He dropped the cigarette from his lips to the floor and ground it out as if it had been lit. It was another fifteen minutes before Lieutenant Wesley Tilson opened the door and invited him in.

The primary function of Room 517 was to host meetings for the grand jury. Bare walls under fluorescent lights, with dozens of armless oak chairs, hard as marble, scattered around.

One ping-pong-size table was set in the center of the room. The tabletop was littered with ashtrays, manila folders, pads of yellow legal-sized notepads, and styrofoam coffee cups. Kordic could see an industrial-size coffee pot on a card table against the far wall. The smell of over-perked coffee permeated the room.

"Sit down, Inspector," Wesley Tilson said as he settled himself in his chair, leaning slightly forward, as if he were fishing. "Tell me about the problems you were having with Lieutenant Sullivan, Inspector."

"I don't understand that statement," Kordic said. He grabbed a chair by the back, swung it around, and sat astraddle, as if on horseback. "There were no problems between us. You know that."

Tilson arched a thin eyebrow. "Really? Lieutenant

Sullivan was getting ready to make out a report on you for Flaherty and the Chief. On your condition. The report was on his desk. He hadn't filled it out yet." His eyes rose to meet Kordic's. "Sullivan had been a supporter of yours, isn't that right?"

Kordic didn't like the emphasis Tilson put on the word *had*. "Yes. We were friends. Good cop. Good man."

"Why did Sullivan go back to the office tonight? To your desk? Were you planning to meet him?"

"What the hell is this, Tilson?" Kordic demanded hotly. "I had no scheduled meeting with Chris tonight. What's this crap about my desk?"

"That's where his body was found, Inspector," Tilson said with grim satisfaction. "Right alongside your desk. Why do you think that was?"

"I haven't a clue. Yet."

"Where were you tonight, Inspector? Between five and eight o'clock."

Kordic could feel heat in the back of his neck. "You ask that as if I'm a suspect in Chris's death."

Tilson picked up a thick black ballpoint pen that looked exactly like a Mont Blanc but which was made in Hong Kong and cost some two hundred and twenty dollars less than the original. He tapped it against a notepad. "I repeat. Where were you tonight, Inspector?"

"Out working. I spoke to Chris just before he left the office. He was going to get a bite to eat, then come back and do some paperwork. That was a little after five. I stopped at the Lineup and had a beer with Granados and Pittman. Then I went and interviewed the family of Pepe Fuentes. Fuentes was killed in a shooting on Hyde Street. He was attempting to put a hit on a woman by the name of Mary Ariza. There had been a prior attempt on Ariza. Perp missed Ariza, killed her friend. There's a strong possibility that Fuentes also killed a merchant on Market Street."

Tilson's head bobbed up and down in unison with his pen as it continued tapping against the notepad. "I see, I see. And how long were you with the Fuentes family?"

"Got there about six-thirty or so, left maybe forty-five minutes later."

"I see, I see," Tilson said, scratching some figures down on the pad. "And how long were you with inspectors Granados and Pittman?"

"Oh, maybe half an hour, something like that."

Tilson looked at Kordic carefully, like a botanist confronting an unknown species. "Something like that. You had a beer? Or more?"

"Just one."

"I thought that you had a problem with alcohol, Inspector. That you are an alcoholic, in fact."

"Nope," Kordic answered firmly.

Tilson waited for Kordic to add additional facts or denials, but Kordic knew the games of interrogation far better than Tilson did. Quick questions, then long silences. The silences were designed to make the suspect sweat, get him to wonder just how much the interrogator knew. The notion of cops beating suspects with rubber hoses was purely fictional, at least in San Francisco as far as Kordic knew, but "sweating them" was a time-honored tradition. Just sit there, a smug smile on your face, and wait for them to volunteer information, something that would contradict their prior testimony.

Kordic rested his eyes on Tilson's receding hairline. The strained silence stretched into a minute. Two minutes. Tilson dropped his pen and flicked an imaginary speck of dust from his pants leg. "Just who did you talk to at the Fuentes's house?" he finally said.

Kordic filled him in on the details of his interview with Pepe Fuentes's brother. "The mother doesn't speak English," he added.

"Hmmmm. Then it may be difficult for her to verify just when you were there and when you left."

Kordic kept his face passive, refusing to rise to the bait. "I doubt it. Telling a mother her son is dead leaves a lasting impression, Lieutenant."

Tilson's eyes narrowed to slits. "We'll see. What did you do upon leaving Fuentes's place?"

"I heard about Sullivan on the police channel and came on in."

Tilson picked up his pen and went back to the notepad, seemingly content to try his silent approach again.

Kordic waited him out, his eyes never leaving the notepad.

Tilson sighed, leaned back in his chair, and stretched. "That's all for now, Inspector. You can go."

Kordic stood up, scraping the chair across the linoleum and setting it under the table. "What about Chris?"

"What about him?" Tilson asked, carefully sliding his pen into his coat pocket.

"The investigation. What do you want me to do?"

Tilson's fox-like face broke into a smile—a cornering a rabbit in a shallow hole smile. "Nothing, Inspector. I do not want you involved in the investigation in any way. Any way at all. Is that clear?"

Kordic trooped down the stairs to the fourth floor. The press had taken off, but the crime lab was still busy in the Homicide office.

Tom Sato saw Kordic, grimaced, and closed his eyes as if in sudden pain. "Unbelievable, huh, Jack? I've been in the business over twenty years. Right here. And Chris, of all guys. Unbelievable."

"Turning anything up?" Kordic said, his eyes roaming over his desktop.

"Yes. Too much. Prints, hairs, bottle caps, hairpins. Probably all belonging to your people. Sloppy bunch. This is your desk, right?"

"Right." Kordic looked at the files spread across his desk. "It wasn't like that when I left earlier tonight."

Sato gave an abrupt nod. "We went over everything. The photographs will show it as it was when we were called in." He pointed at the taped body outline on the floor. "Chris was found here. Way it looks is that he was stabbed right about there." Kordic followed Sato's finger to a spot some four feet from his desk.

"Just one knife wound, Tom?"

"Let the coroner handle that one. But from what I saw, that's what it looked like." He tapped his chest. "Right in the heart."

Kordic stared down at the outline. Sullivan had been a naturally strong man, made even stronger by his exercising.

Sato seemed to be reading his mind. "Whoever did it must have been one strong son of a bitch. Either that or he was high on something that turned him into a superman."

"Yes," Kordic agreed, his attention focusing back on his desk. "Can I go through that stuff now, Tom?"

"Sure. We're finished with it, but be sure and look at those pictures of your desk in the morning."

"Oh, by the way, I'd like to show the silencer, the one found on the perp that got killed on Hyde Street, to someone at ATF."

"Your hunch was right, Jack. Same gun that killed Harry Burris, on Market Street. Pick the silencer up at the lab anytime you want, we're through with it." He took a final look at the room. "Unbelievable."

Kordic sat down carefully, the way a very old man does when he's afraid that something might break. Chris Sullivan dead. Sato was right. A police lieutenant, in charge of Homicide, killed in his own office. Unbelievable. He ground the palms of his hands into his eyes. Christ, Chris, what the hell happened? How could you let someone get the jump on you like that?"

Depression swept over Kordic in a wave—Linda, Danny, now Chris. The people he loved. Gone. And all by violence. Senseless, stupid violence.

Tilson can't possibly think that I was in any way involved with Sullivan's death, he told himself. Can't, but Tilson is going to isolate me from the case, use Chris's murder to somehow help in bringing me down. One thing Tilson said was true. Sullivan supported me, protected me. There was no one else now. He had friends, some good friends, but no one who would go the last mile for him. No one who was in a position to do so.

He needed a rock. Something to hold onto. He'd tried church after the tragedy to his family, but it hadn't worked. Then he turned to the bottle, which nearly turned into a disaster. All he had was his job. He had to keep his job.

He picked up the stack of open case files and spread them across the desk. He selected the file labeled JOHN DOE — AIDED CASE and began reading the first page.

Rene Santos propped another pillow behind his back and switched the TV channel again. The newscaster, a woman with hair the color of pale straw, recited the story of the death of police lieutenant Christopher Sullivan. The story was similar to what was being given out on all the other channels: person or persons unknown had killed Sullivan, then vanished from the Hall of Justice. A message had been called in to the police department and the *San Francisco Chronicle* claiming responsibility for the murder. "According to our sources," the anchorwoman said in a papery-dry voice, "the caller claimed, 'We're going to keep killing those' "—she paused, her eyes flicking up to the camera for a brief instant—" 'blanks, until they stop killing us.'

"Police sources say they have no idea who could have made the call. A press conference is scheduled for later this afternoon." The woman shuffled some papers on her desk, then stared into the camera and said, "And now for an up-to-date report on the weather."

Santos clicked the set off, pushed the covers back, got to his feet, and stretched. Naimat strode purposefully into the room on bare feet, carrying the morning paper in one hand and a steaming cup of coffee in the other. She wore a coral-colored oversize hooded sweatshirt. Her legs were bare. Santos flopped back onto the bed, pulled up the blankets to cover himself, and reached out for the paper.

"You're very interested in the news this morning, Rene," she said, perching on the edge of the mattress.

"Always," Santos conceded. He had no intention of telling Naimat about his killing the police lieutenant; however, her cunning mind would no doubt consider the possibility. "Newspapers are one of our major sources of intelligence." He always made a point of reading the local papers from cover to cover when operating in a new location. The front page, the entertainment, the gossip columns, the want ads. They gave off a flavor of the land, of the people. Today the front page was filled with the story of the dead policeman. Santos read each article. Nothing new. Nothing at all.

Naimat stared at him over the rim of her coffee cup. "When are we going to move, Rene? When are we going to get the job done and get out of here?"

"Soon. What have you found out about the woman?"

"Ariza?" she said disgustedly. "She hasn't been back to the apartment. Do you think the police have her hidden somewhere?"

"Quite possibly, though the police have other problems at the moment. I have another assignment for you. The Russian. Boris Zorkin. He seemed to enjoy participating in your part of the interrogation of Mr. Rose."

Naimat snorted through her nose. "The hardest thing about that was keeping the old man alive long enough to get all the information. The Russians depend on truth drugs. They can always hold something back from the drugs. But not from pain. Apply enough pain, and you get it all. Do you want me to kill Zorkin?"

"No. Something less appetizing. Get close to him." He smiled his mirthless smile. "However distasteful that may be for you. I expect he will be having a visitor soon. The same man that visited us in Peru."

"Petrov?"

"Yes. And we must be ready for him." Santos leaned across the bed, opening the nightstand cabinet door. He retrieved a section of yesterday's newspaper. "See what you miss by not reading?" he chided as he neatly folded the paper in half. "Look at this."

Naimat gave Santos her coffee cup and scanned the article:

SOCIETY WHIRL

Everyone who is anyone will be trying to push their way into the Opera House on Friday—not only for the music, dears, but for the party of the year. This year's hostess, gorgeous Adele Abrams, promises it will be 'extraodinaire.' So what if she had to coax her billionaire husband into filling up the empty coffers of the party committee? What's money for if you can't have fun with it?

An above-the-waist photograph of Adele Abrams showed her gazing at the camera lens as if she were in love with it. Her hair was piled high atop her head, and her strapless gown showed off most of her breasts.

Naimat shook her head and frowned. "I'd like to teach this one something about life."

"Yes," Santos said, knowing full well that Naimat would prefer a liaison with the lovely Mrs. Abrams much more than her assignment with Zorkin. "I just bet you would. But first the Russian. Give Boris Zorkin a call. Suggest that you are less than happy with me. Leak a little information about Abrams. You can tell Zorkin that we will have Abrams in a day or two. Wet his appetite. Feel him out. Maybe he'll suggest a nice quiet dungeon where you can practice for our next guest."

Chapter 19

Mary Ariza cut into the egg with surgical care, watching the yolk yellow the plate and the fried potatoes, and creep toward the two strips of bacon.

"You've heard the news, I guess," Matt Pontar said, whisking a chair away from the table and sitting down. "Just coffee and toast," he called into the kitchen. He was dressed in a dark suit and tie, shaved, smelling of talcum, all ready to head for the office.

"Yes," Mary Ariza said. "Lieutenant Sullivan. He was Jack Kordic's boss. Nobody's safe anywhere."

Pontar nodded in agreement. "I knew Sullivan slightly. Saw him at a couple of parties. Played golf with him once. Good guy. I wonder how Kordic is taking it."

The cook, slim almost to the point of emaciation, came into the room and placed a plate piled high with toast in front of Pontar. She disappeared, then returned shortly with a silver coffeepot. Mary waved away the offer for a refill and went back to poking at her food.

"I am going to call Kordic this morning. I'd like to go back to the apartment. Just to pick up some things."

"Good idea. Do you have something formal?"

The question surprised Mary. "Yes, I do. Why?"

"Big bash Friday night at the Opera House. Don't know if you like that stuff. My wife loves it. The party before show time will be fun. Like something out of a Fred Astaire-Ginger Rogers movie. Great chow, and the fashion show of the year. Feel like coming?"

"I like opera," Mary said, "but I don't want to intrude."

Pontar held up a hand. "You'd be doing me a favor,

Mary. You can talk to my wife while I snooze through all those arias. Give Kordic a call. I'm sure they must be through with your apartment by now." He frowned and reached for a piece of toast. "This Sullivan killing must have them going crazy."

"Yes," Mary agreed. "I just hope they haven't forgotten about Walter's killer."

Charlotte, the receptionist, was in tears when she handed Jack Kordic two pink message slips. She tried to say something, but all that came out of her mouth were sobs.

Kordic murmured sympathies, gave her hand a squeeze, then walked to his desk. It was as he had left it last night. Ray Tracey gave him a wave of the hand. Dave Granados managed a pale smile. Everyone else seemed to be going out of his way to ignore him. You're imagining things, Kordic told himself as he slid into his chair and stared at the two notes the receptionist had given him.

The first was from Mary Ariza, and had both her office number and the Pontar home number listed. He caught her at the office.

"There are some things at my apartment that I would like to pick up," she said. "Is there any reason I can't go back now?"

"No, I can't think of any. Are you sure you're ready to go back?"

He could hear her take a deep breath and sigh. "I'm not sure when I'll move back in. But I do need some things. Is there some kind of lock or something?"

"Yes, there is. But the lab is through, so there's no reason to keep it there. Tell you what. Why don't I pick you up at your office? We can have lunch. I'll drive you over there and open the place up for you."

Lunch. Why not? "On one condition," she said firmly. "I buy."

"Then I'll pick out an expensive spot. See you at noon."

The second message was from Max Freeman at the

Israeli Consulate. Kordic dialed the number. Freeman was in a meeting.

"I'm not sure exactly what it's about, Inspector," Freeman's secretary told him, "but I think it's good news."

"I could use some," Kordic admitted candidly.

Fifteen minutes later, Lieutenant Tilson entered the room and went into Sullivan's office. Kordic took off for the crime lab. Tom Sato was "unavailable." The photographs on the Sullivan case were also "unavailable." Kordic filled out the proper request form and was given the silencer from the .22 Walther found on Pepe Fuentes. Kordic felt the crime lab technician's eyes on his back as he left the room. He shrugged his shoulders, advising himself that he was getting paranoid. Sato was probably in the back taking a well-earned nap. The photographs were probably sitting on the chief's desk. The clerk who had treated him like a civilian probably had been up all night. Just paranoid. Probably.

The Alcohol, Tobacco, and Firearms Bureau had several offices scattered around the Bay Area: Drug Task Force, Permit Bureau, Forensic Science Laboratory, Criminal Enforcement Division. The man Kordic wanted to see worked out of the offices on Brannan Street, just two blocks from the Hall of Justice. The rain had let up, so he decided to walk. The sky was gunboat gray, and the smell of more rain was in the air. The wind tossed around newspapers and food wrappings as if they were wounded birds.

Two security guards greeted Kordic at the entrance to the building. They examined his badge and ID and let him bypass the metal detector. Peter Malone was waiting for him when the elevator opened on the seventh floor.

"Jack," Malone said, extending a hand, "good to see you. Sorry as hell about Chris Sullivan. Anything turn up yet?"

"Not yet, Pete."

Malone was a big, hearty man in the prime of his

mid-forties, with a mop of curly gray hair and bushy jet black eyebrows that turned up at the end. "Come on, let's go someplace where we can talk."

Kordic followed him down a narrow hallway, the doors along the way identified only by numbers. Malone opened the one marked 714 and ushered Kordic inside.

It was a typical government office—government-issued gray metal desk, matching file cabinets, imitation black leather chairs. Malone, an avid fisherman, had brightened up the room with prints of streams and lakes. A map of the bay took up most of one wall. Yellow, red, and blue plastic thumbtacks were scattered around the map. Malone rapped a knuckle by a series of yellow tacks covering an area near San Pablo Bay. "Sturgeon were unbelievable this year, Jack. Unbelievable. Ever fish for sturgeon?"

"No," Kordic said as a sudden memory of his son and him sitting in an old wooden boat in Lake Merced flashed into his mind. Kordic had borrowed an electric motor from a friend. Danny had helped load the boat. One of his chores was to put in a set of oars in case something happened to the outboard motor. Something did happen: the battery went dead. Danny's face displayed pure panic when he discovered that he'd put only one oar on board. He looked as if he expected his dad to drop him overboard. It was a dark, gloomy day, very few other boats on the water, so they had to make their way back to the dock using the one oar, pulling their way along the tules. It had been one of those unexpected father-son bonding rituals, the two of them taking turns with the oar and pulling on the tules, laughing and singing old songs as they made their way slowly back to the dock.

"Fantastic fish," Malone said with open enthusiasm. "Bottom feeders, you've got to be careful. Not sure you've got them, then all of a sudden you've got a hell of a fight on your hands. Monsters. I had a six-footer that jumped out of the water like a half-pound trout." He stared at the map a moment more, then went behind his desk and slumped into his chair, his long legs sprawled out in front of him. "Show me what you've got, Jack."

Kordic handed him the manila envelope and watched as Malone shook the silencer out onto his desk blotter.

"Well, well," Malone murmured as he picked up the black cylinder. "Where did you say you got this beauty?"

"A young hoodlum. He was waiting to use it on a woman in her apartment house on Hyde Street. It was also used to kill a man in his store on Market Street a couple of days ago."

Malone twisted the metal around in his hand as if it were a valuable piece of art. "You know much about suppressors, Jack?"

"Only the homemade kind I've seen on zip guns, or the ones in the movies, Pete. This one looks like it's a pro job."

"Indeed it is. Our friends in Hollywood continue to screw up. I was watching something the other night— not a bad flick, figure it must have cost them a few million to make. They go through all of that trouble, beautiful sets, great stunts, then they show the bad guy, a Mafia hit man, and he's got a revolver with a suppressor on it." He glanced up at Kordic. "Everyone calls them silencers, but suppressor is the correct terminology. This little piece of anodized metal doesn't silence the sound of the muzzle blast, it merely suppresses it. To do that you have to make the weapon gas-leak proof. Can't do that with a revolver, because there is an opening between the barrel and the cylinder in all revolvers. When the hammer strikes the bullet, gas escapes, so noise escapes."

Peter Malone opened a desk drawer, drew out a zippered tool pouch, and began dismantling the silencer. "What type of gun was used?"

"Walther twenty-two automatic."

"Good choice," Malone said, still fiddling with the silencer. "What about the ammunition?"

"I don't really know. I haven't seen the lab report yet. Does it make any difference?"

"All the difference in the world, Jack. You have to use subsonic bullets, something that will travel under three hundred thirty meters per second. Anything over that will produce a bullet blast, no matter how good the silencer, by breaking the sound barrier." He leaned back and smiled. "Few months ago we picked up a couple of cocaine cowboys. They had silencers fitted on their English Sten Mark II machine guns. Got all pissed off at the guy who sold them the beauties. They had fired all their subsonic shells practicing out in the woods. Loaded some regular ammo and caused quite a ruckus. Ah, here we go."

Malone twisted the silencer apart and scattered the pieces across the desk blotter. "See these little do-nuts?" He fingered a series of wafer-thin, quarter-sized washers, pushing one toward Kordic. "High-carbon steel. The problem with the old mesh silencers was that after a lot of firing some wire debris would get in the path and throw off the accuracy of the bullet." He stacked the washers in front of him as if they were poker chips. "Really top of the line. They still put out the best, the bastards."

Kordic fingered the fine metal disc in his hand. "Which bastards are we talking about, Pete?"

"The Russians, of course, Jack. What you've got here is a piece of equipment any KGB or GRU agent would have been proud to carry. Terrorists love 'em too."

"Russian? You're sure?"

Malone pushed the stack of washers to Kordic, like a croupier awarding a winner. "No doubt about it, Jack."

"What the hell is some Mission District punk doing with a Russian-made silencer?"

Malone interlaced his fingers, then pulled at a joint until it popped. "I don't know, Jack. But I don't like it."

Chapter 20

Mary Ariza looked at the small, ramshackle wooden building and said, "If this is your idea of expensive, I'd hate to see what you call cheap."

Jack Kordic pulled to a stop in a red zone in front of the Java House at Pier 40. "First thing I learned on the job. Bribe easy."

There was a break in the weather, patches of pale blue sky showing through the leaden cloud cover. A platoon of pigeons patrolled the restaurant's tar and gravel roof.

"Stick to the hamburgers and you'll be okay," Kordic advised as he held the passenger-side door open for Mary.

They managed to get a table overlooking the glassy bay waters. Tiny sailboats, looking like neatly folded pocket handkerchiefs, slewed and yawed across the bows of huge oil tankers and rust-stained freighters slowly working their way out toward the Golden Gate Bridge.

When the cook called out their order number, Kordic went to the counter and carried the hamburgers back to the table. "You said medium, right?" he asked as he set a huge oval dish down in front of Mary.

"Yes. Ummm, that smells good." As he let go of the plate, Kordic's hand passed under her eyes. With the shirt and coat sleeve pulled back, a jagged scar was visible on the inside of his wrist. She studied Kordic as he went back to the counter for coffee. He looked as if he had put in a tough night—the craggy lines in his face seemed deeper, almost like slash marks. Mary Pontar was right. He was attractive. The combination intrigued her: a homicide cop had to be pretty hard-boiled to survive. Yet Jack seemed so gentle. Was it the tragedy of his wife and son that had turned him that way? What about his suicide attempt?

Matt Pontar seemed to think she should ask for someone else to handle her case. No, Kordic was fine. Just fine.

They small-talked their way through lunch, Mary finishing most of her hamburger, piling the untouched french fries into a napkin.

"Feel like a stroll?" Kordic asked, draining the last of his coffee.

They wandered down the Embarcadero, past a green-hulled ship bearing the name *Greenpeace* on the bow. A solitary seagull stood with military precision on a dilapidated wharf piling. Mary tossed him a fry. Soon another half-dozen gulls joined the parade.

"I think I've started something here," she said, throwing the fries two at a time until they were gone.

"Expensive day for you," Kordic said. "First you feed a cop, then the bird brigade."

"I was so sorry to hear about Lieutenant Sullivan." She pulled up her raincoat collar as a nasty gust of wind swept in off the bay. "Have you got any suspects?"

"No, not a one. I did pick up something on yours, though. The name of the young man who was waiting for you at the apartment is Pepe Fuentes. I had an expert examine the weapon. The gun had a silencer. It's Russian-made. The same type their top spies use."

The news stunned Mary. "Russian? What significance does that have?

"There may not be any significance at all. Since the breakup of the Soviet Union, they're selling off everything from tanks to rockets to small arms. Somehow the damn stuff is trickling down to street hoods like Pepe Fuentes."

"Pepe Fuentes. The name means nothing to me. What time is it?"

Kordic raised his left arm to look at his watch. Mary's eyes again went to his wrist. She was sure she saw the outline of another scar near the leather band. Both wrists. The suicide attempt. She cinched her coat belt tighter and looked out to the bay.

"Twelve-forty," Kordic said. "I guess we better get you over to your place."

Adele Abrams admired herself in the full-length mirror. The dress was perfect, and Armand had guaranteed her that no one else would be wearing anything like it. At a cost of close to eleven thousand dollars, he damn well better be right. It would be a night to shine, to show off in front of those old bitches with their turned-up noses. The smirks on their pinched, wrinkled faces. The envy. God, she loved the envy. They all would have jumped for a chance at Paul, but she had beaten them, them and their frumpy debutante daughters, to the prize. And what a prize! She had known Paul was rich, of course. She would never have gone after him if he wasn't, but she had no idea how rich. One of those dull business magazines put him in the top ten of the wealthiest men in the United States.

She went to the dresser, reached into her purse, and pulled out a pre-rolled marijuana cigarette, smiling as she lit up. Another one of Paul's secrets she'd discovered. His own special patch at the ranch in Mexico. Paul, in that photograph on the mantel, looking so distinguished with his perfectly tailored slacks and sports coat, puffing away on a Meerschaum pipe, a smile on his face, the smile there partly because a goodly portion of his pipe tobacco was laced with grass. Paul's secrets. She'd seen something in him right away, that first meeting, at the beach in Acapulco. The dull gray eyes that hid so many secrets. That's what had won her the prize. Recognizing the secrets.

Paul was a voyeur. He liked to watch. She lay on the beach in her bikini, feeling his eyes on her, even though they were hidden by his mirror-front sunglasses. She let her hand stray down her stomach, the fingers trailing to the small strip of bathing suit, turning over so the bikini top rode down over her nipple. She wasn't the only one invited back to his yacht.

Some of the other girls were just as pretty as she was, maybe even more so. But she was the one who followed Paul as he went below, watching him enter one of the bedrooms. She gave him a moment, then knocked and called out, "Anyone inside? I want to change. Is anyone in there?"

There had been no response, and she'd entered the room confidently. Room. Actually, the correct terminology on board ship was cabin, but it was a room to Adele. Over eight feet in height, with wide windows instead of those little portholes. A king-size bed covered in white silk. She had pivoted in front of the mirrors fronting the sliding closet doors, wondering where Paul had disappeared to. Then she saw a crack in the doors. They weren't closed all the way. She imagined him behind the doors, watching, holding his breath, stroking himself. Walking to the center of the room, she slowly stripped off her bathing suit, then took a tube of Bain de Soleil sun oil from her cotton pull-string beach bag and began rubbing the oil over her body, making sure she was facing the closet doors, her eyes closed, her head tilted back, moaning softly as her hands glided across her body.

When she opened her eyes she saw the framed photograph: Paul in his sports coat, with his pipe and that silly smile. She poured more oil on her hands, stood in front of the picture, and began masturbating, making all those exaggerated grunts and squeals the way they do in the porno movies that Paul loved so much. The pornos. That was another one of his secrets that she didn't discover until weeks later.

After achieving orgasm with a shuddering groan, she'd acted embarrassed, quickly slipping into a pair of white cotton shorts and a yellow tube top. She exited the room in a hurry, and rejoined the party on deck. A Mexican band, all dressed in fringed yellow shirts and sombreros the size of small tables, were playing corny old tunes when Paul came over to her, champagne glass in hand.

"I don't think I caught your name" was his opening line. But when she looked into those eyes, she'd known then that she'd caught him. More important, she could control him through sex—playacting out his fantasies. Her bedroom closets was filled with costumes: nuns, schoolgirls, maids, prison guards, cowgirls. He was so easy. All men were, really.

But once he tired of her, she'd be left with almost nothing. Like his first two wives. Because of that stupid prenuptial contract. She never should have signed it. But would he have married her if she had not? The severance pay was down in black and white. Two hundred thousand dollars a year might seem like a lot to some people. But not to Adele. Not after what she'd gotten used to.

She inhaled deeply on the marijuana, closing her eyes, holding the smoke in her lungs as long as possible before releasing it.

"Enjoying yourself?"

Adele's eyes popped open. It was Paul. Peeking again.

"Darling, this is my dress for the opera." She held the edges of the skirt and did a slow pirouette. "Like it?"

Paul Abrams's voice was flat, completely devoid of expression. It was a voice that had chilled the spines of bankers, attorneys, and millionaire businessmen on numerous occasions. "You told me that you were going to a luncheon at the de Young Museum the other day."

"Yes. A benefit for the Asian Exhibition."

"I spoke to several people that were there. They didn't see you."

Adele held out the remains of the cigarette to her husband, who declined with a nod.

"Oh, Paul, it was so dull. I just couldn't stand it. I stayed a few minutes, then left and went shopping."

"I couldn't find anyone who saw you there at all, Adele."

"But, Paul, I told you, I—"

"Your driver that day says he dropped you at the museum, then came back to pick you up after the lunch."

Adele took a final drag on the cigarette, then ground

it out in a crystal ashtray. Paul had spoken to Larry! Shit!

"He wasn't there when I left the museum, Paul. I don't blame him, he couldn't know I was going to leave. It was just a spur-of-the-moment thing. I took a cab downtown, then cabbed it back. He told you he picked me up after the luncheon, didn't he?"

"Yes, he did," Abrams answered solemnly.

Adele heaved a small sigh of relief. Larry hadn't panicked. All of his brains weren't hidden behind his zipper. "I'm sorry if I worried you, darling, it's just that these lunches are—"

"If you're up to something, Adele, stop it now. If you have been up to anything, I'll find out. Understand?"

"Of course I do," she said, running to him, wrapping her arms around his waist. "You didn't ask what I shopped for." She flicked her tongue into his ear. "A new outfit, darling. All latex rubber. Corset, stockings, head restraint. You'll love it."

Jack Kordic pulled the department's DO NOT ENTER WITHOUT PERMISSION sign from the door, undid the crime lab's padlock, then stood aside as Mary Ariza nervously jiggled the key in the lock. The door swung open and Mary stood there a moment, looking down at the carpet. The outline of the bloodstains was still visible.

Kordic noticed that she took a long stride so her feet would miss the stain as she entered the apartment. "I'll just be a minute," Mary said, starting toward the bedroom, then hesitating a moment, shaking her head and then continuing. "I'm not quite ready to move back in."

"Mind if I use your phone?"

"No, go right ahead," Mary said, skirting the kitchen and going directly to the bedroom.

Kordic called his office. There was one message. Max Freeman from the Israeli Consulate had called again. Kordic dialed the consulate's number and this time made a connection.

"I may have something for you, Inspector," Freeman said. "We got lucky. Those numbers: 2036082. There's a possibility they belonged to a gentleman by the name of Joseph Rosenberg."

"Rosenberg? Do you know where he was living?"

"No, I'm afraid not."

"Do you have any specifics? Middle initial. Date of birth? Anything like that?"

"Yes," Freeman said. "Joseph A. Rosenberg. Born in Bremen, Germany, on May 14, 1921. Liberated from Auschwitz. That's about all I have on the gentleman."

"Where did you dig this up, Mr. Freeman?"

"I'm afraid I can't be specific, Inspector. These records, the ones that we have found, are scattered all around. I just called a friend, someone carried the ball the rest of the way and got back to me. I'm sorry I can't supply more details."

"You've been a great help," Kordic said, "a great help." He took out his notebook and carefully entered the name and date of birth.

"Good news?" Mary asked, coming out of the bedroom with a red garment bag folded across her arm.

"Yes. Worth celebrating. Are you free for dinner?"

They stared at each other for a moment, each reading the other's eyes, knowing this had nothing to do with the case, that it was a step in a different direction.

Kordic broke the silence. "I'm sorry, I didn't mean to crowd you. I haven't asked—"

"Matt Pontar told me about your family, Jack. I'm sorry."

Kordic felt like an embarrassed schoolboy. "Yeah. Let's forget it. I just—"

She dropped the garment bag on the couch. "Right now I could use some tea. Would you care for a cup?"

"Sure."

"Tell me about the good news," Mary said, digging the kettle from under the sink and filling it with water.

"Well, it's a rather gory case. We found a body out by Lands End the other day. The head and hands had been severed. We didn't have much to go on. Just a tattoo. A tattoo of a rose that covered a series of numbers. The man I spoke to on the phone was from the Israeli Consulate. The numbers turned out to be from a Nazi concentration camp. They belong to a man named Joseph Rosenberg. Born in Bremen, Germany, in 1921."

Mary put the water on to boil and set out cups on the kitchen table. "Rosenberg. Is he from San Francisco?"

"Good question. Let me use the phone again."

Kordic dialed the office and got Charlotte, the receptionist, to run a DMV check on Rosenberg. She used the computer at her desk and filled him in on the Sullivan investigation as she entered the information.

"Nothing yet." Her voice lowered. "That Tilson is driving me crazy. I hope he's not here to stay. Everybody else has gone for the day. I don't blame them."

"Me either," Kordic conceded, watching as Ariza put tea bags in a white ceramic pot.

"Forty-one Joseph Rosenberg's on line, Jack. Three Joseph A.'s. None with that date of birth."

Kordic had been counting on an easy hit. Now he'd have to do some digging. "Thanks, Charlotte. I'll be back in a while."

"Hurry back. I'd like to have someone to talk to besides that jerk Lieutenant Tilson."

"No luck?" Mary asked, pouring the tea into dainty china cups.

"No. Nothing on him with California DMV. Could be a tourist. A traveling businessman." He sat down and reached for the teacup, noticing Mary's eyes following his hand. He stopped midway to the cup and upended his wrist. "Did Pontar tell you about my suicide attempt too? Is this what you're looking for?"

When she didn't reply, he upturned the other wrist, pushing the watch band up so the scar was easily visible. He raised his arms slightly, palms upward. "Coward's way out. You'd think that if a cop was going to do himself in, he'd do it with his gun. Isn't that how it is in all the books and movies? 'Swallow the barrel' is the term they use."

She reached across the table, gently grabbing his

wrists in her hands, brushing his scars with her thumbs. "I'm truly sorry, Jack. I didn't mean to pry."

"The doctor said it was a cry for help." He smiled ruefully. "I had been drinking for a solid week. I was dead drunk. Sitting in the bathtub. Seemed like a good idea at the time."

Mary raised her eyes to his. "What saved you?"

"My partner. Ex-partner, he's retired now. Benny Munes. Came by the house. Applied some first aid. Got me to the hospital. When I got out of the hospital I started hitting the booze heavy again. Munes drove me up to Murray's in Calistoga."

Mary's eyebrow cocked in a questioning arch.

"Calistoga is a little town up in the wine country, Napa County. Murray's is sort of a workingman's sanitarium. Nothing fancy, no drugs, no doctors, just a clean room, food, hard talk from a bunch of reformed drunks. Cops have been going up there for years to dry out. Vodka was my squeeze then. Whatever you're drinking, Murray makes sure you have about a triple shot of it waiting for you when you wake up the first morning under his treatment. I woke up with a terrible hangover. Reached out for that glass. Thought it was water. Damn near killed me."

Mary released his wrists. "But it didn't. You fought back, didn't you?"

"I guess I did. At least I started getting my head back together, slowly but surely. Linda, that was my wife, her parents helped. They're from back east. Chicago. They were very supportive. I just decided to come back to the living. A little at a time. I gave up drinking completely for about six months. Now I have one or two drinks a day." His lips twisted sardonically. "Whether I need it or not. It's sort of a personal challenge. I never really had a drinking problem before Danny and Linda were killed."

"And the man who killed your wife and son. He was never captured?"

"Nope. Probably still out there on the streets, causing a lot of pain." He gave her a lopsided grin. "I guess we better get going."

Mary put the teacups in the sink and then picked up her garment bag. As they got to the door, she turned around to take a final look at the apartment.

Their shoulders brushed together, and Mary leaned against the doorjamb, dropping the garment bag to the floor. Kordic started to bend over to reach for it, his eyes stopping when they were level with Mary's.

Their faces slowly drifted toward each other, Kordic stopping when his lips were less than an inch from hers.

He pulled back reluctantly. "Scene of the crime. Not exactly the right place for this, is it?"

"Not exactly, no."

Kordic picked up the garment bag, folding it over his arm. "How about that dinner date?"

Mary nibbled at the inside of her cheek. "Whose turn is it to buy if we go out to dinner?"

"Mine."

"You've got a date, then, Inspector."

No one paid any attention to Rene Santos as he parked the cream-colored pickup in the restricted parking zone on the Grove Street side of the Opera House. The truck bore the insignia of Arrow Electric on both doors. One Arrow employee had been good enough to leave the vehicle unlocked in front of the construction site of a building in the South of Market area. With any luck, the worker wouldn't report the truck missing until quitting time. Even if he did make out a report, Santos knew from past experience that it took the police some time to put the license, make, and owner out to the radio cars and motorcycle patrols. And all he needed was an hour, maybe less.

There was a dirty pair of faded denim bib overalls rolled up in the truck's front seat, and a blue cap tucked in behind the sun visor. Santos had only had to stop at a Goodwill thrift store and pick up a battered tool box, and his outfit was complete.

He lugged his tool box to the building's side entrance. A thick-bodied man in a blue-gray security guard's uniform held up a hand to signal for Santos to a stop.

He had a toothpick-wide gap between his front teeth. "Leave your truck there and the damn meter maids will give you a ticket, buddy."

Santos gave a good-natured shrug of his shoulders. "Tough. The company will pay for it. Shop says you're having circuit trouble in the main terminal."

This time the security guard shrugged. "First I heard of it. I'll find Freddy for you. He'll know about it."

"Save Freddy the trouble," Santos said confidently, walking briskly past the guard. "I've been here before. I know the problem."

The security guard scratched his chin with his thumb, gave a final shrug, and went back to leaning against the wall.

Santos found himself in back of the Opera House's enormous stage. Someone was playing a piano. Scales. A half-dozen men were moving scenery, fake trees and rocks, across the stage under the direction of a moon-faced man dressed in tight white pants and a plum turtleneck. He gave Santos a quick look then went back to his hollering. "No, not there, stupid. We've got to leave an entrance clear."

Santos made his way to the back wall, and within a minute had found one of the refrigerator-door-sized electrical switch boxes. The box was a battleship gray color, which almost perfectly matched the shade of the Frangex plastic explosives Santos took from his tool kit and packed into the box's casing. He inserted a detonator, covering it up with more of the Frangex. Even if someone was looking for explosives, he would have a hard time identifying the thin band of putty-like material as something dangerous.

The time he had spent doing research at the San Francisco Library's History and Archives section had paid off. He knew the Opera House's seating capacity was 3,176. That the building had been constructed in 1932 over a small natural lake, and that although the basement level had been covered with fifteen feet of concrete, water still seeped in at certain spots. There were four seating levels and a tunnel connecting it to the adjacent Veterans Building. He also knew that the fire curtain, a three-foot-wide wall of asbestos and steel construction, fifty feet by fifty feet, that weighed in excess of eighty thousand pounds, designed to be lowered by powerful electrical winches and cables in the event of a fire, had never been needed at an actual performance. But it would be soon, Santos thought as he rode an elevator to the fourth floor. When he was sure he was not being observed, he placed strips of the Frangex and detonators in the massive chain cables securing the fire curtain.

The electrical truck was waiting for him, a parking ticket tucked under the windshield, flapping in the wind.

"Told you they'd tag you, buddy," the security guard yelled as Santos drove away.

Chapter 21

Inspector Dave Granados was disappointed. He'd expected the *Chronicle's* pressroom to look more like the ones in the movies: people in shirtsleeves, ties at halfmast, trudging through ankle-deep litter of crumpled paper torn from typewriter carriages.

Instead it looked like a yuppie stockbroker's office: rows of matching beige metal desks arranged in precise order, each desk fitted with a computer terminal, the computer's screen attached to a metal swing arm so it could be moved to any angle.

The man clicking away at the computer keyboard didn't fit Granados's image either. He had short graying hair carefully parted, a lavender cotton polo shirt with the collar turned up, freshly laundered chinos with a neat crease held up by a leather basket-weave belt.

The man pulled his eyes away from the blue computer screen and said, "Help you guys?"

"If you're Dean Glazer you can," Granados said, showing his badge.

"That's me," Glazer said, crossing one leg over the other. Granados glanced down at Glazer's shoes. Sperry Topsiders. No socks. He sighed, the image completely shattered. Where was Humphrey Bogart when you needed him?

"This about the phone call?" Glazer asked.

"That's right," Barry Pittman said, spiral notepad and pencil in hand.

Glazer craned his neck and looked at Pittman. "How's the case going?"

Granados pushed the computer screen out of the way

and perched on the edge of the desk. "Not as good as we'd like. Tell me about the call."

Glazer leaned back, lacing his hands behind his head. "Not much to tell. I had in-call duty. We get some beauties. You wouldn't believe them." He looked Granados in the eye, then said, "Well, maybe you would. Anyway, the call came in. I thought it was probably another nutcase. I logged it. Wrote down what he said. Didn't you guys record it when he called you?"

"No. Sure it was a he?"

"Yeah, pretty sure. Heavy Latino accent. South American, maybe. You guys come up with anything on that? You think it's gang-related?"

Granados gave him a weary smile. Typical newspaperman. Every sentence ended with a question. "Anything unusual about the call? Background noises. That kind of thing."

Glazer stretched his hands over his head. "Well, maybe. I thought I heard a crash. You get anything on that?"

Pittman made his presence known. "What kind of a crash are you talking about?"

"Car, maybe. Sounded like a car crash. Horn blaring, then ka-boom. You guys got anything on that?"

Boris Zorkin was waiting under the twisted and contorted branches of a sycamore tree near the bandstand in Golden Gate Park. He wore a belted raincoat and a checkered wool cap.

Rene Santos patted Naimat lightly on the shoulder. "He's alone. Let him sweat a bit. Then keep him happy."

Naimat nodded in agreement. "I will see you back at the apartment."

Santos melted into a grove of trees as Naimat continued to observe Zorkin. She was pleased to see that the Russian looked nervous, bouncing from foot to foot, rubbing his hands together. He had a reason to be nervous, she thought. If Rene was right, and Zorkin was Petrov's wet man, then he already had his plans made on just how and when he'd killed Santos. And her. Eliminating Zorkin was going to be a pleasure. She continued to watch him for ten minutes before making her presence known.

"You're late," Zorkin said in guttural Russian.

"Give me one of your little cigars," she demanded, switching the conversation to English.

Zorkin dug a tin from his raincoat pocket and offered it to her.

"These are good," Naimat said, selecting one of the hard-backed Dutch smokes. She put it between her teeth and waited for Zorkin to produce a lighter.

"Mr. Rose certainly didn't enjoy them," Zorkin said with a small chuckle.

Naimat puffed repeatedly until the cigar tip glowed red, then let the smoke dribble out between her teeth. "You can tell your Viktor Petrov that his package will be available shortly."

"Wonderful. How shortly?"

"It could be as soon as tomorrow."

Zorkin's head swiveled around, then he began walking, his feet making harsh, grating sounds on the gravel path. "You cannot be more specific?"

"You will be notified. Slow down, what is your hurry? I'm alone."

Zorkin dug in his pocket for his cigar tin again. "I will have to let Petrov know."

"There is time for that. I thought we could get a cup of tea. Isn't that the Japanese Tea Garden over there?"

Zorkin stopped to light his cigar. Naimat noticed he smoked in the European manner, with the palm of his hand facing upward, the cigar pinched between his forefinger and thumb. "You really want tea?"

"Maybe something stronger. What are your plans with Paul Abrams? Are you going to need help during the interrogation?"

"No, not this time." He clenched the cigar between his teeth and thrust both hands into his raincoat pockets, his fingers moving as if he were counting change. "Where are you taking him?"

"Rene has a safe house. Not the same one we used

for Rose. It is well chosen. You will be pleased, Boris."

Zorkin inhaled his small cigar as if it were a cigarette. "I don't want any delays. As soon as you've got him, I want to know exactly where he is. Is that understood?"

"You know how Rene works. He doesn't even tell me everything."

"Yes," Zorkin said in a mocking tone. "El Cabecilla. How long have you been with him?"

"Not long."

Zorkin started walking again. "It must be difficult. A young woman like you. I mean, hiding all the time. Where will you go when this is over?"

"Do you really want to know, Boris?"

Zorkin worked the cigar thoughtfully from one side of his mouth to the other. "No, I guess not. Just curiosity. What time will he call tomorrow?"

"I don't know yet. He hasn't told me everything."

"But you do whatever he tells you, right?"

Naimat nodded. "Just as you do everything Viktor Petrov tells you to do. Right?"

Zorkin slowed down again, his eyes drifting to Naimat's black raincoat, wondering what was under it. "Where is your car?"

"I took a cab."

"Let's go somewhere. Have a drink."

"Wonderful idea, Boris."

Zorkin dropped his cigar into a puddle of water. "Aren't you afraid that I'll take you somewhere, interrogate you? Find out just where this mysterious safe house of yours is?"

Naimat laced her arm through his. "Maybe that's what I'm hoping for, Boris."

Rene Santos centered the camera's 300mm zoom lens on Zorkin and took a final photograph. He hummed to himself as he pushed the rewind button and headed back to the car.

The crime lab technician accepted the silencer without comment, tucking it back in its evidence folder.

Kordic found Tom Sato sitting behind his desk, his hair rumpled, in need of a shave.

"Jack. Glad you came in." He stood up, dry-washing his face with both hands. "Come on, let's take a look at those photographs we took of your desk."

Kordic followed Sato out of his office and into the photo lab, a long, narrow room reeking of development chemicals.

"Here we go," Sato said, spreading a series of eight-by-ten color photographs across a knee-high table covered with butcher paper. "This is how we found it, Jack. Notice anything special?"

Kordic bent over and examined each picture, a lump forming in his throat. The loafer-clad foot of Christopher Sullivan could be seen in the bottom left corner of the first photo. Kordic's face tightened in concentration—the familiar desk, the folders laid out across the blotter. How had he left them? Were they different? He closed his eyes, picturing himself sitting at the desk, talking to Dave Granados and Barry Pittman. The files were laid across his desk neatly. Overlapping. He had left them that way, then gone to Chris's office before leaving for the day. He opened his eyes. The files were spread haphazardly across the desk in the photo. One file was on top of the others, at a forty-five degree angle. Kordic went through the rest of the pictures. A blow-up showed the typed index tab on the file John Doe—Aided Case.

"Well, anything there that excites you?" Tom Sato asked.

"I don't know what it means, but when I left the office, the files were laid out flat. Someone went through them, Tom. They weren't like this."

"Any reason for Chris Sullivan to look at them?"

Kordic shifted his weight to his heels and crossed his arms. "It's possible. He was the boss. He might have been checking things out to see what was happening. I had talked to him about the cases just before I left the office."

"We didn't find any of Chris's prints on the files. Doesn't mean he didn't handle them. There were lots of smudges. Only identifiables were yours."

Kordic stared back at the photographs, trying to picture the scene in his mind. Sullivan in the office, alone. Wandering around, checking things out. Stopping by the desk, poking through the files. It was all possible. Kordic had done the same thing numerous times, early in the morning or after everyone had left at night. Glancing into a file, seeing what the other teams were up to. Curiosity was almost a vice with cops. As a lieutenant Sullivan had every right to dig through the files. Possible, very possible.

The other scenario was someone else digging through the files. Sullivan coming in and spotting him. Or her, though it would have had to have been an awfully strong her to kill Sullivan with a knife. An awfully strong him, for that matter. Someone Sullivan knew? Chris was too streetwise to take chances with some stranger. Someone who was a cop? Someone he thought was a cop? If someone was after Sullivan, there were easier ways, less risky places to use as a killing ground.

"I got the report back on the twenty-two automatic you found on Pepe Fuentes, Jack," Sato said, snapping Kordic out of his reverie. "The one used on the Harry Burris homicide."

"Anything good?"

"Everything came up negative. Manufactured in Germany. No record of it being shipped into the good old U.S. of A. I gave Inspector Granados the information."

Kordic told Sato of his talk with Peter Malone at ATF.

Sato rubbed a hand across his chin. "Russian silencers, German pistols, sounds like an old *Mission Impossible* script, Jack."

"Foreign intrigue. That's all we need. Anything else come in on Chris Sullivan?"

"No, not on our end. Your Lieutenant Tilson does his Sphinx impersonation whenever I ask anything. What do you hear?"

"Nothing," Kordic admitted. "He's not talking much to me either."

* * *

Lieutenant Wesley Tilson sat in Chris Sullivan's office chair, telephone in one hand, rhythmically swinging his pen with the other.

Kordic passed his line of sight as he made his way to his desk, but Tilson gave no indication of seeing him.

Kordic shuffled the files on his desk, hoping for some sudden blaze of inspiration to flash into his mind, the way it happens in the movies. This wasn't the movies, so he sat there, staring at the folders, picking each up, holding it carefully, as a vet might handle a fragile bird. He settled on the file for the headless corpse. Joseph Rosenberg, according to Max Freeman at the Israeli Consulate. He carried the folder over to the computer, called up the DMV menu, and entered Rosenberg's name and date of birth. The notation NO RECORD showed on the screen, just as it had when the receptionist had tried. He then ran the name for registered vehicles. Again—NO RECORD.

Kordic switched menus, running Rosenberg through CI&I, the California Criminal Index, then the NCIC, National Criminal History. The wait took less than five minutes, the results the same. No record. The information system always seemed to report back more quickly if there was nothing to report.

Kordic trudged back to his desk, his mind wandering. Barry Pittman almost knocked him over.

"Anything up?" Kordic asked.

Pittman tilted his head toward Tilson, still ensconced at Sullivan's desk. "Nothing," he said, quickly passing Kordic and exiting the room.

Kordic turned to Dave Granados, who was on the phone, his eyes tilted toward the ceiling. Everyone else was out on the street, out of Tilson's sight.

Kordic studied the files again, this time selecting the John Doe that Mary Ariza had given first aid to on Montgomery Street. The aided-case report had been filed by Officer Louis Aragon. Kordic knew Aragon, an old-time beat man at Central Station. He called Central, and the duty sergeant told him Aragon was off. He gave Kordic Aragon's home number. It was a Marin county prefix. Probably Novato, Kordic thought. Novato had been at the forefront of the real estate boom in the sixties. It was known as the safest community in the Bay Area, thanks to the flood of San Francisco police and firemen who lived there.

The phone was answered by a woman.

"Lou there?" Kordic said.

"Who's calling?" came the cautious reply.

"Inspector Jack Kordic."

"Just a moment, I'll see if he's in."

Kordic could hear the phone being gently put down. He could imagine the scene at the other end of the line. Aragon's wife tiptoeing away from the phone, finding her husband, and giving him the message in hushed tones. Policemen's wives learn early to screen their husbands' calls.

"Hey, Jack, how's it going?" Aragon asked when he finally got on the line. "Sorry to hear about Chris Sullivan. What a crazy world, huh?"

"Crazy," Kordic agreed. "Listen, Lou. There was a guy who had a heart attack a few days ago on Montgomery and California. Lunch hour. Remember it?"

"Yeah, sure. Didn't think it would get kicked up to you guys. Just looked like a guy whose heart gave out." His voice turned wary. "What's the beef, Jack?"

"No beef. It just may tie into something else I'm working on. The guy had no ID on him. Do you remember if he had any friends there? Anyone who knew him?"

"Nope. Some real good-looking lady was giving him mouth-to-mouth when I got there. She's got a lot more guts than I do. I wouldn't wrap my lips around the pope's, with all this AIDS stuff and everything else going on. The ambulance showed up right after I got there."

"And she gave you her business card?"

"Yeah. Then she took off. In some kind of a hurry. Got to give her credit, though, getting down on the ground and giving that old fart mouth-to-mouth."

"Was there a priest on the scene, Lou?"

"Priest? No, no priest. Just the woman. She was a looker. The usual amount of ghouls standing around, doing nothing but getting in the way. You know how that is."

"Right. Anyone else talk to you about this, Lou?"

"Not a soul. What's the big deal, anyway? No evidence of foul play that I could see. None at all."

"Okay, Lou. Thanks for your time," Kordic said. He put the telephone softly back on its cradle and sat looking at it. The priest. The mysterious Father Torres. How had he gotten to Mary Ariza? There had been nothing in the papers about the incident. He could have called the station house, maybe obtained Mary's name that way, some cop or clerk reading the information to him from Lou Aragon's report. But if he had, then why hadn't he identified the body? Where are you, Father?

The tap on his shoulder startled him. It was Charlotte, the receptionist. "Jack. Lieutenant Tilson wants to see you in his office."

Chapter 22

Barry Pittman called out to the clerk, "I need a list of every accident that took place in the city last night between six and seven o'clock."

The clerk was a busty young woman who spoke with a Spanish accent. She wore tight, acid-washed blue jeans and a snug-fitting orange T-shirt with a jagged hole on the left shoulder.

"What locations?" she asked.

Pittman leaned forward, placing his palms on the countertop. "I don't have any locations. I just want them all."

The girl shook her head, causing her bangs to swish back and forth. "You got to have a location or I can't pull the report."

"Listen," Pittman blurted belligerently, "this is related to the death of Lieutenant Sullivan. I want those fucking reports and I want them now. If you can't handle it, then get me your supervisor."

The girl didn't blink under Pittman's verbal attack. The supervisor happened to be her cousin, and since she had her full civil service ranking, there was nothing the hotheaded cop could do to her. She had heard about the lieutenant's death. It gave her the creeps. Someone coming in and killing him right here in the Hall of Justice. She spoke in a metered tone, stressing each word. "You know, mister, you catch more flies with honey than you do with vinegar."

Lieutenant Wesley Tilson leaned back in his chair, his stomach making a noise like escaping bath water. "I'm not going to record this session, Inspector

Kordic." He waved a hand toward a chair. "Sit down, make yourself comfortable."

Kordic looked around the room, noticing the squares of clean paint where the framed photographs of Chris Sullivan's family and friends had hung formerly.

"I spoke to the Fuentes family," Tilson said. "They verify your being there, but they are uncertain of the time."

Tilson hung his suit jacket on the back of his chair and rolled up his shirtsleeves neatly. The shirt collar was so heavily starched it had scored a red mark around his neck.

Kordic waited until Tilson seated himself before he spoke. "Why would you bother to check with them? Are you telling me I'm a suspect in Chris's death, for Christ's sake?"

"A witness saw a man enter the office. He was a white man, had darkish hair," Tilson answered.

"The janitor. Couldn't he come up with a better description than that?"

Tilson shifted uneasily in his seat. "Who told you the witness was a janitor?"

"Who else could it be? It wasn't a cop, or you'd have gotten a better ID. That time of night the only one wandering around here is the janitor. I still want to know why you're checking on me, Tilson."

"Sullivan was your juice, wasn't he, Inspector?"

Juice. The terminology is different throughout the country. Back East the higher department authority who takes an interest in a cop's career is called a rabbi. In other departments that person might be called a bishop, or simply the man. But in San Francisco he was juice.

"He was a friend," Kordic said dryly.

"Was he? Still? Without a good report from Sullivan, you would have been put back on disability leave. He was the deciding factor."

Kordic felt his face flush. Tilson isn't going to let up, he thought. He isn't going to be satisfied until he's rid of me. He'll keep at it, hoping to unnerve me, push and push, hoping to drive me to the edge, back to drinking, to making mistakes. "There's also my doctor and the police union."

"True." Tilson's face took on that look politicians use when they say they want to help you. "There are going to be a great many changes in the department after the upcoming election. I don't think it's in your best interests, a man with your problems, to be working in a stressful position such as a homicide investigator."

Kordic compressed his lips to hold back a curse, then said, "All police work involves stress. Unless you hide out in an office all day. That's one way to make sure you never screw up by shooting the wrong guy. One of your own men."

Tilson made a catcher's mitt out of one hand, a baseball of the other, and pounded them together. "I want complete review reports of everything you're working on now, Inspector. Detailed reports, including the exact time you've spent on each case. Is that understood?"

Kordic heaved himself to his feet, his temper under control. The only way to beat Tilson was to wear him down. Give him nothing to pick at. "You're the boss, Lieutenant," he said, his tone as bland and impersonal as a computer-recorded telephone answering machine.

"Hey, Inspector. I got an appointment in an hour," Hector Lockhart complained in a small, whiny voice that didn't go with his simian-like appearance. He was tall, several inches over six feet, with a thick head of ebony, tightly curled hair. The same hair covered the fingers and backs of his hands.

"I'll drive you to your appointment, Hector, relax," Dave Granados said. "Now show me where you were when the accident took place."

"Right there," Lockhart said, pointing at Howard Street just before it reached the pedestrian crosswalk for Fourth Street. "I'm slowing down for a red light, and this lady slams right into the back of my truck." He ran a finger around the white foam surgical collar banding his neck. "Goofy broad couldn't drive in the rain, I guess."

"So then what happened?" questioned Granados. "You got out of the truck to see what happened, right?"

"Right. Talked to her. She was scared as hell," Lockhart said. "But she wasn't hurt," he added hastily. "She didn't complain about any injuries, nothing like that."

"And you looked around for witnesses?"

"Yeah. Cars went by, didn't stop, though, the pricks."

Granados said, "Tell me about the man in the phone booth."

Lockhart swiveled toward the pay phone alongside the service station. "Station was closed. I saw some guy in the booth. Thought he might have seen her hit me. I yelled out at him, but he took off."

"What'd he look like?" Granados asked, walking toward the phone booth.

"It was raining. Made it tough to see." A small smile crossed Lockhart's homely face. "And I got good eyes. Twenty-ten. Made All-City at Balboa High School as a junior and senior. Pretty good pitcher, too. Had a cup of coffee with the Dodgers, but as good as I could see, I couldn't get the wood on those curve balls."

"Could you tell how old he was? Was he white, black, what?"

Lockhart rubbed a knuckle in the corner of his eye. "White, I'd say. He had a raincoat and a hat. The kind golfers wear. Never got a real good look at his face."

"Give me an estimate on his age. Fifteen, thirty, fifty, what?"

"I guess maybe fifty."

"How tall?"

"I don't know."

Granados opened the phone booth's accordion door. The odor of urine drifted up from the concrete flooring. "He was here at the phone. Where was the top of his head?"

"Uh, about where yours is."

"Makes him about six feet, right?"

"Yeah, but he had the hat on."

"So, shorter than six feet?"

"Nah, I think about six feet is right."

"Fat? Skinny?"

Lockhart cleared his throat, then hiccuped a few times before declaring, "Not fat. Kind of medium."

"So what did he do when he left the booth?"

"Went that way," Lockhart said, gesturing with his thumb toward Forth Street.

"How did he move? Natural? Have a limp? Anything like that?"

"He moved good. No problems."

"Did he get into a car?"

Lockhart fidgeted with his surgical collar again, grimacing as he swiveled his neck slightly.

"Look, Lockhart," Grenados said impatiently, "I'm not an insurance agent, so don't waste your pain and suffering on me. Show me just what the man did, where he went, after he left the phone booth."

Lockhart grunted something only he could understand, then walked from the booth toward the street. "He got about here," he said at the curb, "then the broad that hit me started crying and I forgot about the guy."

"He was standing just about where you are now?"

"Yeah. Oh, he bent down, I remember that, like he was going to tie his shoe or something."

Granados stood alongside Lockhart and bent at the waist. His eyes were staring directly into a sewer grate.

The two city public works employees seemed remarkably cheerful for men who'd had to wrench a sewer grate loose and climb into the muck below.

Actually, only one of the men had climbed down into the sewer. A rangy man with a long, narrow face sat with his legs dangling over the curb, calling out encouragements to his partner below. "Don't step in too much shit, Artie, or you're eatin' dinner alone."

There was a yelled response from the depths of the sewer. The man sitting on the sidewalk turned to Granados and grinned. "Don't know how much luck we're going to have, Inspector. We find all kinds of junk down there: car parts, dead animals, abandoned babies even. Newborn, dumped right in the sewer. Can you believe it? A gun, hell, it could be way down the line by now. One time—"

A shout from the sewer caused him to pause. He leaned down and yelled, "You find something, Artie?"

All Granados heard was a muffled growl.

"He says he found a gun, Inspector."

Artie was built like a jockey, rail-thin and short, which was probably why he got all the sewer-crawling jobs. He pushed up a rake and a shovel, handle first, then climbed up the ladder, his already dirty overalls covered with more grime and silt. He held a soggy cardboard carton in one hand. Granados could make out the butt of a revolver and a holster. The revolver had oversized combat grips. "Got lucky on this stuff," Artie said. "It was jammed up next to a bunch of newspapers. Think this is what you're looking for?"

Granados took the box from Artie's outstretched hands. Chris Sullivan had carried a Dan Wesson .44 Magnum with a two-inch barrel and combat grips. Wedged into the holster was a black handle, with a round hole the size of a cigarette butt drilled in the end. Granados placed the box on the sidewalk and used a pen to wiggle the handle out. A knife. No more than seven or eight inches in length, he estimated. Light, maybe an ounce. Plastic. Fiberglass. Something like that. He let it slide off the pen and back into the box.

"This got anything to do with Chris Sullivan?" Sergeant Rocky Taylor asked Jack Kordic.

"No, something else I'm working on, Rocky. You know this kid?"

Taylor glanced at Pepe Fuente's mug shot. "Looks familiar. Let's go see what's on file." Taylor was a big, round-shouldered man with a jutting jaw. He walked crab-like, from side to side, the result of too many knee operations resulting from football injuries. He wore washed-out blue jeans baggy at the knees, and a faded flannel plaid shirt. One of the benefits of working the Gang Task Force was that you dressed for the streets, not the office.

"Home address on Folsom," Kordic said as he followed Taylor to a bank of chest-high filing cabinets. "He strayed out of the Mission District, up to Hyde Street, near California. Tried to put a hit on a woman. Neighbor got him first. Pepe was armed. A Walther twenty-two semi-automatic with a silencer."

Taylor stopped in mid-stride. "Silencer?"

Kordic told him what he had learned from the Alcohol, Tobacco, and Firearms expert. "The gun was used to kill a merchant on Market Street too."

"Great," Taylor said disgustedly. "That's all we need. Russian silencers. First time I ever heard of that. These punks, they use a weapon, then pass it on, so maybe Pepe didn't do the hit on Market Street." He pulled out a file drawer, his stubby fingers flicking through the manila folders. "Yep. Here we go." He withdrew one of the folders and paged through it before handing it to Kordic. "You see the autopsy results?"

"No."

"He'll probably have a tattoo, the numbers twenty-two right about here," Taylor said, pointing at his left forearm. "There'll be some other flesh graffiti too. Probably *Rifa*, meaning 'We control.' Then there'll be your usual assortment of daggers dripping with blood. Snake heads. They love that crap."

"Why the numbers twenty-two?"

"That's his gang," Taylor said, pointing at the file. "Twenty-Second Street Gang. The *jefe* of the outfit at the moment is some little cokehead, name of Tony Moreno. Tony from Sony. One of his first big heists was a load of several hundred Sony television sets off the docks. His record's twice as long as Pepe's, but he's been careful lately. Getting his boys to do all the hard stuff. Moreno did a few months at county jail on a possession charge awhile back. Some of the street rumors said they turned him inside, made a *puto* out of him. A fag. Moreno says no, but he's not anxious to go back. He's got the rest of them bullshitted, but he's avoiding what they call *la chinga*, the actual work himself."

"Where am I most likely to find Moreno?" Kordic asked.

"Little punk moves around all the time. Never stays in the same place for long. But El Condado, a bean and beer joint on Valencia, is the gang's main hangout. A lowlife by the name of Gus runs it. Gustavo Melendez." Taylor clasped a hand firmly on Kordic's elbow. "These kids are punks, Jack. But dangerous punks. They're high on crack or coke half of the time. They all carry. The boys like automatics, switchblade knives. The girls carry too. We pulled one in the other night, she had a knife and a zip gun stashed in her hair. You want to go see Moreno, let me know. I'll either pull him in or go with you, okay?"

"Okay," Kordic agreed.

"And keep me posted if you hear any more about this silencer, Jack. We got enough trouble with these gangs without having to worry about silencers." Taylor sighed and leaned back against the file cabinets. "Jane was right all along."

Kordic was sure he knew the punch line, but he played straight man anyway. "Jane?"

"What she told Tarzan—it's a jungle out there, baby. I'll put out some feelers on Moreno."

Chapter 23

Rene Santos had a cup of coffee while he waited for the photographs to be developed. The clerk at the small photography shop guaranteed that they would complete the developing in an hour. They were true to their word. Santos examined the pictures of Naimat and Boris Zorkin. There were only seven of them, and the young photo clerk was very apologetic, claiming that they would have to charge him for a full roll. "Company policy."

Santos paid for the pictures, went back to the coffee shop, and used the pay phone. He dialed the number from memory. He was always good with numbers.

"Ticket Brokers."

"This is Mr. Allen. I called yesterday about some opera tickets."

"Oh, yes, Mr. Allen. This is Charles. How are you today?" Charles spoke in a constant hurry, starting each sentence with an intake of breath, hoping it would last through the out-rush of words. "As I said yesterday, this is an unusual request. We deal mostly in sporting events, concerts, theaters, that kind of thing."

"Did you get them or not?" Santos said bluntly.

"Got them, but it wasn't easy. Especially the admittance to the gala party."

"I assume you received the money?"

"Yes, yes, indeed, and thank you very much. It was generous of you."

Santos had had a delivery service bring a small sealed envelope to the ticket agency the day before. The envelope had contained nothing but a pair of crisp hundred dollar bills.

"When can I pick them up, Charles?"

"Anytime, sir, anytime at all. Will you be paying the balance in cash?"

"Yes. As I said, all cash. Double the regular ticket and gala price plus another bonus for your good work. I'll send a messenger right over." Santos broke the connection and dialed the messenger service.

The messenger, a droopy-faced teenager with a mass of brick-colored hair and a weedy mustache, came to the coffee shop within ten minutes. He turned off his radio long enough for Santos to give him instructions and a sealed envelope.

Santos waited alone in a booth, ordering a piece of pie to keep the waitress happy, and studied the photographs. Zorkin would no doubt try to recruit Naimat—turn her to his side. He concentrated on the Russian—his face, his posture.

It was the way he preferred to work. See the man. Study man. Capture his patterns, his rhythms. Zorkin didn't look like anything special in the pictures, but Petrov wouldn't use a man unless he was uniquely skilled. Skilled with a variety of weapons.

Zorkin's instructions from Petrov would no doubt be to wait until after Abrams was captured—then to eliminate Santos.

Santos was thinking along the same time structure. Capture Abrams, then kill Zorkin. Then see what Petrov was really up to. Viktor was a planner, a plotter, a desk officer whose schemes were carried out by field agents. He didn't like to get his own hands dirty. Or bloody.

The messenger arrived within a half hour with the two opera tickets and separate tickets allowing the bearer into the gala ball. The opera tickets went for two hundred dollars each, and the ball tickets five times that amount. All for a good cause, as the newspaper said.

Santos tipped the messenger, left a five-dollar bill on the table for the waitress, and wandered back onto Union Street.

The rain had stopped, the sky that light powder blue

shade that shows up after a storm. He strolled among the shoppers, checking his image in the windows of clothing stores, antique shops, more restaurants, seeing nothing, his mind on Paul Abrams.

Abrams was not the hands-on type that Rose had been. Rose's company had less than thirty employees. He had started from scratch, coming to this country a poor man and crawling his way up the famous American ladder of success. He was a doer. An inventor.

Paul Abrams had inherited millions of dollars from his father, and, along with his brother, had turned them into billions. A much easier road to success. What kind of man was he? His brother's death at the hands of some incompetent kidnappers hadn't seemed to have slowed him down. Abrams Oil continued to prosper, to expand. Business journals described him as meticulous in his planning, willing to take big gambles—for big profits. Ruthless in his pursuit of a deal. Ruthless maybe, but how strong was he really? How tough? Not as tough as Rose, surely. How would he hold up to Zorkin? Or to Naimat? Or Petrov?

Petrov. The new Viktor Petrov. He was operating on a different scale. The money. The Russians had always worked "on the cheap," as one disgruntled member of the Red Brigade had described it to him in Rome. They doled out the money in dribs and drabs, as if the agent handing it over had taken it from his own savings account. The Arabs were just the opposite. Money was never a problem: American dollars, Swiss francs, German marks, gold. They were willing to pay whatever the cost. And now Petrov was acting like an Arab, not a Russian. Of course, the money no longer came out of Moscow. But where was it coming from? And why was Petrov so free with it?

Naimat checked the map several times, cursing under her breath. San Francisco, with all its hills, one-way streets, and tangle of freeways, was a logistical nightmare. She went back to the map, which showed she was in the Bernal Heights section of the city. She found the street she was looking for, Brewster. The map showed Samoset Street running directly into Brewster. The map was obviously wrong, for she was at a dead end. Maybe this was why Rene had picked the place. No one could find it. She backed up, took a series of right turns, and unexpectedly found herself where she wanted to be, on Brewster. She parked across the street and several doors down from the house, studying the terrain: a mixture of old wood-frame houses, most in need of repair. The street's patchy asphalt was wet from a recent cloudburst and was littered with old rusty cars and trucks. Scrubby bottlebrush trees poked their knobby roots through the cracks in the sidewalks. The house itself was detached from its bordering neighbors, a unique feature in San Francisco, where the houses usually bumped right up against each other. Rene had indeed chosen well, she decided as she got out of the car, picked up a grocery bag, and sauntered slowly across the street, eyes sweeping the area, searching for potential problems and finding none.

The rickety stairs squeaked under her feet as she climbed the steps. The front door was weather-warped, the knob green and crusted. She knocked twice and immediately heard the click of several bolts being undone.

"About time," Cesar Davila said as he pulled the door open, his hands reaching for the grocery bag. He was wearing dark blue overalls speckled with white paint and reeking of thinner.

"Who is it?" a voice called from the back of the house. "The chick with the food?"

Naimat closed the door quickly behind her. There was a musty smell to the place. The floors were hardwood, once painted a dark brown, the paint now faded and worn bare on the heavily traveled paths in the hallways.

She followed Davila to the kitchen. The walls and ceiling were yellow from years of tobacco smoke and grease. There was one table and four mismatched chairs.

Tony Morena sat in one of the chairs, leaning back,

balancing on the rear legs. "Hey," he said loudly, "finally some action. You bring a sister with you? You're a little old for me, *mujer*."

Naimat ignored him and scanned the room. The sink was cluttered with dirty dishes. A supermarket bag crammed with garbage was under the sink. A sandwich with one bite out of it was on the table, alongside an ashtray crammed with cigarette butts.

"What did you bring us?" Morena asked. "Something to eat? Besides you, if you're lucky." He smiled, and she noticed that his teeth had a freckled look.

"Cesar," she said, "there are more bags in the car. In the backseat. Go get them."

Davila's temper flared. He didn't like her ordering him around in front of Moreno. He thought of telling her to get them herself, but decided against it. He dropped the grocery bag he'd taken from her onto the table. "I hope you brought steaks. I'm tired of chicken."

Moreno tore at the bag, plucking out a six-pack of beer. He shook the can before popping the top, directing the spray toward the sink. "Help yourself, lady. Where's the boss man? He keeps telling me I'm going to meet the big boss man, but I never do." His eyes narrowed, then he gave a tambourine laugh. "Don't tell me you be the boss." He laughed again and took a long swig of the beer.

'How is the work on the van coming?" Naimat asked.

Moreno belched and rubbed his stomach. "Good, I guess. That's your boyfriend's job, not mine."

"Do you know what your job is?"

Moreno drained what was left of the beer, then tossed the empty can over his shoulder. He burped loudly, staring at the woman. How old was she? Thirty? Older? Maybe, but in good shape. Hard body. A butch haircut. Probably a dyke. The jacket and leather pants fit her tight. Real tight. He always liked leather. Liked the smell of it. The feel of it. It might be worth a shot, fucking a dyke. Maybe turn her back around once she got a good taste of Tony. One thing he wasn't going to do was let her boss him around. Go get the bags in the car. Fuck her. "Yeah, *ruca*, I know my job. I'm gonna start a riot. What do you think about that, *ruca*? You got a name?"

Ruca. Old lady. Gang chick. Oh, he was going to learn a real lesson. "You can call me Nancy," Naimat said, staring back at him. Rene had told her to handle Moreno any way she wanted to, hard or soft, just make sure he stayed in the house. He was not to be seen until after their operation was over. Santos was worried that the police would connect Moreno to the incompetent that had been killed while trying to eliminate Mary Ariza. What was wrong with Rene? If he had given her the job, Ariza would be dead now. Now she had to baby-sit Moreno. He could talk to his gang, but only by phone—any personal contact with the gang would be made by Davila. Naimat was to make sure that Davila and Moreno were prepared and ready for the job tomorrow night.

"Well, Nancy. Let's see your tits."

The manufacturer of the device labeled his invention a Flicket. Nothing more than a small piece of stainless steel that when attached to the blade of a pocket knife enables the user to open the blade using only one hand. A specially designed holster attaches at the hip, holding the knife vertically. Naimat leered down at Moreno, her tongue flicking out and licking her lower lip as she unsnapped the buttons on her jacket.

Moreno leaned forward in his chair. "Yeah, that's it, let's see those babies. If they're real nice, Tony will let you see his cock."

She moved so fast that Moreno didn't see the blade. But he felt it, felt the tip touch his neck, pierce the skin.

He tried scooting back in the chair, but Naimat was on him, one hand behind his head, the knife blade now across his throat. She scraped the razor-sharp blade across his skin, as if giving him a shave.

"You have no manners, you piece of shit," she said in rapid Spanish. "None at all. You do what I tell you to do, when I tell you to do it, or I'll kill you." She pressed the blade a fraction of an inch farther into his neck. "Understand, piece of shit?"

Cesar Davila came in, easily balancing three full grocery bags in his massive arms. He looked at Moreno and shook his head sadly. "I told you not to fool around with her, didn't I?"

Moreno's voice was hardly more than a squeak. "Put the knife away."

Naimat stepped back, the knife vanishing back into its holster.

Moreno stood up shakily, his eyes shooting daggers at the woman. He brushed the arms of his jacket and pants, then lunged out at her with his right hand.

Naimat moved easily out of the way, letting Moreno's force bring him close. The outside of her foot made contact with his knee, and he stumbled. She brought the heel of her hand up under his chin, sending Moreno spinning to the floor. As he tried to get to his feet, she stamped down on one hand with her heel. Moreno grabbed the injured hand, moaning, balling himself up into a fetal position. Naimat knelt alongside him, the knife out again, the blade rolling up his leg, stopping at the crotch. "You want to show it to me, so I can cut it off, Tony?" she said in a soft, mocking voice.

Cesar Davila said, "Leave him be. We need him."

Naimat patted Moreno gently on the head, as if rewarding a dog for bringing in the newspaper, then went to help Davila unpack the bags, storing breakfast cereal in the cabinets, steaks, beer, wine, and vegetables in the refrigerator.

Moreno got to his knees, then used the table as support as he pulled himself upright, his eyes on the floor. He heard a snap and a fizzing sound. When he looked up, the woman was handing him a beer.

"Got any good *zacate* on you?" Naimat asked.

Moreno accepted the beer and took a long swallow before reaching into his pocket for a ziplock bag of marijuana and cigarette papers.

Naimat expertly rolled two smokes, put them both in her mouth, lit them, and handed one to Moreno. She saw his hand shaking. Good. He was easy. Almost too easy. "We can still be friends, Tony." She inhaled deeply, then turned on her heel toward Davila. "Let's see what you've been up to."

Davila led her to the rear of the house and down an inside stairway to the garage. A large white van took up most of the floor space. Davila opened a door to a small, dark room smelling of mildew. The floor was rough concrete. There was a window, no more than two feet by three feet, at the upper portion of the rear wall. The window itself was covered by aluminum foil. An iron window guard in an elaborate scroll pattern was bolted to the wall, covering the window. The walls were untaped sheet rock, the nail heads visible along the studs. In the corner was a metal-framed single bed, covered by a splatter-marked mattress. A pair of handcuffs were attached to the bed frame by a short, thick metal-link chain.

"Not exactly what our guest is used to, is it?" Naimat asked as she left the room and turned her attention to the van. S.F. AMBULANCE was neatly stenciled on the vehicle's door. She ran a finger along one of the four dark, round knobs bracketing the stenciling.

"Magnets," Davila said, lifting the sign away to show the blank paint beneath it. "We'll put the signs on at the last possible moment. I don't want anyone pulling us over for some medical emergency." He pointed at the basement's ceiling, a scant few inches from the top of the van. "I've got a revolving red light. I'll magnetize it to the roof, work it off the cigarette lighter."

"Very nice," Naimat said, taking another pull on the marijuana. She saw Moreno watching her as she strolled to the back of the garage. A door opened to the backyard. It was studded with three locks. Pieces of two-by-fours in steel brackets were stationed at eye and knee height across the door. "Very nice. Very secure."

Davila wiped his hands on his coveralls. "As long as

we don't have to hold him more than two or three days, it will be fine."

She dropped her reefer to the floor and ground it out with her heel. "Oh, I don't think it will take any longer than that." She walked back to the small room, going over to the bed, picking up the chain that held the handcuffs, running the chain through her fingers.

"Tony," she called out in a strong voice. "Come in here. I want to show you something."

The fax machine chirped on, and Paul Abrams almost stepped on Shylock as he strode over to watch the machine spit out its information.

He anxiously grasped the first sheet, a smile coming to his face when he saw the code name *pyat*. Five. The bidding was down to five organizations, including Abrams Oil.

His faith in Russian mafia connection was proving worthwhile. Abrams waited until the fax machine beeped to indicate the transmission was finished, picked up the three additional sheets and carried them back to his desk.

Shylock rubbed up against his master's leg, but for once Abrams ignored the cat. The information was just what he'd been waiting for. The names of the bidders and the exact totals of every bid were all neatly catalogued.

Now that he knew what the others were willing to pay, the whole deal would fall right into his lap. He picked up the phone and punched the button that connected directly to David Blair's office.

"David, come at once. Bring your people. We have twelve hours to change our bids."

"You've had news?" Blair asked.

"Yes. Excellent news. It will mean restructuring our presentations, but that's not a problem. And what of you? Have you spoken to Rose?"

"No, sir. His secretary says she hasn't heard from him for several days."

"And the last she heard he was in Russia?"

"Yes, sir. Moscow."

Abrams mulled over the possibilities in his mind. Rose was a crafty old devil, but he was loyal. There would be no reason for him to do anything that would jeopardize the current project. They were partners now, and Rose stood to make a fortune. He could be up in the frozen wastelands in the north of Russia—their next project site, stranded in some backward refinery. Rose was well into his seventies. Maybe he was sick. Maybe he had died. What would happen if Rose died? All his plans, his technology, and the patents would revert to Abrams Oil. Rose was worth almost more to him dead than he was alive.

"All right, David. Forget about Rose for the moment. And get over here. Quickly."

He went back to reading the faxed report. Moments later he saw a shadow sweep across his desk.

"Is everything all right, darling?" Adele Abrams asked sweetly.

Abrams leaned back in his chair, locking his fingers behind his head. Adele was wearing a white tank top and a short tennis-style skirt. Her hair was tied back in a bob.

"Everything's just fine. Where are you off to?"

Adele clasped her hands behind her back and straightened her shoulders, the movement causing her breasts to thrust forward. "Nowhere. I'll be home all day. In my room, if you want me."

Abrams put his fingers to his lips and blew her a kiss. "Any other time but now, my love. Work to do. Much work to do. I'll be busy all day. Why don't you go out? Shop. See your friends."

"No, Paul. I'll just stay home. Catch up on my reading." She walked around the desk, planted a kiss on his forehead, then padded barefoot from the room.

Abrams watched as she closed the door behind her. Adele. Always playing a role. Today it was the sweet little homebody, wanting nothing more than to keep her husband happy. Poor Adele. So wonderful in bed, but such a terrible actress. She'd been fooling around. He was sure of it. And he'd find out with whom. And then deal with her. Get rid of her. But not until the Russian deal was completed. He pushed Adele from his mind and turned his attention back to the reports his new Russian friends had faxed on the oil field bids.

Chapter 24

The Pontar house was located on El Camino Del Mar, in what is known as the Sea Cliff District, a small patch of expensive homes on the northwest edge of the city. The abundant cypress and pine trees are all bent in bow-like shapes from the constant winds. The sheer, shrub-covered hills drop straight down to rock-encrusted beaches that have caused the destruction of countless fishing boats and pleasure craft.

A foghorn blared out a warning as Kordic parked his car. A recent attempt by the Coast Guard to upgrade the marine navigational warning system by replacing the foghorns with more modern electronic devices had been beaten back soundly. The money crowd and historical buffs vehemently argued that the bellowing of a foghorn was as much a part of San Francisco as the clanging of cable car bells. Kordic inhaled a lungful of salty air, grateful for the fact that the foghorn crowd had won the battle, equally grateful that he didn't live in an area where you had to listen to the damn things all night.

The front of the house was white adobe, the roof Spanish tile. Kordic pushed the bell, setting off an alarm of barking dogs. Matt Pontar himself opened the door. His tie was undone, his sleeves rolled up.

Two good-sized Airedale terriers flanked Pontar, their tails wagging even as they growled at Kordic.

"Frick, Frack, behave yourself," Pontar commanded as he reached down and patted both dogs on their heads. "Come on in, Inspector. Just fixing myself a drink. Want one?"

"I could use one," Kordic replied, following Pontar

and the two woolly black and brown dogs down a parquet floor to the kitchen. Both dogs came to a halt, skidding past their destination as Pontar held the door open for Kordic. The kitchen floor was tiled in dark blue with black grouting, the adobe walls were white, the beamed ceiling made of tongue-and-groove pine planking. The glass-paned cabinets had sturdy-looking brass latches.

"Gin okay?" Pontar questioned, popping open the door to a double-door freezer. He took a bottle of Bombay Sapphire gin and two frosty tulip-shaped wineglasses from the freezer. "Need an olive? Onion? Lemon twist?"

Kordic accepted the drink. The gin swirled slowly in the stemmed glass, with the thick consistency of mercury. "No, this is fine. Cheers."

"Indeed," Pontar said, and both men sampled their drinks.

The dogs nuzzled Kordic's legs.

"They're hopeless, Inspector. Give them a pat or they'll pout all night."

Kordic roughed the hair of both Airedales.

Pontar hooked a leg around an oak captain's chair and invited Kordic to sit down at the kitchen table. "I was terribly sorry to hear about Lieutenant Sullivan. I met him once or twice. I'm a friend of Commissioner Hayes." He held up a hand when he saw Kordic frown. "I'm not name-dropping or trying to show you I know people. I meant it about Sullivan. He seemed like a hell of a guy. It's a real tragedy. Have you had any luck finding the person who did it?"

"No, not yet." Kordic was usually cautious around attorneys. Especially powerful, successful ones like Pontar. But there was something about the man he liked. A tough, no-bullshit attitude. "We're not having much success anywhere of late."

Pontar took a small swallow of the gin. "I'm not trying to butt into your investigation of the attempts on Mary's life, Inspector. But I'm concerned, naturally. I've spoken to her. She's been wracking her brain trying to come up with a motive. So have I, and I can't find any connection between the attempts and her work at the office. About the best idea she can come up with is mistaken identity. She thinks that whoever is behind this has her confused with someone else."

"Possible, but not likely. The first guy, the man who stabbed Mr. Slager—"

"Walter Slager."

"Yes. The suspect was inside Mary's apartment. Waiting. He was apparently there for some time." Kordic paused, wondering just how much he should tell Pontar. "The second man, Pepe Fuentes, the one who was killed by the neighbor, Mr. Landon. The weapon he was carrying had a silencer. A well-made Russian silencer." Kordic gave Pontar a description of the gun. "Fuente's background shows he was nothing more than a street punk. The gun he carried was used earlier to kill a merchant on Market Street. We have reason to believe that the first man, the one who was waiting for Mary, was wearing a baseball cap and a jacket purchased at that same store."

Pontar shook his head and stared into his glass of gin, his brow furrowed in confusion.

The dogs took advantage of their master's lack of attention and pushed their muzzles into Kordic's legs. He put down his drink and used a hand to scratch each of their heads. The dogs had another location in mind, moving their bodies so that Kordic's hands were on the back of their rumps. The looks on their faces showed just how much of a joy this was to them.

"It just doesn't make a whole lot of sense, does it?" Pontar said, his chair scraping the tiles as he stood up and walked back to the freezer. "A man with a knife messes up, so they send someone with a pro shooter's gun after her." He brought the gin bottle to the table and topped up their glasses. "Doesn't make any sense at all." He snapped his fingers to get Frick and Frack's attention. "Come on, boys. I'll go tell Mary you're here, Inspector."

The restaurant was small, bringing to mind a Parisian bistro: the walls decorated with impressionist watercolors of Paris street scenes. The smell of garlic, sauces, and freshly brewed coffee floated around the small dining room. The soft hum of conversation mixed with the sounds of glasses tinkling, corks being pulled, knives and forks scraping against dinnerware.

"What a charming place," Mary Ariza said as she slipped out of her coat.

The waitress, a stout woman with hair the color of polished silver, greeted Kordic warmly, her French accent adding to her charm as she shepherded them to a table near the fireplace.

"They seem to know you," Mary said once she was seated.

Kordic scratched the side of his nose. "I've been eating out a lot. The food is good and it's close."

"Oh, you live around here?"

"A few blocks away," Kordic said, as if he were relaying confidential information.

They sat in silence until the waitress came back and recited the night's specials. They both settled on the *navain d'agneau*, agreeing with the waitress that the weather almost dictated a lamb stew. They added a raw vegetable salad, onion soup, and a bottle of Beaujolais to the order.

"So, how goes the hunt?" Mary asked after the wine had been delivered and poured.

"Not so good for the hunters." Kordic brought her up to date on the investigation.

"What about Lieutenant Sullivan? Are you working on that case, Jack? Everyone in Homicide must be, I guess."

Kordic's face tightened sharply. "No, I've been kicked off that investigation. There's a certain lieutenant who's after me."

"After you? I don't understand."

Kordic paused, breathing deeply, composing himself. "It's been going on for a long time. He wants me off the force."

"Why? What's he got against you?"

"A grudge. He made a mistake once. A big mistake. I saw it. I more or less forced him to leave the detective bureau. I never mentioned his mistake to anyone. I guess I should have, but I didn't. Even though he's gone on to become a lieutenant and may end up with a chief's job down in southern California, he's got it in for me."

"I still don't understand. How can he cause you any trouble?"

"Simple. My suicide attempt, and when my drinking was out of control, I mishandled a couple of assignments, didn't show up for work, things like that. He was in Internal Affairs then. It was just the opening he had been looking for. One of the doctors the city sent me to, a psychiatrist, made a report stating that I wasn't 'emotionally capable of returning to duty.'

"The police union fought it off with a report from another doctor saying that going back to work was just what I needed, but he wants to get rid of me. He's even trying to infer that I'm a suspect in Chris Sullivan's murder. He just wants to drive me back to the bottle, and out of the job."

"What's his name?" Mary asked.

Kordic shook his head slowly from side to side, sorry now that he'd brought up the subject. "It doesn't matter, Mary. I'm going to handle your case. Find out just what the hell is behind those attacks."

"What's his name?" Mary repeated. "Tell me, please. I'm interested."

"Tilson. Wesley Tilson."

"And how long has he been after you?"

"You're starting to sound like a lawyer," Kordic said pointedly.

"I am a lawyer. And a damn good one. If this man has been harassing you, you should go after him." Mary smiled and lightened her voice. "In those immortal words, 'Sue the bastard.' Emotional harassment. I'd be glad to look into it for you, Jack. Sometimes just the threat of a lawsuit works wonders. Come on, tell me what happened. I won't tell a soul, client-attorney privilege."

Kordic sighed, debating with himself. "It was stupid," he finally said. "We were chasing a rape suspect across a row of roofs. It was dark. I had the suspect positioned. I had lost track of Tilson. Suddenly someone started shooting at me. It was Tilson. He was in shock, I guess. I had to take the gun away from him. I hit him. He made a mistake, but, looking back, I did too, came on too macho. He was under some kind of stress, I guess. The department didn't have a stress unit then. We do now, thank God. They helped me quite a bit after . . . after my wife and son were killed. I made Tilson quit the bureau, he went into an office detail. That's about it, Mary."

"But he's persisting in harassing you, isn't he? Even now, with the investigation of your lieutenant's murder." She hurried on without giving Kordic a chance to respond. "You shouldn't let him get away with it, Jack. Let me help you."

"Okay, Counselor, I'll think about it," Kordic agreed, then picked up a spoon and used its tip to draw a pattern on the tablecloth. "What do you say we forget about all of this and just try to enjoy dinner?"

Mary Ariza smiled and raised her glass. "I'll drink to that."

They avoided talking about anything relating to police matters during the meal, and left after dessert, Mary barely taking a spoonful of the crème caramel.

They drove in silence back to the Pontar house. Kordic parked and they sat, listening to the clicking and creaking as the motor cooled. He reached out and touched her shoulder. She grabbed his hand in both of hers, her fingers rubbing against the edge of his scar. She slid toward him and tilted her head back. Kordic felt clumsy, like a teenager on his first date, as he pulled her to him, his mouth going to hers, gently at first, then with a passion that surprised both of them. Their teeth clicked together, their hands began groping.

Kordic was the first to pull away. "Mary, I—"

She kissed him again, her lips trailing down to his neck. He felt her body shudder, then she looked up at him and smiled, her voice suddenly serious. "That was nice."

"Not my normal form of interrogation, that's for sure. Mary, I—"

She put a finger to his lips. "Let's think about this before we go any further, Jack." She dug into her purse for a compact and lipstick.

"I was married for three years. A long three years, Jack. It ended months ago and was part of the reason for my coming out here. Ric was a nice, sweet man, then he became jealous, imagined things." A hand went to her cheek in a nervous gesture. "He became a different person."

"How jealous is he? You think he could have hired someone to—?"

"No. Definitely not, Jack. I called someone I know back home. Ric hasn't left the area, and he's in love with someone else. Wedding bells will be ringing shortly." She looked into his green eyes. "I'm not sure if I'm ready for anything serious. Do you know what I mean?"

"Exactly," Kordic said, feeling uneasy, wishing he could come up with something better.

"The Pontars have invited me to the opera and a pre-performance party tomorrow night. I'm really looking forward to it. I can ask if they can get an extra ticket. It's black tie."

"Put me in a tuxedo, and people immediately start treating me like a waiter. But I'd like to see you. How about lunch tomorrow?"

"Can't. I've got depositions right through lunchtime. How about after the opera?"

"Sounds great. There's a good restaurant a block from the Opera House. Stars. I'll meet you there." His hand went to her shoulder again, his finger making small circular motions. She leaned over and kissed him again, softly this time, her tongue exploring his. "Damn," she said when she pulled away. "I haven't groped around in a car since college." She opened the car door, the dome light coming on, causing both of them to blink. "It's a date, then. Tomorrow. Stars. After the opera."

"Yes. Assure the Pontars that you'll be under strict police supervision. By me."

She gave him a friendly wave, then ran up the path to the house.

Kordic turned over the engine and drove up the street slowly, checking the parked cars on the way. He made a U-turn and checked the vehicles on the opposite side of the street on the way back. Everything looked fine. Peaceful. No visible signs of menace. Could they, whoever they were, trace Mary to the Pontars' house? He decided to stop at Richmond Station and have them make passing patrols.

The six-story sandstone brick building sat squarely on the corner of Green and Baker Streets, in an area known to old-time San Franciscans as Cow Hollow. it was constructed in 1923, and total living space was 37,500 square feet divided into seventy-four rooms and thirty-five bathrooms. Its original function had been as an apartment house.

On March 27, 1973, the property was purchased by the Union of Soviet Socialist Republics, and for years it was listed in the telephone book as the Russian Consulate. The large number of marching, placard-carrying protesters had necessitated the removal of the listing from the phone book. A polished brass plaque on the door now bore the inscription: Consul of the Russian Federation. When the Russians moved in, they did some extensive interior remodeling, and covered the roof with antennas of all sizes and shapes. Neighbors found that if they had a view of the property, they could rent a room to a government agency, be it the FBI, CIA, military intelligence, or even the San Francisco Police Department Intelligence Unit, at very profitable rates. Neighbors joked that they lived in the safest area of the city, because the building was under constant surveillance.

The security at 2790 Green Street was state-of-the-art. The Russians could still teach the Americans a thing or two about security devices. But with all the electronic wonders strategically placed throughout the building, Boris Zorkin had his eye trained on a thirty-eight-dollar pickup truck side-view mirror that had been purchased from Sears Roebuck, then bolted to the bricks on the Baker Street corner of the building. By looking at the mirror, Zorkin could see the consulate vehicles entering and leaving the building's garage. He watched as a gray Ford backed out onto Baker Street and drove north.

There were two agents in the car. The driver of the vehicle, Eric Vladoff, was the one man in the spy shop who worried Zorkin. Vladoff was relatively new at his post, arriving just three months before. The game of spy-checking-spy was still an integral part of the business. While Zorkin had found nothing in Vladoff to criticize, Viktor Petrov had. "Watch out for him," Petrov warned, and Zorkin had done just that. Only yesterday he had surprised Vladoff as the junior man exited Zorkin's office. Vladoff's excuse was feeble: "I was looking for you, sir. A few questions regarding the Fairchild project."

The infiltration of Fairchild Semiconductor had been ongoing for seven years. A new prospect, a young man who placed the payments for his BMW over his loyalties to his employers, had proved promising. The questions Vladoff had asked about the project had been gone over thoroughly at Wednesday's briefing. So what had Vladoff really been doing in his office? Zorkin did not want anything interfering with his plans. Timing was critical now.

He went to the basement, took a car he had never used before, a new Buick LaSabre, and drove out onto Baker Street. He drove slowly, throttling down to loitering speed, causing the car behind to beep and pull around, the young driver flashing him the universal signal of clenched fist with the middle finger extended. Zorkin took a left turn on Filbert, a right on Lyon, then a quick left on Lombard. He drove through the gates and into the Presidio. There were no lights behind him as he drove deeper into the dark, tree-lined army base, past deserted two-story wooden barracks. The Presidio was one of his favorite detours. The army base was being closed piece by piece as real estate developers and environmentalists argued over the best ways to make use of the acreage. It amused Zorkin no end that the United States government had turned over the Presidio's Fort Point Coast Guard Life Boat Station to none other than Mikhail Gorbachev to be used as his base for the International Peace Mission. Zorkin pulled into the parking area by the Officers Club, killed the engine, and waited. Several cars passed in the next few minutes. Zorkin monitored their comings and goings, lit a small cigar, and waited another five minutes. Finally he hit the ignition switch, drove with the lights off to a stop sign, then pushed the accelerator to the ground, feeling his spine press into the leather seat as he rocketed up Arguello Street. He switched on the car's lights after traveling a few hundred yards, now sure there was no possibility of anyone following him.

Once out of the Presidio, Zorkin turned the radio to an FM classical music station and headed east, toward the downtown area. Ten minutes later, he pulled into the only open space he could find, a bus stop.

The after-theater crowd was out in full force. Zorkin turned left. The well-dressed patrons had thinned out, and the sidewalks were now full of prostitutes braving the chill wind in miniskirts and tank tops. A tall, peroxide blonde wearing a garish tiger-skin spandex dress stopped him as he entered the bar.

"Date, honey?"

The large Adam's apple and grains of dark beard starting to show through the caked-on makeup made Zorkin wonder how the man made a living. Once inside the bar he stopped for a moment, letting his eyes adjust to the darkness. His nostrils twitched at the smell of body odor, spilled beer, and urine. The walls were a dark purple, the ceiling black, sprinkled with recessed fixtures like eyeballs which cast dim pools of light onto the crowded floor. Heavy rock music blasted out of unseen speakers.

Zorkin elbowed his way through the throng ringing the dance floor, seeing several grotesque transvestites that made the blonde outside look attractive. A United

States Navy sailor was gyrating with ape-like gestures on the dance floor, urged on by a half-dozen shipmates. Zorkin spotted his man at the bar and went to him, tapping him lightly on the shoulder.

"Glad you could make it," he said softly, but with enough force to be heard over the music and shouting. "You're sure you weren't followed?"

Cesar Davila swiveled on his stool, swirling a glass of rum in his hand. "I'm sure," he insisted. "You think I'm stupid or something?"

That was exactly what Zorkin thought, but he kept his thoughts to himself.

The bartender was shirtless, an unbuttoned black leather vest stretched across his torso, which glistened under a thick coat of baby oil. Zorkin ordered a bottle of beer.

"What kind?" the bartender queried.

"Anything in a bottle." Zorkin had no intention of touching his lips to a glass. He pointed at Davila's drink. "Another for my friend." He watched the bartender go about his business, one hand going to his pomaded hair, then dipping into the ice cubes.

"What have you got for me?" he asked once he had the beer in his hand.

"It's tomorrow night."

Zorkin had already received that information from Naimat, but he wanted to double-check it with Davila. He wanted to double-check everything. "Where?"

"The Opera House. That's all I know. Final briefing in the morning."

The music stopped momentarily. Two of the sailors got into a pushing match.

"Santos hasn't given you the details yet?"

Davila drained his glass, a small river of rum coursing down his chin as he reached for the fresh drink. "Like I said. It's the Opera House—we go in as an ambulance crew, then take Abrams back to the safe house."

"I didn't come all the way down here for old news, Cesar. If you want your money, you'll have to do better than this."

"Money is one thing. Living to spend it is another."

"You'll live," Zorkin announced solemnly. "And wherever you choose." He decided to take a small sip of the beer. Thin. American. Tasteless. "The new identity papers will be worth as much as the money to you, I would think. Now, talk to me."

"The van is ready." He gave Zorkin the details of the vehicle's identification. "As soon as we've got Abrams, I'm to take him back to the safe house. It's on Brewster Street. Two fifty-six Brewster."

"Where Mr. Abrams will be made comfortable, I assume."

Davila took a long, slurping sip of his drink. "Very. His own room. I fixed it up myself."

"But how is Santos going to do it? How is he going to set Abrams up for you? How will he get Abrams into this ambulance of yours?"

"That he has not told me."

"Will Santos be in the ambulance with Abrams?"

Davila rattled the ice cubes in his glass. "That I do not know. But I doubt it. He will no doubt be watching. From a safe distance."

"Where is Naimat?"

"At the house now. With Tony Moreno. He's scared shitless of her. Rene doesn't trust him, doesn't want him to leave until the job is over. I just met with a bunch of his *cholos*. Naimat is controlling Moreno in her usual way. I'm supposed to be timing the trip from the safe house to the Opera House, checking alternate routes."

Zorkin winced inwardly at the thought of Naimat's powerful legs wrapped around the Mexican drug dealer. He had spent a long, exhausting afternoon with her. Exhausting for him. She had hardly worked up a sweat, and for all her tricks and gyrations, he was sure she hadn't enjoyed one second of it. "What are Santos's orders on Moreno?"

"To kill him. As soon as possible. After we have Abrams."

"I can't understand Santos using someone like Moreno."

"Moreno's gang is going to create a diversion, burn down a school. Shoot up some fire engines. What other choice does Rene have?" Davila asked, draining his glass again, the ice cubes clicking against his teeth. "He doesn't seem to want any help from you."

"Ah, but I'm helping you, my friend. Am I not?"

"Yes," Davila said. "But not as much as I'm helping you."

Zorkin had to concede the truth of the statement. Petrov had checked out Davila prior to meeting with Rene Santos in Peru. Davila was wanted for kidnapping and robbery in Argentina. If he was returned to that country, he would be executed. Petrov's plan had been to wait until Santos was close to Paul Abrams, very close, then put the pressure on Davila—find out exactly what Santos's plans were. But Davila had made things easier by coming to them. He was terrified of Santos. The fear, and his greed, made him the perfect pawn.

"What about Naimat?" Davila said, waving a hand to catch the bartender's attention.

"She will be dealt with."

"I'd like to kill the bitch myself," Davila boasted. "Fuck her, then kill her."

"Be my guest. You might want to skip the fucking part. She's not all that good. But not until Abrams is collected. And delivered to me."

Someone bumped into his arm. He turned to see the blonde in the tiger-skin dress. "Call me tomorrow," he said dismissively to Davila, then turned his attention to the blonde, his hand reaching out, tucking a twenty dollar bill in the top of the dress, then straying downward, touching a breast. It was surprising how real it felt. "My friend here wants to buy you a drink. Have fun, children."

Chapter 25

"Are we all here?" Lieutenant Wesley Tilson asked, standing on his toes and stretching to his full height, poised like a tightrope walker about to step off the platform. His eyes flicked over the assembled members of the Homicide detail, and Rocky Taylor and two officers from the Gang Task Force.

Kordic thought that Tilson's eyes lingered on him longer than necessary.

"This is Friday, gentlemen. I hope you didn't have any plans for the weekend, because you're going to be busy working. Inspectors Granados and Pittman have developed some information on the Sullivan case," Pittman announced in a monotone. "We have found Lieutenant Sullivan's personal revolver, as well as what we believe is the murder weapon." Tilson took a plastic bag from his coat pocket, held it between his thumb and index finger, and waved it above his head. "This is a fiber-reinforced polycarbonate knife. I'll pass it around so you all can see it, but do not remove it from the bag."

He handed the bag to Barry Pittman, who gave it to the man nearest him without looking at it.

"The reason the knife is significant," Tilson droned on, "is that it is one hundred percent non-metallic." He raised his eyebrows. "And you know what that means. Inspector Granados will fill you in on the other new developments."

Granados coughed, phlegm rattling in his throat. "We found Chris's gun and the knife in a sewer at Fourth and Howard. Figure the perp came into the Hall just before closing time. This type knife has been used in airplane hijackings and for the murder of a drug dealer at San Francisco International Airport. Not the best of weapons, but it sure as hell won't ding off the metal detectors. You can buy the damn things almost anywhere: sporting goods stores, gun dealers. All those *Soldier of Fortune*-type magazines advertise them, so there's not much chance of running this one down.

"We got a little lucky," Granados admitted. "Found a witness who saw the perp using the phone booth at a gas station on Fourth and Howard. He probably just finished his calls to the *Chronicle* and Central Station. The witness saw him leave the booth, stop as if to tie his shoe by the sewer grate. He was dumping the gun and the knife."

"Any prints turn up, Dave?" Ray Tracey queried, drawing a frown from Tilson.

"Nope. Not on Chris's gun. Not on the knife. Another interesting bit of information. The gun and the knife were in a holster. Not Chris's holster, he was still wearing his. The holster looked new. The metal snap on the holster had been removed. No metal. We figure he came into the Hall with the empty holster. He wanted to look like a cop. He's a real beauty. Crime lab is going over the phone booth, but you know what the chances are of anything turning up there."

"Zero," some said, amid several disappointed groans from the audience.

Tilson's voice dripped icicles: "Let the inspector finish his narrative before injecting any comments."

Granados grimaced, then said, "It was raining. Our informant is just so-so. He was involved in a car accident. Looking around for witnesses. Sees this guy in the booth. Best he can come up with is a male, could be white, nothing firm there, about six feet, maybe mid-forties to mid-fifties, wearing a hat and raincoat. No unusuals. Walks okay, no limp, nothing distinctive. Any questions?"

"Is the witness firm on the age?" Kordic asked.

Granados waved his hand slowly back and forth. "Like I say, Jack, I figure he's so-so, but he's definite that it wasn't some young kid. That's about as much as we can get. If he's right, I think we can kick out any theory of gang involvement." He gave a slight grin. "Unless we've got some new middle-aged gang I haven't heard about."

Tilson's next statement drew a chorus of moans and groans. "I've asked the FBI to assist in the investigation."

Of all the federal and state law enforcement agencies, the FBI was the least respected by the locals.

Tilson seemed surprised at the outburst. "Is there something I've missed?"

The temptation to give the question a definitive answer caused almost everyone in the room to bite down on their lips.

"That's all we've got," Granados said. "Maybe something will turn up from the phone booth, but I doubt it. This perp is slick. He had a reason for coming into the building. Somehow Chris got in his way. If anyone has any ideas, I'm all ears."

"Come to me first with any ideas you might have," Tilson insisted. "This meeting is now over."

Everyone stood in place, until Tilson was back in his office with the door closed, before descending on Granados and Pittman, wanting to know how they had developed the witness, who he was, and what they knew that they hadn't passed on to Tilson.

When Kordic got his turn at Granados, he asked about the accident, then said, "What about the other party? The one driving the other vehicle?"

"Barry interviewed her. *Nada*. Didn't see anyone. She was scared as hell, thought her husband would give her a bad time for hitting the truck, I guess. But you know what interests me?"

"Same thing that interests me, Dave. That nonmetallic knife. And the holster."

"You're right," Granados conceded. "That kicks out Tilson's goofy theory that a cop or a civilian who worked here at the Hall was involved."

Rocky Taylor came over and draped an arm around Kordic's shoulder while he looked at Dave Granados. "If you want my opinion, the phone call was a red herring. If your witness puts the caller up into middle age, then it's got nothing to do with gangs. If you're twenty-five, you're middle-aged in these gangs."

Granados pressed the butt of his hand to his forehead. "What about the bosses? The suppliers? The mob has got to be involved with these punks, Rock. You know that."

"Sure," Taylor agreed. "They're involved in bringing the stuff into the country. They use the gangs just like they've used the Hells Angels all these years. But they don't go around with a vendetta against cops."

"Could the caller have been the father of a gang member?" asked Kordic. "Maybe one who was killed recently?"

"No," insisted Taylor. "Why go through all this trouble? You take a good look at that knife? Not the kind I'd want to carve the Thanksgiving Day turkey with. Knife was for one reason only, to get by the metal detectors. If it was a gang killing, they'd just drive by and plug the beat man or riddle a radio car with automatic weapons. That's the way these punks operate."

Granados and Kordic nodded their heads in unison.

Taylor gave Kordic's shoulder a squeeze. "Speaking of punks, Jack. Tony Moreno has buried himself in a hole somewhere. Nobody's seen him around the neighborhood."

Lieutenant Wesley Tilson was waving at Kordic from Chris Sullivan's old office—Tilson's office now—his hand formed into a three-fingered claw.

Kordic sauntered over, closed the door behind him, and leaned casually against the door frame. "What's up, Lieutenant?"

"I don't recall inviting you to this conference," Tilson said stiffly. "I told you I don't want you working on the Sullivan investigation."

"There are some other cases I'm working on. I'm still a member of this detail."

Tilson planted his hands knuckles down on his desk. "Get out of here, Inspector. Stay out of my way. And stay off the Sullivan investigation. Handle whatever other matters that have been assigned to you. For now.

There are going to be a lot of changes around here. Soon. You'll be part of those changes, believe me."

"Thank you for your support," Kordic said sarcastically. He headed back to his desk, his attention drawn moments later by the slamming of the door as Tilson marched stiff-shouldered through the Homicide detail.

Within minutes the rest of the staff followed suit and Kordic had the room to himself.

He started a pot of coffee and began digging through his open-file caseload all over again.

At times like this he envied the detectives he saw on television: their ability to pull a rabbit out of a hat at the last moment, some small, overlooked clue that had evaded a small army of forensic experts and teams of inept investigators. Most of the cases Kordic had solved in his career were the result of simple, straight-forward, by-the-book investigations. The vast majority of people who find themselves under arrest for homicide do most of the work for the detectives. The woman who is tired of her husband battering her and beats him to death with a frying pan while he sleeps. The man who, after a beer or two too many, is suddenly fed up with his upstairs neighbor playing the stereo too loud at three in the morning and decides to end the problem with a hunting rifle. The addict who sees the bulge in his supplier's coat pocket as the answer to his dream, and uses a dirty syringe for a weapon. In cases like these the detective acts more like a bookkeeper than a policeman: compiling evidence and presenting it to the district attorney. The only question left for negotiation is what the charge will be. First-degree? Second-degree? Manslaughter?

The criminals who try to be clever usually aren't much better. They make mistakes. Stupid mistakes, for the most normal of human reasons: greed, lust, revenge, or their minds are clouded by drugs, alcohol, or missionary visions.

Then there are the ones who are simply dumb: leaving fingerprints on the murder weapon, compiling elaborate alibis that disintegrate under a close look. IQ seems to have little to do with the error of their ways.

Attorneys, accountants, professors, they almost all
make at least one glaring mistake. An East Bay police
officer figured he had a plan that would have driven
Columbo out of his raincoat. His wife's body was
found strangled in the family car, parked in a ghetto
area famous for gang wars, and the car had been spray-
painted with anti-police slogans. The cop had been a
twenty-year veteran who should have known better.
Gangs don't strangle their victims. Knives, guns, baseball bats, yes. But silk scarves? No. The officer's alibi
melted away like ice cream on hot asphalt.

The smart ones who got away with murder, and
there certainly were far too many of those, kept things
simple. Nothing exotic. No curare-tipped darts. No alibis that fell apart because there was a sudden power
outage to delay the prerecorded message set to go out
on the automatic telephone dialer at exactly such and
such a time. No bomb under the dash triggered by the
car's speedometer hitting the 70 mph mark. No. Keep
it simple. Find the victim's weakness. Then find a way
to have that weakness kill him. Or put him in a position to be killed.

"Smart kills" was the way Kordic's old partner,
Benny Munes, described them, and Kordic could never
remember having this many smart kills on his desk at
one time.

He started the routine that Munes had showed him
years ago, going through each file, making out a four-
by-five index card for each victim. Each suspect. Each
witness. Each contact. It took well over an hour. He
thumbed through each card, adding a fact, a description, a question.

He went through the cards several times, highlight-
ing the names in yellow. Then he shuffled them as if
they were a deck of playing cards and went through
them again. Sullivan's name came up first. Then Harry
Burris, then Joseph Rosenberg, then John Doe. John
Doe. His daughter. He felt responsible for her death.
What was her name? He looked at the card. Rose. He
killed Rose. Rose. Rosenberg. Connection? It was a
stretch.

Kordic heaved himself up from the chair and walked over to the coffee machine. He poured himself a cup as his mind wandered. His eyes came to rest on the office computer. Rosenberg. Rose. Rosenberg was a positive ID. A man who had covered up the Nazi tattoo with that of a rose. Would a man who went through all that trouble keep the same name? If not, what would he change it to?

Kordic punched the computer menu to access DMV information and typed in the name Joseph L. Rose, with the date of birth the Israeli Consulate had given him for Rosenberg. The screen pinged into format mode, and within seconds it printed out Joseph L. Rose, 145 Green Street, Coalinga, California. An exact hit on the date of birth. The height and weight looked right. Kordic squeezed his eyes shut, concentrating. Coalinga. What the hell did he know about Coalinga? Somewhere south. Had more earthquakes than almost anywhere in the world. And there was something about oil.

He went to the bookcase containing reverse directories and telephone books for the immediate Bay Area. Somewhere in the mess was an atlas. Or was supposed to be an atlas. He dug through the books, cursing lightly, finally finding a small touring guide put out by the National Automobile Club in 1972. Nothing like up-to-date research equipment, he mumbled to himself, thumbing the pages until he found the listing for Coalinga, in Fresno County, 191 miles south of San Francisco. Elevation 646 feet. Population 6,161, in the heart of one of the world's largest oil fields.

Kordic remembered driving by the town, maybe even stopping for lunch. There were small oil wells, looking like prehistoric beasts, rhythmically dipping their beaks into the parched brown earth.

He went back to his desk, dialed the operator, and got the correct area code for Coalinga, then dialed information. Rose had a listed number at the Green Street address. The phone rang twice, then a recorded message played, the voice male, old, gruff: "I'm out. Leave your name and number, or call the office."

But there was no mention of the office name. Kordic left a brief message and tried information again. Joseph L. Rose & Company did have a listing, but all he got was an answering machine advising that office hours were from eight to five. The voice was female this time. Kordic again left his name and number.

Damn. He was this close. He didn't want to wait for the morning. Back to telephone information. Coalinga had its own police force. He called the number. The man who answered the phone had a warm, crusty voice. "Sergeant Wilcox."

"This is Inspector Kordic, San Francisco Police Department. I'm trying to contact Joseph Rose or someone at his office. Would you know how I could get a hold of them? I've left messages at both the Rose house and the office, but I want to speak to someone now."

"You kiddin' me, buddy? You really with the S.F. cops?"

"Sure am. Any doubts, you can call me. The number is 553–1145."

"You sound serious enough. Whatcha want with that old bugger Joe?"

"You know Rose?" Kordic queried.

"Much as anyone does. He keeps himself pretty tight. Travelin' all the time. Goes all to hell and back."

"What type of business is he in?"

Wilcox spoke in a voice that seemed to come from his socks. "Oil. What else? Hell, he invented some damn thing that gets oil out of places where it's almost dry. Sideways drillin'. Instead of going down, he drills sideways, gets the stuff the other guy's missed. Then he got a patent on something that takes oil out of ice, up in those frozen places, like Alaska. Man's got more money than God. And he spends about as much as the good Lord does too. Tighter than Kelsey's nuts is old Joe. Keeps pretty much to himself."

"Have you seen the tattoo on his left arm?"

"The roses? Yeah. Kind of funny, when you think of it. Old Joe don't look like the kind to be tattooed, you know what I mean?"

"Sergeant, I've got a man lying on a slab in the morgue with a tattoo of roses on his right arm. His head and hands were chopped off before he was dumped into the ocean."

"Holy shit!" Wilcox responded sharply. "You stay by that number. I'll get Joe's secretary to call you."

Kordic went through two cups of coffee before the phone rang. A woman whose voice sounded similar to that on the Rose & Company office answering machine identified herself as Carol Foster and demanded to know what was going on.

Kordic gave her the same information he'd given to Sergeant Wilcox. "Underneath the rose tattoo was a set of numbers: 2036082. I traced those through the Israeli Consulate. They belonged to a Joseph L. Rosenberg."

"My God," the anguished voice of Carol Foster wailed. "That must be Joe. But it can't be. It simply can't be. I've been getting faxes from him. Not for a couple of days, but I'm sure he's all right."

"Faxes. Where from?"

"Russia," Foster said in a soft voice. "He's in Russia on business. There has to be a mistake."

Kordic swallowed a sudden vile taste at the back of his throat. The tattoo. It had to be Rose. "When did you last speak to him on the phone, Miss Foster?"

"Oh, he called several days ago. I didn't speak to him. He left a short message on the machine."

"Have you actually spoken to him? Directly?"

"Ah, no. No, I haven't. He's left a few messages. The time difference, you know. There's an eleven-hour difference."

Jack Kordic paced nervously from his desk to the coffee machine, then decided against pouring another cup. He was jumpy enough as it was. Rose-Rosenberg in Russia. Sending faxes. What the hell was going on? When the phone rang, he snapped a hand out for it.

"Kordic, Homicide."

"Is this Inspector Kordic?" The voice was dull, flat, devoid of animation.

"Yes, it is."

"This is Felix Lebeau. I'm Joseph Rose's attorney. Carol Foster said you called with some rather disturbing news."

"Yes, sir. We pulled a body out of the ocean." He described the body's condition and the coroner's investigation that led to the finding of the concentration camp numbers.

"That is Joseph," Lebeau conceded reluctantly. "He had the rose tattoo put over the numbers years and years ago. He was tired of answering questions about the numbers. Changed his name about the same time because he thought it would be better for business."

"If it is Mr. Rose in the morgue, then who is sending the faxes from Russia?"

"Good question, Inspector. Joseph has two fax numbers. One is for general business purposes, the other is unlisted, solely for his messages when he's out on the road doing business. I discussed this with Carol. They have a code, so she knows that the faxes are from Joseph. She said the messages looked very authentic. Asked the right questions. Maybe it's just a mistake. Maybe—" Lebeau stopped himself with a sigh. "The tattoo. No, it has to be Joseph."

Kordic said, "The condition of the body shows that he was tortured before he was killed. Whoever did it obviously questioned him pretty thoroughly. They could have gotten the fax codes. Could have made him tape some messages so they could leave them on the business answering machine after business hours. When his secretary wasn't there. Just what is he supposed to be doing in Russia?"

Lebeau paused a few moments. Kordic could picture him weighing the scales on client confidentiality and cooperating with the police. The scales tipped in Kordic's favor.

"Joseph was working on a job in Russia. Can't remember just where, one of those many-voweled places they have over there. He told me it would have been the biggest deal of his life, Inspector."

"Was he working with anyone else?"

"Yes, I think so. Joseph never told me much about the details of his actual work, but I know he felt quite confident about this one." He gave a dry chuckle. "He always felt confident."

Kordic lifted his eyes to the acoustical ceiling and grimaced. With that kind of money involved, how many suspects would there be? "Mr. Lebeau, quite honestly I don't know if I ever would have identified Mr. Rose if it weren't for another case I'm working on. That I think is related to Mr. Rose's death. There have been two attempts on a woman's life. The first by a man with the knife, the second by a young hoodlum named Pepe Fuentes, with a gun. The gun had a silencer. The silencer was made in Russia."

"Surely you don't think Joseph was involved with these people, Inspector?"

"I wish I knew. The attorney's name is Ariza. Mary Ariza. She works for a law firm here in San Francisco, Pontar and Kerr."

"I've never heard of any of these people," Lebeau responded. "And I handle all of Joseph's legal transactions. He was a businessman, Inspector, not some kind of a gangster."

"Yet we found his mutilated body in the ocean, and someone is faxing those messages from Russia, Mr. Lebeau. I'd like to see those faxes. And someone will have to come up here to identify him and claim his remains."

"You're right," Lebeau conceded. "I'll meet with Miss Foster this evening. I'll bring the messages and anything else I think will be of help. I probably won't be able to get to San Francisco until late tomorrow afternoon."

Kordic gave him the address for the Hall of Justice. "I'll be waiting for you," he said, hanging up the phone, then leaning back in his chair. Finally. One John Doe identified. But there was still the man in the street, the one Mary had helped, the one who had died in the hospital. He called San Francisco General Hospital, spoke to the medical records clerk—Dr. Wagner had officially pronounced the man dead. He was off duty, but the supervising nurse was working. Medical records transferred the call to ward four. Dixie Butler was the name of the supervising nurse. It took her awhile to recall the unidentified man who had died in Room 414C. "We get so many of them," she said apologetically. "But then you do too, don't you, Inspector? All I remember is that he seemed to be doing all right. I thought he was going to make it. A priest came to see him, I remember that."

"A priest? Did you get his name?"

"No," the nurse said in a tired voice. "Too bad he didn't stick around. Mr. Annuzio, an old man in the next bed, died a few hours later."

"This priest. You saw him?"

"Just briefly."

"What did he look like?"

"Ah, he was a dish, Inspector. Dark hair, very handsome."

Kordic thanked her, then broke the connection. A good-looking priest. Torres again. Torres. He'd bet his pension Torres was no priest. Had he killed the man at the hospital? Why? What would be his motive?

It had to have something to do with Mary. The man in the hospital. He must have told her something. Something important. Something that made Mary a target. Was she still a target? What would they do? Follow her from work. To Pontar's house. Pontar. He and his wife had invited Mary to the opera. They were there now. The Opera House. He grabbed his sports coat, patting the revolver in the holster on his hip to make sure the gun was in place.

Chapter 26

"We are ready, sir," Lieutenant Frank Harris assured Paul Abrams.

"Good," Abrams responded gruffly. He eyed Harris. A three hundred dollar tuxedo and the man still looked like a cop. The red bow tie lent a jarring note to the tuxedo, which is just what Abrams wanted. "Full crew tonight?"

"Yes, sir."

"Let's go, then."

"Ah, Mrs. Abrams coming with us?"

"Yes, have someone—"

Adele swept into the room. "I'm ready, Paul."

"All right, all right, then let's go," he responded frostily. He had other things on his mind. There were still a few items on the oil deal that needed tightening. He'd much rather stay home and work on those, but he was committed. They'd invited friends.

Abrams didn't like attending public functions. There were too many people. Too many things he couldn't control.

Adele laced her arm in his. "Smile, darling. We're going to have a good time."

A good time. That was a good description of his wife, Abrams concluded. A good-time girl. Only he was tiring of those times. At least with her.

Frank Harris held the back door of the Mercedes open for Abrams, then ran around to the passenger-side front seat, checking to make sure that the Ford Taurus with the two additional guards was behind them.

"Okay, Falore," he said once his seat belt was clicked on. "Next stop, the Opera House."

"You like?" Naimat asked, hands on hips as she paraded across the grimy kitchen tiles like a fashion model on a runway.

"Yeah, wonderful," Tony Moreno said in a forced tone. The dress was black, with shoulder pads and a pleated skirt. The neckline started with a wide V at the shoulders, narrowing down to barely an inch as it reached the belt line. Her wig was shoulder length, an inky black color.

Naimat scraped her nails cat-like across Moreno's cheek, then turned to Cesar Davila. "You are ready?"

"All set."

"Now are you going to tell me just what we're going to do?" demanded Moreno.

Naimat clicked her tongue across her teeth. "You are going to make a fortune, little Tony. Your *pinchis* are going to start a riot, just as you instructed them to do. Now, you just do as Cesar tells you. Go with him. Get the right man. Take him to the ambulance. There may be other injured people." Her smile was a rapid flash. "Many injured people. But we are only interested in one. Paul Abrams."

She saw the blank look on Moreno's face. "You have never heard of Abrams?"

Moreno shrugged and tucked in the corners of his mouth. "Nope. Who is he? Some big shot? What makes him worth all this trouble?"

It was amazing how little the pompous fool knew. Rene was right. He was perfect for his role. Naimat opened her purse and extracted a newspaper photograph of Paul Abrams. She handed it to Moreno. "That's our target. He's a rich man. One of the richest men in the world. A billionaire. Do you know how much money that is, Tony? Just follow Cesar's orders, and you'll do fine."

Moreno examined the photograph. The man didn't look all that important—just another old Anglo. He gave it back to Naimat, then went to the refrigerator for a beer.

Both Moreno and Davila were in their costumes: dark blue pants and white medi-jackets, the outside pockets stuffed with scissors, miniature flashlights, and pens. Their blue and white nylon caps had the universal paramedic star-of-life emblem on the crown. "Your last drink until it's over, Tony," Naimat said firmly. "Then you can party all you want." She turned her attention to Davila. "Let's go."

Naimat made a quick stop in the bedroom, picking up a full-length black mink coat. They all trooped down to the basement, where Naimat gave the van a final inspection. The emergency lights and ambulance identification panels were neatly stacked in the back, along with a portable aluminum gurney complete with crossing black Velcro straps, a bright red plastic case stuffed with assorted bandages, clamps, and first-aid dressings. The final piece of medical equipment was a knee-high black plastic case containing a portable resuscitator, complete with oxygen tank and various-sized resuscitation masks. She had watched Moreno and Davila drill on the unit throughout the afternoon, until she was satisfied they looked professional.

"We're ready," Naimat said, climbing into the back of the van.

"I hope you're enjoying yourself," Mary Pontar said, handing Mary Ariza a flute filled with champagne.

"It's wonderful." Ariza looked around at the spectacularly dressed crowd. The men all wore tuxedos, a good many with tails. The women created a kaleidoscope in their colorful gowns, most set off with jewelry of the type associated with movie stars at the Academy Award ceremonies. She felt slightly underdressed in her charcoal gray crinkled satin ballerina dress and pearls, but it would have to do.

Matt Pontar steered his way through the crowd, one hand clutching two champagne glasses, the other a plate filled with hors d'oeuvre: oysters on the half shell, crustless sandwiches the size of silver dollars, crackers heaped with calorie-laden temptations. "Help me with these, ladies. That's real caviar on those little crackers. At these prices, it sure as hell should be."

Mary helped herself to a bite-sized cracker piled high with the glossy black-gray fish eggs.

Pontar wolfed down several of the crackers, found a waiter passing by, deposited his empty glass, and went to work on a full one. "Better stoke up, girls. Nothing to eat until intermission."

Someone jarred Mary Ariza's arm, causing her champagne glass to tip and spill wine onto the marble floor.

"Sorry," said a crisp voice.

Mary Ariza turned to see a handsome young man in a tuxedo and red tie hurry by, his head twisting rapidly from side to side.

"The celebrities have arrived," Matt Pontar announced in a TV anchorman's voice. "That's Paul Abrams and his latest wife. Not bad, huh?"

"Trophy wife," Mary Pontar chided. "Don't get any ideas, Matthew."

Mary Ariza studied the woman in the clinging gold lamé dress, her tawny hair spilling down to her shoulders. Trophy indeed. She'd read about Paul Abrams in the newspapers. Multi-billionaire. He didn't look all that impressive: tufts of curly gray hair interrupted by a small bald spot in the back, an overlong red handkerchief flopping out of the tuxedo's breast pocket.

"He's got his full troop of bodyguards with him," Matt Pontar said. "Got him surrounded."

Mary Ariza noticed the four tuxedoed men shepherding the Abramses across the room. All were wearing red ties. Three of them looked out of place, as if they'd be more comfortable in Levi's and T-shirts than in the restricting, penguin-like tuxedos. The fourth man, the one who'd bumped into her, he looked right at home.

"Man's a fanatic about security," continued Pontar. "Won't leave home without 'em. Seeing his wife, I'm starting to understand why."

"Stop drooling and get us some more champagne," Mary Pontar instructed, holding out an empty glass to her husband.

Adele Abrams smiled widely as her husband introduced her to an elderly woman with hair so black it had hints of blue in it. Sarah somebody or other. The poor thing almost curtsied as Adele held out her hand. She did feel like a queen, especially when a line of men stood there waiting for her. She inhaled and bent over just a little at each handshake, watching their eyes trail from hers down to her throat and down to her breasts, which were pushed up halfway out of the dress. Paul must be loving this. She wondered if he was hard already. She'd find out when they got to their seats.

"So nice to meet you, Mrs. Abrams," a scholarly looking man with long white hair and a large condor nose was saying, pumping her hand while watching the jiggling of her breasts.

"My pleasure. I hope you're enjoying the evening."

He leaned forward, his eyes peering down the huge nose. "Not as much as Paul is, I'm sure," he said, releasing her hand but not before trailing a finger across her palm.

Why, you dirty old man, thought Adele as she turned to the next party in line. Another senior citizen, but a handsome specimen, with a profile that belonged on a postage stamp. His neatly barbered gray hair was rigorously brushed, with the gleam of chromium.

"This is Dr. Larsen, darling," Paul Abrams said. "You remember Bill."

Adele did indeed. He had given her a very thorough examination prior to the wedding.

"I'm in your box, so to speak," Larsen said, flashing a set of deep dimples. "At least we're sitting together for the performance. Do you enjoy opera, Adele?"

"I'm sure I'll enjoy this one."

Her husband cupped a hand on her elbow. "Let's get seated. We'll have champagne sent to the box."

* * *

Had Mary Ariza kept her eyes on the Abrams grouping just a few seconds longer, she might have recognized a dark-haired man, his arm on the elbow of a sleek, exotic-looking woman in a flowing mink coat. Both trailed just a few yards behind the Abramses. Rene Santos's fingers tightened on Naimat's arm. "Trouble," he hissed, steering Naimat toward a crowd waiting in line for the bar, effectively melting into the tuxedo background.

"What's the problem?" Naimat asked nervously.

"It's Mary Ariza. She's there. Directly behind my back. With the gray-haired man and a woman in red over by the staircase."

Naimat narrowed her eyes, finding her quarry. "What a stroke of bad luck," she said, then regretted it immediately, knowing how superstitious Rene was. "Actually, it could be good luck. I can finish her tonight."

Santos bulged his lower lip with his tongue. "Yes, you do just that. I'll stick with Cesar and Moreno when they come in. You kill Ariza, then meet the ambulance as we planned. Are you ready?"

Naimat patted her hands lightly against her billowy skirt, feeling the hard edges of a small gun and a cellular phone. Rene and Naimat were carrying identical weapons: model 950 Beretta .25 semi-automatics, eight shells in the clip, one in the chamber. The gun was four and a half inches in length, the silencer screwed onto the barrel adding just three more inches to the finished product, which weighed less than eleven ounces.

"Yes," Naimat answered in a husky voice. "I'm ready."

Santos edged around slowly so that he could see Mary Ariza out of the corner of his eye. "You're sure about Davila and Moreno?"

"They're prepared. Cesar is too scared not to do the job, and Moreno is too stupid to back out now." She paused a moment, waiting for Santos to focus back on her. "I can have Moreno tonight?"

"In the ambulance, for all I care," Santos said indifferently.

"And Cesar?"

"As soon as Abrams is safely tucked away. For now, stick close to the Ariza woman. See where she's sitting. Kill her after the bombs go off, then meet Cesar. I'll find out where the bodyguards stray to when the curtain goes up."

Cesar Davila nosed the van into the driveway of a closed auto-repair shop on Grove Street, one block west of the Opera House. He'd skirted the building and found that parking any closer was impossible. Rene had gone over the driving plan with him in detail. As usual, Rene had been right. The front entrance on Van Ness Avenue would be littered with double-parked limousines. The private parking area off Franklin Street reserved for the fat cats, Opera House working staff, and entertainers was jammed. The entrance route would be right down Grove, through the private courtyard. Several security guards were stationed there who would escort them into the lot.

There was nothing to do now but wait for Rene's call. He goosed the accelerator, watching the dashboard voltage gauge rise. Moreno's face was a mere silhouette in the dashboard lighting. The phone rang.

Rene Santos said one word: "Now."

Davila pushed the disconnect button, then handed the machine to Moreno. "Call your people. But boss's orders. Put the speaker on. I want to listen to every word."

Moreno's hands were clenched together so tightly that the knuckles were whitened. He snatched the phone from Davila. "When am I going to meet this famous boss of yours? *Vato* acts like he's too good to see me. Sends that bitch instead." He leaned forward in his chair and began punching the phone's buttons. "Listen in all you want, but I'm warning you, and that dyke and your fucking boss, if you don't deliver what you promised, you'll never get out of this town alive."

* * *

Rene Santos knew just where the Abrams party was heading. The small, select boxes could sit from six to eight people in comfort. And Abrams was certainly a man who enjoyed his comfort. Santos walked up the marble staircase to the mezzanine and into the prime box, N1, at center stage. He was interested in what the bodyguards would do once the Abramses were inside the box. He milled around the crowd, watching as Mrs. Abrams flirted with a tall, handsome gray-haired man. Abrams himself was deep in conversation with an old man with stooped shoulders, seemingly oblivious to his wife's behavior.

The bodyguards kept in their diamond-like formation: one in front of the group, two alongside, one in the rear. They looked relaxed. Except for the young one, the one Naimat said was having his way with Mrs. Abrams. He looked tight. Nervous. Why? Santos wondered. A lovers' quarrel? Upset at the sight of Mrs. Abrams spilling out of her dress, batting her long eyelashes at all the other men? Or something else? Something that could be a problem?

The three other guards were all in their late forties or early fifties. One was tall and lean with a military-style crewcut. The other two had beer bellies, one red-faced, the other ill-looking, his face pale, beads of sweat on his forehead. Santos weighed the possibilities. Sick? Some kind of flu? Or was there trouble in the ranks? A dispute with the young, nervous one?

The Abrams party entered the box, followed within a minute by a white-jacketed waiter carrying a tray holding two bottles of champagne in sweating ice buckets. The bodyguards began milling around. When the waiter came out they started talking. Santos edged in closer.

"You look a little nervous," Frank Harris said to Larry Falore. "What's the problem?"

The problem was Adele Abrams. Falore wished he hadn't gotten involved with her. What he told Harris was that his wife was having trouble with her pregnancy. "Doctor told her not to worry, but this is our first. You know how it is."

"Do I ever," interjected Dick Clancy. "We've had six. None of them were easy. Told Annie I'd get myself fixed, but she wouldn't buy it. Must be the only woman in San Francisco that still goes by what the big guy in Rome says."

Harris turned his attention to the third officer, Phil Mifsud. "You don't look so good, buddy."

Mifsud massaged his stomach. "Lunch. Mexican. Too much hot stuff. I'll be all right. How long is this damn thing going to go on, Frank?"

"After the opera we go back to the house. Big party. Could be a long night." He checked his watch. "There should be an intermission in about an hour and a half. No sense all of us standing around here. I'll take the first shot. One of you come and relieve me in half an hour. We'll work shifts till intermission. We all better be back here then. They'll be parading around, showing off. Tinkle time. Abrams will want to see all of us."

Mifsud rubbed his stomach again. "Maybe something to drink will help. Something carbonated."

Clancy clapped his hands together. "Sounds like you're describing that fancy French bubble water they're handing out downstairs. Let's go get a sample."

Rene Santos sauntered along behind the three policemen, watching them disappear down the staircase. He took a position in an alcove, pulled a wallet-sized cellular phone from his pocket, punched in a number, and, after hearing Cesar Davila's voice, said, "It's time. Understood?"

"Understood," came that staticky reply.

The usher looked at Jack Kordic with suspicion. The badge appeared to be authentic, but he'd been fooled before. The man's dress certainly seemed to indicate that he was a policeman: tweed sports coat, tie loosened under a button-down collar. Not exactly opera togs.

"Well, Inspector, I can let you in, but I'm afraid you'll have to wait in the lobby area. We don't allow standing in the aisle areas."

"No problem," Kordic said, slipping through the door, giving the usher a scornful look. Probably working for minimum wage and acts like he's a beefeater guarding England's crown jewels.

There were several dozen people loafing about the lobby area, all elegantly dressed in tuxedos and evening gowns, glasses in hand, faces flushed from the wine and the excitement of the event.

An attractive olive-skinned woman with the name Marci stenciled on her white plastic name tag sat alone at the opera house box office.

Kordic showed her both his badge and his best smile. "Would you happen to know just where Mr. Pontar's seats are?"

A worried look flooded her eyes. "Is there a problem?"

"No, not really. I have to ask one of his guests a few questions. It can wait until intermission, but I thought if I knew where they were seated, I could find them easier."

"Pontar. That would be Matthew Pontar, right?"

"That's the man," Kordic agreed, watching as she began thumbing through a Rolodex.

"Yes, here it is. He has seats in the upper level. That's on the third floor." She read off the seat numbers. "Almost everyone leaves their seats at intermission, Inspector."

Kordic thanked her and wandered back to the lobby area. Horseshoe-shaped tables were covered in what earlier in the evening had been snowy white cloths. Now the covers were wrinkled and smeared with sauces and bread crumbs. He took in the remains of the elaborately prepared food. Tiger prawns draped around a huge glass bowl. Silver chafing dishes with discreet labels showing the contents to be curried chicken, petrale almondine, quail with herb sauce, and roast goose with new potatoes. Large platters that had once been filled with miniature stuffed tomatoes and canapes of all shapes and sizes were now bare, save a few broken pieces of crust and pillow-sized piles of empty oyster shells. An elaborately carved ice figurine of a long-necked swan with extended wings was melting slowly, the intricate bird's features taking on a bland, glassy appearance.

The caterer must have over-ordered on the shrimp, because Kordic was sure he recognized the two men at the shrimp bowl as no great fans of opera. One was patiently taking shrimp after shrimp from the iced bowl, dipping it into the thick, creamy red sauce, then into his mouth.

"What are you two bums doing here?" he asked, causing Dick Clancy to drop a shrimp on the table.

"Hey, Jack, how's it going?" Clancy reached for another shrimp. "Have something to eat. Not much left." He looked at his partner. "Poor Phil's got a tummy ache. Can't enjoy all this high-cholesterol stuff."

"Hi, Jack," Mifsud said. "What's up? You're not dressed for the occasion."

"I'm working," Kordic replied. "What the hell are you two guys doing, all dressed up in gorilla suits?"

"We've been working for Frank Harris. You know him? Lieutenant at Ingleside. He's got a steady hobby-lobby detail on Paul Abrams, the rich oil guy." He shrugged his shoulders. "Hell, easy money. Not much of it, but it's easy." He pointed to a tall young man at the end of the counter, quietly sipping from a champagne glass. "Hey, Larry. Come over and meet Jack Kordic."

Mifsud supplied the introductions while Kordic and Falore shook hands.

"Yeah," Clancy said, reaching for another of the large shrimp, which would bring his total to an even dozen so far. "This isn't a bad detail, Jack. What are you working on?"

Kordic was about to reply when he heard the explosion. A roar echoed through the lobby. Kordic jammed his hands over his ears. The chandeliers were rocking, causing the lights to flicker. The whole building shook. Later he would testify that he thought he heard two separate explosions, possibly three, before the overpowering sound of the crash.

Chapter 27

Cesar Davila attached the magnetized red emergency lights to the van's top while Tony Moreno fastened the ambulance emblems to each door.

"Come on, come on," Davila urged nervously. "Let's go." He maneuvered the shift lever into the drive position, and the van jerked away from the curb before Moreno was safely back in his seat.

"We're rolling now," Davila said into the cellular phone. "Two blocks away."

"Good," Santos said into the open line. He held a palm over the cellular phone, picked up the pay phone, and dialed 911. "This is an emergency," he said in a slow, clear voice. "A man has just suffered a heart attack. Send an ambulance to the Van Ness side of the Opera House immediately." He repeated the instructions, then hung up. Santos put the cellular phone to his ear, his foot tapping on the marble floor. He could hear the van's engine racing. Finally Davila's voice came over the line.

"Pulling in now. Guard's coming out to see us."

"Remember the parking," Santos said calmly. "Park in a spot where you can get out quickly. Come up to the mezzanine level."

"Right, right." Davila slipped the phone into his breast pocket.

Santos was able to monitor Davila's progress, hearing the big man's labored breathing, the slamming of the van's door. The voice of a security guard.

"Whatcha guys got?"

"Heart attack. Mezzanine level. It came over the radio. We were a block away."

"Shit, man. They just alerted us that there was an ambulance coming to the front," complained the guard. "This another one?"

"Sure is." There was the sound of the van's back door sliding open, then Davila's impatient voice: "Get the gurney. I'll bring the oxygen."

The guard again: "You're blocking the road there, man."

"We'll be out in a minute, pal. Let's go," Davila called to Moreno.

Santos was waiting halfway down the steps leading to the mezzanine. When he caught sight of Davila, he turned and headed upstairs, one hand casually sliding into his pants pocket and pushing the detonator button, setting off the Frangex explosives he had put in place earlier.

Domonica Anzido was already feeling the strain from the tight corsetting that the wardrobe department insisted she wear for her role as Carmen. She regretted the rather large lunch she'd enjoyed at the Aqua restaurant. But who could even think of leaving one spoonful of the classic paella with chorizo broth? That, along with the cigar and red wine breath of the overrated baritone playing Escamillo, had been enough to give her a splitting headache. At least the headache took her mind off the stabbing pain from the corset. She closed her eyes, leaned back, and began her aria just as the explosions went off.

She stopped, frozen in place, one arm thrown out to its fullest extent, the other folded across her forehead. The full weight of the eighty-thousand-pound steel and asbestos fire curtain dropped within four feet of her, crushing the stage and throwing Domonica into one of the cramped torpedo rooms behind the orchestra pit.

The thirty-six members of the orchestra and the occupants of the first twenty-five rows of main-floor seats were saved from death when the massive fire curtain crashed through the stage flooring and continued through to the basement, tipped backward toward the stage, becoming entangled in netting curtains and rigging before powering its way to the ground. The fire curtain trapped several costumed extras and stage hands as it ripped its way through the maze of electrical wiring and fifty-year-old circuit boards, causing several fires to erupt simultaneously. The curtain broke into giant jigsaw puzzle pieces, sending a cement and asbestos dust cloud flowing through the Opera House, filling the air and the eyes of the people fleeing their seats in panic. One thought seemed to enter into everyone's mind. Earthquake. The big one. Screams erupted as the herd instinct took over, sending patrons climbing over chairs and one another's backs.

Lieutenant Frank Harris was as confused as anyone. The door to the Abramses' box burst open, Adele Abrams leading the charge. He saw Paul Abrams following behind his wife. Harris grabbed Abrams by the arm and was about to yell into his ear when a knife blade went into his ribs. He arched his back to scream, but fell to the ground before uttering a sound. Paul Abrams felt an arm pull him away, then a sharp pain as Rene Santos shoved a syringe into his back. There was a sudden rush of heat to his head and stomach, a feeling akin to sudden seasickness. Then everything started spinning, and he felt his legs go out.

Santos stowed the syringe back in his jacket pocket. "I'm a doctor," he shouted. "Let us through." He put a shoulder under Abrams's arms and lugged him back into the box seating area, letting him fall with a thud to the carpet.

"What's going on?" someone cried out. Santos turned to see the concerned face of the handsome gray-haired gentleman Adele Abrams had been flirting with.

"Passed out. Looks like it could be his heart. I'm a doctor, give us some room."

The man knelt down beside Abrams. "Well, I'm Paul's personal physician." His hands went to Abrams's shirt, undoing the bow tie. "Paul's never had any problems with his heart. We've got to get him out of here."

Santos arms moved swiftly, accurately, driving the knife blade into Larsen's chest. He reached down, effortlessly picked the body up, and deposited it over the back of one of the Opera House chairs. Cesar Davila entered the room with Tony Moreno. Moreno looked as if he'd bolt at any moment. He stared at Santos. Then he saw the knife.

Rene slipped the knife back into its sheath. "Quick! Get moving! Get him on the gurney!"

Moreno stood there open-mouthed. Santos slapped him across the face. "Move it!"

Davila gave Moreno a hand with the gurney, unfolding it, snapping the rubber-wheeled legs into place. Then, with Santos's help, they loaded the unconscious body of Paul Abrams onto the gurney, strapping him in, then covering his face with the oxygen mask.

"Let's go! Let's go!" Santos shouted.

"Wait," Davila complained. "The oxygen. I've got to turn the damn thing on, or he'll suffocate."

Rene reached for the regular knob, twisted it, and watched to see the foggy mask clear, see Abrams's chest begin moving at a regular pace. "Get him out of here, Cesar. Now."

They wheeled Abrams out to the mezzanine, now empty, deserted except for the bloody body of Frank Harris.

When they came to the stairs, they had to lift the gurney, the powerful Davila taking the front, Moreno the rear.

"Man's too fucking heavy," Moreno complained, wincing at the effort it took to keep Abrams in a level position.

Rene Santos grabbed the gurney's railing, elbowing Moreno out of the way. "Give Cesar a hand," he commanded.

Moreno dutifully went to the front, again staring at the man in the tuxedo who had pushed him away. Old bastard. Must be forty or fifty, but strong as hell. The boss. The big boss, finally.

The stairwell was a wall-to-wall mass of terrified men and women, and they had to bull their way into the crowd, swinging the gurney as if it were a battering ram.

"Emergency, emergency," Santos screamed as loudly as he could. "Let us through."

Four men, three in tuxedos and red bow ties, were waiting at the bottom of the stairs, trying to wade through the mob, frantically scanning faces as the flood of people rushed by, then broke into a run once free of the confines of the stairwell.

Santos recognized Abrams's three bodyguards. The fourth man, dressed in a sports coat, was the policeman Kordic! He recognized him from the photograph he'd seen in the desk at the Homicide detail. Kordic! What the hell was he doing here? "Go, go, go," he urged, heaving a sigh of relief as they reached the ground floor and were able to set the gurney down.

A group of firemen came rushing in, breathing tanks on, carrying axes and coiled lines of thick canvas hose. One of the firemen stood at the door, holding it open for Davila and Moreno, as Santos backed away, blending into the crowd, making his way outside. Davila and Moreno wheeled Abrams directly to the ambulance. Santos shadowed their moves, eyeing the crowd, looking for problems.

Davila and Santos had the back doors of the ambulance open, and were jockeying the gurney inside when a uniformed policeman grabbed Davila by the shoulder.

"I've got several more injured people. Give me a hand, we'll put 'em on board."

"Can't," Davila said quickly. "This guy is critical. I've got to get him to the hospital right away."

"Shit," the cop exclaimed, taking off his cap and wiping a gloved hand across his forehead. "I've got a half-dozen seriously injureds over here. A couple were damn near trampled to death. Give me some help!"

Santos edged closer, his hand closing around the butt of his gun.

Davila waved an arm in appeasement to the officer. "Okay. Go do what you can do. I'll be there soon as I get this man sedated."

The officer nodded in thanks and took off at a jogging pace.

Moreno caught sight of the boss and gave him a thumbs-up signal.

Get in the vehicle and get out of here, you idiot, Santos said to himself.

Davila jumped behind the wheel while Tony Moreno climbed into the back of the ambulance, closing the doors behind him.

The uniformed policeman saw the ambulance start up and began running toward it. Rene jumped in front of him and said, "Officer, there's a man inside bleeding to death. Someone said he was a policeman."

The officer stopped, following the ambulance with his eyes as Davila weaved through small clusters of people who were staring at the Opera House as if expecting it to come tumbling down at any moment.

"Fuckin' idiot," the cop swore. "I'm going to turn that prick in. I want you to be a witness." He turned to look for the dark-haired man in the tuxedo, but he was gone. "Another prick," he said, hitching up his belt and hurrying toward the door leading into the Opera House.

Mary Ariza had found that she wasn't as fond of opera as she had thought. She began wondering how long until intermission. How long it would be until it was over, and she would meet Jack Kordic at Stars.

Matt Pontar seemed to have little affinity for the opera at all. His head would nod toward his chest, then jerk up as if a puppet master were pulling his strings. Mary Pontar sat enraptured, her lips silently moving along with those of the performers on stage.

The explosions jerked Matt Pontar out of his daze. By the time the fire curtain had plunged to the stage, he was on his feet, a hand at his wife's shoulder. "Let's move, but stay together," he commanded in a strained voice. "Stay close, both of you. Don't fall to the floor, whatever you do."

He had an aisle seat and they were only six rows from the exit stairs, so they made it safely to the third-floor reception area without too much of a struggle. People were moving slowly at first, but there were scattered screams. When someone yelled, "Earth-quake!" it was as if the crowd was energized, the panic a visible thing, infecting everyone like an unseen virus.

Mary Ariza felt herself being pushed and pulled in all directions. Matt Pontar's hand stayed clasped to her shoulder like a vise. "Stay together, stay together, don't panic," he kept shouting. The stairway acted like a funnel, compressing the crowd into a tube of fright-ened humans. An elderly woman fell in front of Mary, and she stooped to help her to her feet, but the crowd pushed her forward, with the steady, unrelenting force of an ocean wave.

She heard someone yelling, "Mary, Mary," behind her, but she didn't have the room or the strength to turn around to see who it was, if it was really her they were calling to. The crowd came to a sudden, lurching halt as the groups from the third floor merged into those fleeing the dress-circle seats on the second floor, who in turn were running into patrons on the mezzanine. A feeling of claustrophobia came over Mary as she stood still, pushing, leaning into the heavyset man in front of her. She turned to see Matt Pontar. He gave her a quick wink, and she experienced a great feeling of relief. They were going to make it. They were going to get out. Suddenly the crowd started moving again, like a train engine, slowly at first, then picking up speed.

Again someone called out, "Mary." She ignored it, concentrating on moving down the steps, down and out to freedom. They passed the second floor in a rush, quickly down to the mezzanine level, where again the crowd stopped momentarily, as if running out of gas, then spurted forward, the pace increasing, until they were running toward the street level, where there was room to separate, to hurry without fear of stepping on the person in front, or worse, being caught from be-hind, falling to the ground. She thought briefly of the woman who had fallen in front of her on the third floor. Had someone else pulled her to her feet? She didn't want to imagine what could have happened if they had not.

Matt Pontar finally released his grip on Mary's

shoulder. She looked over to thank him, trying to get the words out, but she found she was out of breath, winded, as if she'd run a marathon. She bent over and dropped her hands to her knees, drawing in big draughts of air. Again someone called, "Mary."

She turned to see who it was. Mary Pontar turned at the same time, leaning on her husband, stepping in front of Mary Ariza.

"Wha—" was all Mary Pontar had time to say before the pain hit her chest.

Matt Pontar stared at his wife in horror as blood began spilling from her dress. He clutched her, his eyes raking the crowd. He saw a dark woman in a fur coat holding something in her hand, a look of hatred on her face. It was a gun. Or was it? He started toward her but stopped, feeling his wife slipping from his grip. "Mary. Mary. For God's sake, what happened?"

Chapter 28

The night air was filled with the ululating sirens of police, fire, and ambulance units rushing toward the Opera House.

Cesar Davila wrenched the wheel of the van to the right to avoid a group of slack-faced civilians standing alongside the wooden barriers the police had set up along the promenade leading to the Opera House's side entrance.

Davila jammed one hand on the horn, skidding into a right turn onto Franklin Street, barreling through a red light at Golden Gate. He took a looping left turn from the middle lane onto Turk Street, causing a red pickup to swerve to his left and into a parked car.

"Easy, man, easy," Tony Moreno yelled from the back of the van. "This hombre's sliding all over the place." He braced his feet against the van's wall in an attempt to keep the rubber-wheeled gurney from rolling free.

Davila doused his lights, then pulled into an open parking spot alongside Hayward Playground. He kept his eyes fixed on the side-view mirror for a full minute. When he was satisfied that no one had followed him, he exited the front seat, ran to the rear doors, and opened them.

Tony Moreno stared at him with a silly grin. "We made it, man. We made it," he said. "Help me hook this sled to the wall.

Davila jerked a thumb at him as he removed the emergency lights from the roof. "Get the ambulance signs off. Throw them back in here." He climbed into the back of the van as Moreno jumped out. Paul

Abrams still had the oxygen mask covering his face. Davila ripped the mask off, his finger going to Abrams's neck, finding a steady pulse.

Tony Moreno threw the ambulance signs onto the van's carpeted flooring. "Let's go, man. Let's get the fuck out of here."

"In a minute," Davila said. "We've got to make sure Abrams is okay."

Tony Moreno waited until Davila had fastened the gurney to the van's wall before smashing an oxygen tank over his head. Davila's huge body twitched, as if he'd been electrocuted, then he sank slowly to his knees, and Moreno gave him another whack with the oxygen tank. Davila fell to the floor and Moreno quickly frisked him, removing a knife and small automatic pistol.

He stepped over the unconscious body of Cesar Davila, locked the back doors, then ran back to the driver's-side door, glancing at the luminous dials of his wristwatch as he climbed onto the seat.

They were due to pick up Naimat at the corner of Laguna and Fulton streets in two minutes. He drove away slowly, his eyes swiveling back and forth to each of the side-view mirrors. Naimat was waiting at the corner, her hands in the pockets of her mink coat.

Moreno rolled down his window. "Get in the back. Abrams is having trouble breathing. See what you can do."

Naimat started to protest. One hand was stuck in the pocket of her mink coat, wrapped around the butt of her pistol. Her plan had been to kill Moreno right away, then Cesar Davila once they had Abrams tucked away in the safe house.

She kept her right hand on the gun butt as she reached for the rear door handle. The sound of the engine revving up didn't bother her; Moreno would be anxious to pull away as soon as she was in the van.

Tony Moreno kept one foot on the brake as the other pushed the accelerator to the floor. When Naimat disappeared from sight, he slammed the gear selector into reverse, the van's tires burning rubber as it shot backward. He could hear the sound of a heavy thump over the screaming of the engine, feel the rear wheels roll over a body. He continued backward for twenty yards, Naimat's crumpled body squarely in the headlights as he eased the car into low gear and again tramped on the accelerator. He wasn't sure if it was his imagination, but it appeared as if her head rose a fraction just before she disappeared under the bumper.

Mary Ariza tried to make sense of the scene unfolding before her. Matt Pontar was suddenly supporting his wife, arms around her waist, lowering her to the floor.

"What happened, Matt?" she asked, bending down, her eyes suddenly fastening on the blood that covered the front of Mrs. Pontar's dress, the blood on her husband's hands.

"A doctor. Get a doctor, damn it!" Matt Pontar bellowed as he dropped to one knee, his hands ripping the top of his wife's dress away, searching for the cause of bleeding. He looked at Mary Ariza, his face drained of color. "Someone shot her, Mary. A woman shot her." He tilted his head back and yelled again, "Doctor, get a doctor, please!"

Mary quickly knelt down beside him, her hands opening the now torn dress, finding a thickening puddle of blood between Mrs. Pontar's breasts. She dug in her purse for a handkerchief, pressing down on the center of the still seeping path of blood. Mary Pontar's face had gone grainy white, her once bright eyes now looking like raisins thumbed deeply into cookie dough. She tried to speak, causing bubbles of blood to spill from her lips.

Ariza turned to Matt Pontar. His eyes were glazed, his breathing ragged. "Stay with her. I'll get help." She struggled to her feet, and began to run. She caught sight of an ambulance crew carrying a stretcher out the side entrance door. She called to them, her voice drowned out by the nervous uproar of the still stunned crowd. The ambulance crew disappeared from sight, but Mary kept after them, all the while chanting: "Help. We need a doctor. Help."

She saw a uniformed police officer out of the corner of her eye and ran to him. "Inside. A woman's been shot. She's bleeding. We can't stop it."

The officer, a tall, muscular man in his early thirties, tilted his cap back and brought a portable radio to his lips. "Shot? Are you sure? I've got people hurt all over the place, ma'am. We've got calls in to ambulances. There're some firemen outside. I'll see what I can do. Where's your victim?"

Mary turned back toward the auditorium. "Inside. Down to the right. She's bleeding very badly."

The policeman held the radio up to his mouth. "A shooting. That's all we need."

Jack Kordic hadn't performed crowd-control duty since his rookie year in the police department. But that's what he felt like he was doing as he attempted to calm the crowd and direct them toward the exits. The flow of humans down the staircase reminded him of the one time in his life when he'd been on an airplane when a bomb threat came in.

He had been escorting a felon back from New Orleans at the time. Kordic always felt, but could never prove, that the person who made the call did so on behalf of the prisoner. That there was some type of escape plan involved. Nothing ever came of the attempt, but he still remembered the chaos, the helpless feeling as women and children were pushed out of the way by large men who only minutes earlier had been polite passengers reading books or magazines, or dozing. When the bomb threat was announced by the stewardess just minutes prior to landing at San Francisco International Airport, the first grumblings of panic were heard. The flight crew did an excellent job of calmly explaining the evacuation system. Longtime flight veterans who routinely ignored the emergency brochures at takeoff time began speed-reading the laminated crash-survival instructions from the seat pockets in front of them. There was a deathly silence as the airplane made a perfect landing on the runway. Kordic could still remember the sight of bright yellow airport fire engines chugging after the plane as it taxied to a designated spot. Once the plane came to a complete stop, the doors were opened and the emergency chutes inflated. Then everything broke loose: screams, pushing, shoving, fights, the crush to make it to the exits, the patient faces of the flight crew, yelling for everyone to remain calm, just as Kordic was yelling now. And with about as much effect.

He tried looking for Mary Ariza. Wondering where she was now. If she was still upstairs. If there still was an upstairs. The explosions had shaken the building to its foundations. He briefly saw an ambulance crew carrying a victim out and wondered how they'd gotten there so fast. Then, within a few minutes, it was over, the stairway almost empty. He, Falore, Dick Clancy, and Phil Mifsud ran up the stairs.

"Let's check the box first," Mifsud said, puffing at the effort of taking two steps at a time. The corridor was deserted. The heels of their shoes made gun-like barks on the marble as they raced to the Abramses' box.

"Jesus Christ, it's Frank," Clancy said, bending down, a hand going to Lieutenant Frank Harris's side, then pulling back as if it had touched a hot stove. "He's dead. For Christ's sake, Frank's dead."

Falore didn't believe him until he dropped to a knee and felt for a pulse. "What the hell is going on?"

"Where's Paul Abrams?" demanded Clancy. "Where the hell did he go?"

Kordic's eyes blurred as he looked at Harris. Another policeman killed. Sullivan and now Harris. Was Abrams the catalyst? Had Abrams been the target all along? What the hell did Mary Ariza have to do with Paul Abrams?

The car was parked in a red zone three blocks away on Golden Gate Avenue. Rene Santos was striding at a steady pace, covering a lot of ground without appearing to be in a hurry. He waited until he was a full block away from the Opera House before pausing to take the cellular phone from his pocket and call Davila in the van. Busy. He clicked off, then quickly redialed, obtaining the same results. He then dialed Naimat's number. Busy. He began walking, his index finger repeatedly pushing the redial button until he was at the car. Still busy. He ran the van again. Busy. Maybe there was something wrong with the phone.

Of all the recent additions to the terrorists' arsenal, Santos considered the cellular phone to be the best. Easily attainable, the phones could be purchased almost anywhere. A number set up with the local phone company in minutes. Instant communication. The only problems with the phones were that anyone with a rudimentary knowledge of electronics could listen in, and their unreliability, especially in hilly locales such as San Francisco. Was that what was happening?

Was that why he couldn't get through to Davila or Naimat? Possible, but unlikely. He saw the lights of a restaurant ahead: Stars. He went inside. The two pay phones at the front entrance were in use, each with a line of two or three people waiting their turn. Many of the patrons were in their tuxedos and ballroom finery. The buzz was all about the explosions at the Opera House. Rene decided to have a drink at the bar.

The bartender was a lanky, balding man in his forties, his face sporting a yellowish, quick-tan glow.

"Stoli, over ice," Santos ordered, reaching for his cellular phone again.

"You been over at the Opera House?" the bartender asked in an excited voice.

"Yes. Terrible thing, wasn't it?"

"I'll say," the bartender said, pouring the vodka into an old-fashioned glass. "Radio says it was a bomb. You're lucky to be alive, pal."

"Indeed," Santos agreed, punching Davila's number into his cellular phone. Busy. He tried Naimat. Busy. He next dialed the apartment he'd rented under the name of Citron that overlooked Abrams's house. The apartment was empty now, except for a lone answering machine. The machine came on-line. He punched in the code needed to check for messages. Nothing. He looked toward the pay phones, then reached for his glass. *"Salud,"* he said to the bartender's retreating back.

A battery of police, fire, and public works crews went through the Opera House, looking for additional victims. The count was up to twenty-one, including the bodies of Lieutenant Frank Harris and Dr. William Larson.

Chief Arnold Fletcher pointed the toe of his scuffed cordovan brogue at Larsen's body. "Knife get him too?"

"Yes, Chief. Looks that way," said Jack Kordic.

Chief Fletcher looked into the nervous eyes of Dick Clancy. "You were part of Harris's crew, right? Protecting Paul Abrams, right?"

"Right, Chief," Clancy reflected somberly. "Me, Phil Mifsud, and Larry Falore.'

Kordic said, "Mifsud and Falore are out looking for Mr. Abrams now, Chief." He handed Fletcher the wallet he'd taken from the gray-haired corpse. "He's a doctor. William Larsen. Address on Pine Street."

Fletcher squinted his eyes and sighed. "And tell me how you happened to be on the scene, Kordic."

"I was waiting to meet someone after the opera, Chief."

"Just lucky, huh?"

Lieutenant Wesley Tilson burst into the room. "Crime lab is on the way up, Chief."

"You got a count yet?" Fletcher asked.

Tilson took a leather-jacketed notebook from his pocket. "Nineteen that we know of." He pointed a chin at the ground. "In addition to Harris and this man. The fire department is still digging through the rubble. One woman was shot. She's been taken to San Francisco General." He wagged his head slowly back and forth. "Doesn't look good."

"Shot?" Fletcher exclaimed. "What the hell we got going on here? Bombs, stabbings, now a shooting. What's the shooting victim's name?"

Tilson went back to his notebook. "Pontar. Her husband's an attorney."

"Pontar?" Kordic cried out in a wounded voice. "Mary Pontar?"

Tilson's eyes narrowed, like a cat's. "You know the woman?"

Kordic reached out for a chair to steady himself. "Yes, I do. The case I'm working on, the murder of Walter Slager and attack on Mary Ariza. Ariza works for Pontar's law office. She is staying with the Pontars at their house in Sea Cliff. Ariza came to the opera with the Pontars tonight. It was Ariza I was waiting to see."

Chief Fletcher's eyes turned inward, like a blind man's, trying to digest the information thrown at him. "What the hell is the connection, Kordic? I want—"

The thudding of heavy feet caused Fletcher to cut his sentence short. Phil Mifsud came into the crowded box, his face a sheen of sweat.

"Chief. Paul Abrams. He's not around. No one's seen him. Not his wife. Not no one."

"Where's Mrs. Abrams?" Wesley Tilson demanded.

"Out at their car. Larry Falore's with her. She says the last time she saw her husband was after the first explosion. He told her to run. She thought he was behind her coming down the stairs."

"That's not all, Chief," Tilson said. "There's rioting out in the Mission District. Mission High School's on fire, and some snipers are shooting at the firemen."

Fletcher let out a low groan. "What the hell have we got here?" he demanded of no one in particular. He took a deep breath, then began issuing orders: "Tilson, get the crime lab up here. And the medical examiner. I want a full scope on Harris and this doctor fast. Clancy, you go back to Mrs. Abrams. Take Falore with you. Go to their house. See if her husband somehow got separated, took a cab or a friend gave him a ride home."

"Chief," Mifsud said, "Paul Abrams wouldn't take a cab, believe me. He don't go nowhere without bodyguards. There's always two or three of us with him anytime he moves out of the house."

"You weren't much use to him tonight," Wesley Tilson volunteered. "Not much use at all."

Chief Fletcher gave Tilson a withering look. "Let's not start calling each other names. We've got to make sense out of this. Tilson, call in the troops. I want everyone who's available on this. If Abrams doesn't show up, it'll give the FBI an excuse to take over."

"They have people out in front already, Chief," Tilson said. "And the fire department called in the Alcohol, Tobacco, and Firearms explosive experts."

"Shit," Fletcher cursed. "It's going to be a circus. Tilson, after you get me a full count on the fatalities here, I want you get over to Abrams's house. Don't let those FBI jerks in the front door unless you get clearance from me." He turned to Kordic. "Inspector, follow up on this woman who was shot. What's the name?"

"Mary Pontar, Chief."

"Yeah. Follow up on that. Keep in touch. Gentlemen, let's get busy."

Mary Ariza watched Matt Pontar climb slowly into the back of the ambulance with his wife. The fire department rescue squad, then an ambulance crew, had responded quickly, going about their grisly tasks in a quick, professional manner. They applied bandages, administered oxygen, and hooked up an intravenous tube, all in a matter of a couple of minutes.

Matt Pontar looked as if he was going to pass out at any moment, but he insisted on going to the hospital with his wife, and the ambulance crew was too busy to argue with him.

Mary thought about what to do next. She could go to her apartment, but she wasn't sure she was ready for that. She'd have to find Jack. Would he still go to Stars? Or was he somewhere in the Opera House? It must be swarming with policemen by now. She started walking, scanning the crowd, looking for Jack's face. The news and television people were on the scene now, setting up searchlights. The police were pushing the crowd backward as a crew of city workers unloaded a truckload of wooden sawhorse barriers.

Mary stopped to ask a policeman if he knew where Inspector Kordic was.

He didn't have time for her question. "Not now, lady, not now. Just stay back, please."

A light rain started to fall, adding to the confusion. Her coat was still in the Opera House cloakroom. She decided to go to the restaurant. She hurried her steps as the rain showers picked up in intensity, her mind going back to the tragedy. The confusion. Someone had been calling her name. Mary. A woman's voice. Or had she been calling for Mrs. Pontar? She remembered the last call, almost a demanding yell: Mary! She'd been winded, almost exhausted from the short, terrible trip down those stairs. Her head bent, hands on knees, taking in deep gulps of air. As she started to straighten, to turn toward the voice, Mrs. Pontar had stepped in front of her. In front of her. God, that was it. It was meant for me! The blood coming from Mary Pontar's chest. They meant to shoot me! She started to run.

There are two entrances to Stars. The front, where the cabs stop and the parking attendants are stationed, and a back entrance on Redwood Street, more of an alley than a street. Mary was familiar with the back entrance, having gone to lunch at Stars several times while attending trials at nearby City Hall. She hurried up the back steps, grateful to be inside, to hear the noise of a crowd, to be among people again. Her eyes searched the crowd for Jack Kordic, but there was no sign of him. Where was he? She dug in her purse for his card. Maybe his office could get a message to him. She remembered the phones were up at the front, near the rest rooms. She made her way through the excited diners seated at their tables, toward the telephones. There were lines in front of both of them.

She tapped her foot impatiently while waiting, closing her eyes, tilting her head back, breathing deeply.

Rene Santos hung up the phone and swiveled toward the exit. He caught a quick glance of the woman standing in the queue next to him. It was her! The attorney. He made his way back to the bar. She hadn't seen him. But she was alive! Naimat had missed her. Where was Naimat? Where was Davila? And why weren't they answering their phones?

Jack Kordic had left his car in front of a fire hydrant near the Polk Street entrance to City Hall and walked to the Opera House. Now he sprinted to the car and, as soon as the engine kicked over, used the radio to ask the communications operator to check with San Francisco General on the condition of Mary Pontar.

"Be a while," the harried voice said. "We're backed up, Inspector."

Kordic could imagine the confusion going on in the small, cramped communications center. "Thanks," he said. "Anything you can do." He made a U-turn and drove up Polk Street, parking in the crosswalk at the corner of Golden Gate Avenue. There was a chance that Mary Ariza had gone to the restaurant rather than the hospital. He saw her as soon as he entered the doors. She was on the phone. He tapped her lightly on the shoulder, and she jumped backward, holding the receiver in her hand as if it were a club to hit him with.

"Easy, Mary. Are you okay?"

"Oh, Jack," she said, dropping the receiver, letting it dangle from its cord. "I was trying to call you. You won't believe what's happening."

"Yes, I would. I heard about Mary Pontar. I'm on my way to the hospital now."

Mary clutched his hand. "Jack, I think it was me they wanted to shoot. Not Mary Pontar. Me."

Kordic was bumped from behind by a long-chinned man in a wet overcoat. "Mind if I use the damn phone?" he said irritably, pushing Mary out of the way.

Kordic had a sudden urge to hit the man. To hit somebody. Something, even if it was a wall. He reached for Mary's shoulder. "Come on, we'll talk on the way to the hospital."

* * *

"You want another drinker, mister?" the bartender asked.

Santos ignored him, his eyes anchored on the figures of Mary Ariza and Inspector Jack Kordic, his hand unbuttoning his shirt collar, reaching for the silver cross. The woman was a *bruta*. A witch.

Tony Moreno checked on both Paul Abrams and Cesar Davila. Abrams looked fine, but Davila was breathing heavily, through his mouth. His face was a gray, clammy color. Moreno tested the ropes on Davila's arms and feet, then adjusted the gag around his mouth. He'd live. Maybe not for long, but he'd live.

He turned his attention back to Abrams, reaching out and running his hands through the man's thinning gray hair.

"They went through a lot of trouble for you, Paulie. But I think you're going to be worth it. To me, anyway." He climbed out of the van, made sure the doors were locked, then trotted over to the bar.

The blaring of salsa music greeted him like an old friend as he pushed his way into El Condado. He was recognized immediately and welcomed like a war hero returning home to a mini-parade. He shook a few hands, patted a few behinds, then waved a hand for Gus, the bartender, to follow him into the men's room.

Two leather-jacketed males, neither older than eighteen, were doing a cocaine deal near the urinals. They both recognized Moreno right away.

"Out," he commanded, and the two began stuffing money and powder packets into their pants, departing without a word of protest.

"Where have you been, Tony? It's been like a war out there," Gus Melendez exclaimed once they were alone.

"Yes, I know. Relax. I've got everything under control," Moreno said. He pulled a rat-tailed comb from his pocket and began rearranging his hair. "I've been busy. What have you heard about Mission High School? Did they burn the fucker down?"

"That's what I hear," Melendez said nervously. Why

did Tony want a school burned down? What was the sense? Where was the profit? A couple of firemen got shot. There's going to be hell to pay."

Moreno said, "I told you to relax. *Rifamos,* man. We're in control. We're the best. I'm going to need some help in moving some packages. Get someone to take over for you behind the bar. The packages are heavy."

Gus wiped his lips with the back of his hand. "Hey, Tony, I'm not into moving the—"

Moreno pointed the tip of the comb at Gus as if it were a gun. "I said I need some help, Gus. You telling me you don't want to do it?"

"No, no, Tony. You know me better than that. It's just that usually you have your boys do the camel work."

Moreno's face split into an obscene grin. "No camel work this time. You know how many million dollars it takes to make a billion?"

Gus Melendez's hands flew through the air like two frightened birds. "What you talking about, Tony?"

"A thousand million. I figured it out, man. A thousand million. Well, I got something that's worth a couple of billion. Whatcha think they going to pay to get it back, huh?" He pressed the tip of the comb into Gus's chest. "Huh? How much?"

Chapter 29

"They're late," Viktor Petrov rasped irritably. "You're sure they are bringing Abrams here?"

Boris Zorkin shifted uncomfortably in the sedan's front seat, then turned around to look at Petrov. "Both of them, Naimat and Davila, assured me they would take Abrams directly to the safe house."

"Turn up the radio," Petrov commanded, reaching for the thermos of hot tea. He poured himself a cup, then, with little enthusiasm, asked Zorkin if he wanted one.

Zorkin declined, switching through radio stations that were either playing commercials or music until he found one broadcasting a story of the "explosions at the Opera House."

Both men listened as the excited reporter gushed out facts of the damage done by a bomb as well as the unconfirmed report of a shooting victim.

Petrov gave a sarcastic murmur. "Old Rene, he does have a knack for the dramatic, does he not? Opera House. Bombs. You would think he could have come up with something a little simpler, a little neater. But that is not his style. Always the dramatic." He took a sip of the tea, which was sweetened with jam, then smacked his lips. "Rene is slipping badly, Boris. There was a time when he would have brought this all off perfectly. Now he can't trust his own people. That's the problem when you deal with mercenaries. No loyalty. You can't trust anyone these days. You have handled both Naimat and Davila well, Boris." He leaned forward. "You are sure they are both unaware of your contacts with the other?"

"Positive," Zorkin said with more enthusiasm than he actually felt. "They are both too greedy to worry about the other."

Petrov leaned back and sipped his tea. "I don't like this, Boris. Too much time. Where are they?"

Zorkin adjusted the starlight scope attached to the car's dashboard with suction cups, and zeroed in on the house on Brewster Street. Petrov monitored the scope's vision through a ten-inch portable TV set on the seat beside him.

"I don't know what's keeping them," Zorkin confessed.

Petrov grumbled a Russian curse, then lit up a thick Cuban cigar, blowing the smoke toward the front seat. "You should have had someone follow them from the Opera House. If they do not show in ten minutes, I'm afraid we can assume that we have a problem."

Zorkin felt a chill down his back. Petrov would blame him if something went wrong, even though it was Petrov who had vetoed Zorkin's plan to tail the ambulance from the Opera House. Petrov had been afraid that Santos would spot a tail. What had gone wrong? Had there been a last-second change of plans? Both Davila and Naimat had cellular phones. They would have called him. Unless Santos had pulled a trick. A rabbit out of the hat. The thought that Davila and the woman might have led him by the nose caused Zorkin to break out in a cold sweat.

They sat in silence, listening to the radio broadcast. The victim who had been shot had still not been identified, other than being a woman "still in critical condition at San Francisco General Hospital."

"I wonder who she is?" Viktor Petrov called from the backseat. "Maybe Rene found out about you and Naimat, and—" Petrov broke off, his eyes riveted to the TV monitor. "A car!"

Boris put the scope to his eye. A dark sedan had passed the house, made a U-turn, and parked some fifty yards away. Nothing happened for two long minutes. Then the car's door opened and a man got out. The car's interior lights had been removed, so Petrov wasn't sure it was Rene Santos until he was almost to the house.

He tapped the ashes of his cigar into the now cool cup of tea. "Santos. Alone. Major problems, Boris."

Rene Santos walked swiftly toward the house, on the balls of his feet, ready to dart back to the car at the first sign of trouble. He stopped at the garage door, peering inside through the mailbox flap. The interior was dark. If the van was there he would have been able to see its outline, even in the dark. It was all the evidence he needed. He sprinted back to the car.

"He's not even going inside," Boris Zorkin said in amazement.

"No need," answered Petrov angrily. "Find that van, damn it. Find that damn van and Paul Abrams!"

Rene drove to Laguna and Fulton streets, where Davila had been scheduled to pick up Naimat. A black-and-white police car was parked at the intersection, its red light revolving into the blackness. Santos slowed down and pushed the button to slide down the driver's-side window. He could see several people dressed in shabby street clothes clustered around the sidewalk. A policeman in a black slicker was waving a flashlight in a circle.

"Keep moving, buddy. Nothing to see. Keep moving."

Santos slowed to a stop. "I was looking for a friend of mine, Officer. A woman. We went to the opera together. I haven't been able to find her."

The policeman turned his flashlight beam in the direction of a lump covered by a dark blanket. "What's your friend look like?"

"Fifty, red hair, heavyish. Wearing a mink coat."

"Well, you're lucky this is not your friend. Mink coat, all right, but she was younger, dark hair, and packing a gun."

"Thank God," Santos said, taking a final look at Naimat. "Was she shot?"

"Nope. Hit-and-run." The policeman pulled his rain-coat collar up. "What a night, huh? Not even a full moon, but all the crazies are out." He circled the flash-light beam again. "Good luck with finding your lady friend, but you better get moving."

Rene pulled away slowly, driving straight for several blocks before parking under a street lamp. Naimat dead. The police had her gun. There would be no other ID on her, and her fingerprints wouldn't be on file in America. Would the police check further? Her prints were certainly on file in Israel. Perhaps with Interpol, but Interpol was a poorly run organization, and their files had been discredited so often that the Mossad had stopped cooperating with them years ago.

He could think of no way the police could trace Naimat to him. Unless they had help from the Russians, Zorkin and Viktor Petrov. What must Petrov be thinking now? There was still nothing on the radio about Paul Abrams. He gripped the steering wheel be-tween his hands, pulling outward in an isometric drill, pulling until his shoulder muscles began to ache.

Think, Rene, think, he goaded himself, fingering the cross as he tried to put the pieces together. Naimat gone. She was too well trained to fall victim to an auto accident, so somehow that fool Davila had killed her. Why? Fear. It had to be fear. Davila was smarter than Rene thought. He must have known that Naimat was going to kill him. That if Naimat didn't, Rene himself most likely would. But what would he do with Abrams? What good was Abrams to Davila? The Rus-sians. He must be trying to make his own deal with the Russians. But why? Why would Petrov go to Davila? A double cross obviously.

His fingers drummed across the steering wheel as different scenarios flashed through his mind. Boris Zorkin. Naimat was the contact with Zorkin. Was Naimat involved too? With Cesar? No. She would never betray me for Davila. Unless she made a deal with Zorkin, then dragged Cesar in with her. Cesar is afraid of Naimat. But he is much more afraid of me. What made him turn?

Naimat was not someone easily fooled, or easily killed. Why had she become so vulnerable on the street? It had to be Cesar. Cesar coasting up to her, then running her down. Then there was the Mexican punk, Moreno. His body would be found on the street, in an alley, or floating in the bay. Or perhaps never found. While Cesar Davila was no mental giant, he was skilled in the art of disposal. Or was he? Santos thought of the mutilated body of Joseph Rose. The bad luck had started there, when the body had not gone out to sea.

But what of Paul Abrams? What would Davila do with him? Where would he take him? It had to involve the Russians. Which meant they have no more use for me.

Santos made a U-turn and retraced his way to Laguna and Fulton. The same policeman was in the middle of the block, directing traffic with his flashlight. It might be some time before the body was removed. The radio was broadcasting an urgent message from the mayor for citizens to remain calm. There were thoughts of bringing in the National Guard. Fires were still burning in the Mission District. There were reports of snipers firing at both police and firemen in the ruins of Mission High School. Victims were still being removed from the Opera House. Guest commentators ranging from elected state and city officials to former police chiefs were brought on the air to voice their opinions.

He headed downtown, driving into a public garage on Mason Street, taking the long, spiraling driveway up to the sixth floor. He gave the car's interior a quick inventory, then did the same for the trunk. Satisfied he was leaving nothing behind, he took the elevator to street level. Santos stood at the corner, across from the Hilton Hotel, got his bearings, then walked south, toward Market Street, into the area listed in the city guidebooks as the Tenderloin, usually described as "undesirable."

Prostitutes of both sexes accosted him at intervals of thirty seconds. Rene kept his eyes straight ahead, ignoring the populace, his mind whirring at high speed, plotting his next move. He was so engrossed that he went right past his destination, not realizing his error until he was a half block away. He did an about-face.

The bottom three floors of what was once an old hotel had been converted into a self-storage warehouse. The clerk, a square-jawed man with a bullet-bald head, verified his locker pass, pointed a thumb down the hallway, and said, "You know where it is, mate," in a dusty Australian accent.

The lockers ranged in size from cubicles three feet by three feet to bedroom-sized caverns. Santos's locker was six feet in height, three feet deep, and more than adequate for his needs. He opened the locker, plucked out a soft vinyl suitcase, and placed it between his feet. He glanced around to make sure no one was watching. He quickly slipped out of his raincoat and tuxedo jacket, tossing the jacket to the dirt-encrusted cement floor. He added his tuxedo pants, bow tie, and glossy shoes to the pile, then unzipped the suitcase and retrieved a dark blue blazer, gray slacks, and black loafers. He donned them quickly, then squatted on his toes, examining the suitcase contents closely.

Snuggled in among sweaters, ties, socks, and underwear was a brick of Frangex explosive; a handful of various-sized detonators; four bundles of cash, neatly stacked and rubber-banded, the bills twenties and fifties and totalling twenty-two thousand dollars; and a wallet containing five thousand dollars in traveler's checks, a New York driver's license, Visa, Mastercard, and American Express cards, all in the name of Phillip Simpson.

Satisfied, he zipped the case closed, ran his fingers through his tuxedo pants and jacket, retrieving all that was there, then jumbled up the garments and dropped them on the floor before replacing the lock. He hurried out of the building, walking in the general direction of Union Square. He remembered there was a first-rate hotel across from the square. It would do for the night.

"He's not here, I told you he wouldn't be here," Adele Abrams screamed at the top of her lungs.

"Where were you people? You should never have let him out of your sight. It's your fault!"

Dick Clancy pawed at the Persian carpet with his foot. "We know, Mrs. Abrams, we know. Just so you know, however, Lieutenant Harris was killed trying to protect your husband."

Adele Abrams picked up an eighteenth-century French vase clock from a circular Cuban mahogany table and smashed it against the table. Clancy winced, rightly figuring that the clock was worth a year's salary.

"I can't help that. I'm lucky I wasn't killed." She turned her eyes on Larry Falore, who was leaning casually against a priceless Mortlake tapestry depicting a knight on horseback charging a dragon. "And where were you?"

Falore spoke directly to Clancy. "You better get back to the chief on this. Looks like Abrams has been snatched."

"Lieutenant Tilson's going to be in charge. He should be here any minute. Let's see what he wants to do."

Adele's throat muscles tightened. "What he wants to do. What he wants to do. What about what I want to do?" she demanded.

"You find Tilson, Dick," Falore said. "I'll stick with Mrs. Abrams."

Clancy looked uncertain for a moment, then hurried from the room. Falore walked over and closed the door behind him. "Adele," he said as he turned around. "You better get control of yourself. This is going to get rough."

He crossed to the glass and silver drink tray, selected a bottle of Martel's cognac, and poured a hefty measure into a balloon snifter. "Here. Take a swig."

Adele accepted the glass reluctantly, then placed a finger on the rim of the glass and ran it around a couple of times. "You act like you're taking charge, Larry."

"Nope. Just trying to be helpful. If someone did snatch your husband, they went through a hell of a lot of trouble to do it. If he has been kidnapped, you should be ready. There will be calls. Ransom demands."

Adele stared into the cognac. "Paul was always afraid that something like this would happen. I thought he was just being foolish."

Falore moved behind her, undoing the neck clasp that held her cape together. His hands glided across her bare shoulders. "There will be more police units here any minute. Maybe you should change into something more—" He paused for a moment. "More appropriate."

Adele stared at Falore as if seeing him for the first time. There was something different. A shrewdness in the eyes. "You think someone will call in a ransom demand?"

"It's the usual procedure in situations like this," Falore said, walking to the drink tray and pouring himself a small snifter of the cognac. He held the glass up to her in a brief, silent toast. "I'll be happy to stick around during the crisis, Adele." He sampled the cognac. "Paul's brother was killed in a kidnapping, wasn't he?"

"Yes. Years ago. In New York. Paul left New York right after that. He never went back."

"Adele, if the people who snatched Paul are responsible for the bombings and the murder of Dr. Larsen and Lieutenant Harris, you can be sure they're going to go for a huge ransom. You're going to have to prepare yourself for the worst possibility. We don't even know if your husband is still alive. In less than an hour this place will be swarming with all kinds of cops, reporters, television people. It'll be a circus. I want to help you as much as I can."

Adele took a deep breath, releasing the air slowly. "And exactly how can you help me, Larry?"

"Tell whoever is in charge—my department, the FBI, whoever—that you want me right here. With you. That you trust me."

"Can I trust you, Larry?"

"Yes. To do whatever you want, Adele. Whatever."

* * *

Jack Kordic questioned Matt Pontar in a small office down from the intensive care unit, where Mary Pontar was being operated on. He probed gently, like a dentist trying to avoid a nerve.

Mary Ariza cringed inwardly at the way Matt looked: eyes red-rimmed, lines of weariness running from the corners of his mouth to the wings of his nose. His normal, almost swaggering walk was reduced to an old man's shuffle.

"Long, dark hair, thin. Coat was fur. Is that right, Mr. Pontar?"

"Yes. Yes, I think so."

"What about race?"

"I don't know. She had tan skin." Pontar settled onto a folding chair with a thick-bodied slump. "The coat was fur. Dark. That's why it took me a second to see the gun." He ran a finger down his cheek hard enough to leave a red mark. "I'm sure it was a gun, but I didn't hear anything."

"A silencer," Kordic said.

Pontar glanced up at Kordic, his eyes drifting to Mary Ariza's. "Yes, I guess so. I certainly didn't hear a shot. Did you, Mary?"

"No. No, Matt, I didn't."

Pontar held her eyes. "A silencer. Another silencer. Like the man who tried to kill you." He made a clucking sound with his tongue, then covered his face with his hands. "The woman was after you, wasn't she, Mary? Not my wife. She was after you."

Mary Ariza could not think of a response.

Kordic broke the tension. "That's a strong possibility, Mr. Pontar. What about Paul Abrams? Do you know him?"

Pontar shrugged impatiently. "Abrams? What the hell has he got to do with this?"

"I'm not sure," Kordic admitted. "We believe he was kidnapped tonight. From the Opera House. Do you know Abrams?"

"I saw him there, earlier." Pontar nodded at Mary. "She did too. But I don't know him. Never did any business with the man."

"Yes," Mary said. "I remember Matt pointing him out to me. He—he had several bodyguards."

"Friends of mine," Kordic said. "San Francisco policemen. One of them was killed. In Abrams's box. Do you know Abrams, Mary?"

"No," she said quickly. "No, I don't."

Kordic tapped his pen against his notepad. Another dead end. "Can I get you anything, Mr. Pontar? Drive you somewhere?"

"No. Thanks. I'm sticking around. Doctor says it could be a couple of hours before I can see her." He put his hands on his thighs and pushed himself clear of the chair, swaying slightly as he stood up. He reached out and wrapped his arms around Mary, burying his head in her shoulders. "Pray for her, Mary. Pray for her."

Kordic backed away to give them some privacy. Mary was silent as they walked to the car. As Kordic was unlocking the door, she said, "God, Jack, I feel awful. Just awful."

Kordic opened the door, waited for her to get in before putting a hand on the roof and leaning down so that his face was just inches from hers. "It's not your fault. That bullet was meant for you. It was luck. Nothing more than that. Bad luck for Mrs. Pontar."

"Luck." Mary spat out the word.

"Did the description Pontar gave of the woman mean anything to you?"

"No. I can remember someone calling out Mary a couple of times, but when I turned around, all I saw was Mr. Pontar holding his wife. I didn't see this woman at all."

Kordic squinted at the radium dial of his watch. Just past midnight. "I've got to get down to the Hall of Justice, get this file going, see what developments have been made on the Opera House. It'll take a couple of hours. I don't want to leave you alone. Where do you want to go?"

"Home, really. Get on a plane and try to forget all of this." Her voice turned serious. "I can't go back to the Pontars' house, Jack. Not now. I just can't."

"I know how you feel. And we don't want you going back to your apartment." Kordic hesitated, his throat muscles tightening. "How about my place?"

The clerk at the St. Francis Hotel greeted Rene warmly, advising him that there was a room available. However, it was one of the principal suites and went for almost six hundred dollars a night. Santos told him that would be no problem and handed him the Visa card made out in the name of Phillip Simpson. Sixty, six hundred, or six thousand dollars—it made little difference to Santos, since the bill would never be paid. Mr. Simpson, an archaeologist, was thought to be on an expedition in the Peruvian jungle. Rene had killed him a few days before leaving South America— burying his body in the jungle. Perhaps another archaeologist would dig it up one of these days.

A bellboy offered to take his bag. Santos slipped him a five dollar bill and told him to forget it. He was still clinging to the smallest of hopes that the reason he hadn't been able to get a hold of Naimat or Davila was that there was a problem with the cellular phones. There was a bank of pay phones on the far side of the lobby. Santos was disappointed. Usually, he could depend on hotel lobby phones. The phones in Europe, the Mideast, or South America were nowhere near as efficient as their American counterparts, but the booths were often large, sumptuous affairs that provided a great deal of privacy. Here were mainly open phones, each within inches of its neighbor.

He dug into his pocket for coins, finding none. The concierge broke a five dollar bill into a roll of bright, shiny quarters. "Part of the service." She smiled. "We wash the coins every day."

That might have impressed some of the hotel guests, but not Santos. Dirty or clean, money was money. He went back to the phones, found an available one between two businessmen in pinstriped suits who covered up their notebooks as if they contained state secrets when Rene wedged himself in between them.

He again tried the numbers of the two cellular

phones that should have been in the possession of
Cesar Davila and Naimat. Davila's was once again
busy. Naimat's was answered this time, by a tentative
male voice.

"Hello?"

"Who is this?" Rene demanded.

"Deputy Coroner Gilleran."

Rene's first instinct was to hang up. He hung on,
waiting.

"Maybe you can help us, sir. We're trying to identify
a woman who was injured in a traffic accident. She
had no identification on her. What's your name?"

"Is the woman badly injured, Deputy?"

"You called her phone, you must know her. Can
you—"

"Is she badly injured?" Rene repeated, heat rising in
his voice.

"Yes. Perhaps you could help us in the identification. I'd be happy to send a car for you. Where are you
calling from, sir? I—"

Rene broke the connection.

A finger tapped him on the shoulder, and he swiveled around, left hand going up with fingers curled,
palm rigid, the other reaching for his knife.

An intoxicated man with brown hair that stood up
and away from the dandruffed collar of his suit jacket
leered at Rene. "You through with the phone, pally? I
got a call to make."

Santos stepped away without a word, thinking how
lucky the drunken fool was. He walked outside the hotel, waited for a cable car to clang by, then ran across
Powell Street to wide-open Union Square. The wind-
blown palm trees looked curiously out of place to Santos. He used his cellular phone to call the rented
apartment above the Abrams mansion. There was one
message on the answering machine. Boris Zorkin's
voice. "Problems? Call three."

Three. A code. Viktor Petrov was here. Was Petrov
calling to gloat? To tell him he had Abrams? Or had
something happened? His fingers stabbed out the emer-

gency number Petrov had supplied him during their meeting in Lima.

Petrov picked up the phone on the first ring.

"Rene. Congratulations. I must say you do put on a good show. Always the dramatic. It must have been your circus background. When can I see my package?"

Rene felt a surge of energy. Petrov didn't have Abrams! "Tomorrow, Viktor," he said coolly. "I'll call you in the morning."

"I want him now," Petrov declared.

"Tomorrow."

"You worry me, Rene. What is the problem?"

"No problem at all," Santos said, his voice full of false confidence. "I just want to make sure everything is right when I turn him over to you."

"That is totally unacceptable, Rene."

"You will have to live with it, Viktor. Just for a little while longer."

"It is in perfect condition?"

"Perfect. Still a virgin."

Petrov grunted into the phone, then said, "I don't like this stalling, Rene. Don't try to be too clever. Not with me."

Santos broke the connection. Clever. Cesar Davila was trying to be clever. He had Abrams. But where?

Chapter 30

The call had come in just ten minutes before Lieutenant Wesley Tilson made a personal appearance at the Abrams residence. The phone rang softly. It had one of those throttled croaks designed to spare the nerves.

Larry Falore had answered. The voice was young, male, Latin accent.

"Get me Paul's wife."

"Who's calling?"

"Paul's drinking buddy. We're sitting here having a couple of shooters right now. Get the woman."

Falore waved Adele over to the phone, holding it between them, their foreheads pressed together as they listened.

"Now, mama. You want to see Paul again, all you got to do is pay up. Five million and he's all yours. How's that sound? Not too much for getting Paulie back, is it?"

"How do we know you actually have Mr. Abrams?" Falore asked.

"Who you, man? The fucking butler? Some cop? 'Course I got the man. Hold on."

Falore could hear the sound of a phone being put down, rattling on a solid surface.

The voice came back on the line. "Here's Paulie's wallet." He read off Abrams's driver's license number, the list of his credit cards. "Picture of a blonde in a bikini with big tits. That you, mama?"

Adele cleared her throat. "Let me speak to my husband."

"Paulie ain't up to talking to anyone now, mama. But I'll get him to send you a message. You got any doubts? Hey, butler man. You want me to send you a finger? One of his balls? You'd recognize his balls, huh, mama?"

Adele pulled the phone away from Falore's grasp. "Listen, I want—"

"You listen, mama," Tony Moreno shouted. "It's not what you want. It's what I want. You keep the *chotas* out of this, or I'll kill old Paulie. I'll call you tomorrow. Get the money, mama."

Adele Abrams looked down at the receiver in her hand. She was holding it carefully, as if it were one of her husband's valuable pieces of art. She handed it to Falore. "Five million dollars. He's crazy."

"Yes," Falore agreed. "He sounded like he was high on something, but he's got Paul's wallet. That's for sure."

"What are *chotas*? He told me to keep the *chotas* out of it or he'd kill Paul."

"Spanish slang for cops. What are you going to do?"

"Five million dollars. He expects me to just turn over five million dollars to him."

"What are you going to do, Adele?" Falore repeated.

She walked to the drink cart. "Tell the police, of course. That's what you people get paid for, isn't it?"

The hotel suite was large, done in ivory, with gold filigree panels. A glass-topped coffee table covered with vases filled with a profusion of flowers was set in front of a marble-faced fireplace. Chairs covered with heavy tapestry material were scattered around the room.

Santos stepped into the adjoining room. More of the same French furniture, a large bed, an elaborate telephone, and fax machine on the bed stand. He studied the printed phone instructions for a moment, then dialed room service, ordering a large steak, potato, spinach salad, and a pot of coffee.

The wide-screen TV in its plastic cabinet seemed a bit out of place amid the stylish furniture. He turned the set and used the remote control to flip from channel to channel, picking up little new information.

Abrams's name was not mentioned. The police were withholding the names of the dead until their relatives were notified.

Room service arrived with his order, and he sat on the edge of the bed, chewing slowly, flipping TV channels. The fires at Mission High School had been extinguished, and the shooting had stopped. There was no doubt it was arson, the cameo-faced announcer said as she stood at the corner of Eighteenth and Dolores, the wind blowing into her microphone. "Parts of Mission High School have been completely destroyed, but the fire department has been able to prevent the fire from leaping to nearby private housing."

"Good for them," Santos said dryly. At least Moreno's gang had carried out that end of the bargain. He continued clicking through the local channels, then picking up the story on CNN. Theories of social unrest and comparisons to the riots in eastern cities and Los Angeles were bandied about by pontificating reporters. "The fact that they went after such a firmly established upper-class culture icon as an opera house shows just how far the decline between rich and poor has escalated in this city," pronounced one pompous expert. Santos chuckled wryly. It was the first laugh he could remember in days.

He kicked off his shoes, propped his head against the pillows, and dozed off. He woke up a few minutes after five in the morning with the television still on.

A fresh crew of reporters was on the story. A stocky, glum-looking man bundled up in an overcoat, his eyes squinting against the glare of the lights, was speaking in a hushed, authoritative tone. "This reporter has learned that industrialist Paul Abrams has been kidnapped. Police are now huddled at the Abrams residence. No details of the kidnapping have been released, but confidential sources speculate that Mr. Abrams was abducted during the bombing catastrophe at the San Francisco Opera House, and that a large ransom has been demanded for his release." The TV screen switched from the announcer to a view of the Opera House.

Santos leaped to his feet. Large ransom! Davila. The

fool. Was that little idiot Moreno in it with him? He had to be. The two of them working together, killing Naimat. That had to be it. Davila and Moreno. Santos hurried into the bathroom, stripping off his clothes, dropping them in a trail on the thick eggshell-colored carpeting. He turned on the shower, and while waiting for the water to warm up, he studied his reflection in the mirror. His luck was back. He could still salvage the mission. Where would they take Abrams? Somewhere that they felt was safe. Cesar would know I'd be after him. It would have to be someplace they thought I knew nothing about. Moreno's boat? Yes, that would be the perfect place. He stepped under the hot water and began soaping his body. The boat. With any luck, that's where they'd be. If not, he'd find them. Wherever they were.

Jack Kordic appeared almost embarrassed when he let Mary into his oceanfront apartment: living room-dining room combination, two bedrooms, kitchen. It was obvious he hadn't been expecting company—clothes strewn on the couch, dishes in the sink.

Kordic gave her a brief tour before rushing off to the Hall of Justice. After he'd gone, Mary put a pot of coffee on the stove and began wandering around. The walls were pale beige, devoid of paintings or photographs. The master bedroom was sparsely furnished: queen-size bed, bedside nightstands, two dressers, all of straight-line Danish design. The small second bedroom was nothing more than a storage room, overflowing with cardboard boxes bearing the stamp of Bekins Moving & Storage Company. The boxes were stacked all the way to the ceiling.

The dining room set was old and expensive, the wood a deep ruby cherry color. A large-screen TV took up one corner of the room. In front of the television was an imitation leather rocking chair. Mary carried her coffee over to a floor-to-ceiling bookcase made of simple, unpainted pine boards. The top two shelves were jammed with books, police procedural nonfiction works, one of which she was somewhat familiar with:

the California Penal Code. The others related to DNA, fingerprints, arson, and the like.

The next two shelves were a mixture of fiction from classics to pulp: *Moby Dick, The Three Musketeers, The Razor's Edge,* Louis L'Amour, LeCarré, Wambaugh, paperback westerns, and a large collection representing the various Peanuts characters and Calvin and Hobbs.

She knelt down to look at the bottom shelf, which was taken up entirely with cookbooks, mostly soft covers published by Sunset, covering everything from seafood to party breakfasts and brunches. The hardbacks ranged from Julia Child's *Classical French* to Graham Kerr's *Mini-Max Cooking.* She began pulling out books at random, flipping through the pages, finding a personalized stamp on the inside jacket page of the cookbooks: "Property of Linda Kordic. Please return when you're through with it. Thanks."

She sampled a *Christmas with Charlie Brown.* Here there was a simple signature, a large, loopy scrawl: Danny Kordic.

There were a half-dozen videocassettes stacked neatly on top of the TV: *Casablanca, North by Northwest, The Pink Panther, Gunga Din, The Quiet Man,* and a Peter Sellers movie she could not recall seeing, *The Party.*

Mary replenished her coffee, then made her way back to the spare bedroom. One of the boxes caught her eye. It was filled with grasspaper-jacketed photo albums. She sat cross-legged on the floor and pulled one of the albums from the box. In slightly more than an hour, she had gone through all twenty-two albums, seeing pictures of a young, smiling Jack Kordic, the wedding pictures, his wife, a stunning blonde with soft blue eyes. The boy, Danny, starting life quite fat and cuddly-looking, growing up into a smiling, happy-looking boy with a crew cut in sports uniforms of every stripe: baseball, basketball, soccer. Pictures of Danny smiling at the camera, holding up a fish almost as big as he was. The later pictures showed him with longer hair, the same pale blond as his mother's, the happy, sometimes toothless smile replaced by a quiet, confident grin. She slipped the albums back into the packing box, feeling slightly guilty for intruding on Jack's past.

God, it must have been difficult losing them like that. Both so young. So beautiful. So full of life. The barely touched coffee was cold now. She took it to the sink, dumped it, rinsed the cup, and washed the pot. She yawned widely and made her way to the bedroom, kicked off her shoes, and climbed under the bedspread.

Mary was dreaming she was at the Opera House, reliving the trip down the stairs, the crowd pushing her, closing in around her—she could hear someone calling her name. The touch on her shoulder brought her out of the dream. She bolted into a sitting position, arms raised over her head as if to ward off blows.

"Easy, easy," Jack Kordic said, holding out his hands in front of him.

Mary shook her head to clear away the lingering image of the dream. "Oh, I'm sorry, I thought . . . hell, I don't know what I thought."

She reached out for Kordic's hand. He looked haggard. Stubble on his chin, bags under the eyes, jaw slack. Pale sunlight was making its presence known through the curtains. "Did you just get in?"

"Couple of hours ago," Kordic said with a lopsided grin. "You were out like a light."

Mary looked at the far side of the bed. The cover was smooth.

"I flopped out in the chair." He rubbed a hand across his whiskered jaw. "It's been confirmed. Paul Abrams was kidnapped. Someone called his house. They want five million for him."

Mary dug her elbows into the mattress and wriggled herself up into a sitting position. "Do you think that someone would go through all that trouble, kill all those people, just to get their hands on Paul Abrams?"

"That's the theory. The whole charade at the Opera House was just to get to Abrams. The riots and fires in the Mission District could have been part of it too, diverting attention and personnel away from the Opera House. Away from Abrams."

Ariza leaned forward, elbow on knee, chin cupped in her palm. "But it just doesn't make sense, Jack. What about Mary Pontar? Shooting her, or rather, trying to shoot me. That certainly doesn't have anything to do with Paul Abrams."

"Doesn't it? I think it does. I think it was about Abrams all along. And Joseph Rose, also known as Joseph Rosenberg. Rose's business was oil, or at least getting it out of the ground. Abrams's business is oil—finding, buying, selling, refining it. It's my gut feeling that that's the link. I think you became involved purely by accident, Mary. That man on the street. The words he confessed to you. Whoever is behind this is worried about what you were told. Rose wasn't the man's daughter. He was confessing to the killing of Joseph Rose. They still want to kill you, that's why the attempt was made last night. It was all because of the man's supposed confession to you. What else did he tell you? There must have been something else."

Mary pinched the bridge of her nose between thumb and forefinger. "He just babbled on and on." She pulled the fingers away. "His father. He spoke of his father, that he was afraid of his father, the conductor."

"Conductor?"

"Yes, he called him El Cabecilla. Conductor. The man who said he was a priest told me the man's father used to conduct an orchestra. I think that's what he said." She shook her head from side to side. "It's all so confusing, Jack."

"Conductor. What the hell could that mean?"

"Well, it could mean something else. Sort of a leader, or a boss."

Kordic sighed, then handed Mary a Polaroid photograph. "Recognize this woman?"

Mary winced while studying the picture: dark hair, the eyes closed, the face bloodied, the features grotesquely arranged, as if she'd been beaten with a heavy object. "Who is it, Jack?'

"I think she's the person who shot Mrs. Pontar. She

was found a few blocks from the Opera House. Run down in the street."

Mary handed him the picture. "What makes you think it was her?"

"She had a gun on her. With a silencer. It may take till the end of the day before the crime lab has time to do a ballistics test, but I'm sure she's the one who shot Mary Pontar."

"Who is she?"

"No identification yet. She had nothing on her except the gun and a cellular phone. No purse, no cosmetics, no cash. Just a spare clip of ammunition for the pistol. None of these people carried an identification. The man you helped on Montgomery Street. The punk who your neighbor Mr. Landon shot. Now this woman. It's all a well-organized plot, Mary." Kordic reached out for her hand. He forced a grin. "There is some good news."

"I sure could use some," Mary said earnestly.

"Mrs. Pontar's going to make it. The brooch on her dress deflected some of the bullet's impact. She's going to be okay."

"Well, that's about the only good news to come out of this mess," Mary said. "Except for you and . . ." She stretched out to him, guiding his hand closer, running the tip of her tongue across the scar on his wrist, then tilting her head to the side, her lips reaching toward his. The first kiss was soft, their lips barely touching; then the intensity increased, mouths opening, tongues crossing. She reached her arms around his neck, pulling him down to her.

"It's him," Boris Zorkin whispered, his hand over the receiver.

Petrov stopped stirring the jam in his cup of tea, letting the spoon fall to the saucer. He snatched the phone away. "I was wondering when you would call. You're being foolish."

"Not me, old friend. A renegade. But it is all under control."

Petrov's silky eyebrows arched up toward his forehead. "Is that right? Then when can I have my package?"

"Soon."

"Why not now?" Petrov insisted.

"Delivery problems. I have never disappointed you before. Trust me."

Petrov's laugh boomed from deep in his chest. "Trust. What an odd word coming from you. Or me, for that matter. No, trust is not sufficient. Power is a better word. And remember the power I have, Rene. If I do not get my package today, I will have to talk to certain people."

"That would be foolish for both of us," Rene Santos suggested.

"No. Just for you, Rene. Believe me. Just for you."

"I'll be in touch," Santos said.

"Where will delivery take place?"

"I'll call you, Viktor. But if, just by chance, you already know the location of the safe house, it's been booby-trapped. Remember Paris."

Petrov hung up the phone and looked across the desk at Boris Zorkin with a wan, humorless smile.

"What was that all about?" Zorkin asked.

Petrov blew air through his lips, then went back to stirring his tea. "He was telling me that the safe house on Brewster Street is booby-trapped. Reminding me of an operation he handled in Paris. He kidnapped a high-ranking NATO officer. The French found out where the man was. They were warned not to enter the building, but you know the French. They had their so-called experts check it out, went in through the roof—cut a hole right in the middle of it—slid down ropes, found the man tied to a chair, gagged, shaking his head like crazy. The bomb squad had determined that there was no sign of explosives. A French agent rushed over to untie him. As soon as he did, the bomb went off. Rene had given the brave NATO officer a plastic explosives enema." Petrov chuckled dryly. "Blew all their asses off. But that was a long time ago. I want you to kill Rene."

"But what about Paul Abrams?"

"If Santos cannot deliver Abrams on schedule, then Abrams is already dead," he said in a stony voice. "Find Santos and kill him."

Rene had started his morning by slipping out of the St. Francis Hotel unnoticed. Two mini blasting caps and several finger-size strips of Frangex were stuffed in his raincoat pockets. The Beretta was tucked in the waistband of his pants. He remembered walking by a drugstore on Powell Street that sold everything from perfumes to sporting goods and baked goods, in addition to row upon row of packaged medicines.

There wasn't much in the line of men's clothing, but he found what he needed: a San Francisco Giants baseball cap and windbreaker, a pair of cheap, Korean-made tennis shoes, sunglasses, a small carryall grip, and, from a counter that displayed camera equipment, an inexpensive Polaroid, film, a pair of binoculars, and a pack of AAA batteries. He added a half-dozen chocolate candy bars to his shopping basket, stuffed his purchases into the grip, then walked back to the garage on Mason Street. The car was still there on the sixth floor. He was slightly annoyed by the parking fee of forty-one dollars.

He stopped before getting on the freeway, studying the maps before heading south. He exited at the Sierra Point off-ramp, undercut the freeway, cruised past three buildings of totally different architecture. One had a tight, oily black outer skin, the next was a mini-skyscraper of mint green, the third a sprawling white complex that looked like a space station to Santos. He saw an array of boat masts in the distance. The parking area was neatly laid out. The cars were of all sizes, shapes, makes, and colors. There was just one van, white, no markings. He immediately recognized the license plate, heaved a sigh of relief, and pulled into a space directly across from the van.

The van was there, but what about the boat? Would Davila be clever enough to up anchor and move across the bay? It would be difficult to track down but not impossible. He left the car and casually strolled by the van, hands in his raincoat pockets. He looked around carefully. No one was paying him any attention. He wandered to the back of the van, peering in the window. The gurney was still there, and a blanket lay crumpled on the floor.

Sloppy, he told himself. Cesar, I thought I taught you better than that. He returned to his car and drove it toward the far end of the parking lot, where the view of the docks was better. A derrick floated out in the water three hundred yards away, pile-driving logs into the soft bay mud, constructing a sea break. The pounding sound reverberated over the water in a steady, boring rhythm, almost like the beat of a slowed-down Latin song: cha cha boom, cha cha boom. Be there, he prayed softly to himself as he leaned over the steering wheel, focusing the binoculars. He found the pier Naimat had told him of, holding his breath until he saw the boat. The *Olé*. A big white cruiser, stern to the dock, with a dark blue canvas awning pulled back to allow access to the boarding steps. Just as Naimat had described it.

He leaned back and thought about just how to get to Abrams. He couldn't wait until dark. The *Olé* might pull out at any moment. Davila wouldn't be alone. He'd have that fool Moreno with him. Maybe some of Moreno's gang. He got out of the car and studied the yacht harbor. A two-story building, gray with blue trim, rose directly in front of the four piers. The offices of the harbor master. Santos focused the binoculars on the building. A pretty raven-haired woman was behind the counter, talking to a middle-aged man in foul-weather gear.

There was a path, set between a well-trimmed lawn and the seawall, leading out to a concrete bridge connected to the piers. Thin Italian poplars were being blown around by the wind. They would give no cover at all. A small brick building was at the end of the path. Rene focused the binoculars on the building's sign. MEN'S ROOM. There would be a woman's room on the opposite side. A vending machine was in front of the little building. Alongside the vending machine was a pay telephone.

To the left of the harbor master's building was a long, narrow concrete pier jutting out into the murky bay waters. A lone fisherman in a bright red parka was slowly reeling in his line. Rene could see no way to get to the *Olé* without being seen. He dropped the binoculars, letting them hang from his neck by their thin plastic cord, then went back to the car. He popped the trunk and made a quick change of clothes, donning the baseball cap, replacing the raincoat with the jacket, and slipping on the tennis shoes. He fingered the Beretta. Very little firepower, but in this case, size meant everything.

He slipped the knife from his belt and unscrewed the gun's checkered walnut handles, then slipped the weapon into his waistband. He went to work on a mini-sized blasting cap and a detonator, checking them carefully, making sure the detonator's battery was operable.

He stood up, hearing the bones in his knees pop, and slammed the car trunk shut. Santos pulled the beak of the baseball cap over his forehead, slipped on the sunglasses, rolled a handkerchief around his right fist, then walked quickly to the harbor master's office.

The woman greeted him with a smile. "Can I help you, sir?"

"Yes. I'm a doctor. Rather silly of me, but I was getting my fishing gear together and I cut my hand."

The woman's expression mirrored her concern. "Shall I call an ambulance?"

"No, that's not necessary. If I could just get some bandages."

She left the counter and came back with a small first-aid box. She opened the box and Rene picked through the supply of tape, gauze, and ointments.

"This is all I should need," he said, selecting a roll of half-inch tape, some square gauze pads, a tube of ointment, and a pair of scissors. "Is there a room I can use?"

"Surely. The rest room is right there, Doctor. Let me know if I can be of any help."

Santos thanked her for her kindness. Once inside the rest room he turned on the basin's faucet, then tore off several bands of tape in ten-inch lengths. He took off his coat and rolled his shirtsleeve up, then taped the Beretta to his left forearm, the tip of the silencer resting against his leather watchband. He pulled up his right pant leg and used a strip of the tape to anchor the detonator to the back of his calf. He took his time, making sure the switch was free of the tape. He armed the detonator and carefully lowered the pant leg.

There was a knock at the door.

"Everything okay in there, Doctor?"

"Yes. Just fine, thank you. I'll be right out."

Santos used the scissor blade on the inside seam of the jacket, cutting the seam open from a few inches above the cuff to the elbow. He ran a piece of tape under the opening in the coat sleeve, pressing the tape down lightly so that it barely held the material together.

He took a quick look at himself in the mirror, then exited the room, his supposedly injured hand jammed into his jacket pocket. He again thanked the pleasant woman for her good deed.

Rene strolled slowly over the small bridge and onto the concrete pier, whistling a tuneless melody in time to the pile driver's action, the blasting cap in the palm of his right hand. As he approached the bow of the *Olé*, he bent to one knee, pretending to adjust a shoe string while dropping the blasting cap into the center of a neatly coiled mooring line. There was no sign of life from within the *Olé*.

"Cesar," he shouted. "Come on out. We need to talk."

There was nothing but silence. "I'm alone, Cesar, so show yourself."

Slowly the hair, forehead, then eyes of a man showed over the window of the ship's cabin. Santos's eyes narrowed. The face was unfamiliar, a big, burly man. Who the hell was he? Someone Cesar had picked up to do his dirty work? Maybe one of Moreno's men.

"Tell your boss I'm here," he said angrily.

The man's eyes bored into Santos's, a mixture of fear and hatred.

Rene climbed up the ladder slowly, and once on board he sat down on the boat's railing, legs spread apart, hands resting on his knees, the palms in an upright position. The man came up on deck, a long-barreled pistol dangling from his right hand.

"I'm not armed," Rene said. "Get Cesar."

A head popped up from the ladder leading down below. It was Tony Moreno, wearing stained jockey shorts and a V-neck white T-shirt, the front splattered with yellowish stains, a heavy gold cross dangling from his neck. "You—you son of a bitch," Moreno declared. "How did you find me?"

"Where's Cesar Davila?"

"Down below. Come, I'll show you." He motioned with his head to the man with the gun. "Gus, if he doesn't move his ass, shoot him."

"You may want to reconsider, Tony. I have a man in the parking lot. He's an expert marksman and has the boat zeroed in. Anything happens to me and he'll start shooting, and that'll be the end of the both of you. And Paul Abrams too."

"You think I'm stupid? That I'd fall for such a story?" Moreno demanded with a sneer. "That's *puro caca*. Pure bullshit."

"You're obviously not stupid. You got Abrams away from me, didn't you? But at what cost?" He turned to look at the other man. "Stand still. You might get my man with the rifle nervous."

"He's full of shit, Gus. Don't worry about it. Grab him." Moreno was still covered by the cockpit leading to the cabins below, out of the vision of a possible sniper.

"Let's not fight," Rene said, calmly, leaning backward, folding his arms over each other. "We're all after the same thing. How is Abrams?"

"None of your fucking business," Moreno grumbled nastily.

Gus Melendez looked from Rene Santos to the parking lot. He thought he saw the sun glinting off something, perhaps a telescopic sight. "I don't think he's kidding, Tony."

"You seem to be the one in charge now, Tony. How much do you want for Abrams?"

Moreno scratched his crotch. "More than you've got."

"Maybe not. I have a client. I made a deal with him. He still wants Abrams. You have him now. I'm willing to deal with you."

Moreno's laugh was like a dog's bark. "Yeah, you got five million dollars lying around?"

"Sure," Santos answered quickly. "That figure is not a problem. Let's do it."

Santos could see the doubt in Moreno's eyes. Moreno twisted his head to look behind him, down into the bowels of the boat.

Santos timed his movement with the pile driver, jamming his right calf back against the bulkhead at the booming sound. The blasting cap exploded, and Gus and Moreno ducked instinctively. Rene tore his coat sleeve apart, pushing his left palm away from the line of fire, his right index finger latching onto the Beretta's trigger. He felt the powder burns on his wrist. The first bullet went wide, the next four caught Gus in the stomach and chest. He dropped to the teak deck, spinning around in a circle as if one foot were nailed in place.

Rene walked toward Tony Moreno slowly, exposing the gun on his wrist. "Get down below! Drag that man with you."

Moreno bent over at the waist, his hand groping for one of Gus's legs, his eyes wide open, staring at Rene.

"Don't think of trying for the gun, Tony," Santos warned. "Come on, damn it! Get him down below!"

Moreno followed orders, straining at the effort required to pull Gus down the stairs. Rene glanced up and down the dock. No one had made an appearance. He picked up the gun Gus Melendez had been holding.

"Where's Abrams?" Rene barked once they were all down below deck.

"In—in the cabin, there."

"Where's Davila?"

"With Abrams. They're both okay," Moreno babbled. "I didn't hurt them. I didn't—"

"Shut up." Rene stuck a toe into Gus's body on the floor. There was no response. He kicked hard at the man's bleeding stomach. Still no response. He pointed the gun at Moreno's right eye. "Who else is on board?"

"No one. Just Dolores. A girl. That's all, just a girl."

"Who else?" Santos demanded.

"That's it. I swear!"

"If you're lying, I shoot your balls off one at a time. Show me Abrams."

Moreno walked crouched over, his hands above his head, almost bumping against the ceiling. There were three teak cabin doors. He opened one. Rene could see Paul Abrams on a bed, face up, head on a pillow, ropes tied across his chest and legs. A gag was placed in his mouth, a black scarf across his eyes. Cesar Davila was on the floor, trussed up like a pig ready for slaughter, mouth taped shut, dried blood caked on his head. He opened an eye, saw Rene, and tried to move, his efforts obviously causing him pain.

"Sit tight, Cesar," Rene said, flashing a smile. "I'll be back. We have much to talk about, old friend." He turned to Moreno. "All right. Now the girl. Dolores. Where is she?"

Moreno pointed at a door on the opposite side of the narrow hallway. "In there."

"Let's pay a visit."

The girl was lying in the middle of a large bed, naked, her legs twisted over each other. She opened her eyes slowly, shaking her head, causing her long, dark hair to sway in front of her face.

Sixteen, seventeen, at most, Rene estimated. She groaned, her mind still clouded from the drugs consumed the night before. She put her arms behind her back and struggled into a sitting position. "What's the matter? What's happening, Tony?" she asked softly in Spanish.

Santos could see the traces of white powder under her nostrils. It was a shame, but she'd seen him now. He had no other choice. He pushed Moreno against the wall.

Dolores was blinking, trying to focus her eyes. She barely heard Santos say, *"Vaya con Dios,"* before he pulled the trigger.

Chapter 31

The sound of the shower running woke Jack Kordic from a deep sleep. He blinked his eyes at the dappled sunlight streaming through the curtains. He started to get up, but flopped back against the pillow, listening to the running water and wondering what would happen when it stopped. When Mary Aliza would come out of the bathroom. What would she say? What would he say? He tried to think of something witty, sophisticated. Nothing came to mind. The water stopped. He could hear her moving around. The tap turned on and off. He could picture her, a towel wrapped around her beautiful body, staring into the bathroom mirror, perhaps wondering how she had gotten herself into this mess.

He pushed the bedcovers back and got to his feet and slipped on his pants. He was looking for his shirt when she came into the room, her head turbaned in a damp towel, his shirt around her shoulders, buttoned at the bottom, the top gaping open, drawing his eyes.

"Good morning," she said cheerfully. "God, I'm hungry. How about you?"

"Famished," Kordic acknowledged, surprised at just how hungry he was.

Mary fingered the shirttail. "I had to borrow this. I don't have much else."

Kordic crossed to his closet, pulling out a dark brown flannel robe. "Sorry about that. I'm not really set up for visitors."

Mary took the robe, her hand touching his.

Kordic felt the same electricity that he had during

their lovemaking. He pulled her close, his lips searching for hers.

Mary broke the kiss after a while, rocking lightly back on her heels. "I'll get the coffee going."

By the time Kordic had showered, shaved, and slipped into a fresh shirt, the coffee was poured. Mary had donned her satin dress and stood with a steaming cup in her hand, staring out the front window at the Pacific Ocean breaking onto the beach.

"This is nice, Jack. Have you been here long?"

"No, just a few months." He took a sip of the coffee. "This whole area used to be an amusement park. Playland at the Beach. Roller coaster, fun house, carnival games. They tore it all down years ago." He tapped a sheetrock wall. "Put in these things."

Mary decided to be direct. "You sold your house after your wife and son were killed?"

"Yes. Too big. Too many ghosts."

There was an uneasy pause, after which Mary said, "Talk is cheap. What about breakfast?"

Kordic was glad to have something to do with his hands. He had always enjoyed cooking, helping his wife prepare the evening meal, sharing a glass of wine while they made a salad, chopped vegetables, went over the news of the day while preparing the chicken or making a marinade for barbecuing steaks. Then helping with the dishes. Danny flashed into his mind. One of his son's birthday parties—the sink a jumble of ice-cream-smudged glasses and dishes—Kordic trying to get them all into the dishwasher. "Don't worry, Pop," Danny had reassured him. "Mom can get a Volkswagen in there."

On his own, he had found cooking a form of therapy, a time killer, a hands-on experience that kept his mind away from all the dark images. He expertly assembled a pair of Spanish omelets, warming tortillas in the microwave, slathering them with butter while both of them listened to the portable TV, picking up the latest news of the bombing at the Opera House and the Abrams kidnapping.

Mary mopped up the last of her omelet with a piece

of tortilla. "That was great. If you do windows, I may never let you out of my sight."

"Before I start on the windows, I better call the office, see just what I'm supposed to be doing."

The Homicide lines were busy. He finally got through after the eighth try.

Charlotte, the office receptionist, answered in a harried voice, speaking so fast the words ran together, "Homicide, how can I help you?"

Kordic identified himself. Her voice dropped to that of a conspiratorial whisper. "Jack, Lieutenant Tilson has been raising hell. He wants to talk to you."

"Is he around now?"

"No. He's with the chief, I think."

"Well, tell him I came in and left. Any messages?"

He could hear the sound of rustling papers as Charlotte rummaged through the stacks of notes on her desk. "I don't see any, Jack. But it's been bedlam around here. Wait a minute." There was more rustling, then Charlotte came back on the line. "There was a call for you. Max Freeman from the Israeli Consulate. He's called twice. Said it was urgent." She gave Kordic the number.

Kordic thanked her, then said, "Don't forget to tell Tilson I was in. Talk to you later."

When Kordic hung up, Mary said, "Is that lieutenant still giving you a bad time?"

"Yep, he's still at it."

"I need a change of clothes, Jack. Can you drive me back to my apartment, then to the office?"

"Sure. Let me make one quick call."

Max Freeman sounded anxious when they were connected.

"Inspector Kordic, we have to get together. I have some information that will be valuable to you."

"I should have called you earlier," Kordic apologized, filling Freeman in on his identification of Joseph Rosenberg as Joe Rose from Coalinga.

"Yes, I'm aware of that. There is someone you should meet. A colleague. He has more information on Mr. Rosenberg. He's here at the consulate now. You

should meet with him. I think you will find it inform-
ative."

Santos tied Tony Moreno to the bed, next to the life-
less body of the young girl. He made the knots extra
tight, using a particular type of truss he had learned
years ago at a PLO training camp in Libya, the ropes
looping from the hands behind the back, through the
legs, up to and around the neck. The more the victim
struggled, the more the pain increased and the closer
he came to strangling himself. The trick was to remain
motionless as long as possible. The training camp in-
structor, a battle-scarred Libyan with a swooping mustache, had used captured Israelis as guinea pigs. The
longest Santos had seen a victim last was slightly more
than an hour.

He explained the situation to Moreno. "You are going to talk. Tell me everything you know, or I am
going to leave you alone here with your young friend."
He patted the dead girl's thigh. "In about ten minutes
the pain will be so intense that you will beg me to
shoot you, like I did her. But I won't do that. I'll simply stuff one of your filthy socks in your mouth and let
you strangle yourself." He gave a slight pull on the
strand of rope, causing Moreno to cry out in pain.

"Talk," Santos commanded.

Moreno talked continually for several minutes, telling Santos many things he already knew. He ran his
fingers lightly across the rope.

"You spoke to Mrs. Abrams directly. From where?"
Santos feared the idiot had called from the phone
booth near the rest rooms on the dock.

"From a phone booth. In San Francisco. I'm not a
fool."

Santos twinged the rope again, as if it were a guitar
string. "Wrong. You are a fool," he said over Moreno's
gasps. "What made you think you could get away with
all of this?"

Moreno's voice was almost a croak. "You were going to kill me, weren't you? You. Or Cesar. Or the
dyke."

Maybe I was too quick to judge, Santos thought. Maybe he wasn't a complete fool. "Who else knows about your calls to Mrs. Abrams?"

"No one. It was just Gus and me. Gustavo. The man you shot. He's the bartender at El Condado. He works for me. The girl was just for party time."

Santos remembered Cesar mentioning the bartender, but not giving him the name. "What was your impression of Mrs. Abrams? Does she plan to pay?"

"Please," Moreno begged, biting down on his lower lip. "Loosen the knots. Please."

Santos gave the rope another flick with his thumb. "Answer the question. Does she plan to pay?"

"What choice has she got? Sure, she'll pay." A look of hope filled Moreno's watery eyes. "She knows my voice. I talked to her. She's expecting to hear from me."

Rene ran his hands up and down the rope, seeing terror flood into Moreno's features. He adjusted the knot behind Moreno's back, slacking off the tension an inch or so. It would still be uncomfortable, but Moreno wouldn't strangle himself. He slid one of Moreno's soiled socks from his foot, holding it in his hand as if it were a mouse, then stuffed it cruelly into Moreno's mouth. He then unclasped the chain holding the large gold cross on Moreno's neck, examined it briefly, then leaned over and placed it around the neck of the dead girl.

Cesar Davila looked every bit as frightened as Moreno had as Rene entered the cabin, knife in hand. Rene first checked Paul Abrams, pulling the soggy gag from his mouth.

Abrams shook his head as he attempted to spit out tiny bits of cloth he'd chewed from the gag.

"Be patient, Mr. Abrams," Rene advised him. "I will release you in a moment. Let you regain your circulation. Relieve yourself. Have something to eat." He put the tip of the knife's blade against Abrams's nose. "But keep your blindfold on at all times. Your only hope of surviving is if you do not see me. If the blindfold slips, you're a dead man. Understood?"

"Yes, yes," Paul Abrams said, his voice sandpaper dry. "Water, please. Something to drink. Please."

"In a minute," Santos said, stooping over Cesar Davila, the knife flashing down and cutting through the ropes across his chest. "First I have to talk to your friend here. Then we'll get you something to drink. And then we'll talk."

Jack Kordic looked into the small surveillance camera above the entrance to the Israeli Consulate as he announced himself. "Mr. Freeman is expecting me," he added.

The door buzzed open. Max Freeman was inside, dressed in a tweed suit, matching vest, tattersall shirt, and brown bow tie. He looked nervous as he pumped Kordic's hand vigorously and led him down a corridor of cream-colored walls. Freeman stopped in front of an unmarked door, knocked twice, then opened the door and waved Kordic through.

The room was a large square box. A walnut table ringed with dove gray leather chairs took up most of the space. The table was littered with foolscap notepads, ashtrays brimming with cigarette butts and piles of pipe ashes. A pink carton of donuts and a liter-sized thermal carafe surrounded by paper cups were at one end of the table. There were no windows, no posters. A bank of telephones and a fax machine were set along a counter rimming one wall. There was one man in the room. He looked up at Kordic and nodded, reaching for a donut. "Help yourself. They're not bad."

Kordic put him at one or two years from either side of fifty. He had short, Brillo-pad gray hair. His skin was tree bark brown. He dunked the donut in a coffee cup and munched away, watching Kordic through curiously pale blue eyes under broadly arched brows. He was wearing a short-sleeve white shirt with a dark blue knit tie unbuttoned at the collar.

Max Freeman made the introduction. "Inspector Jack Kordic, this is Mr. Weeks."

Kordic slid into a chair directly opposite the man

eating the donut. "Does Mr. Weeks have a first name? Or a title? Captain? Lieutenant? Ambassador?"

Weeks chomped down the rest of his donut, brushing the powdered sugar from his hands. "No, no title. Just Weeks is fine." He smiled at Freeman. "Thank you, Max. We'll be okay now."

Freeman backed out of the room. The door closed behind him with a solid click. The two men stared at each other, both taking stock, looking for obvious strengths or, more important, weaknesses.

"Nice office you have here, Mr. Weeks," Kordic finally said.

Weeks pursed his lips, picking through the donuts, settling for one covered with a thick coating of chocolate. "Shouldn't do this. Bad for the blood. But what the hell. No one lives forever. Sure you won't have one?"

"You look like a busy man," Kordic said. "I don't want to waste your time."

"Well put," Weeks said, dropping the donut back into the pink box. He shook a cigarette from a pack of Lucky Strikes, scorching it halfway down with a battered Zippo lighter, letting the smoke out of his lungs slowly, waving it away with the flat of his hand. "You did a good job on Joe Rosenberg. Very good."

"I wouldn't have gotten anywhere without that date of birth Freeman supplied me with."

"I wonder," Weeks said, staring at the chocolate donut.

"I'm not very skilled at international politics, Mr. Weeks. I don't know if you're part of the consulate, if you're with the Israeli version of the CIA, or what. You're some kind of a cop. So tell me what you want."

"I admit I have you at a disadvantage, Inspector. I know quite a bit about you. Just to make things a little even, I'll give you my credentials. The official name of my organization is the Central Institute for Intelligence and Special Assignment. Back home it's known as Sherbut Habitachon, or just Shin Bet. You've probably heard of us by the name Mossad." He reached for the thermos. "Coffee?"

"Sure," Kordic said, knowing there was no sense in trying to rush Weeks into his story. He had the solid look of a professional who knew his business and wasn't about to be pushed around.

"Tell me what you know about Joe Rosenberg," Weeks said as he poured the coffee.

Kordic gave him a brief rundown on the investigation to date, ending up with the information that some-one was sending fax messages to Rose's unlisted number in Coalinga. "The faxes are coming from Russia."

"Russia? My, my. Isn't that interesting? And these were received after you found Rose's body?"

"Right. Rose's secretary says they were worded just the way Rose would have worded them. They had some kind of a code. She's been faxing material to whoever was using the Rose code in Moscow. Another clever touch, there were messages on the company an-swering machine—brief messages from Rose. They must have made Rose record them before they killed him. Rose's attorney is supposed to come to town to-day. I don't know if I'll even have time to meet with him."

"Is he coming to identify the body?"

"There's not much left of it," Kordic pointed out.

Weeks worked his lips to remove a strand of tobacco from his teeth. "The tattooed number is enough. After we got your request for the number from Max—"

"This was in Israel?"

Weeks chalked a line in the air. "One point for you. Yes, it was in Israel. We did some checking on our own. He changed his name to Rose legally. Years ago."

"Mr. Freeman didn't relay that message to me."

"Mr. Freeman wasn't aware of it, or I'm sure he would have, Inspector. We knew of Rose, but never coupled the names." He held up a hand. "I know it sounds sloppy, but there was never really any reason to. Joseph Rosenberg came to America, disappeared. Joe Rose became a successful businessman. Rose trav-eled to Israel often. He also traveled to the Mideast, to Russia. They may not like Jews in those places, but when a Jew can help them, they make room for him. Rose's business was oil. Finding it, squeezing the last drop of it from a well. Warming it up so it could flow out of ice packs. He'd been traveling to Russia quite a bit lately."

Weeks stubbed the remains of the cigarette into a butt-filled ashtray, laced his fingers together, and cracked the knuckles. His eyes roved to the donuts again. " 'True it is that politics make strange bedfellows.' Do you know who first said that?"

"Can't say I do," Kordic said, becoming impatient.

"A man called Charles Dudley Warner. Wise man. Said all kinds of important things. But nothing quite so significant as that statement. Oil makes even stranger bedfellows, Inspector. God, for all his wisdom, chose to enrich the lands around Israel with oil. But for reasons known only to Him, he left us out. So we've had to make bargains with the devil to survive. Mideast devils, western devils, and devils farther north."

"Russia."

"Why not?" Weeks said, running a finger around the chocolate donut, then pulling it back to take a lick. " 'He must have a long spoon, who shall eat with the devil.' John Heywood." He smiled apologetically. "Excuse the quotations. I once had to spend almost a full year in a hospital. You wouldn't believe the things I read. Anyway, Russia is where it's at right now. For oil, I mean."

"And the Russians will sell to you?"

Weeks brought his hands together in one quick, derisive clap. "Not directly. They still hate our guts. But there are ways."

"And Rose was your man."

"He was a Jew," Weeks said bluntly. "An *altekoker,* a tough, independent oil bird who had paid his dues in the camps. He wasn't an agent, but he passed along information once in a while. Not to me, or my organization directly. But he let people in Israel know what was going on." He leaned back in his chair, waiting to see what Kordic would come up with.

It didn't take long. "Paul Abrams is your man."

"Abrams is not 'our man.' He's a Jew too, a *shtarker*. A big shot, but he's never supplied us with any intelligence, though I know he has excellent sources. He'll work with anyone to make a buck. But he has been supportive of us in some ways. If he gets into Russia, gets his oil fields and his refinery, once the oil is out of the country, on a tanker, it can go anywhere. A lot of it will go to us. We'll have to pay retail, but we'll get the oil." His hand moved reluctantly to the box of donuts again, selecting a glazed one this time, examining it as if it were a rare jewel. "Tell me about the kidnapping."

"You should be talking to my chief, not me," Kordic protested.

"There's no time for that, Inspector. You scratch my back, I'll scratch yours."

"My back's a little itchy right now."

"Touché," Weeks said grudgingly. "The kidnapping was an elaborate affair, right? Mr. Abrams is known to be extremely nervous about security. A fanatic would be a more accurate description. He had no regular time schedule, often wouldn't leave his home for days or weeks at a time. The house was a fortress. Members of your own department worked for him."

"One of whom was killed last night," Kordic said solemnly.

"Exactly. It was a bold, daring, ruthless plan. And it didn't come cheap. Not only in lives, but in the planning. The operation. This was no spur-of-the-moment group of Mafia hoodlums. Am I right?"

"As far as I know, you are."

Weeks stood up and walked over to the counter by the fax machine, coming back with a manila envelope. He pulled a photograph from the envelope and sailed it across the table to Kordic. "Ever see this man?"

Kordic studied the picture. It was black-and-white, grainy, obviously blown up from a much smaller negative. The head of a man. The skin sallow. The face round, the nose slightly pronounced, the cheeks puffy, riddled with pockmarks. His hair was receding at the temples. His eyes focused on something straight ahead,

out of sight of the camera. They were hard, dark eyes.
"Not exactly a happy camper," Kordic said.

"He wasn't aware the picture was being taken. It's
old, but it's one of the few we have of him without a
mask or stocking over his face." Weeks dug back into
the envelope. "How about this one?"

The second picture was also black-and-white, the
man older, darker, with thick, shoulder-length hair, a
full beard. "He looks like a lot of people I've seen, but
no one in particular."

"Part of his charm," Weeks said dryly as he pulled
another picture from the envelope and handed it to
Kordic.

The third man was older still, gray hair plastered
across his forehead curling around his ears, dark eyes
curtained by tufts of gray hair. "This looks like a mug
shot," Kordic said, sliding the picture back across the
desk.

"It is. Frederick Kroder. A German. A fanatic."

"None of them rings any bells with me," Kordic
said, standing up and rubbing the small of his back.
"You think one of them is involved in the Abrams kidnapping?"

"They are all possibilities. All major league terrorists. You Americans were once immune from these
types of gentlemen, but no more, eh? You've joined
the rest of us. The rest of the world that has to put up
with this scum."

"It seems we have. But I don't see how any of this
helps me."

"Each of these men is a professional, but they all
operate differently. Fill me in on the details of what
happened at the Opera House, then maybe I can help."

It was Kordic's time for show and tell. He gave
Weeks a brief rundown of what he knew, ending with:
"A woman was killed by a motor vehicle about two
blocks away from the Opera House. She was armed.
The gun had a silencer." Kordic handed Weeks the picture of the accident victim and went into detail on the
attacks on Mary Ariza.

Weeks was patient. He sat listening, asking the occasional question, lighting one cigarette from the butt of another.

"Go back and tell me about this lieutenant. The one who was killed in his office," Weeks said, splitting the remains of the coffee between them.

When Kordic was through with his narrative, Weeks held up one of the pictures. The first one. "I'm betting this is your man. It's his kind of operation. He likes to use local people, a few of his own men to work with the locals, so he remains hidden, unseen. He doesn't like to leave witnesses. We got a tip that he was in South America, but we couldn't pin him down. I'd do anything to get my hands on him."

"Why all the interest?" Kordic asked. "What did he do?"

Weeks's voice grew harsh. "What didn't he do? Years ago you Americans were obsessed with one terrorist. Carlos. Remember him?"

"Yes. He got a lot of press."

"Carlos, real name Ilich Ramirez Sanchez. A Venezuelan by birth. Yes, he was a big item. But the ones that get all the press aren't the worst ones, Inspector. It's the ones that you never hear about that you should fear the most. This man goes by many names. The latest we have is Rene Santos. He's a terrorist for hire. He worked for them all—the IRA, Baader-Meinhof gang, the Japanese Red Army, the Cubans. The targets didn't matter to him, but in those days a lot of the targets were Jews. Qadaffi used him often. So did the Syrians, the Iraquis, the Popular Front for the Liberation of Palestine. All those *mumzers*. He was responsible for killing several of my comrades. We want him quite badly."

"What's a *mumzer*?"

"A bastard," Weeks explained. "A real bastard."

Kordic turned the picture over. A list of the man's criminal activities, his description, date of birth, and a.k.a.'s, also known as, were neatly printed on the back of the photograph. Alongside the foreign names were English translations. He ran his eye casually down the list.

"What is it?" Weeks asked when he saw Kordic's facial features freeze.

"El Cabecilla. The conductor."

"Yes. Because he likes to play the orchestra leader. He picks the notes, lets the others make the music. A symphony of terror."

Kordic studied the photograph. "I think we've found the right man. Mary Ariza, the woman I told you about, before she was attacked she stopped to help a man who had an apparent heart attack. He was in shock, thought she was a priest, told her his confession. One of the things he mentioned was being afraid of El Cabecilla. The priest who—"

"What priest?" queried Weeks.

"A priest visited Ariza at her office, asking about the man who died on the street. Mary mentioned the man being afraid of El Cabecilla. The priest told Mary his father was an orchestra conductor."

"Priest," Weeks snorted. "That was no priest. What'd he look like?"

"The description was handsome." Kordic held the photograph up. "Nothing like this guy, that's for sure."

Anatoly Weeks got to his feet. "Listen, if you looked like that, you'd have some plastic surgeon do you over. And Santos has more than just one reason to change his appearance. Come on. Show me what you've got in your morgue."

Chapter 32

There was a possibility that one of Moreno's gang would show up looking for the boat, so Rene Santos felt it necessary to move the *Olé* from the Brisbane Marina. The navigational charts on board showed that the Coyote Point Marina was just a few miles south.

Santos had no problem navigating the powerboat to Coyote Point. He docked in a guest slip, arranged the canvas deck cover so that it covered the *Olé*'s markings, and listed the boat with the harbor master under the name *Fortuna*. Which was exactly what was on board. He paid in cash, indicating that he'd be there no more than a day or two.

Santos felt good. *De buena suerta*. Luck was with him. It was coming together. He could feel it. Taste it.

The *Olé* bobbed easily in its slip as a good-sized sailboat maneuvered past it, disappearing into a hive of similar craft.

Rene climbed aboard, ran below, checked his passengers, then undid the mooring lines and got the *Olé* under power again. He steered north, under the monstrous shadows of jet liners approaching the airport. He found a stretch of calm water the charts described as an old seaplane harbor that was adjacent to the airport's northerly landing strips, then dropped anchor.

Cesar Davila was trussed up uncomfortably between the dead bodies of Tony Moreno and the girl, Dolores. Davila's enormous strength didn't help a bit now. He stared at Rene with popping eyes, the tendons of his neck standing out like strands of wire. He'd made Davila watch while he had interrogated Moreno. Made him watch Moreno die, after Rene was sure he'd gotten all he needed from the foolish young man.

Abrams was alone in the next cabin, tied to the chair. Santos loosened the ropes so he could maneuver a bit.

"I'm back," Rene announced. "I'll take out the gag."

"Thanks," Abrams said once the gag was removed. "I could use a drink."

The *Ole*'s small galley was crammed with hard liquor, wine, and beer, as well as a supply of marijuana and cocaine, but the food consisted only of canned soups, chips, and peanuts.

"I'll get you a beer." He took two Coronas from the galley fridge and brought them back to Abrams. "I'll undo your left arm. Don't touch your blindfold."

Abrams chugalugged most of the first beer down, pulling the bottle away from his lips reluctantly, wiping his sleeve across his mouth. "That gag is very uncomfortable."

"Things could be worse," Santos advised him.

"What's next? Did you contact my wife about the ransom?"

"No. That was another man's idea, though I think I'll go along with it. How much do you think they'll pay for you?"

"Another man? Is he the one you killed?"

"What makes you think that?" Santos asked sharply.

"The screams. When the screams stopped, I figured he was dead. He wasn't very smart, you know. I hope you're smarter. You sound like an intelligent man. A businessman. Just listening to you, it's obvious that you are a man used to being in charge. There was a screw-up, right? Those men I was with last night, they were idiots. Vulgar. At one point I thought they were going to kill me. I tried to make it plain to them that I was worth more alive than dead. But they were like two drunken sailors, only interested in the woman. Boasting of how they had fooled everyone." Abrams pulled his shoulders up toward his ears. "I know how these things can happen. The most carefully planned business transaction, months of preparation, all jeopardized because of one stupid fool. It happens. All too often. But you are in control now. What's your next move? Pretend you are going to deliver me to my wife? Take off with the ransom? Then deliver me to whoever it is who planned all this?"

"That doesn't sound like an unprofitable scenario."

Abrams drained the rest of the beer from the bottle. "Could I have another?"

"Certainly." Santos handed him the second Corona.

"The other man. The one you killed. I made a deal with him. I hope I can make one with you too."

"Tell me about the deal."

"He was unrealistic. He wanted five million in cash. I suggested that wasn't plausible. Coming up with that amount of cash in a short time is a problem. Even for me. But he insisted. Under the circumstances, however, I couldn't argue with him."

Santos snorted. "And just how was this ransom to be paid?"

"There was a great deal of arguing between the two men as to just how and where the delivery would be made. My wife was to deliver the money, but I don't know if they ever settled on a plan."

"I don't think the police would just let your wife waltz out the front door with five million dollars tucked under her arm."

"Why not?" Abrams queried. "I haven't been kidnapped. I call my wife. My attorney. Tell them that I'm fine. That I had to leave on a confidential business matter. That the Opera House business had nothing to do with me. I would claim that whoever made the phone call saying I was kidnapped was just some crazy taking advantage of a terrible situation."

"The police would never believe that."

"Who cares what they believe? If my attorney tells them to back off, they'll back off."

"Just like that," Santos said scornfully.

"Yes. Just like that, believe me. They'll do as they're told."

Santos was impressed with the man's bravado. Ordering the police around as if they were a bunch of waiters. "I'm going to untie your other arm. Your legs are still tied to the chair, but you can stand up and stretch if you want."

Abrams did just that, getting to his feet unsteadily, then moving his arms around, an athlete stretching his muscles before a contest.

"Sit back down," Santos ordered, pleased when Abrams followed his instructions immediately.

Abrams took a sip of the beer, swishing the liquid around his teeth before swallowing. "How did you become involved in all of this?"

"I'm an independent. I was paid to get you, Mr. Abrams. It's as simple as that."

"By who?"

"Are you sure you want to know?"

"I'll know sooner or later, won't I? Unless you plan to kill me. And that would be a mistake."

"Why's that?"

"Because I am worth money. A great deal of money. So who was it?"

"Why should I tell you?" asked Santos.

"I'd like to know who went through all this trouble. Who was it?"

Santos considered the question. How much should he tell Abrams? Could he squeeze something out of the man? The ransom deal. As dumb as Moreno was, there was no sense in letting that much money pass him by. He thought about what had happened to Rose, and what they probably had in mind for Abrams, and for him too if they had their way. "Russians," he finally said.

Abrams relaxed, the tension slowly leaving his body. Russians. The oil deal. Of course. "Can you give me a name?"

"No, I think not."

Abrams blinked his eyes behind the blindfold. It had to be a major player. Someone he knew. Someone who knew him. "Let me guess then. Lotkin? Atikan? Petrov? Buchanic? Fedelchak?"

"That's quite a list."

"Yes," Abrams agreed hurriedly. "All former Russian intelligence officers. The whole of Russia is awash with them. Was I right? Is he one of them?"

"Yes. Now pick the rabbit out of the hat, and I'll get you something to eat."

Abrams rolled the beer bottle across his forehead. Which one? It could be any one of them. All were cutthroats who wouldn't hesitate to kidnap, or kill, to gain their objective. Who was the best of the bunch? Or, more practically, the worst? The most ruthless. Petrov. He'd seen Petrov briefly in St. Petersburg! In the hotel lobby of the Grand Hotel Europe. Petrov, his hair neatly trimmed, a stylish cashmere topcoat. He had looked more like a rich Swedish tourist than a former spy. It had to be him. He had been with the GRU's fifth directorate—operational intelligence. Petroleum was his speciality—and he discreetly peddled his contacts and information to the highest bidder. It had been five years since they'd done any business together. They'd met in Moscow, then Istanbul. The Russian supplied him with information on the new refineries being built in Izmir. The information had been well worth the price Petrov demanded. "Viktor Petrov," he said with confidence.

Santos was impressed. "Was that a lucky guess, or are you a mind reader?"

"Petrov. He's working for one of the other oil companies. That's it. He wants to know what I'm bidding on." The confidence drained from Abrams's voice. Petrov would get the information. Then kill him. He was certain of that. He couldn't let him live. "Let's make a deal. You kill Petrov, and I will give you the five million dollars those fools thought they were going to get for me."

Santos laughed out loud. "Five million. Is that what you think your life is worth?"

"Yes. Petrov can't be offering you that much."

"Maybe he's offering more than money, Mr. Abrams."

Abrams blew air through his lips. More than money. The man certainly couldn't be an idealist. "He has something on you, then. Well, Petrov will either use whatever he has or kill you. That's the way he operates."

"You sound as if you know Petrov quite well."

"Oh, I do. I've dealt with him before. I've never trusted him. I need someone I can trust. Someone to carry out operations for me. You could be that person."

"You would trust me?" Santos scoffed. "After what I've done?"

"Why not? Especially if you save my life. You're a businessman. I'm a businessman. Let's do business."

"You mean you have people kidnapped and murdered? I thought you were in oil."

"I am. And it involves dealing with some rough characters. I'll give you five million dollars for killing Petrov and setting me free."

"I'd like to see some of that money before I make a decision, Mr. Abrams."

Abrams maneuvered himself to the edge of the chair, as if he were going to jump up and run at any moment. "Yes, yes. Of course. I understand. I don't blame you at all. I want you to be able to trust me, so that we can negotiate future dealings."

He's clever, Santos admitted. Very clever. Not just a fool with billions. "Why should I trust you anymore than I'd trust Petrov?"

"Because I'm a very rich man. I want to live, and the only way I can accomplish that is by making a deal with you. I can help. Not just with money. Whatever it is Petrov has on you, we can get to. I want your help now. And in the future."

"You're also a ruthless bastard."

"Yes. But I'm a man of my word. You can't say that about Petrov. I've never reneged on a business deal. You set me free, kill Petrov, you'll get the money. That's a promise."

Santos fingered his cross, twisting it until the chain around his neck tightened. "Do you know a man named Joseph Rose?"

Abrams stiffened in his chair. "Rose! Shit! Petrov has him, doesn't he? I own Joe Rose. At least forty-nine percent of his company. He's working for me. Where is he?"

"He's dead."

The news shook Abrams. "Dead? Did you—"

"No. I just picked him up and delivered him to Petrov's people."

"They interrogated Rose before they killed him, of course."

"Of course. They picked his brain clean."

"Perhaps," Abrams conceded, "but not just anyone could pick Rose's brain. It would have to be someone who—"

"How about a couple of geotechnical engineers?"

Abrams's head sank to his chest. "Russian geotechnical engineers. You were there?"

"For a while. It got a little too technical for me. And too noisy. Rose did not give up his information easily. They kept at him for two days. I saw him work with the Russians, blueprints, diagrams, photographs. But I'm intrigued about you. Why does he want you? What is it that you have that Petrov wants to badly?"

"Me. Mostly. He'll want to know who I've bribed. But mostly he wants me. If I'm not around, Abrams Oil is out of the bidding."

Santos sifted the information. "What about the other companies involved?"

"I know the amount of their bids. No doubt Petrov, or the company he's working for, does too. The others are corporations. It takes a board meeting and dozens of conferences for them to come up with a counteroffer if there is a stalemate in negotiations. That's one of the reasons I've been so successful. One man, one vote. With me out of the way, and with the information Petrov got from old Joe Rose, he's a sure winner."

Santos rose to his feet, the scratching of the chair's legs on the floor causing Paul Abrams to twitch slightly.

"Relax. There are some things I have to do. I'll have to tie you up again."

When Abrams was bound to the chair, Santos wadded up a clean handkerchief. "The gag will have to go back too."

Abrams opened his mouth wide, a patient anticipating the dentist's drill. He quickly snapped his jaws shut. "Do we have a deal?"

"Possibly."

"What do I call you?" Abrams asked, once again stretching his mouth wide.

"What's in a name? You pick one."

"Well, since my life is literally in your hands, how about Savior?"

The phone was picked up immediately, as though they were waiting at the other end. "Your package will be ready tonight," Rene Santos said.

"You surprise me, Rene," Viktor Petrov said truthfully. "From what I see on the television and hear on the radio, it is hard to believe you still have possession of our mutual interest."

"You above all people should know that you cannot believe what you see on television, Viktor."

Petrov cocked his head and looked up as Boris Zorkin hurried into the room. "When will I take possession?"

"I'm not certain yet. Perhaps by eleven," Santos answered.

Petrov studied the Regency-style long-case clock opposite his desk. "Why so late? Why not right now?"

"The package has to be delivered to the right destination. The package can then be examined at leisure. You will bring the items we discussed? The money and the documents?"

"Yes, yes, of course," Petrov said hurriedly. "What is the address?"

"You already know, Viktor. Cesar told Zorkin. But I wouldn't try to get there before I do. Say hello to Boris for me," Santos said before hanging up.

"What do you think?" Boris Zorkin asked once Petrov had cradled the phone.

Petrov held up one finger to signal the answer would be forthcoming.

Zorkin waited impatiently, shifting from one foot to the other. "Do you think Santos has Abrams?"

"I don't know," Petrov admitted reluctantly. "Rene is an actor. I can never tell when he's telling the truth. How long will it take to get to Brewster Street?"

"Twenty minutes, perhaps a little longer."

Petrov drummed his fingers on the desktop. "Go. Observe. Don't get too close. I'm sure Rene has the house booby-trapped. Let me know when he shows up. What he is driving. If he's alone. You've heard nothing from Davila?"

"Not a word."

Petrov's long fingers started drumming faster, a pianist pounding out the same notes over and over. "And the woman? Naimat."

"Not a word," Zorkin said again.

"Then we have to assume Santos killed them. What we don't know is just what they told dear old Rene before they died."

"They could have been killed during the kidnapping," Zorkin volunteered.

Petrov considered the suggestion. One might have died. There was talk on the news about a woman being run down but no details. All the speculation had been about Abrams.

Had Davila or Naimat succeeded in snatching Abrams from Rene, only to find Rene waiting, taking him back? It made no sense for Santos to promise Abrams if he couldn't produce him. He looked up to see Zorkin staring at him. "What are you still doing here?" he demanded. "Go, damn it, man. Go."

"You do have a first name, don't you?" Jack Kordic asked as he showed the Israeli the way through the coroner's office to the refrigerated body cubicles.

"Sure. Anatoly. Tough one to shorten. An doesn't work, neither does Toly. So let's just stick with Weeks, okay?"

The wall of stainless steel body cabinets stretched down to the end of the tiled corridor. Kordic checked the ID tags on each slot, finding the coded number the clerk had given him for the woman killed by a vehicle at Laguna and Fulton. It was a bottom drawer. He bent down and gave the drawer a tug. It rolled out smoothly on a row of casters. The body was covered by a sheet, once white, now tinged gray and ringed with bleach stains.

Weeks pulled the sheet back and studied the body. "Santos has had a woman as part of his team for years, though he's said to be asexual. Loves no one but himself. The woman was described as a Palestinian. This could be her." He took a palm-sized ink pad and several pieces of playing-card-sized paper from his jacket pocket and reached for the dead woman's right hand. "You don't mind if I print her, do you, Inspector?"

"I can get you a copy of the coroner's prints."

Weeks smiled without putting much effort into it. "Thanks, but if you don't mind . . ." Weeks didn't finish the sentence or wait for Kordic's permission. He expertly ran the thumb and all four fingers over the ink pad, then carefully rolled one of the pieces of paper around each finger. "Lot easier getting prints when they're alive." When he had finished the job he added, "Lot easier on them too. Let's see the next one."

"You'll have to narrow that request down," Kordic said dryly.

"The guy who collapsed on the street. The one who told his confession to Mary Ariza."

Kordic had to go back to the office to get the right shelf number. When he returned, Weeks was leaning casually against the wall, an unlit cigarette dangling from the corner of his mouth.

Kordic found the correct drawer, and stood back watching as Weeks went to work again.

"Getting ripe, even with all this refrigeration," Weeks reported, his nostrils pinched tight. "This guy looks a little familiar, Inspector. I've seen his picture somewhere before. Can't say where." He went through the fingerprinting procedure in the same professional manner as he had on the woman. He pocketed the ink pad and paper and backed away, shaking his body like a dog shaking off water. "I'll fax these back home.

Sometimes we can work off a fax, sometimes not. But I'll bet you a steak dinner that both of these stiffs turn up as terrorists who work for Rene Santos."

Kordic pushed the body drawer closed with his knee. It closed with a solid thunk. "I'm not sure if I want to win or lose that bet, Anatoly."

Chapter 33

Mary Ariza pushed herself away from the table, stood up, placed her hands on her hips and arched her back, then rotated the trunk of her body slowly. The conference table in the Pontar & Kerr law library was littered with bound legal journals, four years of issues of the biweekly *Jury Decisions* magazine and stacks of the daily *Legal Recorder*.

She'd been researching harassment suits, trying to find a precedent for Jack Kordic's problems with his superior officer.

The vast majority of the suits related to female plaintiffs going after male defendants for sexual harassment, or job-advancement restrictions under the ever present glass ceiling.

There were a handful of male vs. female cases, and a few like-sex filings, any one of which more or less fit the bill. A Los Angeles police sergeant had sued his lieutenant for harassment, claiming that the lieutenant was blocking his advancement out of spite, due to the fact that the sergeant had once written a less than laudatory report relating to the lieutenant's handling of evidence seized in a narcotics case.

It wasn't a perfect fit, but it was a starting point. A junior police grade suing a senior rank. It had been done, and could be done again.

Mary sat back down and began writing out notes in longhand. She felt that Jack was reluctant to actually initiate a suit, but just waving a threatening letter under Tilson's nose might be enough to get him to back off.

She stopped writing and began doodling aimlessly, her mind wandering. When she looked back down at the foolscap tablet, she saw she'd been making an extended line of interlocking circles. She smiled inwardly. What would a psychiatrist make of that?

The trip by taxi back to the Brisbane Marina was a risk, but Rene Santos considered it one worth taking. He needed the van, and the electronic garage door opener to the house on Brewster Street. Leaving both Abrams and Cesar Davila alone on the *Olé* was another risk, but one he had minimized. Both men were securely bound and gagged. He'd forced several Halcion pills down Davila's throat, enough to keep him in a stupor. Abrams had insisted he didn't need the sleeping pill, but Rene had convinced him. And had told him that if he struggled to get free from the bed and put so much as one foot on the floor, the whole boat would blow up.

Rene had the cabdriver circle the area before letting him off. There was no sign of any police activity. He paid the driver and went directly to the white van. The keys he'd taken from Cesar Davila slid into the door lock and the ignition. It would have been easier just to rent or steal another vehicle, but if his plan was going to work, he'd need this van. He studied the maps in the glove compartment and found his way back to the freeway. He drove south, pulling off at an exit marked San Bruno. There was a large plot of land marked Tanforan Shopping Center on the map. The Americans couldn't seem to live without a shopping center every few miles. He had no problem finding the items he needed. He purchased a two-suit carry-on suitcase, a portable radio, a roll of aluminum foil and, at a fast-food outlet, four pre-cooked hamburgers that were wrapped and shoved into a bag almost as soon as he'd given his order.

He headed back to the freeway, but the sight of a string of hotels bordering the airport caught his attention. He drove slowly past the hotels, finding the one that best suited his purpose, the Radisson. He made a quick reconnaissance of the hotel, then went back to the van and got on the freeway and drove to the Coyote Point Marina. He parked the van and carried his purchases to the boat.

Abrams was still groggy from the pill. Rene removed his gag and lightly slapped him across the face.

"Wake up. Dinner is served." He waved the hamburgers under his nose.

Abrams licked his lips. "I hate that gag," he said in a thick, slurred voice.

"If you really are a man of your word, it won't be needed much longer. I've decided to take you up on your offer. But just to make sure, I want to continue along the lines with the ransom you set up with my . . . predecessor."

"The same figure?"

"No. Since this is just a gesture of good faith, I'll settle for, oh, say, five hundred thousand. Your people shouldn't have any trouble getting that amount together. We're going to go for a short sail. I have some items to dispose of. Then I want you to call your banker, your attorney, whoever handles these things for you. Set up the payment we discussed. When Petrov is eliminated—and you will receive proof that he's dead—I expect the balance of the money, four and a half million dollars, to be sent to my bank. I'll give you the name of the bank and the account number."

"I like it. It's a deal." Abrams licked his lips again. "I'm hungry."

Santos untied one of his hands, cautioning Abrams not to touch his blindfold.

Abrams dug into the hamburger with gusto. "Ummm, wonderful." He wiped the back of his hand across his mouth. "How did you come up with the figure of five hundred thousand dollars?"

"It's a reasonable amount. Portable, and not likely to cause your people to do something stupid. I want to see just how much I can trust you. How much power you really have. I want your wife to deliver the money to me, and I want the police out of the way."

"Why use my wife?"

"The two of you have been under surveillance for

weeks now. I know what she looks like, what car she uses, and her favorite bodyguard."

Abrams almost gagged on a mouthful of the burger. "Really. How interesting. We must discuss your findings soon. But Adele is hardly the one to make the delivery. I can have—"

"No," Santos commanded. "She will do it."

"She'll be terrified. You don't know Adele."

Perhaps I know her better than you do, Santos thought. "She can bring one person. One of her guards. No more. If she is followed by your people, by the police, or if the money is marked, or counterfeit, the deal is off and I dump you in Petrov's lap."

Abrams took another large bite of the burger. "Yes, I believe you would," he said between chews. "But tell me. The money for killing Petrov. You'll have to trust me on that, won't you?"

"No, I don't have to trust you. You were somewhat more difficult to kidnap than some others, but you would be very easy to kill. I had you in the cross hairs of a rifle scope many times. In your beautiful garden while you were admiring your roses. When you parked in the garage at your office, and on the way to the elevator.

"Your bodyguards are professional policemen—but not professional bodyguards. I could have shot you any number of times at the Opera House. Could have poisoned your champagne, blown up your car, your house, your airplane.

"You could change your ways. Develop a bunker mentality. Never leave your house. Never go near a window. Have a food taster, wine taster, woman taster. But by failing to live up to your offer, killing you would become my obsession, Mr. Abrams. And I'm very good at killing, believe me."

"Oh, I believe you, Savior. Yes, indeed I do."

Santos watched Abrams's face. He could almost see his brain computing the problem. There was one simple solution. Abrams grasped it right away.

"Of course, I could kill you. If I find out who you are, what you look like. There can't be that many people in the world with your particular skills."

"You could try," Santos granted. "But I would get you first."

"That's a distinct possibility. It seems that I'll be much better off keeping you on my side, Mr. Savior. Did you just bring the one?"

Santos was confused a moment, then grinned and gave Abrams another hamburger.

David Blair pushed his way past Lieutenant Wesley Tilson. "I'm Mr. Abrams's lawyer. I have to speak to his wife."

Tilson jerked a finger toward the double doors leading to the library. "Well, I'm Lieutenant Tilson, and I'm in charge here. Mrs. Abrams is in there. But I want to talk to you, mister. Have you—"

"All in good time, sir," Blair assured him, hurrying to the library. He opened the door and saw Adele seated, a man hovering over her. He recognized him as one of Paul's bodyguards. "Adele, we have to talk. Alone."

Adele looked at Larry Falore, waving him away with a hand. "You can go now."

Blair closed the door after Falore, shaking the handle to make sure it was secure. "I heard from Paul. He called the office."

"Is he free?" Adele blurted.

"No, not yet, but he sounds fine. Definitely fine. Sharp as ever. Very businesslike." He looked at Adele, who was perched on the edge of an eighteenth-century gondola chair, her legs crossed at the ankles. "Adele, Paul wants you to deliver something for him."

"The five million dollars? He's going to pay the five million?"

"No, apparently Paul has been negotiating. The figure is down to five hundred thousand."

"Why didn't Paul call me?" Adele demanded.

"He thinks the police are monitoring all calls coming into the house. And he's right as usual. He does not want any police involvement. None whatsoever. He says he is not in any danger."

"Fine with me," Adele said. "I'm tired of them telling me what to do. But you're sure, David. Paul is all right?"

"Paul says he is, Adele. That's good enough for me. This is the scenario he wants put to the police and the press. He was never kidnapped. He left town on a business trip. Whoever called about the ransom was either sick or trying to put one over on the police."

"Yes, but they're not going to believe that, Paul."

"We don't care what they believe. We just give them Paul's scenario, all right?"

Blair waited until Adele had nodded in understanding, then went to the door, opened it, and crooked a finger at Wesley Tilson. "Lieutenant, could you join us for a moment?"

Tilson hurried into the room. "Something up?" he asked eagerly.

"Yes, Lieutenant. Good news. I heard from Mr. Abrams. He called the office less than a half hour ago. He's fine. There's been a terrible misunderstanding. I blame myself. Paul told me he had an important meeting set up right after the opera. In all the confusion I'd forgotten. He was upset by the tragedy, of course, but he left for his meeting. He never was kidnapped. We apologize for the inconvenience you and your men have been put through."

Tilson threw up his hands in a gesture of contempt. "What the hell are you saying?"

"I think I've made it clear," Blair said sharply. "Paul Abrams was not kidnapped. There is no longer a reason for the police to be looking for him."

"Hey, this is bullshit," Tilson protested. "He was snatched. His doctor was stabbed to death, and one of our men was killed trying to protect him."

"Lieutenant Harris was one of Mr. Abrams's employees, also. There is a life insurance policy worth a half million dollars that will be paid immediately, and Mr. Abrams will set up a trust fund for their children. I will notify Mrs. Harris personally of this."

"Why all the hide-and-seek games? Where the hell is he?" asked Tilson.

"That's Mr. Abrams's business," Blair said in an authoritative tone. "He expects to be back home in the next day or two. If you knew Paul as well as I do, this all wouldn't sound so mysterious."

Tilson put an edge on his voice. "They're still pulling bodies out of the Opera House."

"Yes. We're just fortunate that Mr. Abrams is not one of those bodies."

Adele Abrams rose to her feet abruptly. "I've got things to do, gentlemen."

"Sure. And I bet one of those things has to do with a ransom delivery. You must think that I'm some kind of a—"

"I think," Blair said quickly, "that we would appreciate it if you and your men, along with your equipment, were to leave as soon as possible. We thank you for your efforts and apologize that you were unnecessarily put upon. Mr. Abrams intends to make a generous donation to the Police Charities. If you choose not to leave, I can assure you that we will take efforts, including civil action, against the department, the chief, and you individually, Lieutenant." He smiled and lowered his voice. "If you want, I can call the mayor, or the governor. They're friends of Mr. Abrams, and I'm sure they'll support his position. I'm also sure you have other matters to attend to."

"Other matters, yes," Tilson said, bunching his hands in his pockets to curtail the shaking. "Mrs. Abrams, do you back this up? Do you want us out of here?"

"Yes, I certainly do."

Tilson bared his teeth in frustration. "All right, but I want to see Mr. Abrams when he comes home. If he comes home."

Blair acknowledged the request with a tight grin. "I'll be sure to inform him of your wishes, sir."

Tilson stormed out of the room. Adele started to speak, but Blair held a finger to his lips. He went into the next room and watched as Tilson supervised the removal of the telephone recording equipment.

Tilson gave him a final withering glance before leaving.

Blair went to the window and watched Tilson and several plainclothes officers enter a dark green van parked in front of the house. Only after their van disappeared down the street did Blair finally speak.

"Paul will be calling here within the hour with instructions, Adele. Are you up to it? Delivering the money? You can take one of the bodyguards with you."

"Yes, yes. I'll be fine, David. Just fine. I'll have Officer Falore drive me."

The call came an hour and ten minutes later. Blair answered, the relief in his voice readily apparent. "Paul, I was afraid something had gone wrong."

"Everything's fine. Have the police gone?"

"Yes, they'll stay out of it."

"You've done well, David. Let me talk to my wife now."

Blair handed Adele the phone, then retreated to the liquor cart and poured himself a stiff bourbon. He was happy to let Adele Abrams handle things from here on.

Mary Ariza closed the office door behind Jack Kordic and wrapped her arms around his waist. He looked exhausted, which didn't surprise her, remembering that he'd gotten no more than a few hours' sleep. "Good news on Mary Pontar, Jack. She's doing much better." She tilted her head back and kissed him. "Much, much better," she said when they broke apart.

Kordic glanced around her office. "Very impressive. How's Mr. Pontar handling things?"

Mary moistened her lips with the tip of her tongue. "Matt looks like hell. He was . . . cordial, I guess you could say." Her fingers slid down his arm, grasping his hand. "Here, I've got something I want you to look at."

She plucked a sheet of paper from the computer printer's tray. "This is just a rough draft. A notification of intent to your Lieutenant Tilson."

Kordic frowned as he read the document. "Wow. I don't know, this is pretty strong, I—"

"You wouldn't have to go through with a lawsuit, Jack, but believe me, this will intimidate Tilson, and quite possibly get him off your back."

"Yes," he said uncertainly. He looked up and saw her staring at him. "You must have put a lot of work into this."

"Yes, and I'm ready to represent you in court, Jack, if it comes to that. But I really don't think it will. Let me present this to Tilson. I want to see his reaction, see how he takes it. My bet is that he backs off."

Kordic handed the document back to her, then conceded with a curt nod. "Okay, Counselor. Let's give it a try."

"Good. Now, how's everything going with your investigation?"

"There's a new player in the game," Kordic said wearily. He slumped into the leather client's chair. "His name is Anatoly Weeks. He's involved with Israeli intelligence." Kordic handed Mary the photograph of Rene Santos supplied by Anatoly Weeks. "Do you think this could be the man who came to your apartment with the knife? The one who killed Walter Slager?"

Mary crossed to the window, holding the picture up to the natural light. She thought for a moment, one finger brushing her lips. "This is not a very clear picture." Her shoulders twitched nervously. "I really couldn't say for sure, Jack."

"Turn the picture over," Kordic suggested.

Mary ran her eye down the printed names, her head snapping up when she saw the notation, El Cabecilla. "My God. The Conductor. It has to be him, doesn't it, Jack? It has to be him."

Kordic crossed one leg over the other, leaning back and closing his eyes. "It fits. Except for one thing. The priest. He was here, right here." His hands patted the chair's arms.

Mary murmured her agreement. "Right there." She

ran a fingernail down the photograph. "Maybe the priest worked for this man."

Kordic leaned forward, placed his hands on his knees for leverage, and pushed himself to his feet. "Maybe. Weeks throws a pan of water on the theory. He says if Santos was going to kill you himself, he wouldn't have missed. Look at the picture again. Could this be the priest before cosmetic surgery?"

Mary Ariza went back to the photograph. Nothing fit. The nose too fat, the skin too tough, too pocked. The eyes, the hairline, all wrong. "It's a completely different face, Jack. No resemblance. That's all I can say."

Kordic placed his hands on his back and pushed his lips out as if giving great thought to his next words. "Where are you staying tonight?"

"Do I have a choice?"

"I still don't think it's safe for you to go back to your place. You might not feel comfortable with Pontar."

Mary pressed her lips into a kiss of worried disapproval. "No, I don't want to impose on Matt. Any suggestions?"

"My place?"

She reached out to him again. "Yes. That sounds like a good idea."

Kordic dug a key ring from his pants pocket, threading one key from the metal loop. "Take this, just in case I can't get back in time to pick you up. Take a cab, Mary."

"You know, Inspector," she began in a husky voice, "after all this is over, I'm going to cook you one of the best meals you've ever had. At my place. Is that a deal?"

"When it's over," Kordic agreed. He paused for a moment, as if marshalling his thought. "When it's all over."

"You left?" Chief Arnold Fletcher screamed at the top of his lungs. "You just took off?"

Wesley Tilson rocked back on his heels. "What was

I supposed to do, Chief? Abrams's attorney ordered me out of there. His wife backed him up. What the hell was I supposed to do?"

Fletcher did an abrupt about-face and folded his arms across his chest. "Paul Abrams is playing games with us. He was snatched, all right. Frank Harris was killed trying to protect him. His doctor was killed right in their opera box. And the death toll is still coming in from the Opera House, and he expects us to just fade away."

"His attorney claims that Abrams called. That he's fine. Never was kidnapped. What the hell was I supposed to do?"

Stop whining for a change, Fletcher thought. He turned back and glared at his red-faced lieutenant. "Do we have anyone out at Abrams's place now?"

"No one, Chief. I called everyone off."

Fletcher waited for the familiar "What was I supposed to do?" but for once Tilson knew when to shut his mouth.

"What about our guys working for him? The bodyguards?"

"Yeah, that's right. Larry Falore stayed behind, I think."

Wrong, Fletcher wanted to say. You don't think. That's the problem. Falore. At least he still had a man on the inside. "Who witnessed the attorney—what's his name?"

"David Blair, sir."

"Blair, yeah. Who witnessed him telling you to go take a flying fuck for yourself?"

"Ah ... Mrs. Abrams was in the room the whole time."

Fletcher chewed the inside of his lip. Abrams. If he turns up dead, I'm in shit. If I try to find him, I'm in shit. If I interfere with whatever Blair and Abrams's wife are up to, I'm in shit. The only good news was that one of the punks that was shooting at the fireman at Mission High School had been caught and arrested. A member of a local gang. The 22 gang. Fletcher had sat in on the interrogation. The little Mex was scared, but when Abrams name was brought up it meant nothing to him, and he denied having anything to do with the Opera House. They had leads to the rest of the gang, the name of its leader, Tony Moreno. Maybe something would turn up.

He looked back at Tilson. He was standing at attention, like one of those old calvary officers expecting to have his epaulets ripped off. "Get in touch with this Blair guy. Right now. I want something in writing. Telling us we're not wanted. Get it notarized. And get it right now!"

Anatoly Weeks liked the restaurant Jack Kordic had suggested. Sam's was one of the best fish places in San Francisco. Located in the downtown area, just a block from the Israeli Consulate, Sam's was an old-time establishment with a busy bar and serious-faced waiters who didn't tell you their names when they took your order or chirp "Have a good day" when the check was presented.

Weeks followed Kordic's lead and ordered fresh sand dabs, a celery Victor salad, and fried zucchini.

The seating suited Weeks even more than the atmosphere and the food. They settled into a private booth with a curtain that could be drawn.

"Great fish," Weeks said, dabbing up the last of the sauce with a piece of crusty sourdough bread.

"Yes. Now what did you get on those fingerprints you took at the morgue?"

Weeks ran a tongue around his mouth. "Plenty." He opened a battered leather briefcase, rummaged around, and selected two documents. "We got a match on both of them. The woman is the Palestinian. Naimat Hamdan. A PLO princess. The man is an Argentinean. Alejandro Liberto. Bad boy." He checked the documents, then handed them somewhat reluctantly to Kordic. "Bad girl. Bad boy. Hell of a combination together. She was a stone-blooded killer. Liberto was an all-around craftsman: burglary, kidnapping, bombings."

"So you think they were both working with this Santos guy?"

"Sure as can be."

The waiter cleared away their plates. Weeks ordered a brandy. Kordic stuck to coffee. It had been a long day, and he was afraid if he had a drink he'd fall asleep in his chair.

"What do you think we should do next?" Weeks asked, after the coffee, brandy, and check were delivered.

"I've got to pass this on to my lieutenant. I should have done it already."

Weeks leaned forward, his elbows on the table. "Say you do that. What will he do? Pass it on to a captain, or a chief, right? Nothing personal, now. You guys are doing a good job. But this is a little out of your league, Kordic. Admit it. You don't run into international terrorists every day. Maybe ever. Am I right?"

"Right," Kordic agreed. "But you're forgetting one thing." He banged a knuckle on the table. "This is my ballpark. San Francisco. You're as lost here as I would be in Tel Aviv. So don't get too high and mighty, Anatoly."

"Hey, I agree a hundred percent," Weeks said, laughing. "I am lost out here. That's why I think we should work together. The two of us." His voice quickened and gathered strength. "I want Santos caught. I don't care who gets him. Me, you, the FBI, any of them. I just want him caught.

"But in my opinion, and it's an opinion I value very highly, the more people looking for Santos, the greater the chance that he gets away. He's got a sixth sense. Don't laugh. I really believe he does. I know him as well as anyone in law enforcement does, Kordic. If he gets an inkling that his cover has been blown, he'll go underground. And this guy can bury himself deep. It may take years to find him again. We're close. Real close. Let's just you and me work together for a while, okay? We'll pick the brains of anyone we can, but we just don't dump what we have."

Weeks held a hand across the table. "I'm taking a chance with you, Kordic. How about it? Deal?"

Kordic studied the dark, rough-skinned hand a moment. It wasn't really a big decision. Either try to explain their theory to Lieutenant Wesley Tilson or stick with the Israeli. He grabbed the hand. "Deal. For now."

Chapter 34

Charlotte, the Homicide detail receptionist, knocked lightly on Wesley Tilson's door. "Someone to see you, Lieutenant. An attorney. She says she has some information on the Opera House." She dropped a business card on the desk.

Tilson grimaced. An attorney. He picked up the card. MARY ARIZA, ATTORNEY AT LAW. Ariza. The name sounded familiar. "Okay, send her in," he said in a forced tone.

Mary entered the office, pleased to see that Jack Kordic was not at his desk. In fact, Tilson seemed to be the only one in the office other than the receptionist.

"Thanks for coming in, Ms. Ariza. Just what information do you have about the bombing at the Opera House?"

Mary gave him her best smile. "I was there that night, Lieutenant. But that's not what I wanted to see you about." She placed her briefcase on his desk, reached in, and pulled out an envelope. "This is for you."

Tilson's eyes narrowed. "Just what's this all about? You—"

"I advise you to read the contents of that envelope, Lieutenant. It contains a civil document that may well be filed in court today."

Tilson ripped the envelope open, silently cursing himself for allowing the woman in his office in the first place. "I've got too much on my mind to be playing games, lady, and—" His mouth snapped shut as he read the document. *Kordic* v. *Tilson*. Complaint for damages. He went back behind his desk and sat in his chair, reading the three-page complaint thoroughly before looking up at Mary Ariza. "You've got to be kidding. This is some kind of a joke, isn't it?"

"No," Mary said firmly, pleased at Tilson's reaction. He looked as if he'd been kicked in the stomach. "It is not a joke, Lieutenant. I plan to file this case in San Francisco Superior Court if we cannot come to a mutually beneficial agreement right now."

"Agreement?" Tilson protested. "What the hell is there to agree about?" He rolled the document into a ball and threw it across the room. "This is all bullshit."

Mary reached back into her briefcase and brought out another envelope. "I recommend that you give this copy to your attorney, Lieutenant. It will save him the cost of having one made at the county clerk's office."

"My attorney! I haven't got an attorney, lady. I don't need one. I—"

"You do need an attorney, Lieutenant. I don't know your financial circumstances, but I assume you have a home, some savings. You certainly have a salary, which can be attached, if necessary to satisfy our judgment. And I'm quite confident there will be a judgment in our favor."

Tilson stroked his chin for a few moments. "Let me get this straight. Kordic is suing me for harassment? I mean, is he going to say I patted him on the butt or something? He'd be a joke. The whole department would be laughing at him. You better tell him that—"

"Don't advise me what to tell my client, Lieutenant. I will give you some free advice, however. You can pass it on to your attorney. Have him research a Los Angeles County civil case. *Sellers* v. *Trigone*. A sergeant sued his lieutenant for harassment. The judgment was seventy-five thousand dollars. I think I can do a lot better than that."

Tilson leaned back in his chair, suddenly snapping his fingers. "Ariza. Aren't you the woman in the investigation? The one Kordic's handling. Someone shot at you, didn't they?"

"There were two attacks, Lieutenant."

"And that's how you met Kordic, huh?"

"Yes, but it has nothing to do with this, Lieutenant."

"Yeah," Tilson scoffed. "I'll bet. I think you're bluffing, lady." He pointed at Mary's briefcase. "This is all a bunch of crap. You and Kordic are probably—"

Mary slammed a fist on the desk. "If you want to add another action to this one, then by all means make your accusations, Lieutenant. But I'm telling you that this case is not 'a bunch of crap.' I'm going to sue you. I'm going to win. I'm going to empty your pockets. And in addition, you can kiss good-bye any ideas you have about promotion, here in this department or in any other police department. Unless we can come to an agreement right now, you'll be the one the department is laughing at, not my client. Do you understand that, Lieutenant?"

Tilson looked at his hands, twisting his wedding band slowly. In his entire life he had never been involved in a civil law suit. Never even had an accident claim with his insurance company. Now he had Abrams's attorney and this damn woman threatening him. "What do you mean by an agreement?"

Rene Santos was sure no one was following Adele Abrams after only two stops: first the Fairmont Hotel, then the Clift Hotel. Apparently Paul Abrams had scared off the police. Apparently.

The problem was the big gray Mercedes. He'd spotted the driver, the young policeman whom Naimat had said Mrs. Abrams was screwing. But because of the car's dark windows, there was no way of telling if anyone else was in the back of the vehicle with her.

He was surprised at Mrs. Abrams's tone when he had her paged at both hotels: a bit hostile, pugnacious, definitely not frightened. The third stop was another hotel, back up California Street to the Mark Hopkins, catercorner from the Fairmont Hotel.

This time Mrs. Abrams was definitely hot under the collar when he made contact.

"This is ridiculous. I'm tired of running around like a fool with this money. Where is my husband?"

"Patience," Santos cooed in the cellular phone. "I

have to be sure you're alone. Abandon the car. Take a cab, alone. Leave your bodyguard behind and go to——"

"No way," Adele Abrams announced firmly. "Larry stays with me. And if we don't make contact right now, I'm going home."

"Your husband wouldn't be pleased, Mrs. Abrams. All right, bring your bodyguard with you. I know you're fond of him. We've been watching you for weeks. Take a taxicab. Go to the Radisson Hotel by the San Francisco airport. You're very close now. Keep your nerve. And, Mrs. Abrams, we haven't told Paul about you and your bodyguard. And we won't as long as you cooperate. If the police are still involved, if there's a transmitter in that piece of luggage, then we'll change all of our plans."

Santos watched from the lobby-level coffee shop at the Fairmont Hotel as Adele Abrams came stomping out of the Mark Hopkins lobby. She got into an agitated argument with Falore, dropping the case to the ground, waving her arms in the air, and signaling for a cab. Falore picked up the case and began negotiating with the hotel doorman about what to do with the Mercedes. Adele Abrams rolled down the cab window and began waving her hands again. One of the skills Santos had learned years ago in those desert training camps was lip-reading. It was a skill he had kept in good practice. An amused grin came to his face as he digested Adele Abrams's dialogue. Her bodyguard carried the case into the cab. Santos watched patiently for another five minutes. No sign of any police activity. The Mercedes was driven away by a valet parking attendant. Santos stood and paid for his coffee, leaving a large tip. It was going well. Very well.

"I'm tired of this," Adele Abrams said, arms folded across her chest, her lips in a pout.

"They have to be careful," Larry Falore advised her.

"They're probably going to kill him anyway," Adele said, pushing her hair from her forehead and looking at the cabdriver's long ponytail. Could he be one of them? she wondered. "This better be the last stop. I mean it."

Adele Abrams stormed into the Airport Radisson Hotel's lobby while Falore paid the cabdriver. She went immediately to the white in-house phone bank, expecting to be paged any minute. It took almost fifteen.

"Now what?" she demanded, picking up the phone as soon as her name was announced on the paging system.

"You're almost through. Take the case from your boyfriend. Walk quickly to your left, down the hallway to the elevators. Get in the elevator with the out-of-order sign. Push the buttons for each floor. When the elevator doors open and you see a black suitcase on the floor, throw the case out. Don't get out! Continue up to the tenth floor. Do it, Mrs. Abrams. Now."

"No way. Where's my husband, I—"

"You are being watched. And listened to." Rene repeated some of the language Adele had used in front of the Mark Hopkins Hotel. "You are being monitored every step of the way. I'll kill you if I have to. Paul is very close. After you drop off the case, go back to the lobby and go to the bar. Paul will call you. Do it! Now!"

Adele looked around the lobby. There were several dozen people—any of them could have been holding a gun. She walked straight to Falore, grabbing the case from his hand. "Stay here, Larry." She swiveled, confused for a moment, then found the correct hallway and stalked off, glancing over her shoulder to make sure Falore was following orders. Damn it, the bastards were thorough. They had been close enough to overhear her at the hotel. Had there been a listening device in the cab? Or had the cabdriver been part of the plot? Her hunch had been right. He must have been in on it.

She pushed the Up button on the elevator with the out-of-order sign taped to it. The door rasped open and she stepped inside, feeling vulnerable, looking up at the ceiling. Someone could be up there. With a gun. She'd seen a movie like that once. She pushed the button for each of the ten floors. The door opened on the second floor. The black suitcase was there! She used both hands to toss the case out, then backed away as far as possible, eyes riveted on the closing doors.

Rene Santos scooped up the case and quickly inserted it into the suitcase he'd purchased at the shopping center, the interior of which was doubled-lined with aluminum foil and held a portable radio. The radio was tuned to a heavy metal FM station. He turned the radio on and zipped the suitcase closed. If there was a bug in the case Adele Abrams had thrown from the elevator, the aluminum foil would block any tracing attempts, and the music would certainly do damage to the eardrums of whoever was listening in.

It was his one moment of vulnerability. The odds were heavily in his favor that there was nothing inside the case but the money. Very little money to Abrams, Santos reminded himself as he hurried down the hallway, to the back staircase, down and out to the rear parking lot. The van was still in its spot against the fence. He pulled slowly out of the lot, past the hotel's front entrance, and out onto the freeway again. He drove north for a mile, took the Millbrae off-ramp, and drove into the parking lot of yet another of the numerous hotels bordering the airport. He rummaged through the suitcase, extracting the neatly packed money and tossing away the expensive-looking suitcase out the window. He then drove for several blocks, pulling into the parking lot of a deserted office building.

He checked his watch. Eleven minutes since he'd picked up the suitcase at the hotel. He took a notepad from his pocket and dialed the number he'd written down for the Radisson Hotel. When he was connected to the hotel's lobby bar, he asked for Adele Abrams. "She's an attractive woman in a red jacket who probably looks mad as hell," he told the person on the other end of the line.

Moments later she came on the line. "This is Mrs. Abrams."

"You did quite well. Your husband is no more than two or three miles from you."

"You'd better not be lying, whoever you are, because if you are—"

"Shut up," Santos said harshly. He gave her detailed instructions on how to find the *Olé,* then said, "Tell your husband I'll be contacting him shortly." He severed the connection and swiveled around in the van's bucket seat. "It went well. Very well, Cesar," he called out to the bundled lump lying under a blanket. "You should have stayed on my side, my friend. You would have been a rich man. But don't despair. You still have an important role to play."

"Who'd you say he was?" Lieutenant Wesley Tilson asked suspiciously.

"Name is Weeks," Jack Kordic replied. "Heavy hitter in the State Department."

Tilson walked to his office window and ran a finger between his neck and shirt collar. "State Department. What's their interest?"

"You know how well connected Paul Abrams is in Washington."

Tilson was standing so close to the window, his breath left cloud marks on the glass. He watched the small, dark man reading through files on Kordic's desk.

"Well, send him home. Haven't you heard about Abrams? He's telling everyone the whole idea of him being kidnapped was a mistake. That he was involved in a complicated business deal, that he was never abducted. Never in any danger. Abrams is barricading himself behind his lawyers. We'll be working day and night on this for a month. The TV people have been all over me." His face flushed. "This State Department guy hot to get on TV?"

"No. From what I gather, he's strictly a behind-the-scenes troubleshooter." Kordic saw doubt creeping into Tilson's features. "Sort of a minor league Oliver North type."

Tilson reached for his raincoat. "Your attorney stopped by to see me, Kordic. We came to an understanding. I guess she told you, huh?"

Kordic hadn't heard a word from Mary, but he didn't want Tilson to know that. "I spoke to her."

"I think you handled it the wrong way. We could have worked it out between us. There was no need to bring an attorney into it, but done is done." He looked up at Kordic expectantly. "All right?"

"As long as you get off my back, I'm satisfied, Lieutenant. I want to stay here. In Homicide. And I want to see my evaluation report before it goes to the chief."

Tilson drew a handkerchief from his pants pocket, wiped his face, and nodded all at the same time. "Yeah, yeah. Your attorney made that clear. I've got to get a few hours' sleep. You handle this State Department character. Just keep him out of the way."

Kordic waited until Tilson was out of the office before rummaging through his desk. Chris Sullivan's bottle of Jack Daniels was still in the bottom drawer. He picked up two paper cups and carried the bottle to his desk.

Weeks smiled at the sight of the whiskey. "I could use one of those. You square things away with your boss?"

"I told him you were a heavy hitter with the State Department. I just didn't tell him it happened to be the state of Israel."

"Good thinking." Weeks watched as Kordic poured some whiskey into the cups. "I thought you were off the sauce for the night."

"I thought so too." Kordic picked up the cup and drained it. "Paul Abrams has called his office, saying the whole thing was a mistake. He was never kidnapped."

Weeks held the cup under his nose and inhaled. "And your people believe that, I take it."

"No, but they've dropped the kidnap investigation."

Weeks leaned back in his chair, digging in his pockets for cigarettes. "Santos is clever, isn't he? He kills all these people at the Opera House, including Abrams's doctor and your police lieutenant. What was his name? Harris, wasn't it?"

"That's right. Frank Harris."

Weeks lit up, drew deeply on his cigarette, and

puffed the smoke toward the ceiling. "Santos's got them all running in circles, my friend. Us too." Weeks tapped a finger on the files piled on Kordic's desk. "And he killed your other cop too. The one in this room."

"Chris Sullivan? I'd like to be able to prove that. It's Sullivan's booze we're drinking."

Weeks picked up his cup and made a toast: "Mr. Sullivan, I hope that St. Peter was in a good mood when you got to those pearly gates." He swallowed the whiskey and followed Kordic's lead by tossing the empty cup into the wastebasket. "I hate to say it, but it looks like all we can do now is wait for his next move. Abrams will be one of the keys. Alive or dead, he'll be one of the keys."

"What's the other key?"

"Santos's client. Who the hell is he working for this time? That's what I want to know," Weeks said, attempting to blow a smoke ring but creating something similar to a mushroom. "Abrams may look like a wimp, but he's a tough customer. Especially when it comes to making a buck. A real tough customer. No one amasses that kind of money without being tough. But he's not in the same league as Santos. Santos went to a hell of a lot of trouble to snatch him. Someone paid him to do it. Either Abrams made Santos a better offer, or he's already as good as dead." He looked around for an ashtray. Finding none, he leaned down and rubbed the cigarette out on the inside of the waste-basket. "Waiting. God, the older I get, the harder it gets." He looked up at Kordic and grinned. "Can't say that about everything, can you?"

The sound of the key in the lock startled Mary Ariza.

"It's me," Kordic called through the door.

By the time the door opened, Mary was there waiting, a smile on her face. The smile faded when she saw the other man.

"Mary, this is Mr. Weeks, the gentleman I told you about from the Israeli Consulate."

Weeks's teeth flashed white against his dark skin. "My pleasure," he said, pumping her hand. "Jack tells me you've been through hell. Maybe we can figure this all out together."

"Just give us a minute," Kordic said, cupping Mary's elbow and leading her back to the bedroom. "I saw Tilson. You must have rattled his cage pretty good. He almost kissed me."

"He folded like a deck chair," Mary said with enthusiasm. "He won't be giving you any more trouble, Jack. No more harassment. You can stay in Homicide, and Tilson guaranteed me that your upcoming evaluation report will be a good one. He was really worried about the possibility of being sued. I almost felt sorry for him there at the end."

"An attorney feeling sorry for someone?" He kissed the tip of her nose. "Thanks," he said softly, pecking at her nose again. "Come on, let's go back and talk to the Israeli spy."

The three of them sat around the dining room table, and Mary reassured Weeks that his cigarette smoke didn't bother her. They discussed the generalities of the bombing at the Opera House.

Mary could see Jack's head nod, then jump up. "You look exhausted," she told him. "Why don't you take a rest? It'll do you good."

Kordic looked at Weeks through red-rimmed eyes. "You'll be polite to the lady, won't you?"

Weeks raised a palm, like a Boy Scout taking an oath. "I'll be on my best behavior if she promises to do the same."

Mary laughed out loud. She decided she liked Anatoly Weeks. Something about him gave off a feeling of confidence. Much like Jack.

Kordic dragged his chair back and got wearily to his feet. "Wake me if you two come up with anything interesting."

Mary watched him trudge into the bedroom. When she turned to look at Weeks, he was smiling. "Nice guy, isn't he?"

"Yes. Very nice."

"Tell me all about this priest of yours, Mary," Weeks said, lighting up a fresh cigarette.

Mary gave Weeks as much detailed information as she could recall about Father Torres. "Jack showed me that photograph. It doesn't look anything at all like Father Torres."

"Yeah, he told me. Still, the picture was taken years ago." Weeks pulled the photograph from his jacket pocket. "Hell, if I looked like this, I'd go in for some plastic surgery myself. And I'd want to come out looking like a stud. Think about it, Mary. Could it be the priest?"

Mary looked at the picture again. "It's possible, I guess. Tell me about this Santos man. In spite of everything, he sounds like he's extremely intelligent."

"He is," Weeks acknowledged. "He's a chameleon. An actor. He speaks a dozen languages and can blend in just about anywhere. Africa, Asia, Europe, South America. That's why this operation at the Opera House smells so much like him. In Tel Aviv he did much the same thing, but it was at a tourist hotel. Bombs, a fire, seven tourists machine-gunned on the beach. Confusion everywhere. During all that confusion he, or one of his agents, was able to get close enough to our headquarters to plant a bomb. Killed four of our top people. It's the way he works. Confuse and conquer."

Larry Falore was at Adele Abrams's heels as they left the bar. "I'm going to call David Blair now," he said.

"Not yet. It may be another wild goose chase." She pushed her way through the lobby doors.

Falore grabbed her elbow, but Adele quickly pulled it away. "Come on. Let's grab this cab."

Adele grabbed Falore's shoulder as he opened the cab door. She peered in to make sure it wasn't the same driver they'd had before, the one with the ponytail. "Do you know where this place is?" she asked Falore. "The Coyote Point Marina?"

"Sure. It's just down the road."

Adele looked Falore in the eye before making up her

mind. "All right. Let's go," she said, sliding into the cab's backseat, staring daggers at the driver.

Falore gave the driver their destination. The rest of the trip was made in almost complete silence, the only noise being the muffled sound of Adele's toe tapping against the floor of the cab.

Adele Abrams had her door open before the cab came to a complete stop. Falore told the driver to wait and ran to catch up with her. "Slow down. You don't know if Paul's here. You don't know who is waiting for you. They could be out to snatch you too."

Adele paused in mid-stride. "Why would they want to kidnap me?"

"For your hot little body and all that money. Think about it, Adele. Slow down. Let's get some help down here."

The piers were all well lighted. Painted signs showed the dock markings. Adele gestured with an arm toward the pier marked VISITORS. "Let's see if the boat's really there before we call anyone."

They passed several groups of people as they walked down the raw wooden pier. They all seemed to be in their thirties, dressed in yuppie-style mariner gear. Half were holding beer cans in their hands.

"There it is," Adele said, grabbing Falore's arm. "Right where he said it would be. The *Olé*."

Falore studied the white cruiser. A light was on in the cabin. More light could be seen coming from a porthole just above water level.

"Okay," he said. "It's here. Let's get some help."

"No! Are you armed?"

"Sure, but—"

"Give me your gun."

Falore grabbed her by her shoulders and shook her. "Get real, Adele. This isn't a game. I'm going to call for help."

"No! What if Paul's not there? What if this is just another trick? Maybe there's a note in there, or something to tell us where Paul is. If we bring in anyone else now, it might spook them."

Falore chewed at the corner of his lip. She was right.

It could be just another ride on the merry-go-round. "Okay, I'll take a look."

Adele shook her head violently, sending her hair across her eyes like curtains. "No, I'm going."

Falore started to protest.

"Remember who you're working for, Larry. Me! Now give me your gun."

"No, I can't—"

"Give me the gun or get your ass out of here. For good."

Falore unbuttoned his jacket and hesitated. "No. I can't give you the gun, Adele. You'd—"

"All right, you stay here. I'll go check it out."

"No, Adele—"

"God damn you," she said, her voice razor-sharp. "Those were the orders on the phone. I go on the boat alone. That's what I was told. Now, you do what I tell you to, or just go sit in the cab and wait like a flunky!"

Falore stepped back, as if he'd been physically hit. "All right, Adele, all right. I'll be right here."

Adele's shoes rattled the gangway planks as she hurried to the boat, climbing the stairs and taking the small jump to the deck in a graceful, athletic move. She saw the hatchway leading down below. A small overhead fixture cast a circular pool of light on the carpeted decking. There was a rank smell she couldn't identify. The cabin door on the left was open. She looked in. Her husband was tied to a chair, blindfolded, a gag across his mouth. His head was cocked, listening to her approach. She touched a finger to his damp forehead, and he jumped, mumbling something against the gag.

Adele stared at him for a moment, then went back outside. Larry Falore was standing anxiously, one hand on his gun butt.

"Paul's dead," she called to him. "Call David Blair. Not the police. Call David."

Falore started to climb on board, but she pushed him back. "Please, Larry. Go call. Now. Please!"

She watched Falore lope down the docks, then retreated back to the cabin. Taking a handkerchief from her purse, she clamped both fingers across Paul Abrams's nose, cutting off his only supply of air. Abrams tried pulling away, but she clasped the back of his head in one hand and held the nostrils shut, feeling him trying to buck free from the chair, feeling the strength ebb from him, his life slowly drain away. "I'm sorry, Paul," she whispered hoarsely. "I really am. But you were planning on getting rid of me, weren't you, darling?"

"He was alone?" Viktor Petrov asked after watching the white van disappear into the garage of the house on Brewster Street. He leaned forward in the car's backseat. "I couldn't see anyone else, just the driver."

"Santos was driving the van," Boris Zorkin replied, dropping his infrared binoculars to his lap. "He used the automatic door opener to gain entrance to the garage."

Petrov grunted, stretching his arms, rotating his shoulders. He felt stiff from the long stakeout. He had decided to join Zorkin rather than wait for Rene Santos to call him. "Paul Abrams had better be in the back of that van. Are you ready?"

Zorkin nodded his head. A Czechoslovakian VZ 61 Skorpion 7.65 machine pistol, complete with a sound suppressor permanently welded to the barrel, a twenty-five-cartridge clip, and a collapsible metal shoulder stock, was attached to a Velcro strap on his right shoulder. His raincoat draped over his shoulder like a cape, the weapon out of sight but ready for instant action. "Ready," he said.

"Don't forget about the possibility of booby traps," Petrov warned him. "Don't kill Santos until we are sure Abrams is safe and that we can get out of the damn house without it blowing up. Let's go."

They crossed the street together, then went up the front stairs single-file, with Zorkin in the lead. As they reached the landing, the front door suddenly swung open, causing Zorkin to reach for the Skorpion.

"Gentlemen, quick, come in," Rene Santos said. "Abrams is downstairs. He's having trouble breathing.

I don't know what the problem is." He turned his back on the two Russians and strode quickly to the door leading downstairs, pausing a moment, waving for them to follow.

All three men descended in a hurry, the thump of their feet shaking the wobbly wooden stairs.

"In here," Santos said, holding open the door leading to the cell.

Viktor Petrov pushed past him, reaching out to the blanketed body on the cot. He skidded to an abrupt stop when he saw that the hair was different. The body was too big to be Abrams's, but it was too late. The unmistakable cough of two gunshots from a silenced weapon and the thud as a body hit the floor told him all he needed to know. Zorkin was out of the picture. He raised his hands slowly. "Are you going to kill me too, Rene?"

"I may have to eventually, Viktor. It all depends on what you have to tell me."

Paul Abrams was rocking back and forth in the chair, savagely shaking his head, screaming futilely, silently into the gag. Twice he had succeeded in breaking his nose free from her grasp, but she had him now. One hand entangled in his hair, the other clamping his nostrils shut.

Adele Abrams could hear footsteps, could feel the boat rock as someone climbed aboard. She pressed down harder on the handkerchief, her eyes on the door. As the footsteps got closer, she pulled the handkerchief away.

Larry Falore came lumbering into the room, out of breath. "I called. Blair is on his way, but we're going to have to call the cops, Adele." He strode toward Paul Abrams, stooping to look at the flushed face, his middle finger instinctively moving to Abrams's neck.

"Jesus. He's got a pulse, Adele, he's alive!"

Adele slapped his hand away and jammed the handkerchief back on Paul's nose. "Get out of here, Larry. Get off the boat!"

Falore watched Paul Abrams's body twitch, the chest surge forward. Adele's eyes blazed into his.

"Get off the boat, Larry. I'll take care of you. I'm going to be rich—"

Falore grabbed her hand and twisted hard. She cried out in pain, falling backward, bumping into the cabin wall. He quickly tore the tape off Paul Abrams's mouth, then dislodged the wet gag. The blindfold came off next. Paul Abrams's pale gray eyes blinked rapidly. He coughed, then stretched his mouth wide, gulping air in huge drafts.

Falore tried to untie him, but the knots were too tight. Abrams's breathing was returning to normal.

"Mr. Abrams, I'll have to get a knife to cut these ropes. Are you all right?"

"Yes, yes," Abrams said between gasps. "Do that. But don't leave me alone with that woman. Is that understood? Don't leave me alone with her."

Adele Abrams shouldered her way past Falore without a word, walking toward the cabin door with her head dropped to her chest, arms straight at her sides, like a prisoner approaching the gallows.

Chapter 35

"**Y**ou are a very big disappointment," Viktor Petrov stated harshly. "This is all very foolish, Rene. What happened to Abrams? You lost him, right?"

"No, no. In fact, we became good friends, Viktor. He told me all about you. Well, not all. No one knows all, do they?" Santos bent down, running his hands over Boris Zorkin's body, jerking the Skorpion strap free. He dug the barrel of his Beretta into Petrov's back, finding a silencer-fitted Makarov 9mm pistol in Petrov's shoulder holster. The Makarov was a standard issue to GRU agents and a weapon Santos was very familiar with. He shoved Petrov's gun into his jacket pocket. "You and Boris certainly came prepared. Come. This way."

Petrov moved slowly, his hands above his head, judging the distance between him and Santos.

"Don't think about it, Viktor," Santos cautioned. "You and I are going to have a little talk."

Petrov followed Santos's instructions, up the stairs, into a room at the back of the house. Santos snapped on the light, revealing a small room, the furnishings consisting of a bed with a rumpled blanket covering most of the bare mattress, an unpainted pine chest, and one club chair, the once red upholstery faded to the color of a dying rose. A small portable TV was set on a metal tray alongside the chair. The walls were a dingy gray, unpainted in the spots where shelves had been ripped away. The windows were covered with pine boards.

"Charming," Petrov said, slowly lowering his arms.

"Turn around," Santos ordered.

Petrov turned slowly. "Now what, Rene? How long before my men come barging in? Is that what you want to know?"

"There are no men, Viktor. So let's not bore each other with silly games." Santos turned on the TV. The screen fluttered, like a flag in the wind.

Petrov settled himself carefully in the chair. "You and Abrams must have gotten along quite well."

"Indeed. He's safe and sound. Waiting for me now. He wants to make a deal. You know how they are when they think they're going to die. They'll tell you anything."

Petrov grunted. "Some will. Some won't."

"Exactly. But Abrams did. What about you, Viktor? What have you to tell me?"

"Take me to Abrams now. Stop this foolishness."

Santos leaned casually against the door frame, his Beretta dangling from his hand. "The stakes have been raised a bit. You're bidding against Abrams now. What have you to offer?"

"I've already made you a deal," Petrov protested. "Money. A new identity. Your files from the Kremlin wiped clean. What more do you want?"

"What we all want, Viktor. More. Abrams is offering five million. All I have to do is kill you. What do you think of that?"

Petrov stirred in his chair, as if to relieve a muscle cramp. "There's an old Russian proverb, Rene. Fuck you!"

"Now, now, Viktor, you do want to get out of here alive, don't you?"

Petrov grunted. "What are the chances of that? Do you take me for a fool?"

"No," Rene responded casually. "No more than you think of me as one. Cesar Davila told me all about your plans, Viktor. You had Cesar. And Naimat too, no doubt. I was to be killed as soon as you took control of Abrams."

Petrov waved the accusation away with a hand. "No. Of course I took control of Davila and the woman. I wanted to monitor you, Rene. That is all. There was never a plan to kill you. Why the hell would I want to kill you?"

"To pin the blame of the Abrams kidnapping on someone. You needed someone with no connection to the oil deal. An aging terrorist would fit the bill perfectly."

"You're being stupid, Rene. I suggest—"

Petrov's calm voice turned into a pain-filled snarl as Santos fired a single bullet into his left knee. Santos waited patiently as the Russian fell from the chair, clutching his leg.

"You can still lead a good life with one leg, Viktor. With two gone, much of the fun is gone." He bent down, picked Petrov up, and heaved him back into the chair. "So what's your offer, Victor? Do you have my files? The masters? You accuse me of being stupid. I would have to be stupid to think you didn't have a half-dozen copies of those files floating around. Who has them, Viktor?"

"No one. I swear."

"Did you bring the money?"

"No, I was going—"

Santos lashed out with his foot, catching Petrov in his wounded knee. "There never was any money, was there?"

Petrov groaned out an unintelligible answer, and Santos kicked his leg again.

"No, no money," Petrov cried out in pain.

Once again Santos kicked out at Petrov's leg. "Who else knows about me, Viktor?"

"No one."

Santos placed the tip of the silencer against the bleeding knee. "How did you find me in Peru?"

"Luck. We had an operation in Colombia. With one of the drug cartels. There was talk of a man in Lima who was making a reputation as an assassin. I decided to check him out. I was thinking of using him. The more I looked, the more he reminded me of you, Rene. The same techniques, the same thoroughness, but the description didn't fit." He looked at Santos through pain-filled eyes. "I liked you better when you were ugly, Rene. I still wasn't sure. Then I tapped your phone. Your voice, Rene. You can change your face, but not your voice."

Santos took careful aim and shot Petrov in his right elbow. When the Russian stopped screaming, he grabbed him by his hair, pulling his head back. "Tell me! Who else knows about me? Tell me or this is going to go on all night."

Petrov's eyes darted around the room. There was nothing. Nothing to grab. No weapons of any type within reach. No chance of mounting a charge against Santos. He squeezed his eyes shut. "No one, Rene."

Santos put the Russian out of his misery. One shot to the temple, then he emptied his pockets, checking the wallet, removing most of the cash, leaving the identification. He went to the kitchen, retrieved the Polaroid camera from a cabinet, came back and took several photos of Petrov to send to Abrams to prove Petrov was dead, then walked downstairs and rifled through Zorkin's personal belongings, again taking all but a little of the money and leaving the identification. Santos walked over to where the bulky figure of Cesar Davila lay on the cot. Davila was stirring. Rene whipped out his knife, the blade slashing through the ropes at Davila's wrists and ankles. He watched as Cesar rolled off the couch, falling to his knees and elbows, lying there, an exhausted hand going to his mouth, working the gag free.

He started to say something when Santos took Viktor Petrov's Makarov pistol from his pocket and shot Davila twice in the chest. He fired once more just to be certain, the bullet entering Davila's right eye, then wiped the gun clean and placed it in Zorkin's hand. He pulled the trigger one more time, aiming at nothing in particular. He then repeated the procedure, placing the gun he'd used to kill both Petrov and Zorkin in Davila's hand, firing a shot into the wall.

He picked up a can of gasoline, dousing Davila's hands and legs with the gas, drenching the area that was marked by the ropes. He kneeled down, opened Davila's mouth, and filled it with gas until the liquid spilled out onto his chin. He then went about setting up the Frangex explosive and blasting caps around the basement. The Russians' car would be somewhere close. Not more than a block away. It wouldn't take long for the police to locate it. He debated about the van. It would be so much easier to take it with him, but then the police would find just the one vehicle. The Russians'. No, the van would have to stay, to explain the third body—Davila's. He went over it carefully, wiping everywhere his hands had touched as well as places he had never come near, just to be sure. Satisfied at last, he folded the light wire butt stock of the Skorpion machine pistol over its barrel and slipped it into the suitcase with the money and exited the house through the garage door. He walked almost a full block before activating the blasting caps. The sound was a dull, muffled roar at first, then a resounding boom. He could see flashes of the fire briefly through cracks in the garage door, then smoke. Lots and lots of smoke.

Mary Ariza could understand why Anatoly Weeks would be a great success in his line of work. He had the ability, like a great actor or comedian, to leave his audience hungry for more. He would tell a story, an anecdote, and leave something out, something missing, so the listener would not be satisfied until more details were revealed. His account of the life of the terrorist he suspected was behind the attempts on her life was fascinating to Mary. She willingly fell into Weeks's interrogation traps, providing him with information by asking questions.

Mary studied Weeks through half-closed eyes. "What will he do next?"

"Who knows? If—" Weeks's head snapped back, his attention diverted to the low rumbling of the radio. The announcer had cut into the soft classical music being transmitted. A news bulletin.

"Paul Abrams, the billionaire oil executive who was reportedly kidnapped from the Opera House the other night, has been seen returning to his residence here in San Francisco within the last hour. Abrams spokesperson David Blair was on hand to announce that Mr. Abrams is sorry for any confusion caused by his disappearance, which, according to Mr. Blair, involved an urgent business trip to Alaska. Mr. Abrams himself was not available for comment."

Anatoly Weeks pounded his hand on the table in frustration, causing Mary's coffee cup to fall to the floor.

Jack Kordic padded barefoot into the room, rubbing his eyes with both hands. "What's going on?"

"Abrams," Weeks announced with an air of confession. "He just turned up. He made his deal with Santos. Now we may never get him."

"What are you going to do now, Jack?" Mary asked.

"I don't know." He looked at Weeks. "Any suggestions?"

"Just one. Let's go get something to eat."

Jack Kordic goosed the accelerator. The streets were empty. The dark forest of Golden Gate Park bordering Fulton Street was half hidden under a low fog.

Anatoly Weeks dug in his pocket for a cigarette. "My guess is that Paul Abrams will be taking a trip out of the country. Very soon." He tapped Kordic on the shoulder. "You guys aren't even going to get to talk to him."

Why not?" Mary Ariza twisted around to look at Weeks, alone in the backseat. "He'd have no reason to protect the people who kidnapped him."

"He and Santos made a deal. Otherwise Abrams would never have gotten away alive. Part of the deal will be Abrams's silence."

The radio cackled, the police communications operator's voice excitedly reporting an 811, a bombing, on Brewster Street. "Fire department and radio car units are on the scene. Bomb-disposal team responding."

Kordic applied the brakes, and the car skidded into a right turn on Stanyan Street. "More bombs," he said out of the side of his mouth. "What a coincidence. I bet it has something to do with Santos. Want to take a look?"

Mary's hands began groping for the seat belt.

* * *

Brewster Street was blocked off at both ends by radio cars. Kordic held his badge out the window and squeezed his way through a narrow opening between two fire engines. He drove slowly as the car bumped and weaved over charged hose lines.

"Your town looks like it's turning into a war zone," Weeks said when they pulled to a stop.

Kordic recognized the fire department arson investigator, Joe Delfino.

"What's it look like, Joe?"

Delfino walked over to the car, pushed his helmet to the back of his head, and wiped his forehead with the back of a gloved hand. His eyes took in Weeks and Mary Ariza.

"They're with me, Joe. No problem."

"Okay. With all this going on, you don't know who you're talking to. Chemical explosion of some type. No doubt about it. Concentrated explosion patterns. I'd bet it's the same thing that was used at the Opera House. Where's all this stuff coming from?"

"Wish I knew," Kordic answered. "Okay if we take a look?"

"Sure. But be careful. Three fatalities so far. Two are in the basement. One of them is just a lump of charcoal. Hard to believe it was ever human. The other one's in bad shape too. Guy upstairs is pretty much intact." Delfino gnawed at his upper lip. "Looks like your line of work, Jack. Ambulance crew said he was shot."

Kordic swiveled around to the backseat. "Mary, maybe—"

"I think I'll stay right here," she said wearily. "I've seen enough bomb sites for a while."

Kordic and Weeks picked their way through the debris: snakelike layers of fire hose, still smoldering bits of wood, plaster, sheetrock. The floor was slick from the mixture of water and blackened wood. They walked by the burnt carcass of a vehicle, the frame blown almost completely apart, the wheel struts resting on puddles of melted rubber. The entire rear and right corner of the building was blown away. The wooden posts and foundation bracing showed heavy alligator charring, indicating them to have been ignition points for the fire.

Firemen carrying axes, salvage covers, and grimy lengths of hose passed them without saying a word.

Weeks bent down and picked up a small, jagged piece of charred wood. "Explosives, all right," he said. "Look at the size of the shearings." He pointed at a heavy support beam flying on the floor. "See the end of the post? Jagged but abrupt. Heavy explosives do that."

Kordic pointed his badge at a white-helmeted firefighter. "Safe to go upstairs, Chief?"

"Yeah, sure. Just don't step where there ain't no floor."

Kordic saw what the fireman meant when they reached the second floor. Pieces of flooring were blown away or chopped open to reveal the basement level. He saw a city ambulance crew standing by a doorway in the back.

"Body in here?" he asked the steward.

"Yep. No hurry to move him. He's room temperature."

Kordic stooped to examine the body sitting back in the chair, the head tilted to the right, crusted blood surrounding the wound in his left temple.

Weeks took one look and said, "Well, I'll be damned."

"You know him?" Kordic asked. "Is this Santos?"

Weeks continued staring at the body in disbelief. "No, not Santos. Viktor Petrov. Used to be a heavy hitter in Russian Intelligence. Ex-GRU. A *paskudnyak*. A no-good son of a bitch. There's your fax connection. One of Petrov's boys in Russia was no doubt sending those faxes to Joe Rose's office."

Kordic felt a wave of nausea come over him. GRU? Who would show up next? James Bond? "You're sure?"

"Positive. What's he got on him?"

Kordic felt inside the man's jacket, pulling out a

thick alligator leather billfold. "There's a passport. French. Emile Dutil. Address in Paris." He passed the billfold to Weeks, who examined it carefully.

"Beautiful," Weeks said. "No one does them any better. Not us, not the CIA. No one."

Kordic patted down the body, retrieving some American coins, a comb, handkerchief, fountain pen, and a small, razor-sharp pocketknife. He dumped all of the items in the handkerchief and folded it, then dropped it on the dead man's lap.

Weeks handed him the billfold. "Usual stuff in there. Credit cards, French driver's licence, all in the name of Emile Dutil."

"Well?" Kordic said, dropping the billfold alongside the handkerchief.

"Let's check the bodies downstairs," Weeks suggested.

Chapter 36

"We can have those pants hemmed by tomorrow, if you wish, sir," the slim, distinguished-looking salesman said.

"Yes, that will be fine," Rene Santos said. "Now let's see some sports coats."

Santos was finding San Francisco to be what others proclaimed it to be, a tourist's delight. Especially a rich tourist, and since the credit cards under the name Phillip Simpson were still good, there was no reason not to push them to their limit: luggage from Bali's, Gucci shoes, shirts from Mark Cross, a blazer from Dunhill's, and now suits, slacks, and sports coats from Burberry's. All these wonderfully overpriced stores located within two blocks of the St. Francis Hotel. He'd felt no need to move from the hotel. There was no way to trace him there and, judging from the news reports he'd been carefully reading and screening for the past day and a half, no reason to think anyone would be looking for him.

Even if they were, they'd be canvassing the air terminals, car rental agencies. He remembered the time he'd killed an Iranian ambassador in Paris. The police hunted the killer with what the newspapers called a "holy vengeance." All the while Rene enjoyed the comforts and room service of the Ritz Hotel.

Besides, he still had unfinished business in San Francisco. Mary Ariza. She was the only one left. The final loose thread in the blanket. Liberto, Davila, Naimat, Moreno, the unfortunate girl on the boat, Zorkin, Petrov. Those who could recognize him. They were all conveniently gone. Except for Ariza. Was it worth the risk to wait in town and kill her? Rene thought so. Ariza and that policeman—Kordic. The way they had hugged each other in the bar after the explosion at the Opera House. There was something between them. He could picture the two of them naked, her body sweating, her legs wrapped around his back, just like Sister Angela and the priests. Would Kordic keep digging? Even after Abrams was no longer in jeopardy? It would be perfect if he could catch them together. Eliminate them both.

The news reports let on that the police now knew that Tony Moreno, the leader of the 22 gang, was responsible for the fire at the high school. The police were looking for Moreno now. They'd need divers to find him. Moreno, his friend the bartender, and the hapless girl were all together on the bottom of San Francisco bay. Santos had bound and weighted their bodies down himself. There was no chance of their surfacing as Joseph Rose had.

The police were trying to determine if there was a connection between the Opera House bombing and the three bodies found at the house on Brewster Street. Both Petrov and Zorkin had been identified. The third body was still a mystery. Burned beyond recognition. Would that satisfy Ariza's policeman? Would he believe that it was the body of the man who attacked her? Or that of Father Torres? Would he put the puzzle together in a manner that linked the body to the kidnapping of Paul Abrams?

Abrams was successfully avoiding contact with the press and, according to disgruntled reporters, was being less than totally cooperative with the police. Abrams's doctors had formally pronounced him to be suffering from fatigue and exhaustion and in no condition to be interviewed.

Yes, Abrams, Santos thought as the salesman held up the subtle plaid coat for him to try on. It was time for Mr. Savior to contact Abrams.

"I think the gray suits you perfectly, sir," said the overly polite salesman.

Santos studied himself in the mirror. He liked what

he saw. "Yes, it does. Let's look at some raincoats next."

He settled for one of the store's famous trench coats, taking it with him and instructing the salesman to send the other items to his hotel. He wandered back onto Post Street, in no particular hurry, strolling along until he found an unattended pay phone in front of a jewelry store. He eyed the slim gold watches as he dialed the number Paul Abrams had given him.

A cultured English voice answered and advised that Mr. Abrams was not taking any calls.

"Tell him it's Mr. Savior. I'll call back in ten minutes." Santos broke the connection, then looked at his watch. It looked rather shabby against the fine Egyptian cotton shirt and sleeve of the camel hair coat. Ten minutes. He looked at the jewelry store window. Just enough time to buy a new watch.

"Bad kidneys, young fella. You'll have the same problem when you get to be my age. Wait and see."

Jack Kordic made small sounds of agreement. "You're sure you saw this man, Mr. Folger?"

Randy Folger stretched to his full height of five feet five and pulled at the suspenders holding up his faded jeans. "I'm seventy-eight, mister, but I ain't senile yet. Sure I seen him." He nodded his head toward the bathroom window. "He was standing right there, out in the street. Then that damn bomb went off. Scared the hell out of me, I can tell you that."

Kordic studied the old man. There was a horseshoe of white hair around his freckled scalp. His arms were stick-thin, his stomach pushing over the top of his pants. He looked as if he hadn't shaved in a week. A pair of thick black plastic-framed glasses perched on the end of his bulbous nose.

"Did you have your glasses on, Mr. Folger?"

"Sure did."

"You put your glasses on when you get out of bed in the middle of the night to go to the bathroom?"

Folger smiled, showing a broad range of tobacco-stained teeth. "Yep." A magazine lay on the top of the toilet tank, showing an advertisement for scotch whisky. Folger reached out and turned the magazine over, revealing a young redhead in a bikini. *"Playboy,"* Folger said with a roguish laugh. "Sometimes I got to stand there quite a while 'fore I get my plumbing going, if you know what I mean."

Kordic stood in front of the toilet and looked out the window. "Tell me what the man looked like."

"Well, can't say for sure. Kinda tall, I guess. Wearing a dark jacket. Had a hat. Baseball cap. Giants maybe, too dark to be the Oakland A's. He walked, then stopped, turned around. Then I heard the damn house explode."

"What did the man do after that?"

"I went to the window, stuck my head out to get a better look. House was in flames. I looked back, the man was still standing there, then he took off. Walking that way. Down toward Esmeralda."

"Was the man carrying anything?" Kordic asked.

Folger scratched the whiskers on his chin. "Yeah, he was. Some kind of bag, like a suitcase or something. He wasn't runnin' or nothing. Just walking. I was kind of surprised he didn't stick around to see what happened with the fire and everything. You think he may have had something to do with it?"

Kordic put a leg over the rusty tub and stuck his head out the window. The view was directly down the hill to the house, situated a good half block away. "Did the man have a car? Did you see him get into a car?"

"Nope. He just was walking away, like I said. I didn't see no car."

"You stay right here, Mr. Folger. I'm going outside. You tell me when I'm at the spot where you saw this man."

Kordic went out onto the street, following Randy Folger's waving hand. "Right there. That's the spot," Folger called out in a voice that could have announced boxing matches from ringside.

Kordic stared down at the fire site, still ringed with police units and a lone red fire engine. A man on the street, carrying a bag, at one-fifteen in the morning. He swiveled around. Folger was waving from the window again. "He went that way, mister. About halfway up the block when I last seen him."

Kordic began walking up the street. A car. Where would he park the car? Why so far away? The lab had identified the vehicle in the garage from the VIN number on the chassis. A van, stolen weeks ago. The lab was able to piece together enough of the license plates to determine they had been stolen from another vehicle, one that had been sold to a salvage yard and junked. The Russians' sedan was found parked just a block away.

Had there been another car waiting in the street? If not, what would the mysterious man with the bag have done? Where would he have gone at that time of the morning? Had he rented a nearby house? Was he looking out a window at Kordic now? Laughing? Maybe there was no third car. What if he had arrived in the van found in the basement? Maybe he had come to the house with the third victim, the one almost totally destroyed by the fire.

How much of what Mr. Folger had told him could he believe? An old man taking a leak, reading *Playboy*. Kordic shrugged his shoulders. What a witness he'd make. He started back toward his car, then stopped. If there was no third car, if there was no nearby house, what would the man look for? A phone? The arson investigators had reported finding the remains of two cellular phones in the debris. A cab? Kordic started walking.

"Mr. Savior. I was wondering if I'd ever hear from you again. The stories of the fire—I thought perhaps I had been saved four and a half million dollars."

"No such luck. I've sent you two photographs of your old Russian friend."

"I look forward to receiving them. As far as I'm concerned, you carried out your end of the bargain. Where do you want me to deposit your fee?"

Santos looked at the new wafer-thin Baume & Mercier watch on his wrist. He'd been on the phone long enough. "I hear that the banks in Berlin are excellent. I'll be making arrangements for the transfer."

"Berlin is a good choice. Don't worry. The money will be deposited wherever you wish. We had a deal. You kept your end of the bargain." He paused, then added, "I am not at all interested in living in what you called a 'bunker mentality.' "

"I hope I didn't scare your wife," Santos said.

"Not at all," Abrams assured him. "Almost nothing frightens Adele."

The bartender behind the plank at the Indian Head Cocktail Lounge had the thick neck and heavily muscled shoulders of a wrestler and a beef and bourbon complexion. He looked at Kordic's badge through eyes as bland as a cat's. "Yeah, so what's the big deal? The night of the fire, right? That's what we're talking about?"

"That's right. Around closing time. Anyone come in? Man in dark clothes, wearing a baseball hat, carrying a bag?"

"Hell, closing time's always busy. I have to throw out half the bums that are in here."

Kordic knew the bartender wasn't exaggerating. The Indian Head was a well-known "bucket of blood" at closing time. He remembered responding all the way from Mission Station while on patrol duty, helping the cops from Ingleside Station break up street fights in front of the bar shortly after it shut down at two in the morning. "All those sirens, you must have heard them from here. You're only a few blocks away from the fire."

The bartender picked up a stained towel and began wiping down the bar. "You want a drink or what?"

"Sure." Kordic looked at the draft pump handles. "Make it a Michelob."

The bartender poured the beer, then scooped up Kordic's five dollar bill, dropping it directly into his apron pocket. "It got pretty exciting. We were watching some movie on the TV. They broke in with news of the fire."

Kordic sampled his beer. "What about a new customer? Like the one I described to you."

"Yeah, some guy did come in. Ordered a straight vodka, used the phone."

"Didn't happen to hear who he called, did you?"

The bartender's upper lip tightened and rode up over his teeth. "How's your beer?"

Kordic dug out his money clip and deposited another five dollar bill on the bar, holding it down with an index finger. "You'll have to work for this one."

"Well, yeah. I know who he called. Yellow Cab. He had another vodka while he waited."

"Describe him," Kordic said, releasing his hold on the bill.

"Just a guy, you know. Wearing a Giants cap, like half the other clowns that come in here."

"Had this particular man been in here before?"

"Don't think so. He ordered Stolichnaya, that Russian stuff." He reached down into the bar well and held up a bottle of vodka. "I sell this crap most of the time. They make it right down the road, in Fremont. Good as that Russian stuff. All that vodka tastes alike. This jerk wants to spend extra dough for the Russian rotgut, it's his business. You want another beer?"

"I can't afford it," Kordic said, walking toward the pay phone. He dialed the office of Pontar & Kerr.

"Jack," Mary Ariza said, the happiness in her voice apparent. "I was just getting ready to leave and go home."

"Home?"

"Yes. Back to my apartment. There's no reason not to now."

"I don't know. We're still not sure about this Santos guy. Weeks and I are working on—"

"Jack," she said firmly, "he's not going to bother me now. There'd be no point in it. If he's still alive he's miles away. In Europe, or the Mideast. He's not going to hang around here."

"Mary, listen, Weeks says—"

"Weeks will talk your head off if you let him. I'm going home. No arguments."

Kordic chuckled dryly. "Is that a sample of your courtroom persona?"

"Yes. And I usually win." She lightened her tone. "When am I going to see you?"

"I've got a few more things to wrap up, Mary. Soon as possible, though."

"I still owe you a home-cooked meal. You're not forgetting, are you?"

"No, I'm not forgetting. I'll call you as soon as I can."

Jack Kordic's next phone call was to the Yellow Cab Company offices. They had one of those complicated voice-mail machines handling incoming calls, and Kordic had to listen to the dull, recorded voice advising him of his options, then to select one of three choices and listen to additional instructions before he was finally hooked up to a dispatcher.

He identified himself and explained his needs, giving the dispatcher the name of the bar and approximate time of the pickup.

"You ain't one of those private eyes working a divorce action, are you, pal?"

"No. You can give the information to my office if you want: 553–1906."

The dispatcher's voice had a nasal tone and a New York accent. "Nah, you sound legit. Hold on."

Kordic surveyed the bar's daytime crowd as he waited. All male, ranging in age from early thirties to the seventies, all with weary, slack faces. Most were drinking hard liquor, either straight up or with water. No one made small talk as they stared at the TV on the wall or straight into their glasses. This was no *Cheers* rerun. There was no Norm or Cliff cracking jokes, no Sam behind the plank devising schemes to get Rebecca into bed. Just lonely, melancholy men with no home, no family they wanted to be with, nowhere else to go. Kordic remembered being a member of their club not too long ago.

The dispatcher came back on the line. "Here ya go. Pickup at one-forty a.m. From the Indian Head bar to O'Farrell and Taylor. Driver was a Johnny Henderson.

Recorded fare, six bucks and change. That all you need?"

"Is Henderson working today?"

"Hold on, buddy."

Kordic could hear the phone being dropped, pages being shuffled. "Yeah. Comes on at two this afternoon. Now I guess you want his home number, huh?"

"You guessed right," Kordic advised him.

Mary Ariza hadn't realized how much she missed her apartment until she was home again, alone, with her things, her space. She wandered through the rooms, checking the refrigerator, the kitchen cabinets, running a hand across the clothes in her bedroom closet, touching each as it were an old friend, slowly settling back to normal living.

But what was normal? Certainly Jack Kordic was playing a big part in her future plans. She hadn't felt this way about a man in a long time. If people had told her just a couple of weeks ago that she would be having an affair with a policeman, she would have laughed in their faces. A cop? No way. But Jack had changed all that. She found herself thinking about him often: the way he could be so gentle and so caring, yet so tough, so dedicated at the same time. A lawyer and a policeman. What a combination. Could it last? Mary hoped so. But time would tell. And she did need her own space. But was it going to be this space? The apartment suited her needs and her expenses, but there were those memories. She flopped onto her bed and stretched out, staring at the pale ivory ceiling. The bloodstains from Walter Slager's body were still partially visible on the carpet by the door. Would they fade away? No. There would always be a trace there, a speck to remind her of what happened.

I'll move, she decided suddenly. As soon as possible. Check the papers, see what's available. I'll start looking now. Today. She could afford an uptick in rent. The million-dollar out-of-court settlement had proved her worth to the firm. What was it going to be like working for Matt Pontar now? Mercifully, Mary Pontar was going to survive. Survive, but would she be the same person? One fellow attorney killed on her doorstep and the boss's wife shot. So perhaps it was time to make another major move. To another law firm. Perhaps to another town. A lot depended on Jack Kordic and how their relationship developed. She hugged her arms to her chest and said a simple prayer, no elaborate Hail Marys or Our Fathers. Just a small prayer of thanks. Thanking God that she was alive. That Rene Santos was gone. For good.

Santos felt restless. He decided to go for a walk. He roamed the streets of San Francisco, finding himself in front of a Catholic church. The bells were announcing mass. Curiosity got the better of him, and he went inside, sliding into a pew, sitting next to a weeping woman in a soiled raincoat. It was the first time he'd heard mass said in English. It sounded bland, impersonal. The smells were the same, though. The candles and incense. Always the candles. He stayed through the Gospel reading, the priest's Irish brogue droning through St. Mark, Chapter 8, Jesus Feeds Four Thousand.

A small, hunchbacked man in a tattered blue suit came with the collection basket, giving Rene a gap-toothed smile as he shook the basket, the coins clinking together. Rene had reached for his wallet, but then changed his mind, abruptly standing up and hurrying to the exit. He'd given enough. More than enough.

He hurried back to the hotel, scooping up an armful of local and international papers in the lobby. He stretched out on the bed and started thumbing through the papers. Paul Abrams's disappearance and reappearance, and what was being called the "Opera House Tragedy," still dominated the news.

A photograph on the second page of the *Chronicle* caught his eye. He stood, carrying the paper over to the window, holding it up to the natural light. A picture of what remained of the bombed-out house on Brewster Street. Several men were shown walking from the house. Santos immediately recognized one of the men as the policeman, Jack Kordic. Standing next to Kordic was a short, dark-skinned man. The man had his hands out, palms upturned, as if trying to explain something to his companion. Santos compressed his bloodless lips. It was the Jew. Weeks. Anatoly Weeks. The bastard from Mossad. Weeks was here, in San Francisco. Or had been. What brought him?

He looked back at the photograph. What had Weeks and Kordic been talking about? How had Weeks picked up the scent? Petrov? Had the Russian tipped Mossad off? Tipped off Weeks? Weeks. He should have been in that building in Tel Aviv. Should have been one of the causalties. He was a thorough man. He'd keep digging. And now with Kordic's help. And through Kordic, Mary Ariza.

He'd have to move quickly. Get rid of her now. Right now. He'd hoped to let things cool down, let her begin feeling comfortable, safe. That's when they were easy. It was a luxury he couldn't afford. She could identify him. Now. He had to eliminate her now!

He went to the bed stand and dug out the phone book, flipping through the pages for the law firm where the woman worked. Pontar & Kerr. He dialed the number and asked for Mary Ariza.

"She's not in today, sir. Can I take a message?"

Santos hung up. Not in. But where was she? At home? He closed his eyes, slowed his breathing. Ariza didn't have a listed telephone—he'd found that out when he had originally located her address. Think, damn it. The newspaper stories, the neighbors. The name of the man who'd shot Moreno's hoodlum. What was it? A town. A city. Something like a city. London! Landon, that was it. Landon. He got the phone book. Landon was listed. John Landon, Hyde Street.

His eyes drifted to the TV set. A handsome black man was giving the news on Channel 2. The station's logo came on, showing the location. Jack London Square, Oakland. Oakland. Just across the bay. He started forming a pretext in his mind, the droning of the TV set helping him to think. He picked up the phone book. The call letters for the television station in

Oakland were KTVU. Even though it was an Oakland listing, it was there, in the San Francisco book, 2 Jack London Square in Oakland. He called the TV station first.

"Hi, I'm meeting someone from your station later today. I'd like to take him to dinner, somewhere close by. Could you recommend a really good restaurant?"

"Who are you meeting?" the receptionist asked.

"One of the gentlemen in sales. I'm embarrassed. I'm not at my office, and I left his name there. Don, or Joe—"

"Don Paulson?"

"Right. Where would you like to go if it were you I was meeting?"

"Shenanigan's is nice. It's just down the street a couple of blocks, in Jack London Square, on the bay—"

Santos pushed the disconnect bar and quickly dialed Landon's number.

"Yeah, this is John Landon."

"Mr. Landon. How are you, sir?" Santos said in his best American accent. "This is Mr. Paulson, KTVU television in Oakland. We want to congratulate you on your actions the other night. That took real courage. We're wondering if you'd be interested in being interviewed for one of our shows on local heroes. We'd go into some details about just how you single-handedly saved Mary Ariza's life."

"You want me on TV?"

"We certainly do, sir. We've been trying to get a hold of Miss Ariza, but she hasn't been at work, and I can't catch her at home."

"Nah, she's been away, came back today," Landon said amiably.

Santos's hand squeezed the receiver tightly. "Is Ms. Ariza there now?"

"She was earlier. I think she went out. I can go check if you want."

"No, no. It's you we want, not her. In fact, now that I'm thinking of it, I'd appreciate it if you didn't mention my call. We'd like to get you on first, get your story, then maybe later we'll get her side."

"When's this going to happen?"

"Would you be available this evening, Mr. Landon?"

"Sure, no problem. Can I bring my wife?"

"Absolutely. She was there at the time of the shooting, wasn't she?"

"Yes, sure was. Didn't want me to go outside and take that punk on. You know how women are."

"Yes, I sure do," Santos agreed. "Can both of you be here at, say, six o'clock? I'd like to meet you before we go on. There's a restaurant just down the street. Shenanigan's. I'd like to buy you and your wife dinner. We can talk while we eat."

"Sounds great," Landon said enthusiastically.

"All right, sir. But once again, let's keep this just between us, all right? And if I'm not there right at six, have a drink. Have them run a tab, so it'll go on my bill when I get there."

"He should be here any minute," Jack Kordic said, scanning the streets for the Yellow Cab from the front steps of the Hall of Justice.

Anatoly Weeks drew a crumpled pack of cigarettes from his jacket pocket. "How'd you get along with Felix Lebeau, Rose's attorney?"

"He's an attorney. His client is dead. There are heirs to think about. He's the executor of the estate and one of the heirs."

"So you got nothing."

"Not really," Kordic admitted. "The lab didn't come up with anything positive on that charred body from Brewster Street. Nothing much left of it. They estimate he was about six feet in height, big-boned, so he could be the man who killed Walter Slager."

"Yeah, Santos is hoping you'll settle for that, and that you'll pin the body to the Abrams kidnapping. Tie it up in a neat package for you." Weeks shook a cigarette loose and counted those remaining in the pack. Just two. He was about to go back into the Hall and buy another pack when the cab pulled up.

The driver, John Henderson, was a tough-looking redhead in his thirties. "One of you guys Kordic?" he called from the driver's seat as the two men approached.

"Right." Kordic held open the door for Weeks. "We want you to take us to the Indian Head bar, then drive the same route you took this man, okay?"

Henderson swiveled around so he faced both men. "You guys are cops. You're getting paid. I'm not."

"Pull down the meter," Kordic said. "Let's go."

Henderson flashed a smile, flipping the meter level as the cab jumped forward and edged into the sparse afternoon traffic.

Both Kordic and Weeks shot questions at Henderson during the drive to the bar and back to the drop-off spot at O'Farrell and Taylor streets. The answers were simple, honest, and not very helpful. The customer had been waiting in front of the bar when Henderson got there. He got in the backseat, told Henderson where he wanted to go, and didn't say another word. He paid in cash, adding a five dollar tip. "That's about all I remember of him. Good tipper."

The description Henderson gave was just as useless: medium height, medium weight, dark clothes, baseball cap. "The suitcase was not so hot. I notice cases. They can tell you a lot about your customer. How he's gonna tip. This looked like some cheapo job."

"Did it look heavy?" Kordic asked. "Did he have any problem carrying it around?"

Henderson's eyebrows met above the bridge of his nose, and his forehead wrinkled in thought. "No, not too heavy. Not too light, you know what I mean?"

Kordic and Weeks exited the cab. Weeks paid the fare, and the cab took off in a squeal of burning rubber.

"I hope you left him a good tip," Kordic said.

"Told him not to play the horses. Best tip he'll get all his life." Weeks put his hands on his hips and took in the sights. "Hell of a shitty neighborhood you got here, Inspector."

"This is where Santos got off. Carrying a suitcase. What's in it? We both agree that he wouldn't have let

Abrams go without a payoff. A big payoff. Let's say cash. So let's assume the payoff is in the suitcase. Where would a man with a suitcase full of cash go at two in the morning?"

Weeks stood on his toes to look over the top of a truck parked on the corner. Both sides of the street were filled with older eight- to ten-story apartment houses that advertised monthly, weekly, and daily rates. "If he's holed up in one of these flophouses, we may never find him. He could have just walked a block, got another cab, and headed for the airport."

"Is there anything to keep him in town?"

Weeks dug his last cigarette from the pack. "Not that I can come up with, unless he made some deal with Abrams, or unless he's playing it cute. He's done it before. Pulled off a job, then buried himself right in the same city. He did it in my town. Tel Aviv. We had all our agents and half of the damn army running around at the airports, blocking roads, boarding ships. I found out later Santos had holed up six blocks from my office in some dumpy apartment behind a shoe store for three weeks. But my bet is he's gone. In a car. No planes for Rene. Not out of here, anyway."

"I hope you're right. I hope he's long gone. But if he isn't, if he stayed around, for whatever reason, where is he? This is the last spot we're sure of." Kordic stamped his foot on the sidewalk. "He was right here. At two in the morning. Where'd he go to, Weeks?"

Weeks plucked at the skin of his throat. "Okay, let's give it a run. You take the right side of the street, I'll take the left."

They expanded their search in a classical, systematic box search, moving block by block. It was slow, hard, and unproductive work. The only thing Anatoly Weeks learned was that flophouses in San Francisco exuded the same stench of urine, moldy carpets, and over-fried foods as those in Tel Aviv, Paris, Singapore, Bombay, and Algiers. His knowledge of Spanish, Farsi, Arabic, and Hindi came in handy, but the results were still the same. Negative.

He and Kordic stopped for a cup of coffee at a diner on Mason Street.

"Maybe we're going about this the wrong way, Anatoly."

Weeks stirred sugar into his cup and made a face at the no-smoking sign. "What's your brainstorm?"

"Our man has made some kind of a big deal with Abrams. Why would he bother holing out in some dump? Why not go first-class?"

"Such as?"

"A major hotel. Caviar and champagne from room service. He just struck it rich. He's got it. He's home free. Why not flaunt it?"

Weeks dumped another spoonful of sugar into his cup. "How many major hotels within walking distance from here?"

"Oh, half dozen or so."

Weeks sampled a spoonful of the coffee. "There's something else a major hotel would have that might appeal to our friend. A safe."

Chapter 37

Rene Santos walked back to the same drugstore on Powell Street where he'd purchased the binoculars, Polaroid camera, baseball hat, and windbreaker. This time he headed for the hardware and kitchenware aisles. He hailed a cab and transferred the purchases from the bag to his suitcase as he sat in the back of the cab. He directed the driver to drop him off at Polk and California streets, some three blocks from Mary Ariza's apartment on Hyde Street. Ariza. Kill her. And Kordic. Just to wrap things up tightly, he'd kill the policeman too.

It had been raining when he left the hotel, but there was just a light mist now. He approached the apartment house cautiously, moving slowly from doorway to doorway, noticing the flow of pedestrian traffic. The weather made his frequent stops appear perfectly reasonable. When he was sure that the apartment house wasn't under surveillance, he ran across the street and up the stairs, stopping to ring the bell for John Landon's apartment.

He kept his gloved right hand slipped through the inner hole in his raincoat pocket, firmly wrapped around the grip of the silenced Skorpion machine pistol he'd removed from Boris Zorkin's body. The weapon hung from its suspender strap around his right shoulder, under the new Burberry trench coat. There was always a chance that Mary Ariza would come traipsing by and he could complete his task right then and there.

He pushed the bell again, then went to work, inserting the edge of a flexible metal cooking spatula purchased from the drugstore above the door's lock, and worked it down smoothly. The door popped open in a matter of seconds.

He surveyed the hallway and decided to take the stairs to the fourth floor.

Picking locks was not one of his strong points. He examined Ariza's lock. No, it wasn't worth taking the risk of another tenant spotting him. He went directly to the Landons' door, this time taking a foot-long iron pry bar from the suitcase's side pocket, jamming the tool's edge into the door frame and giving it a hard shove.

There was a cracking noise as the door gave in. Santos went inside the Landon apartment quickly, closing the door behind him. He stood still, listening for any commotion in the hallway. Hearing none, he opened the door and checked the damage. Not bad. The crack in the frame was noticeable, but only if you were really looking for it. He pushed the splintered wood together as best he could, then closed the door and surveyed his surroundings.

As a matter of routine, he checked the apartment for an emergency exit. The only viable alternative to the front door was a four-story drop from the kitchen window to the street below.

A telephone was set on a small table alongside a reclining chair. On the table was the Landons' personal address and telephone book. The final entry under the letter A was for Mary Ariza, 555–3490. He dialed the number, his finger resting on the disconnect bar, ready to hang up if Ariza answered. Only she didn't answer.

He went to the bedroom and found the wall separating the Landon apartment from Mary Ariza's. He pressed his ear to the wall, closed his eyes, and listened. Nothing. He looked at his watch, estimating that the Landons wouldn't figure they were being duped for at least another two hours. The drive across the bridge in commute traffic would probably take an hour itself. He placed the suitcase on the bed, selected an ice pick from the items he'd purchased at the store, and started chipping away at the plaster.

* * *

The lobby of the St. Francis Hotel was mobbed, the desk clerks busy with a bus load of Japanese tourists checking in.

Kordic was about out of patience when he finally got the floor manager to help him. He identified himself and introduced Weeks as his partner.

The manager was a clean-cut man in his thirties with black hair that was carefully groomed and frozen with a ruler-straight part on the left side. The discreet brass name tag on his dark blue blazer jacket identified him as Jason.

"Jason, we're working on the bombing at the Opera House. I want to know if a man checked into the hotel last night, after two in the morning. Alone. Carrying one piece of luggage. Possibly wearing a dark jacket, perhaps a Giants baseball cap."

Jason raised his eyebrows amiably. "Well, we can certainly look and see if we had any check-ins at that time, Inspector."

He led Kordic and Weeks to a small, cramped office out of sight of the lobby desk, and began punching the keys of a Hewlett-Packard computer. The amber screen came to life, and Jason scrolled down a long list of names. "After two o'clock, you say?"

"That's right."

"No, nothing until almost three. That was a couple from Wisconsin, Mr. and Mrs. McGowan."

"Can you tell us what Mr. McGowan looked like?"

The manager's face crumpled into a rueful smile. "Sorry. We certainly don't log that type of information. The McGowans are still here if you want to talk to them."

Kordic moved from one foot to the other, debating with himself if it was worth the time to check out the McGowans.

Weeks said, "Can you tell us if anyone checked a case into the hotel safe last night, after two?"

The manager's mouth twisted wryly as he fed more codes into the computer. "Yes, here we are. One of our guests, a Mr. Phillip Simpson, did check in one piece of luggage at two twenty-five a.m. Removed his property about an hour ago."

"Is Simpson still registered?"

Once again Jason went to work on the computer. "He hasn't checked out. Room 1146."

"Call him up. See if he's in," Kordic said in a tight voice.

They watched as the manager dialed the room. He let the phone ring ten times, then hung up. "No answer."

To the dismay of the manager, both Kordic and Weeks had their guns out as they approached Room 1146. Kordic gestured with his fingers for the key.

Jason handed the small plastic card to Kordic, who inserted it into the lock and pushed the door inward, then ran inside, gun in hand, arm extended. Weeks dropped to a crouch and followed closely.

They searched each room. There was a breakfast tray in the bedroom. Weeks stuck his finger into the coffeepot. "Ice cold," he said.

Kordic went through the closets, then dropped to his knees to look under the bed.

"Do you really think all of this is necessary?" Jason called from the hallway.

Both Kordic and Weeks looked at each other and shrugged their shoulders. Was it? Simpson could be a jewelry salesman, a precious coin or stamp dealer, the suitcase his merchandise which would be routinely checked in and out of a hotel safe.

"What more can you tell us about Mr. Simpson?"

"Nothing," the manager responded. "We can check his room charges, of course."

They went back to the crowded office and the computer. Jason pulled up all charges to Room 1146, and pushed the print button. The laser printer spat out the results almost immediately.

Kordic snatched the document from the manager's hand. Room service, room service, room service. Telephone calls.

"You log all local calls?" he asked.

"Yes, sir. There's an additional charge of seventy-five cents for all local calls. Guests dial directly from their room, but our computer records them in case there's a dispute in the billing."

Weeks peeked over Kordic's shoulder. "Let's try them."

Kordic used the phone on the desk. The first call was to the 510 area code, the East Bay. A recorded message came on the line. "This is KTVU Television. Our office hours are nine a.m. to five p.m. If you—"

He hung up quickly and dialed the San Francisco number. Another recording. "Hi, this is John and Paula Landon's home. Leave a number and we'll get back to you."

The police department's radio communication system is broken up into four channels: Channel 1 covers the Bureau of Inspectors, Southern, Central, and Potrero stations. Channel 2 takes in Ingleside, Mission, and Taraval stations. Channel 3 handles the motorcycle and accident-investigation units, and Channel 4 covers Park, Richmond, and Northern stations.

Kordic switched the channel selector to number four as he swerved through traffic, siren blaring, barreling down Sutter Street. "This is Inspector Jack Kordic, for Northern Station. Are McCarthy and Monroe working?"

"This is Northern two," came a scratchy reply. "Greg Monroe, Jack. What's up?"

Kordic dropped the microphone as he wrenched the steering wheel to the right to miss a pedestrian crossing against the light. Anatoly Weeks grabbed the mike and handed it to Kordic once he was through the intersection.

"Remember the 187 on Hyde Street, knife job? Perp shot by neighbor?"

"Sure do," Monroe replied.

"Someone is going to try again. Same apartment number. He'll be armed. Could be waiting outside for the woman. Repeat, armed and dangerous."

"We're about ten blocks away," came the reply. "Be there in a minute."

Kordic let the microphone drop to his lap again.

Anatoly Weeks put his feet on the dashboard and wrapped his left arm around the seat for support as the car swerved through another intersection. "What's a 187?"

"Penal code number for homicide."

The St. Francis Hotel was no more than a dozen blocks from Mary Ariza's apartment, but the weather made driving treacherous. The windshield wipers thumped out a steady tune, clearing the rain away. Kordic cut the siren when he reached California and Leavenworth. He turned left on Sacramento and skidded to a halt at the corner.

The black-and-white radio car with Monroe and McCarthy pulled in front of the apartment house just as Kordic and Weeks were running up the steps. Kordic rang Mary's bell with his right hand while his left rattled the door handle.

"Let me get it, Jack," Officer McCarthy said, expertly slipping a piece of celluloid into the door and pushing it open.

The hole on the Landons' side of the wall was a circle roughly one foot in diameter. The plaster was old and crumbly and broke away easily with the aid of the keyhole saw Santos had purchased. He sawed through the rotting wooden lath behind the plaster until there was nothing separating him from Mary Ariza's apartment but a thin layer of plaster. Santos worked the tip of the ice pick through the wall. A drill would have done a much neater job, but he wasn't really worried about appearance. It wasn't at all like the covert surveillance jobs he'd worked on, when tiny, 2mm spy scopes were meticulously augured through walls, allowing the viewing or filming of an entire room.

His main concern was that the ice pick would come through behind a wall painting or mirror. The pick's tip punctured the wall. He twisted it around, enlarging the hole, then worked the blade of the keyhole saw until he had a hole the size of a donut in Ariza's wall, more than enough room for him to see over the Skorpion's barrel and take aim as Ariza came into her apartment. He'd let her get well inside before pulling the trigger. If Kordic happened to be with her, all the better.

He heard the sound of sirens but paid them little attention. San Francisco was a city of alarms: police, fire, ambulance. The sound of footsteps thundering up the apartment's stairway was a different matter. More than one person. And in a hurry.

He fought down a surge of panic, knowing there was no way for anyone to suspect he was in town, much less in this building. His eyes widened in fear when he heard a loud crash, then saw the door to Ariza's apartment burst open and a uniformed policeman roll into the room, tumbling to his knees, gun at the ready. Another uniformed cop quickly followed, walking in a duck-like crouch, gun out, waving back and forth in a short, deadly arc.

Two men in plain clothes followed. Santos couldn't believe it. Anatoly Weeks. And the policeman. Kordic. How had they found out? How did they know?

Kordic ran through the kitchen, toward the bedroom, shouting, "Mary! Mary! Where are you?"

Santos placed his palm over the hole, blocking out whatever light was spilling into Ariza's apartment from his side of the wall. When would they notice the hole? The plaster droppings on the floor? He peeked through the cracks in his fingers. Kordic came running back from the bedroom.

"She's not here. Let's try Landon's apartment."

How do they know? Santos asked himself again as he lined up the Skorpion on the nearest policeman and pulled the trigger.

Officer Greg Monroe cried out in pain, falling forward on his face. McCarthy looked down at his fallen partner, unable to fathom what had taken place. "Greg, what—" His question was cut short when a bullet ripped through his throat.

Anatoly Weeks's head swiveled around to take in the two fallen officers. Kordic was at the door when he heard Monroe scream. He turned to see what was going on, watching in horror as Weeks's shoulder exploded in blood. Then holes suddenly appeared, as if by magic, puckering the wooden door. Kordic dived out to the hallway. He glanced back into Mary's apartment. Weeks was crawling slowly toward the door. Kordic reached for his ankles and dragged him into the hallway.

"Next door," Weeks gasped in pain. "He's got to be next door."

Kordic got to his feet, his revolver cocked and aimed at the dead center of the door to the Landon apartment.

"Police emergency!" he yelled as loud as he could. "Call 911. A police officer's been shot! Call 911!"

A woman in a bright red brocade robe, her hair in rollers, opened her door at the far end of the hallway. She peeked out cautiously and saw Kordic holding his weapon. She quickly slammed the door shut.

Kordic dropped to one knee and tried to catch his breath. He thought back to when he had been in the Landons' apartment. It had seemed to be a duplicate of Mary's place. One bedroom, a kitchen, living room. The windows. Did they open out onto the street? Was there a fire escape? He'd taken no notice at the time. What was the man inside thinking? He couldn't wait much longer. He'd know that half the city's force would respond to a call for help when an officer'd been shot.

"Get him, damn it," Anatoly Weeks cried out. "Get the bastard. It's Santos. Get him!"

As soon as Rene Santos saw that he'd missed the fourth man, Kordic, he stripped the sheets, blanket, and spread from the Landons' bed and ran to the kitchen window. He tied the bedding material together, adding a slip knot every few feet for traction, all the while keeping both eyes on the front door. He didn't have far to travel, maybe forty feet to the ground, which meant he could get perhaps twenty-five feet with the bedding and jump the rest of the way. He fastened the end of a sheet around the radiator near the window and shoved the bedding material out the window. Santos slipped the Skorpion over his left shoulder, the suitcase with the money over his right, took a deep breath, and climbed outside, his hands holding firmly to the knotted sheet. The rain-slick bricks made it difficult to get any footing. He wrapped his feet around the makeshift rope, hands moving down, searching for the next knot. He looked down to the street, releasing the pressure on his feet so he could move faster.

Jack Kordic knew he couldn't wait any longer. He fired into the lock once, then put his foot to the door, dodging back out of sight when it opened with a bang.

He counted to ten, dropped to one knee, edged up to the door, and peered into the apartment with his right eye. He spotted the open window and the sheeting tied to the radiator. He rushed into the room. Reaching the window, he could see a darkened figure some twenty feet below him. "Freeze," he hollered.

Santos felt his feet move past the final knot. He looked up, directly into the barrel of Kordic's revolver. "Help me," he pleaded. "I'm falling." He hung on for a last second, then shouted, "Help." It all depended on luck now, he thought as he let go.

Jack Kordic tightened his finger on the trigger as the man dangled, then fell free, landing on the street with a sickening thud, lying still. Then suddenly he was getting to his feet and limping away. Kordic snapped off two shots, then ran out of the apartment and down the stairs, cursing himself. The bastard suckered me. I had him and he suckered me.

Santos knew his ankle was broken and that one of Kordic's shots had grazed his neck. He could feel blood running down his shirt. He dropped to the ground and rolled into a kneeling position, then crawled to the side of the building, put his back to the wall, and inched his way into a standing position. He took a tentative step, almost crumbling to the ground. The leg was useless. But he still had the Skorpion and the suitcase full of money. He bent over, jamming the barrel of the machine pistol into the ground as if it were a cane and hopped over to a telephone pole, rubbing his face against the rough wood. Hang on, damn it, he commanded himself. Hang on. You can still do it.

Kordic hit the lobby on the run. Weeks had told him that Santos had been some kind of a circus acrobat. A trapeze artist. Slipping down that rope was second nature to the man. He slammed open the apartment house's front door, then hurried out to the street, arms extended, his gun cradled in both hands, sweeping nervously back and forth. He hugged the edge of the sidewalk, near a line of parked cars. Cars. Did Santos have a car? Was he in it now? Getting away? Monroe and McCarthy? Were they still alive? How about Weeks? Where was the goddamn ambulance? Where was Santos?

The sirens were getting closer. He'd have to get away before the reinforcements arrived. A car. He needed a car. There was no time to break into one. Hot-wire it. His eyes blurred. The neck wound was worse than he thought, the blood now spurting out with each beat of his pulse. He felt his strength draining away. He looked around desperately. A cab was coming up the street.

"Must be some five-alarm fire or something," the cabdriver said, slowing down as he passed a cable car on California Street. "When you hear that many sirens, it's usually a big one."

Mary looked out at the rain. She should have brought an umbrella. She took a white scarf from her purse and put it on. "This is it, driver. Hyde Street."

"Yeah, I know," he answered, making a cautious right turn. "Hey, look. There's a cop car right there."

Mary Ariza looked over the driver's shoulder. A black-and-white patrol car. Parked in front of her apartment. What now?

"How much do I owe you?" she asked hurriedly, digging in her purse for some money.

"Seven-eighty, lady. Okay if I stop right here?"

Mary shoved a ten dollar bill at him and yanked on the door handle. "Keep the change."

Santos hopped across the street on one leg. He opened the taxi cab door and shot the driver in the head twice, his blood splattering the seat rest. He reached in, grunting at the effort it took to drag him out from behind the wheel.

He heard the car door slam and looked across the cab's roof. A woman. He squeezed his eyes open and shut several times, trying to clear them. It was Sister Angela. Her beautiful face a mask of terror. Her eyes wide, the mouth a round circle. Her white habit hiding her hair. She had called him *carantamaula*. The ugly one. His laughter rode with the wind. Ugly no more. After all these years he had her. His revenge was complete. He raised the barrel of the Skorpion and laughed again. How lucky could he get?

Kordic blinked against the rain. The damn rain. It was bad enough that—a figure. Across the street. A taxi cab. A figure moving awkwardly toward it. Santos! He saw him open the cab's door. Saw the flash from Santos's gun, the driver being pulled from the cab.

He started running. Then he saw Mary. She was there! "Santos! Santos! Freeze!"

Kordic's first shot whined off the cab's fender. The noise caused Santos to whirl around. Still running, Kordic pulled the trigger again, and again. One of the bullets caught Santos in his right shoulder, another hit his chest.

Santos dropped the Skorpion, then the suitcase, grabbing the cab door with both hands. His fingers gradually loosed their hold. He hit the ground knees first, then fell on his side.

Mary Ariza ran to Kordic's side. "Jack, Jack. Jesus, it's him, isn't it? The priest. Santos!"

Kordic wrapped his arms around Mary, hugging her so tightly it hurt her ribs.

"It's him," he said between labored breaths, pointing his gun barrel at the figure on the ground. "It's him. El Cabecilla, Rene Santos, Father Torres, whatever his real name is, it's him."

Mary stared in disbelief at the pale, pain-wracked face on the ground. His lips were moving. One hand groping at a chain around his neck. She dropped to her knees, pushing his hand from his neck, feeling for his pulse. It was then she heard him whisper in Spanish.

"Perdone, Padre, porque e pecado." Forgive me, Father, for I have sinned.

Chapter 38

"I had hoped that I'd never have to see this place again," Mary Ariza proclaimed flatly.

Jack Kordic made a left turn, then backed into the spot marked SAN FRANCISCO GENERAL HOSPITAL. EMERGENCY VEHICLES ONLY.

He switched off the ignition key, and the motor died with a jerk and noisy sigh. He could understand Mary's feelings. She'd been brought to the hospital after the attempt on her life, when Walter Slager had been killed. Rene Santos had no doubt murdered his henchman on the hospital's fourth floor. Mary Pontar had been treated in the emergency ward for her gunshot wound. Now Anatoly Weeks was in the intensive care unit, recovering from the bullet Santos had fired into his shoulder.

Rene Santos had made a brief second appearance at S.F. General, the paramedics transporting him from the street in front of Mary's place. But Santos had died somewhere en route, officially pronounced dead on arrival at the hospital.

"Actually, I think it's kind of a romantic place," Kordic said with a grin. "It is where we met." He led her into the building. He knew the way to the intensive care unit only too well. While he and Mary waited for the elevator, he asked about Mary Pontar.

"She's doing great. They've transferred her to Mt. Zion Hospital. Matt says she'll be home in a few days."

"And how are things at the office?" Kordic inquired. The elevator pinged and the doors opened. Two smiling nurses hurried out, walking briskly, their shifts over for the day.

Kordic pushed the button for the third floor.

"Things seem to be okay," Mary said cautiously. "Matt has gone out of his way to get everything back to normal. At least as normal as possible. Finally catching that man has been a relief to everyone. You're sure it was him, aren't you, Jack? That the killer was really Rene Santos? He didn't look anything like that picture you showed me."

Kordic nodded. "We're sure it was Santos, Mary," he said, trying to make his voice sound more confident than he felt. "The autopsy showed he'd gone through a lot of plastic surgery. Hair transplant. The works." Kordic still wasn't completely satisfied about the ID. The problem was that no one had his fingerprints on file. No dental charts. Even the Mossad had no prints or charts for Santos. He'd shown all the information to Anatoly Weeks. Weeks was positive that Santos was the man Kordic had shot to death. Kordic hoped so. That morning he'd awakened from a nightmare, seeing Santos hanging from the bed sheets, crying for help.

Mary's first sight of Anatoly Weeks in his hospital bed made her stomach muscles tighten. His whole left side was bandaged. Clear plastic IV tubes were stuck into his right arm. But the most worrisome thing was his coloring. There was a distinct gray cast to the deeply tanned face.

Weeks cautiously opened one eye. When he saw Kordic and Mary Ariza, he popped the other eye open and smiled, crinkling his face into hundreds of wrinkles. "Heard the footsteps. Thought it was that damn nurse and doctor again. They're crazy. Came in the middle of the night and woke me up. Wanted me to get up and be weighed. Can you imagine that? Middle of the damn night to get weighed. What the hell difference does it make if I'm losing weight now? How the hell could I put on any weight with the crap they're feeding me anyhow? Garbage. Pure garbage." He fixed his gaze on the bag in Kordic's hand. "I hope you brought me something to eat."

"You sound like you're feeling pretty good," Kordic said, setting a white paper bag on the side of the bed.

Weeks could see the grease stains on the bag and smiled again. He looked at Mary. She was carrying a bouquet of multicolored, sweet-smelling flowers. "Thanks. They're beautiful. Put them right over there," he said, nodding his head toward an enamel-topped table. "I'll have the nurse put them in water."

"When will you be getting out of here?" Kordic asked, digging in his pockets, taking out two packs of Lucky Strike cigarettes and dropping them alongside the white bag.

"I'm not sure. It's all up to the docs." Weeks winced as he tried to shift his body into a comfortable position. "Bullet didn't hit any bones. Flesh wound, like they call them in the movies. Problem is, it killed a lot of flesh. And muscle, and nerves, and cartilage." He ran his right hand over his heavily bandaged left shoulder. "I don't think the arm will be much good anymore." He grimaced again as he tried to move his fingers. "What's new on the case?"

"Not much," Kordic said, dragging a chair over to the bed for Mary, then another for himself. "A lot of inquiries coming in for information on Santos. CIA, FBI, police in France, Germany, Peru, Argentina. All over the world." Kordic paused. "But not from your people. I guess they came directly to the source."

"Someone came by to talk to me about it," Weeks admitted grudgingly. "What the hell. Santos is dead. That's about all anybody needs to know. What about Paul Abrams? You get to talk to him?"

Kordic gnawed at his upper lip. "Nope. He took off for Mexico. Under his doctor's orders. We didn't get close to him."

"I saw a news story on TV," Mary said. "He is divorcing his wife."

Weeks chuckled lightly. "Yeah. Great timing, huh?"

Kordic said, "Maybe she'll tell us something. After the divorce."

Weeks reached out for the white bag with his right hand. "Fat chance. She'll be paid enough to keep quiet.

If she talks, they'll turn off the money tap." He peeked into the bag and flashed his teeth. "The cash in the suitcase. Abrams's. He'll never claim it, though. It was about oil all the time, wasn't it, Jack? Petrov, Santos, Abrams, Rose. All about some damn oil in the ground in Russia."

Mary Ariza shook her head angrily. "God, it's all so wicked. All those innocent people dying: Walter Slager, the people at the Opera House. Those policemen. For oil. For money. It's like a war."

Weeks drummed his fingers on the paper bag. "Wicked. There's a word I haven't heard in a long time, Mary. But it's a good one."

They chatted for a few more minutes, turning the conversation to small talk. What they would do when Weeks was released from the hospital. Restaurants to go to. Places to see.

"That'll be nice," Weeks said wearily, "but truth be known, I'm starting to run out of gas."

Mary leaned over and kissed him on the cheek. Kordic shook his good right hand and promised to drop in on him tomorrow.

Weeks leaned back against the pillows and watched the two of them leave the room, walking slowly, their shoulders touching, their hands dangling along their sides, brushing against each other. Nice couple, he thought. But what were their chances? A cop and an attorney. Not exactly a perfect marriage of careers. But who knows? He opened the white bag and heaved a sigh of relief. Real food. Donuts. Good old greasy donuts. He selected a chocolate-covered one, took a big bite, then slid the bag under the sheets, just in case the nurse came in.

TERROR ... TO THE LAST DROP